TELL ME
WHAT
YOU WANT

OR

LEAVE

ME

ALSO BY MEGAN MAXWELL

Tell Me What You Want

Now and Forever

TELL ME
WHAT
YOU WANT

OR

LEAVE

ME

MEGAN MAXWELL

Translated by Achy Obejas

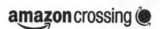

Previously published as *Pídeme lo que quieras o déjame* by Planeta in Spain in 2014. Translated from Spanish by Achy Obejas. First published in English by Amazon Crossing in 2020.

Published by Amazon Crossing, Seattle

www.apub.com

Amazon, the Amazon logo, and Amazon Crossing are trademarks of Amazon.com, Inc., or its affiliates.

ISBN-13: 9781542043113
ISBN-10: 1542043115

Cover design by PEPE *nymi*, Milano

Printed in the United States of America

With love to all my crazy and wonderful Maxwell Warriors.

As you say, there's no two without a third!

I hope you'll fall in love with Eric and Jude again.

A thousand kisses,
Megan

1

Riviera Maya Hotel, Mezzanine

White sand beaches . . .

A dazzling sun . . .

Delicious cocktails . . .

And Eric Zimmerman.

I'm insatiable!

That's the word that most accurately describes the hunger I feel for him—for my awesome, handsome, sexy, and kinky husband. I still can't believe it. I'm married to Eric! My Iceman!

We're in Tulum, Mexico, savoring our honeymoon, which I would like to go on forever.

Settled into a hammock, I'm sunbathing topless. I love feeling the sun's rays on my skin as my Iceman talks on the phone just a few yards from me. I can tell by his furrowed brow that he's focused on business.

Eric is tanned and virile in his blue bathing suit. I watch him carefully . . . and the more I watch, the more I like him and the more excited I get.

I notice that a handful of women sitting at a lovely bar nearby are also watching him. I totally get why. I consider calling out to them, "Hey, hyenas, he's all mine!"

But I know it's completely unnecessary. Eric *is* mine, all mine, without any need for me to shout it out to the four corners of the earth.

Three days after our wedding in Munich, my husband surprised me with this stupendous and romantic honeymoon. So here I am, on this exotic beach on the Mexican Caribbean coast, delighting in these excellent vistas and longing to go back to the intimacy of our room.

I'm also thirsty. I get up from the hammock, pluck out my earbuds, put on my yellow bikini top, and head for the beach bar.

Suddenly, I hear Alejandro Sanz's voice, and I sing along as I walk.

The soft breeze plays with my hair, and I keep singing along until I reach the bar.

I ask the bartender for a giant Coke with extra ice, and when I take a sip, a pair of hands encircle my waist.

"Hey, sweetheart."

His voice . . .

His nearness . . .

His way of calling me sweetheart . . .

Mmm . . . he drives me crazy and, smiling broadly, happier than a clam at high tide, I lean back, and he kisses me on the forehead.

"Do you want some Coke?"

He nods and settles on the stool next to me, grabs the glass I offer, and takes a long swallow.

"Thanks. I was so thirsty." After running his blue eyes over my chest, he gives me a teasing smile. "Why did you put your top back on? You're denying me a marvelous view."

"I'm just not really comfortable being topless here at the bar."

I can feel his heat. The music suddenly changes, and a romantic ranchera plays. Hooray for rancheras!

What a playlist. So much feeling. Eric, who has turned into the most romantic person I've ever met in my life, looks at me slyly and takes me by the waist again.

"Will you dance with me, sweetheart?"

I love it when he gives in to his impulses and just thinks about him and me.

It's so crazy.

I'm so head over heels in love.

The song Dexter dedicated to us at our wedding comes on. Eric comes down off the stool, and right there, in the middle of the bar at the beach, not caring about the tourists, completely besotted, we dance before an audience of jealous women as Luis Miguel sings.

Oh God . . . what a moment!

This is what I want, for everyone to let Eric and me be happy—actually, for us to let ourselves be happy. Because if we've learned anything, it's that we're fire and water, and although we love each other madly, we're always charged, ready to go off.

We haven't fought since the wedding though. We're both on a cloud and just kiss, whisper sweet nothings, and devote ourselves to each other.

Hooray for the honeymoon!

The song keeps playing, and we keep dancing. We enjoy the moment. We forget about the world and gaze at each other adoringly.

His blue eyes cut right through me, and he tells me how much he loves me and wants me, and when the song is over, my husband, my lover, my crazy love, kisses me. Settling me back on the stool, he whispers just a few inches from my mouth.

"Like the song says, I'm going to love you my whole life."

Mother of God . . . he's so beautiful. I just want to eat him up bit by bit!

Five minutes later, after we've exhausted ourselves with sweet caresses and cuddles, and under the indiscreet eyes of the women watching us at the bar, I ask, "Was that Dexter you were talking to on the phone?"

"No, Dexter's business partner. He wants us to meet tomorrow at his office to take care of a few things."

"Where's his office?"

"About thirty minutes from here. At Carmen Beach. So, tomorrow morning we'll—"

"We?" I cut him off. "No, no . . . you mean you. I'd rather stay here."

Eric raises an eyebrow.

"Alone?" he asks.

The look on his face amuses me.

"Eric, I won't be alone. The hotel is full of people and so are the beaches."

He furrows his brow. The return of the Iceman!

"You'll be by yourself, Jude, and that doesn't please me."

I laugh aloud.

"My love—"

"No, Jude, you'll come with me. I've seen too many predators hunting for pretty women, and I'm not going to let them have mine," he says, quite seriously.

That makes me laugh even more. Obviously, he isn't amused. I love his jealous side, and, getting up from the barstool, I put my arms around his neck.

"I'm not interested in a single predator except you! So, chill because I know how to take care of myself. In any case, if I know you, you'll be up at the crack of dawn, right?" My sweet thing nods and circles my waist with his arms yet again. "I don't want to get up early. I want to sleep and sunbathe until you get back. What's the problem?" I ask.

"Jude . . ."

I kiss him. I love kissing him.

"Let's go back to our room," I say guiltlessly.

"We're talking about—"

"It's just that when I see you so serious," I say, cutting him off again, "I want you so much."

Eric grins. "Good!"

He pulls me toward him and kisses me . . . and that kiss is filled with adoration, which leaves the women at the bar gobsmacked.

Then he takes me in his arms and walks us back in the direction of our room.

By the time we get to our door, my personal predator is in a hurry. Laughing, I open the door with the key card, and he closes it with his foot. He drops me on the bed.

"I'm going to start the Jacuzzi." I watch him walk over to the round tub just a few yards from our bed and turn on the water. "Get naked, or that bikini is going to end up torn to shreds," he says, clearly excited.

Wow!

I tear that thing off me at the speed of light. The bikini is beautiful. I bought it yesterday at a crazy expensive store in Tulum, and I don't want it to end up like most of my underwear.

Eric grins when he sees my urgency. He bites his lip as he watches me, and, once I'm fully naked, he signals for me to come to him with his index finger. I go. My breasts collide with his taut chest.

"Show me how much you want me," he whispers in a raspy voice. Oh yes!

Hot and horny, I untie his swim trunks. My hands slip inside as I kneel before him. Once I get the trunks from around his feet, I lift my eyes and stare at his penis.

My mouth waters when I see he's ready for me. I look up at Eric's face. "I'm all yours, sweetheart."

Without hesitation, I take his hard cock in my hand and rub it on my face and neck as I watch him and the look of delight on his face.

Ready to enjoy this tempting morsel, I run my tongue from one end of it to the other.

Eric smiles as I nibble—not once taking my eyes off him—until he moans with satisfaction and puts his hand on my head. My breathing gets faster—I want him! Anxious for more, I bring him into my mouth and feel his hands tangle in my hair. He sighs. Oh yes!

I love his cock: hard, hot, and smooth. Our game continues for a few more minutes until he can't take it anymore. He pulls on my hair to make me look up at him again.

"Get in bed."

I get up off the floor and do as he says. My knees are trembling. Eric, my powerful god of love, comes to me breathing heavily and gives me an order. "Spread your legs."

I gasp and my breathing picks up. I know what he's going to do, and it drives me crazy.

Eric gets up on the bed and kisses me. He's on all fours, like a lion, and brings his mouth close to mine; I can't wait to devour him.

Kisses . . . bites . . . my husband knows I'm willing to do anything for him, and he glides down my body until he's perfectly positioned between my legs and makes me cry out.

His mouth is moving and making demands at the very core of my desire!

His fingers open me up and slide inside me over and over as I begin to pant.

"Don't stop . . ."

Oh God . . . he's not listening to me. I could kill him. And then, suddenly, his tongue—his magnificent, wet tongue—enters me and makes love to me.

Oh yes, he's so good at this! I gasp and grab the pretty bone-colored sheets as I jerk and moan over and over while enjoying what my love is doing to me.

When I think I can't take any more, Eric rises from between my legs, leans over me, and penetrates me. His thrust is quick and strong, and I arch up to receive him, dying of desire.

He gives me no break as his hands grab my hips, and he slams into me once and twice . . . over and over. I take it all in. My legs are shaking. My body is vibrating as he takes me, and when the heat, the passion, and the delirium all hit my head at once, I hear a long, satisfied groan.

Right after, I groan too, and, sweating from the effort, my man falls on top of me.

Thirty seconds later, I'm overheating because of the giant laying on my body. "Eric, I can't breathe."

He rolls off to my right on the bed. This time, he takes me with him so that in the end, I'm on top.

"I love you, sweetheart." And then, like always, he adds, "Everything all right?"

Delighted and in love, I grin. "Everything's perfect, Iceman."

We spend the afternoon laughing and playing in our little love nest.

That night, as we're finishing up a wonderful meal at the hotel restaurant, Eric's cell rings. He answers, speaks only briefly, and then leaves it on the table when the call is finished.

"That was Roberto. We're meeting at his office tomorrow at eight in the morning."

"That means you'll get up at first light!"

He's about to say something, but I don't let him.

"Oh no . . . I said I'm not going. I want to sunbathe."

"Jude . . ."

"C'mon, don't be jealous, silly. I just want to sleep and lie in the sun," I say. "And then, when you return, we'll go back to our room and back to our fun, just you and me. What do you think of that?"

Eric smiles. He knows I'm not going to change my mind.

"Fine, stubborn girl," he says finally. "I'll come back with a pink-labelled bottle. What do you think of that?"

2

I wake up at six thirty in the morning and hear Eric in the bathroom. I want to give him a kiss before he goes, but I'm so sleepy, I decide to wait until he's finished. When I finally awaken, it's ten thirty.

"Fuck."

Stretching out once more on the enormous and luxurious bed I share with my love, I pick up my cell.

Everything OK? I type.

I worry about my guy as much as he worries about me. A minute later, I get a response.

As soon as I'm with you again, everything will be all right. I love you.

I smile like a fool, roll around in bed, and enjoy his smell on the sheets. I loaf for a while and then open Facebook on my laptop and upload a photo of Eric and me at the beach. Two seconds later, my wall is chock-full of comments from my friends, the Maxwell Warriors. "Eat him up!" "If you don't want him, I'll take him!" "I want an Eric in my life!"

I laugh. The Warriors are girlfriends I met online, and they're happy about my wedding and can't stop teasing me about my honeymoon.

After a quick shower, I decide to call my father. I glance at the clock and calculate the time difference. It's evening in Spain, but I know he's still up. Like Eric, he doesn't sleep much.

I sit on the bed and punch in the number. He picks up after two rings.

"*Orale*, Papito, hello!"

"Hi, my love. How is my sweetheart?"

"Great, Papá. Everything's great!" I hear him laugh. "This is a dream, and I'm having an amazing time with Eric."

"I love hearing that, sweetheart."

"Seriously, Papá, you have to come here. You should tell Bicharrón and Lucena that you're taking your next vacation here. You're going to love it."

My father laughs again.

"Listen, we couldn't drag Lucena out of Spain even with a crane! He went to your wedding in Germany only because it was you. Don't even think about another trip!"

"He didn't have a good time?"

"Oh no, sweetheart, he had a great time. But he's hung up on food. According to him, there's no place he'd rather eat than home."

"Then include Bicharrón's wife on your next trip—I'm sure she'd love it!"

"That's true . . . and he'd probably like that."

We talk for a good while. I tell him a thousand stories, and he tells me how things are going there. He's a little concerned about the economic crisis. He had to lay off one of his mechanics, and it broke his heart.

"Is Flyn behaving?"

"Like a lamb, and let me tell you what a great caretaker he's turned out to be for Lucía. He loves her! Seriously, my dear, he's having a lot of fun with the kids from the neighborhood and with Luz. Those two are dangerous together. And what an appetite that kid has. And great taste. If I don't give him top-of-the-line ham, he quickly looks over and says, 'Manuel, this ham is no good.'"

"Oh my God."

"I'm telling you. And Pachuca's chilled tomato soup is driving him crazy."

I laugh.

"We can't put one foot in the restaurant without that boy asking for a bowl. And he's like two peas in a pod with Luz. She taught him how to ride a bike and—"

"Oh God, Papá. He might fall."

Crap. I sound exactly like Eric.

"Easy, sweetheart . . . that kid is tough. Even though he's had two spectacular crashes against the fence."

"Papá!"

"It's no big deal, girl. He's a kid. A couple of bruises and scratches, and everything's all right. But you should see him on that bike."

I smile as I picture them. Luz and Flyn: Who would've thought?

I still remember the first time they met and how disastrous that was. But they've gotten to know each other since, and now they can't get enough of one another. So much that Flyn begged to go to Jerez while we were on our honeymoon.

"How's Raquel?" I ask.

"Your sister is driving me mad, sweetheart."

I feel for him. After my wedding, when my sister went back to Spain, she decided to spend some time with my father in Jerez. I offered her the house Eric gave me so she could live there with the girls, but neither she nor my father accepted my offer. They wanted to be together.

"So, what's going on with her?"

"She is ruining my life. Can you believe she's taken command of the remote?"

I laugh.

"I am so sick of shows about gossip, soap operas, and other stuff like that. How can she like that trash so much? And just so you know, she said that when you guys come back to get Flyn after your honeymoon, she's going to talk to Eric about a job. She says she has to start her life anew, and she can't do it without a job. And, needless to say, she's also dealing with Jesús's constant calls."

"Jesús! What does that imbecile want now?"

"According to your sister, he's checking in on the girls and wanting to talk to her."

"Do you think she wants to go back with him?"

I hear my father sigh. "No, thank God she's clear about that."

I'm not in the least bit amused to hear about these calls. My stupid ex-brother-in-law abandoned her while she was pregnant so he could live his crazy life. I just hope Raquel keeps it together and doesn't fall for that wolf in sheep's clothing again. I know my father worries about that too.

"About getting a job, Papá, I get that—and she's right."

"Oh, c'mon, sweetheart, with what I earn, I can support her and the girls. Why does she want to work?"

"Listen, Papá, I'm sure Raquel is happy living with you and is very grateful for all you do for her. But she doesn't want to stay in Jerez, and you know that. When we talked about it, she told you it was a temporary move and—"

"But what is she going to do all alone in Madrid with the girls? Here, she's got me, and I take care of them and make sure all three are OK."

I can't help but smile. My father is super protective, like Eric. "Papá . . . Raquel has to get her life back. If she stays in Jerez with you, it'll just take her longer. Don't you see that?"

My father is the best and the most generous person on the planet, and I understand what he's going through. But I also understand my sister. She wants to get ahead, and, knowing her, she will.

Nearly an hour later, after I hang up with my dad, I fill up at the hotel buffet. Everything is delicious. I'm wearing a green bikini that accentuates my tan, and when I finish my meal, I head for the beach. I look for a free hammock and umbrella, and, when I find one, I immediately drop into it.

I love the sun!

I pull out my iPod, put on my earbuds, and hit Play, and my beloved Pablo Alborán begins to sing.

I sing along and watch the waves come and go.

It's the perfect song with which to contemplate the sea.

I'm happy right now and I open my book. Sometimes I can read and sing along at the same time. It's a rare talent, but I can do it. Twenty minutes later, just as Pablo sings "La Vie en Rose," my lids are getting heavy, and the tender breeze makes me close my book. Without realizing it, I fall into Morpheus's arms. I don't know how long I'm asleep when I hear a voice.

"Miss . . . miss . . ."

My eyes pop open. What's going on?

Not sure what's happening, I pull out my earbuds, and there, in front of me, is a smiling server offering me a margarita.

"This is from the gentleman in the blue shirt up at the bar."

Eric is back!

Thirsty, I take a sip. It's so good! But when I look up at the bar with one of my most enchanting and sensual smiles, I'm horrified to discover the man who sent me the cocktail is not Eric.

Oh my God.

The gentleman in the blue shirt is in his forties, is tall with dark hair, and is wearing a striped bathing suit. When he sees me smile, he smiles back, and I want the earth to swallow me.

What do I do now? Spit out what I just drank?

Trying to make as little of it as I can, I thank him, stop looking at him, and open my book again. Out of the corner of my eye, I see him smiling, then sitting at one of the stools at the bar, drinking.

For about a half an hour, I focus on reading, but the truth is nothing registers. The man at the bar is making me nervous. He doesn't make a move, but he won't stop staring at me. I finally close my book, pull off my sunglasses, and decide to take a dip in the water.

The water is fresh, and I love it.

I walk in a few yards, and, when the water is about at my waist and I see a wave coming up, I launch myself like a siren and dive into it.

Oh yes . . . what a feeling!

When I get tired of swimming, I flip over and float on my back. I consider taking off my top but decide against it. Something tells me the man at the bar is still looking at me and could misinterpret that as an invitation.

"Hello."

Surprised to hear a voice at my side, I jerk and almost drown. A pair of unknown hands quickly pull me up and let go as soon as I stand. I wipe my face and blink and realize it's the man who's been staring at me for nearly an hour.

"What do you want?"

"For starters, for you not to drown," he says with a teasing smile. "I'm sorry if I scared you. I just want to talk, pretty lady."

I can't help but smile. His Mexican accent is very sweet, but, recovering, I step away from him.

"Listen, thank you for the drink, but I'm married, and I'm not really into talking with you or anyone, OK?"

He nods. "Recently married?"

I'm just about ready to tell him to take a walk. What does he care?

"I just told you I'm married, so would you please leave me alone? Before you insist, let me tell you that I can easily go from a pretty lady into something of a beast. So, just walk away and don't make me mad."

The man nods and steps back. As he creates some distance between us, I hear him say, "Wow, what a babe!"

I keep an eye on him and watch as he gets out of the water and goes directly to the bar. He picks up a red towel, dries his face, and leaves. I'm pleased and swim back to the shore. I sit on the sand and play around, dropping handfuls on my legs.

That's when a little girl comes to sit by my side.

"Shall we play?" she says, offering me a bucket.

"What's your name?" I ask, nodding and filling the bucket with sand.

"Angelly," she says with a beautiful smile. "And you?"

"Judith."

"I'm six years old," she says, still smiling. "And you?"

Well, that's the kind of question my dear niece Luz would ask. I smile and ruffle her hair and pick up the bucket once more.

"Shall we build a castle?"

I play as the sun dries my skin. I'm getting very, very dark; as my father would say, like a gypsy.

An hour later, the girl leaves with her parents, and I return to my hammock. Two seconds later, a much younger man sits by me on the sand.

"Hello," he says in English, "my name is George. Are you by yourself?"

I can't help it and start to laugh. There's so much flirting going on!

"Hi, I'm Judith, and, no, I'm not by myself."

"Are you Spanish?"

"Yes." But I know this game and get ahead of him. "I'm sure you like paella and sangria, right?"

"Oh yeah?"

I recognize his accent. "German, right?"

He stares at me.

"How did you know?"

I want to say Frankfurt! Audi!

"I know a few Germans and am very familiar with that accent."

I start to put on some lotion.

"Shall I do that for you?"

I stop. I look him up and down.

"No, thank you. I can do this quite well by myself."

George nods. He wants to talk.

"I've been watching you all morning, and no one has come to sit with you except me. Are you sure you're alone?"

"I already told you."

"I saw you playing with a little girl and shutting down some guy."

Incredible. Has this guy been spying on me?

"Look, George, I don't want to seem rude, but what the hell are you doing keeping tabs on me?"

"I don't have anything better to do. I'm on vacation with my parents, and I'm bored. Will you let me buy you a drink?"

"No, thank you."

"You sure?"

"Very sure, George."

His insistence and his youth make me laugh at precisely the moment my cell rings. A message.

Flirting, Mrs. Zimmerman?

I immediately sit up. I look around until I see him. Eric is at the bar, and he's watching me. I smile at him, but he doesn't smile back. Uh-oh.

I can tell from his face that he's wondering who this stranger is here. But I want nothing more than to get this over with.

"Do you see that tall blond man who's looking at us from the bar?" I ask the young man.

"The one with the sour look?" asks the boy as he follows the direction of my index finger.

I laugh and nod.

"The very one. I want you to know he's German, like you."

"So what?"

"And he's my husband. From the look on his face, I'd say he doesn't like it one bit that you're here."

He flinches. Poor man!

Eric is bigger, stronger, and taller than he is. Now very serious, George immediately gets up. "I'm sorry, my apologies. I'm going," he says as he steps away. "I'm sure my parents are wondering where I am."

I give him a smile as he takes off, and I look up at my husband, but he's still unhappy. I roll my eyes and wave at him to come join me. He doesn't. I pout, and then, eventually, I see the right side of his mouth starting to curve.

Finally!

I signal him again with my finger to come over, but he refuses so I decide it's my turn. If the mountain won't come to Mohammed, then Mohammed must go to the mountain.

As I get up, I have an idea.

Feeling Machiavellian, I take off my top, drop it on the hammock, and, ready to give my husband a feast of a view, slowly walk up to him.

I'm getting so shameless!

Eric stares at me. He eats me up with his eyes, and I blush and my nipples stand at attention.

My God . . . he really gets me revved up when he looks at me like that.

I stand on my tiptoes to kiss him on the lips.

"I've missed you," I whisper.

He doesn't move and just stares at me from above. He's my very own Mr. High and Mighty.

"You were having a very good time talking to that fellow. Who is he?"

"George."

"And who is George?"

"Let's see, my love. George is a young man on vacation with his parents," I say, noticing his furrowed brow. "He was bored, so he decided to come and talk to me. Don't start up again about predators."

Eric doesn't say anything, and I remember the man with the blue shirt.

That guy really was a predator. George, who's much too young, is one thing, but the guy who offered me a margarita is another.

After a few seconds in which the Iceman simply looks at me, and I'm practically breaking my neck trying to look back at him, he finally cracks a smile.

"I have something with a pink label on ice back in the room," he says.

I laugh and, without hesitation, run back to the hammock. I grab my things, and, when I dash back to him, panting and with my breasts bouncing in the open air, Eric takes me in his arms and gives me a soft kiss on the lips.

"Let's go have some fun, Mrs. Zimmerman," he whispers.

That night there's a party at the hotel. After dinner, Eric and I grab a couple of comfy seats so we can enjoy the show. The dances are so colorful and everything is so Mexican and I'm having a great time singing along with the music.

Eric looks surprised. "You know this song too?"

I nod and lean over. "My love, I've been to so many Luis Miguel concerts in Spain, I know all his songs!" I tell him.

We kiss. We enjoy the moment while the mariachis sing "La Bikina" and slide right into the next song. One of the elegant cowboys in the band asks me to dance, just like they've asked some of the other tourists, and, neither shy nor lazy, I accept. "Lucky me!"

He leads me to the dance floor where the rest of the dancers and the tourists do what they can to the beat of the music. Loving every minute, I do the same. I'm never embarrassed to dance—I love to dance. Eric watches me and grins. He looks so relaxed while enjoying the show, and I feel like I'm going to burst from happiness.

And then, as I turn, my eyes connect with the man who offered me a drink and pursued me in the water this morning.

The man in the blue shirt! Oh God . . . oh God, I hope he doesn't try to flirt with me again because that would really be asking for it.

I'm nervous, but I don't know why.

Quickly, I look at Eric, and he winks at me. That's when I see the stranger walk over and greet him. If it weren't for my dance partner holding my hand, I might have fallen flat on my face.

I watch as Eric talks warmly with him and has him take my seat. My seat! A few minutes later, the song is over, and the dancer escorts me back to my table. Eric welcomes me with a kiss.

"You dance beautifully."

I nod and force a smile.

"My love, let me introduce you to Juan Alberto, Dexter's cousin. Juan Alberto, this is my lovely wife, Judith."

Teasing, the other man takes my hand and chivalrously kisses it.

"Judith, it's a pleasure to meet you . . . at last."

"At last?" asks Eric, surprised.

But before I have a chance to say anything, Juan Alberto clears the air.

"My cousin has spoken very highly of her."

I blush.

Oh my God . . . my God. What did Dexter say to him?

Eric grins when he looks at my face. He knows what I'm thinking.

"But, really, I mean 'at last' because I tried to meet her this morning. Dude, your wife has a hell of a temper. She kicked my ass and warned me that if I bothered her again, I'd be in even more serious trouble."

Eric cracks up. He likes hearing this although I can tell he's bothered that I didn't mention it to him.

"I told you I could defend myself from any predator," I say.

Juan Alberto laughs. "Oh yes. I will testify to that, my friend. She really scared me off."

Eric sits down and pulls me on his lap. He puts his arms around me protectively and gives me a teasing smile.

"So, this guy tried to flirt with you?"

I smile, but it's Juan Alberto who responds.

"No, dude. I was just trying to meet my friend's wife. Dexter had mentioned you were staying at this hotel, and, when I saw this beautiful young woman, I knew it had to be Judith."

Eric grins, as does Juan Alberto and, finally, I do too. Everything has been cleared up.

The three of us keep partying, drinking exquisite margaritas while listening to the delightful music at the bar. Juan Alberto is as much fun and as lively as Dexter. They look quite a bit alike too. They're both dark and attractive but, unlike his cousin, this guy does not look at me with desire.

We talk and I discover Juan Alberto will be going with us to Spain and then traveling through Europe. He is a consultant and designs security systems for businesses.

Finally, at two o'clock in the morning, Juan Alberto stands up. "Well," he says, "I'm going to sleep so you two can enjoy yourselves."

Eric and I get up too, and Eric extends his hand.

"Are you going to the dinner Dexter is having at his house in Mexico City?" Eric asks him.

"I don't know," responds Juan Alberto. "He mentioned it, and I'll try. If I don't make it, I'll see you guys at the airport, OK?"

Juan Alberto gives me two quick kisses on the cheek and leaves.

Once we're alone, Eric brings his mouth to my neck. "I like knowing you can defend yourself from predators."

"I told you, my love."

"What do you think of Juan Alberto?"

When I see the look on his face, I arch an eyebrow.

"What do you mean?"

"As a man, do you find him sexy?"

I know what he's getting at.

"I only find you sexy."

"Mmm . . . that excites me," he whispers into my mouth.

We gaze at each other. We're mere inches from one another, and I know what he wants and what he desires. His breathing picks up and so does mine.

The two of us! Suddenly, I feel his hand under my long skirt, and I blush.

"What are you doing?"

My Eric grins mischievously.

"Here?" I add in the thinnest little voice.

He's so playful. And I'm getting so hot.

He wants to get me off here?

The people around us are laughing, having fun, and drinking margaritas as we listen to the sound of the waves and the music. I'm sitting with my back to everybody in front of my love, and his hand reaches my thigh. He draws circles with his fingertips until he reaches my thong.

"Eric . . ."

"Shh."

Excited and nervous, I grin.

Oh God . . . oh God . . .

I very carefully look both ways. Everybody's doing their thing.

"Sweetheart, nobody's looking at us," Eric murmurs playfully.

"Eric . . ."

"Easy . . ." He pulls the thin fabric of my thong, and, quickly, one of his fingers begins to play with my clitoris. I close my eyes and my breathing gets heavier. Oh God . . . I love what he does to me.

I love the feeling I get when we do what's prohibited. It gets me very excited, and, when Eric slides one of his fingers inside me, I gasp. Popping my eyes open, I find his naughty smile.

"You like it?"

I nod like a bobblehead while my insides go crazy.

I don't want him to stop!

He smiles back while his finger plays with me, and the people around us, unaware of our hot little game, continue with their own fun.

He is so shameless!

But I like it . . . I like it, and, finally getting into it, I grin and move in search of more depth and more bliss.

My look of surrender makes him grunt.

Yes . . .

I drive him crazy too.

Yes . . .

He brings his mouth close to mine.

"Don't move, or everyone will know what's going on," he whispers, voice thick with arousal.

God . . . God . . . oh God, how very naughty.

How can I possibly stop moving?

The way he touches me makes me want more, and my face gives away what I'm thinking so Eric pulls his wet fingers from under my skirt, stands up, and takes me by the hand.

"Let's go," he says.

Excited, nervous, and full of desire, I follow. I would follow him to the ends of the earth!

I'm surprised when I see we're not headed for our room. He's headed to the beach instead. Once we are beyond the lights of the bar and wrapped in the breeze and the darkness of the evening, my love kisses me desperately.

I'm dying to touch him and unbutton his shirt. I'm overcome by my husband's body. It's smooth, sinewy, and hot.

I touch him; he touches me.

The heat between us grows with each second.

Between the kisses and the groping, we bump up against the bar on the beach, that little place where they make those stupendous margaritas during the day. It's closed now, and Eric wants to play. He unknots the bow at my waist to open my blouse.

"This is what I want," he murmurs once my breasts are exposed to the night air.

Hungrily, he kneels before me and kisses my nipples. First one, and then the other. My blouse falls to the floor, and I'm left wearing only my long skirt. Aroused, I look over to the bar, where everyone is having

21

fun. They're just a few yards from us, but I don't care if they can see us; I grab him by the hair and bring my right breast to his mouth.

"Taste me," I whisper.

He's thrilled and focuses his attention on my breasts as his hands run up and down my legs and slowly, very slowly, lift my skirt. When my nipple stiffens, I don't need to ask. Eric turns his attention to my other breast.

"Yes . . . Like that . . . That's how I like it," I say between breaths.

I'm all stirred up, and as his hands squeeze my ass, I feel my thong ripping.

"You don't need that," he says, teasingly.

I laugh aloud, but, once he tears my skirt off, it turns into a nervous giggle.

I'm just a few yards from the tourists at the hotel, naked and with a ripped thong but ready to go. And then, in that instant, we hear a woman's laughter—but not mine—close to us. Eric and I glance at each other when we realize a man and a woman are in our exact same situation on the other side of the bar.

We don't say a word. We don't need to. Without acknowledging each other, each couple continues their own kinky dance.

We're turned on by each other's presence.

Eric kisses me. He longs for my mouth in the same way I need his. His hands take hold of my wrists, and he lifts them above my head. His body is pressing mine against the bar's wooden boards, and I can feel his erection on my belly. That incites me even more.

He's throbbing violently. I want him inside me.

"You drive me crazy," he says.

I grin. I close my eyes. I'm so happy.

Suddenly, the woman's moans make us turn our heads. She's on the floor on all fours, and her companion is fucking her over and over from behind.

I can't take my eyes off this spectacle, and I'm particularly entranced by the woman's expression. Her mouth, her face, her gaze show she's enraptured. I can see how much she's loving it, and that makes my own temperature rise.

I love to watch.

Watching gets me worked up.

Watching makes me want to play.

"Do you like what you see?" Eric murmurs in my ear.

That question brings back memories of our first visit to Moroccio, that very special restaurant he took me to in Madrid. I smile when I remember how scared I was back then, and I sigh as I try to imagine what my face looks like right now. Everything's different. Thanks to Eric, my perception of sex has changed—I think for the better.

I'm now a woman who relishes sex. Who talks about sex. Who knows how to play and no longer sees it as taboo. As the woman's cries get louder, and her partner's thrusts become harder and more assured, we watch, and Eric's voice breaks a little.

"Now I want to hear you moan," he says.

I can't take my eyes off the scene before us, but I notice when Eric undoes the knot on his linen pants and takes them off. He turns me toward him, parts my legs, and after rubbing his cock on my butt, he locates my sex and thrusts into me.

Oh yes . . . yes.

His stroke is heavenly and fearless. The way we both like it. His hard, smooth, stiff penis buries itself completely in me, and I suckle it and squeeze, delighted to receive him.

The pleasure is so intense . . . The heat is bracing . . . I pant and my love, my lover, my German, holds me by the waist, having too good a time as he lunges at me over and over, drawing moans from me that drive us both crazy.

I turn and realize the couple who was tussling before are watching, and I know now it's me who's showing the other woman the depths of my desire.

Oh yes . . . I really want her to see.

I want her to know just exactly how much I'm savoring this.

Because of Eric's height and force, he lifts me off the ground a couple of times, and I have to hold on to the bar's wooden boards so he can come in and out of me. I like how he possesses me.

He does it again and again. I love it. He loves it. The strangers love it, and then my body weakens, turns to jelly, and I let myself come with a long and delicious cry. Eric follows the instant after my climax with a raspy groan.

For a few seconds, we're quiet and don't move. We're exhausted now. And then the other couple waves at us as they get dressed and go, and we come back down to earth.

Still holding on to me, Eric pulls his cock from inside me. He kisses my ribs, and when he sees me cringe, he squeezes me tighter in his arms.

"Do you want to take a little swim?"

Oh yes . . . I like doing everything with him, and I accept without reservation.

I love it when he's so relaxed. When he loses his arrogance. His solemnity.

Naked, happy, we run toward the water, holding hands. We both dive in, and when we emerge from the water, my lover takes me in his arms and kisses me.

"I'm crazier about you every day, Mrs. Zimmerman," he says.

I smile broadly.

How could I not smile . . . drool . . . shout out my happiness. What a husband I have!

I curl my legs around his body and notice his erection growing again. I give my insatiable, kinky, and hot husband a certain look.

"Tell me what you want," I say.

3

After twenty days in our own personal paradise where everything is magical and fun, I look out the car window in Mexico City, and I'm surprised to discover the streets are choked with people. Eric's on his cell, with his usual serious expression, as the driver navigates our impressive limousine.

When we arrive at a very modern building, a man in a uniform opens the car door. He greets Eric and quickly calls for an elevator. When the elevator doors open on the eighteenth floor, Dexter is there to meet us. His warm smile lets me know how happy he is about our visit.

"Look at how pretty and tan the lovers are," he says. We all laugh, and then Dexter takes my hand. "Goddess, what a delight to see you again."

"Hey, what about me?" Eric protests.

Eric fist bumps him.

"Sorry, dude, but I like your woman more than I like you."

Because he's in a wheelchair, I have to lean down to give him a kiss on each cheek. After our initial greetings, Dexter introduces us to a woman who's been standing near him. "This is Graciela, my personal assistant. Eric, you've already met."

"Welcome, Mr. Zimmerman," says the brunette.

Eric shakes her hand and responds warmly. "Good to see you again, Graciela. Everything going OK with this jerk?"

The young woman looks over at Dexter with a shy smile. "Right now everything's fine, sir," she says.

"Judith is Eric's wife, and they've come to visit us after their honeymoon," he tells her.

"Delighted, Mrs. Zimmerman, and congratulations," she says.

"Please," I say, "call me Judith. All right?"

The young woman looks over at Dexter for approval, and he nods.

"Please, you don't need their blessing to call me by my first name, OK?"

I smile and she smiles back.

"Now you know, Graciela," says Eric. "Just call her Judith."

"Of course, Mr. Zimmerman." She turns to me. "A pleasure, Judith."

I don't particularly care to be called ma'am or Mrs. Zimmerman all the time. In fact, I don't like it at all.

I think Graciela must be a few years older than me. She seems meticulous and, from my point of view, attractive. She has dark hair, captivating eyes, and a sweetness about her. And yet, she doesn't really look like a woman of today. Her beauty feels old-fashioned and not like that of someone my age.

Once we've been welcomed, we retire to a simple room. There are no obstacles so that Dexter can move around with ease in his wheelchair.

For about an hour, the four of us chat and talk about the wedding. Dexter asks about my sister, and when he mentions her for the fourth time, I decide to be crystal clear with him. "Dexter, don't go anywhere near my sister," I say.

He and Eric crack up, and I get it. I can't even imagine what would happen if Dexter made a date with my sister and proposed any of his games. She'd slap him so hard, she'd knock him off his chair. I laugh the more I think about it.

"Easy, Jude," says Eric when he realizes what I'm thinking. "Dexter knows very well with whom he can and cannot mess around."

I nod. I want to make sure I'm clear, but Dexter gets ahead of me. "Got it. Are you a little jealous of your pretty sister?"

I just stare at him.

Me? Jealous of my sister?

Please! "No, I'm simply protective of her," I respond, again trying to make things clear.

Dexter smiles.

"You're so sweet, my dear Judith."

"Thank you; you too," I say, teasing him. "But your promise means you'll leave my sister alone. Remember: you were warned!"

The three of us laugh, clear about our understanding, and then I realize Graciela isn't laughing. She doesn't smile. Her eyes briefly moisten, and she stares at the floor. She takes two deep breaths and lifts her head, and then her eyes are back to normal.

Wow . . . what an incredible recovery but, even more impressive, what I just realized is so intense!

Graciela is obviously head over heels for Dexter. Poor woman. I feel terrible for her.

In an instant, she says goodbye and leaves.

When it's just the three of us in this huge room, Dexter asks how we were treated at the hotel during our honeymoon. Eric looks over at me, and I smile like a fool.

It was fantastic. The best trip of my life. Eric loves me in a way I never imagined a man could love, and I'm desperately in love with him.

As we laugh and chat, Dexter asks if we played during our honeymoon, and I tell him we played a lot—a whole lot—but that these were games strictly between my husband and me. God, just thinking about it makes my heart beat faster.

The hotel . . .

The bed . . .

His eyes . . .

His hands . . .

All those hot, kinky talks . . .

As he listens to me, Eric smiles. He says he can tell exactly what I'm thinking by the look on my face, and I'm sure he's guessed my thoughts more than once.

"Goddess, whenever you want, I'm ready to play," says Dexter, joking around, like always. He winks at me and admires my tanned legs.

That makes me blush. Eric's games are always hot and kinky, and when I look over at him, I can see he's ready—my husband's always ready to go. But our stimulating conversation is cut short when we hear a phone ring, and an instant later Graciela comes in, holding it in her hand.

Dexter takes it, and Eric leans toward me. "I see you're a little flushed, my love. Is everything all right?"

He's so shameless.

I can't help but grin, but before I can respond, he caresses my leg with his hand.

"If you want, I'm willing," he says in a honeyed voice.

Wow, I'm getting so hot . . . so very hot!

As happens every time, I get butterflies in my stomach and wet in a fraction of a second. There's no question: I'm turning into a sex fiend. Who would have ever thought I would love this game so much?

The truth is, I like it. I enjoy it.

My man grins. I do too.

I whisper to him so Graciela won't hear me. "Tear my thong off."

Oh my God, what did I just say?

The Iceman's blue gaze turns ardent. Wow! I've gone from top speed to supersonic, and, from what I can see, he's breaking all kinds of records.

I'm well aware that both my shamelessness and my surrender drive him crazy. I give him a smile I know will push him even further.

He responds with a word Mexicans love to use: *"Sabrosa!"*

When Dexter finishes with the call, he hands the phone to Graciela, and she leaves the room.

"Dexter, when do our dinner guests arrive tonight?" asks Eric.

They give each other a look, and I know they've communicated perfectly. Those two!

"In about three hours," he responds, clearly delighted.

Dexter arches his brow and stares shamelessly at my erect nipples. "What do you say we go someplace more private?"

My pulse quickens.

I stand up, and Eric holds my hand tightly. I like that feeling. We walk behind Dexter, and I'm surprised when we find ourselves in his office. I thought we were going to a bedroom.

Once Eric closes the door, I'm astounded when Dexter pushes a button on the bookshelf, and it suddenly slides to the right. I can't hide my amazement.

"Goddess, welcome to the pleasure dome," says Dexter.

Eric guides me by the hand. Once the bookshelf closes behind us, there's a tenuous and yellowish light.

This is kink in its purest state.

My eyes adapt to the shadows, and I see a bed about thirty yards from me, a Jacuzzi, a round table, a cross on the wall, boxes, and several things hanging from the walls. When I come near, I realize they're straps and sex toys. S&M! I don't like S&M.

My face must have given me away because Eric steps up to reassure me. "Are you scared?" he asks.

I shake my head. I'm never scared when I'm with him. I know he won't let me suffer or have me do anything I don't want to do.

Dexter rolls his wheelchair over to a sound system and puts on a CD. An instant later, the room is filled with a very sensual instrumental music. It's pretty hot. He positions himself by the round table while Eric kisses me. I let myself enjoy his tongue inside my mouth . . . I'm loving it as he plants his hands on my butt and squeezes it with delight.

The heat rises, and my body responds to his touch in a matter of seconds.

We kiss and grope for several minutes. I know Dexter is enjoying watching us. And once I'm totally and completely turned on by my handsome husband, he abandons my mouth and sits on the bed.

"Undress, my love," he says.

Both men stare at me, and I notice neither of them are undressing. They just watch and wait for me to do what he's requested.

Without hesitation, I undo the button and zipper on my skirt and let it fall to the floor.

They both center their gaze on my thong, but I leave it on for the moment.

Dexter makes a movement with his hand, and, once I get his meaning, I turn and show off my ass.

"Mamacita," he murmurs.

When I turn back to them, I very slowly drop the straps from my top and pull it off so I'm just standing there in my underwear and high heels. I know these two, and I know they love that.

"Put your hands on your waist and open your legs a little bit," says Dexter.

I do as he says, and my breathing accelerates.

"Touch your breasts," says Eric.

I put my hands over them, on top of my bra, and I squeeze and rub them while the two of them watch, and I burn with desire.

I'm being watched by two men who want to fuck me.

I'm being watched by two men who want to taste me.

I'm being watched, and it excites me.

I'm agitated. I want them to touch me.

"I still remember that woman in Germany having her way with your body and the way you were panting," whispers Dexter as he comes up close to me. "That was amazing. I can't wait to see that again."

Remembering that turns me on too. I like Diana, the German woman Dexter's referring to. Her way of taking me was so exacting that I get wet just thinking about her.

We talked about it during our honeymoon, and Eric's as excited to see her again as I am. "Oh, you will, my friend," says Eric once he recognizes the look on my face. "I can assure you Jude wants to do it again."

Dexter sighs and nods. He moves to the back of the room where there's a small fridge and pulls out a bottle of water and a jar of something red.

My curiosity gets the better of me. "What's in the jar?"

Dexter opens it and shows me. "Cherries. I love them!"

He drops one in his mouth, chews, and savors it. "Mmm . . . they're so sweet."

Seeing my expression, Dexter grins and places the jar of cherries on the table. He opens the drawer of a small dresser, pulls out a box and a mask, and hands it to Eric.

"Put this on her."

Eric brings the mask over to me and, after giving me one of those looks that drive me crazy, kisses me and pulls the mask over my face. My world turns black. I can't see anything.

"Sit her down at the table," I hear Dexter tell him.

My man leads me, and, once I'm situated where Dexter wants, he puts his hands on my knees. "Lie down, my love."

I do as he says.

The table is hard, and I can't see. I don't know where Eric is, and that disorients me a little bit. There's a finger running on my thong, and my tummy flips. I'm hot. Excited and totally exposed to them, I hear Dexter's wheelchair doing circles around the table.

"Goddess, the smell of your sex drives me crazy, but I want it to be your man who takes your thong off for me and invites me to do whatever I please with you."

An instant later, I feel Eric's mouth on my navel. He kisses me all the way to the top of my thong, touches my thighs, and pulls the thong off me.

"I'm thirsty," I say, my mouth dry and panting.

Suddenly, I feel an ice cube on my lips. I open my mouth, ready to be refreshed.

"Dexter, be my guest and take what you want from my wife."

"I'll be delighted to do so."

My mouth, which had been moistened by the ice, now goes instantly dry when I feel fresh water on my sex. A soft towel pats me dry. "Now you're ready, my love."

I feel my heart in my throat. I'm incredibly keyed up and blinking under the mask.

"Do you like what you see?" I ask.

Carefully, Eric lies down next to me on the table, undoes my bra, and lets my breasts out into the open air.

"It drives me crazy, sweetheart."

Once I'm completely naked on the table, I feel Eric move away, and Dexter, in his wheelchair, takes a place between my legs. He lifts them on his shoulders.

"What a mouthwatering feast you're offering me, beautiful."

I shake. I know what's going to happen, and I moan in anticipation. Without pause, Dexter rubs his hand on my tattoo, and, I imagine, reads it.

But he surprises me. "I'm going to ask that you surrender yourself to me," he whispers.

I'm trembling from being so desired and anxiously waiting to be devoured.

"Put your feet on the floor and stand up," Dexter says suddenly. "Turn around and lie back down on the table."

I do as he says. I turn around, and once my face is back on the table and my ass is exposed, he slaps me a couple of times.

"Red . . . Like that . . . Red for me."

My butt stings from the slaps. I know Eric is watching and controlling everything when I feel Dexter's hand separating my butt cheeks and rubbing gel on my anus.

"We're going to play a different game today."

A different game? What game? I'm about to protest when I feel Eric's hands on my shoulders.

"Don't move," he whispers in my ear.

His voice calms me down as I realize Dexter has inserted something in my ass.

"These anal beads will increase your and our pleasure . . . You'll see," says Dexter.

Still on the table, I let him push in bead after bead, getting more excited by the second.

My God . . . I love being their toy!

Dexter is having fun with the beads in my asshole. He gives me a little lash after each bead and then a little bite and rubs my cheeks. Oh yes . . . I love what he does to me.

Once he's finished, my ass feels full. It's a strange sensation, but I like it.

"Goddess, lie down on your back on the table the way you were before."

My butt is red and jammed with beads, and I'm still blindfolded, but I do as he asks.

"Eric . . . may I taste your woman now?"

My heart is going a mile a minute.

These two are expert players, experts in kink, and they're driving me crazy while barely touching me.

"Taste her as much as you want," I hear Eric say, and I gasp and pant.

I can't see his expression.

But I can imagine it and the tone of his voice lets me know how much he's enjoying the moment. I am panting like mad, and I can hear my breathing echo in the room.

Oh yes . . . yes . . .

I don't want them to stop.

I want them to play and play.

I want them to taste every part of me.

I want them to fuck me.

Eric parts my thighs, and I'm completely exposed. That's when I notice something round and slick on my clitoris.

"Cherries and Judith," says Dexter. "An explosive and ambrosial combination."

He places the cherry between his teeth and presses it against me. The cherry is smooth and hard and slides around on my clitoris, and I'm breathing so hard. Dexter skillfully moves his mouth, and the cherry sparks my desire in seconds. He drops the cherry, and I feel it roll off my sex as he brings his tongue to my clit. He picks up the cherry again and repeats the action.

Oh God . . . oh God!

My body responds.

I can barely breathe . . . and I can't believe it when Eric puts his mouth on mine.

He kisses me . . . He luxuriates in me . . .

He makes me crazy . . .

Dexter is sucking on my swollen clitoris when I lift my hips off the table, ready to offer even more.

"Like that, my love, like that," murmurs Eric as he notes my surrender with approval.

For a few minutes, I'm their banquet, their blindfolded banquet. One is enjoying himself between my legs, and the other is enjoying my mouth. But the best part is that I get to enjoy them both. This is extraordinary! Suddenly, Eric pulls away from me. I lift up, searching for him, but I can't find him, and I can't see because of the mask.

I want his kisses . . .

I want his touch . . .

And when I feel them pouring water on my sex again, I know the game is about to change. Dexter retires, and I hear the wheelchair coming around the table to where my head is. He takes my hands and kisses my knuckles.

"Now you're going to get what I can't give you," he says.

Eric's hands touch me. I recognize them. I smile as he firmly and forcefully takes hold of my thighs, and then he's inside me with one mighty thrust.

His groan drives me crazy.

I'm breathing so heavily. Dexter lets go of my hands as Eric lifts me up off the table and pulls off my mask.

"Hold on to me."

I'm shaking . . .

As the man I adore vigorously penetrates me over and over, I look into his eyes without his needing to ask me.

Oh God, his gaze!

His eyes look right through me, they speak to me, they tell me they love me as Dexter slaps my ass and makes it even redder, just the way he likes it.

Once more, Eric goes in and out of me, and, in that instant, Dexter pulls on the anal beads. I release one, and he slaps me. I can't believe what I feel, and I scream. I'm out of my mind.

Eric grins and presses me against him, thrusting into me again.

Another onslaught.

Another yank on the beads and another slap. Another scream from my throat.

One by one, the little beads come out of me, and I'm raving as Eric holds me in his arms.

"Like that, my love, like that . . . Just look at me and enjoy yourself."

Once Dexter has pulled all the beads from inside me, he moves aside, and Eric takes over. He walks me over to the wall and leans me against it, and, taking my mouth the way only he knows, he fucks me over and over so intensely that I think he's going to split me in two—but I like it. His hands squeeze my ass as I take him and open myself up more and more for him.

Our pleasure is so immense, I don't want it to end. I want his lunges to last forever. His groans make me crazy, and just when I think we're both going to explode, we release at the same time, and, after one last blitz, we both succumb.

With his cock still inside me, I put my head on his neck. I love how he smells. I love the feel of him. I close my eyes and hold him closer as he holds me back and feels everything I'm feeling.

After a few minutes, when our breathing returns to normal, he asks what he always asks. "Everything all right?"

I nod and smile.

Eric walks me back over to the table and positions me on top of it. Dexter comes up and takes my hand and kisses my knuckles.

"Thank you, Goddess."

I smile and, without the slightest bit of shame, pick up my thong from the table and put it on.

"Thank you, handsome," I say. I need to wash up.

Two hours later, after a quick shower in the room we've been assigned, we dress for dinner, and my prince and I return to the big room, which is already overflowing with people.

I don't know anyone, but they all greet me with great big smiles. They're Dexter's friends and family. Eric knows everybody, and I'm surprised to see him so relaxed and happy.

Of course, when he wants, he can be a real charmer!

Dexter's family is wonderful, and his parents are beautiful people. By the way they treat Eric, I can see they're really fond of him. When he introduces me as his wife, they hug me, and, in their sweet Mexican accent, they welcome me and compliment me every which way.

They're followed by Dexter's aunts and uncles, cousins, and friends, who all make me feel very special. They remind me of the sweet and warm people back in my hometown. Eric picks up Dexter's sister's baby and looks over at me.

Oh God, my neck is starting to itch!

When he sees me scratch, my Iceman cracks up, and I do too.

And then, suddenly, I see a familiar face: Dexter's cousin!

Juan Alberto and his captivating smile.

"Can I say hello without putting my life in danger?" the new guest asks.

I laugh every time I remember the things I said to the poor man that day, but I like that he's so good-humored about it. If the tables were turned, considering how sour I can be, I'm pretty sure I'd still be holding it against him.

The reception is very nice, but I soon notice Graciela, Dexter's assistant. The young woman isn't treated in the same way. Just then, Dexter's mother takes her nephew Juan Alberto's arm. The family calls him Juanal.

"Is it true you're leaving for Spain with them in two days?"

"Yes, Auntie."

"If I might ask, what for?"

"I want to visit Spain and several other European countries to see about expanding my business," Juan Alberto says, smiling warmly at his aunt.

"But you're coming back, aren't you?"

"Of course I'm coming back, Auntie. My business is here; my life is in Mexico."

I see his aunt nod. I don't know what she's really thinking, but she doesn't seem too convinced.

"I'm going too, Mamita," says Dexter with a wide grin.

I laugh. Dexter's such a rascal.

"I can't imagine what you're going for, you scoundrel," says his mother. "You spend half your life abroad anyway."

"Mamá . . . Mamita linda, I run an international business, and it forces me to travel a great deal. In fact, this time—and I know this will make you feel better—Graciela is going with me."

Dexter's mother's face completely changes. She absolutely beams.

"Oh, I like that. She'll bring some balance to your schedule."

I laugh again.

Not even God could bring some balance to Dexter!

"My dear," she says to me, "please find a good woman for my nephew. My Juanal needs someone who is pretty and loving and who'll spoil him and take care of him."

"Hey, while you're at it, find me one too," Dexter says, teasing.

His mother stares at him. "If you wanted, you'd already have one," she says in a low voice but in front of everybody. "I've told you a thousand times."

Dexter rolls his eyes.

"Mamita, don't say that," he says, looking over at Graciela, who is now holding his baby nephew.

"Auntie, the last thing I need is a wife," says Juan Alberto, looking around expansively. "Now that I'm single again, I can have as many as—"

"Oh, cut the BS and find yourself a good woman. That's what you need!" she says, and then, to me, in an aside, "I don't know what it is with youth today; nobody seems to want the kind of beautiful thing you have with Eric."

"Cristina, that's because Judith is a love," says Eric, taking me by the waist. "There aren't a lot of women like my sweetheart, believe me. That's why, when I met her, I wouldn't let her go until she agreed to be my wife."

Uff!

What my husband said is so beautiful and romantic, I could just eat him up with kisses!

Head over heels, I lean my head on his arm.

"It's wonderful to meet a special person, and I was lucky enough to meet Eric," I say, looking up at Cristina's tender face.

My man presses me against him.

"You don't happen to have a sister for my Dexter, do you?"

Eric's laugh is absolutely monumental.

"Yes, Mamá, she does, but, according to Judith, there's no way her sister is for me," says Dexter.

"She's that bad?"

Now it's my turn to bust out laughing.

"No, Cristina," I answer, "it's just that she's too good and too innocent for your son."

Before she has a chance to ask me any more questions about my sister, Dexter takes his mother by the arm and leads her to the table where we're all sitting down for dinner.

During the rest of the evening, we keep company with several of Dexter's gal pals. They're a little too much for my taste and, I think, for Cristina's too. They're a little too familiar with Dexter and Juan Alberto, and when they try it with Eric, I give them a look that says "I'll cut you." They still completely encircle him, and Eric grins.

After dinner, we keep on drinking and talking, and, as often happens at these family gatherings, in the end Dexter pulls out a guitar. His father takes it, and his mother serenades us with a ranchera.

I'm sure if the party were in Spain, my father would be singing a *bulería* with Bicharrón.

So much talent! I listen attentively to Dexter's mother, and her voice reminds me of the late Rocío Dúrcal.

That woman could sing anything!

My father has all her records, and I remember how he used to sing along with my mother. Those are beautiful memories.

Once the song is over, I clap and quickly request "Si Nos Dejan." Eric glances over, and I grin. It's the official song of our honeymoon.

Cristina doesn't hesitate, and Dexter joins her for this one. Oh God, amazing! They have incredible voices.

I'm sitting on my husband's lap, and he holds me close as I listen to this romantic and passionate song. When it's over, Eric kisses me.

"I love you, sweetheart," he whispers in my ear.

After a few more songs, they want me to sing. I'm the Spanish girl! Oh man . . .

Eric grins. He knows I know how to have a good time. I sing "La Macarena," and they all laugh uproariously. They know the words!

Once we finish the song and its corresponding choreography, Dexter's father, who plays guitar very well, plays a little rumba. Happier than a pair of castanets, I hit the floor and dance like Rosario Flores and let my hair down and completely let go.

When it's over, Eric claps with pride, and everyone congratulates him.

Once we've all settled down, I notice Graciela again as her gaze follows Dexter all over the room. I feel bad for her. I know what it's like to suffer because you're in love with your boss, and there's nothing you can do about it.

While Eric talks to Dexter's parents, I take a stroll and end up by Graciela's side. She looks my way and smiles, and I notice something in her eyes I hadn't seen this morning: resentment. Of course, when she looks at Dexter, it's pure adoration.

Poor girl.

"Have you been working for Dexter for very long?" I ask.

"Four years."

Four years is a long time to yearn for somebody.

"What is Dexter like as a boss?" I ask.

"He's a good boss," she says, pulling a strand of hair from her face. "I make sure he's good at home and that he doesn't need anything."

I realize that, even if he were a tyrant, she wouldn't tell me. Goddamn it, I feel a cramp in my belly. I think I'm getting my period.

"Sometimes, he's a little disconcerting," she says, bringing me back to the conversation, "but right now, with your visit and the party, he's very happy. He really appreciates this."

"You know what? Eric was also my boss, and he used to behave exactly the way you describe Dexter," I say in an attempt to bond with her.

"Mr. Zimmerman was your boss?" she asks, stunned.

"Yes. I worked in his office though, not at his house."

I see her attitude change. All of a sudden, she sees me as an equal.

"Well then, it makes me doubly happy to see that your love is real. That's great!"

"Thank you, Graciela."

Eric and Dexter look at us from across the room. They're whispering about us, and I smile but Graciela blushes. There are many things I want to ask this young woman, but I hold back. I don't want to be nosy like my sister.

"I have to go to the bathroom," I say to keep myself from asking more questions. "Do you know where it is?"

"I'll go with you," she says.

We walk down a long hallway until she stops and opens a door.

"I'll wait for you here, and then we can go back together, OK?"

I go in by myself. Goddamn it, I got my period.

"Graciela, do you happen to have a tampon?"

"Yes, I'll get it for you right away."

She vanishes. I stay in the bathroom, well aware of all that comes with my period, until Graciela comes back. I don't have cramps right now, but I know I'll be doubled over in pain in a couple of hours.

When I come out of the stall, Graciela has a look on her face I recognize.

"What is it you want to know? C'mon, just ask."

Red as a beet, Graciela lowers her voice. "Dexter goes to Germany a lot. Is there someone special there?"

Oh, poor girl. Now I understand her anguish even more. I want to hug her.

"If you mean a woman, no. There's no one special."

Her face changes. My answer has made her smile.

"It's only taken me a few hours to realize how much you like Dexter."

"Am I so easy to read?"

"Women's intuition, Graciela. It's almost always on point."

We both smile, well aware of our sixth sense.

She is blushing a bright red. I've taken a great weight off her.

"Does he know?" I ask.

Embarrassed, she shrugs. "I don't know," she says. "I sometimes think he must, because of the way he treats me, but other times, I honestly don't know if he even knows I exist. I liked him from the instant I saw him lying in bed. He reminded me of a Mexican singer named Alejandro Fernández. Do you know who I'm talking about?"

"Oh yes. He's quite a hunk."

"I used to work as a nurse in a hospital, and when his family offered me this job, I didn't hesitate. It was a way of continuing to be near him. It was love at first sight for me. But I don't think he's ever noticed me. He treats me well, he is very proper about everything, but there's nothing more."

"He's never insinuated anything?" I ask, surprised by Dexter's professionalism.

"No."

"Not even a little?"

"No, nothing."

"Nothing?"

"Absolutely nothing. And it's not because I haven't tried."

I laugh. I can't imagine Dexter avoiding sexual possibilities.

"Listen, Judith, I'm not made of stone, and I have my needs. But it's clear he's not attracted to me. I don't exist to him."

The wistful tone of her voice touches my heart.

"You're not Mexican, are you?"

"I was born in Chile, in a beautiful place called Concepción," she says with a smile. "But I've been working in Mexico for many years. My father was from here. I am a mix of Chilean and Mexican."

I'm very sympathetic to this girl who has so sincerely opened up to me after hearing that Eric was my boss even though she barely knows me. She's nice looking but totally asexual. The dress she's wearing and the way she's gathered her hair in a bun don't do anything for her.

"Listen, Graciela, I don't know if you know that Dexter can't . . . ."

Her eyes widen.

"I know. Remember that I met him at the hospital. I know everything about him."

"So, you know he can't . . . do that . . . and you still want something with him?"

Even redder than she was just seconds before, she nods.

"Not everything in this life has to be conventional sex."

Well, well, well, so much for her asexuality.

"Oh no?" I ask now that I see she's not so innocent.

"On a few occasions, I've seen him with his girlfriends and his friends in his office or in the room next to his office," she whispers. "That same room where the three of you were today. I know exactly what goes on in there."

"You do?"

Graciela nods.

Now I'm the one who's as red as a tomato, and I understand the look of reproach on her face.

"God, Dexter is so hot . . . so exciting!"

I laugh with incredulity, and the poor woman recoils, embarrassed.

"Please . . . please . . . What am I saying? Why am I telling you this?" she says. "I'm sorry . . . I'm so sorry."

She's horrified and covers her face with her hands.

"It's OK, Graciela. It's OK," I say, feeling sorry for her. Still, I want to know what she knows.

"And what do you think of the games Dexter plays with his friends?"

Graciela sighs, smiles, and whispers, "Very kinky, very exciting."

So much for our Sweet Miss Innocent. Who would've thunk it?

"Have you ever played the same kind of games?" She's nervous and sighs and so I try to help her trust me with her confidences.

"I have, although if you ever told anyone I said so, I'd deny it. What about you?"

Surprised, she blinks a few times. "After I saw what he does, I did some research, and I met up with some people with whom I play and fantasize that it's him," she says. "But I've never dared with Dexter."

"But would you dare?"

She nods without hesitation.

"Don't worry. You've entrusted me with a secret, and I'm not going to reveal it," I say. "I hope you'll keep mine too."

"Have no doubt about that, Judith."

"Now if you like Dexter," I say, "you need to do something to get his attention."

"I've done everything, but he doesn't notice me."

"Maybe if you dress differently, that would change," I say, afraid I might have offended her. "Don't you think?"

She touches the bun on her head.

"If I have to look like those ridiculous girlfriends of his for him to notice me, forget it!"

"That's not what I'm talking about, Graciela," I say. "Is it true you're going with Dexter to Spain and then Germany on this trip?"

She nods.

"That's great! Tomorrow you and I will have a girls' day out. We'll go shopping while they talk business."

"You'd do that for me?"

"Of course. We women are here to help each other, even though it may not always seem that way," I say, sure I've now overstepped.

We hear a knock on the door. When we open it, we find Eric with a worried look on his face.

"Why are you taking so long?" he asks. "What's going on?"

I give him a sweet kiss on the lips.

"My love, I just got my period." The poor man furrows his brow. He knows I turn into a beast during my period. "Also, listen, I'm going shopping with Graciela tomorrow, OK?"

Eric is surprised by our sudden friendship. He knows I'm up to something, I can see it in his eyes.

"No problem on my part, and I doubt on Dexter's part either."

I grin. Nothing gets by him.

4

The next morning after a terrible night of cramps, I open my eyes, and all my discomfort is gone. Fantastic! I know it's just for the moment and that it'll come back later, but I'm used to it.

I get up, and, after breakfast with Dexter and Eric and letting them know about my plans with Graciela, Dexter insists someone go with us. He refuses to let us go alone anywhere in the city. He gets on his phone, and, an hour later, we have a very charming driver to take the two of us to the most exclusive stores.

We go from shop to shop. I love being able to buy whatever I want for my family and for Eric. I love giving him gifts. Although I know him well enough to know he'll never wear this red T-shirt that says "Viva la morenita," I still buy it just to see his face.

Hours later, when I'm bogged down with stuff and Graciela hasn't bought a thing, we come to an enormous store. I try to encourage her.

"Let's see, Graciela, what can we buy you."

"I don't know," she says. "Something pretty to wear during our trip; price is no obstacle. I've been saving for so long, I think today is a good day to spend it on a new wardrobe."

I love her sweetness.

"Why don't we start by getting you a pair of jeans that fit you so well they'll make men cry?"

"I don't think I've worn jeans since I was a teenager."

"Seriously? I couldn't live without them. It's what I wear most, and I can tell you they go with everything."

Graciela grins. She's in a good mood.

"We could buy several things to combine—cool, trendy things; a few pairs of jeans; maybe a dress; and perhaps something more elegant in case we go to a party like the one last night."

"Fantastic!" Her eyes are bright.

I'm ready to help her conquer Dexter so I start looking around. In the background I hear Jessie J's "Price Tag," and I sing along.

I pick up a pair of low-waisted jeans, a top with purple straps, and a pair of tall black boots.

Knowing Dexter, he's going to love these boots. In fact, I'm going to buy myself a pair of red ones and drive my own man insane.

"Try this. I think it's going to look great on you."

Graciela stares at what I've handed her as if it were an astronaut suit. It's not her style, but, if she's going to have an effect on Dexter, this is the way to go. When I realize she's not moving, I push her into the dressing room. Once she's on her own, I try on the boots.

They're great!

Heels, soft, all the way up to my knees, and red. My Iceman will love them. They look amazing with the jeans I'm wearing, and I decide to keep them on. They're beautiful. I get a text at that precise moment.

I miss you, sweetheart.

I hope you're buying everything you want.

I love you.

Oh, my love. I really do just want to eat him up. He's concerned about my well-being every minute.

The Visa card is burning up.

I love you back.

I press send. Eric is so marvelous that merely thinking about him makes me smile.

Just then the dressing room door opens, and, exactly as I expected, Graciela looks incredible.

What an amazing body this girl has!

My mouth drops open.

"If Dexter doesn't notice you now, he's deader than I thought he was."

Graciela grins. "Isn't it a bit too much?"

I shake my head; this girl has tremendous potential.

"I promise that, once he sees you, Dexter is going to get up and walk."

We both laugh. I really want her to try on more things.

"C'mon, let's see what else we can find to drive that man crazy."

After the first batch, I make her try on a long black skirt that gathers in the back along with a sexy pistachio-green blouse that's knotted at the waist and a pair of pretty high-heeled shoes in the same color. The result is spectacular. Even Graciela is surprised when she looks in the mirror.

"You can wear this to any party, and you'll always look impressive."

"I love it." She claps when she sees herself in the mirror.

As soon as she undresses, I hand her a sleeveless black dress with a low neckline. I also bring her a pair of black high-heeled shoes; she looks so lovely.

The sales clerk is very happy. She's going to get a good commission, and when I ask about lingerie, she points the way. Graciela mutters when I hand her an eggplant-colored set.

"Oh God, it's going to be difficult for me to try this on."

"Why?"

"Because it's lingerie," she says with a sly smile.

I laugh aloud.

I pick up an electric-blue bra and thong combo and show it to her.

"I'm going to try this on," I tell her. "Let's just say I'm buying Eric a little birthday gift."

We both laugh as we go back to our dressing rooms.

Minutes later, we're done.

"How did it fit?"

"It could be a nice little gift for Dexter," she says naughtily.

It's late when we leave the store. We're hungry. My cramps are back, and I need to contain them before they become unbearable.

As we look over the menu at the restaurant, I notice several men looking at us, and I grin. They mouth the word "sabrosa," and Graciela and I laugh.

If Eric were here, he'd give them one of his death-ray looks, and they would all shrink away.

But he's not, so I just enjoy the admiration. I notice a beauty shop after we finish lunch and suggest we get our hair done. Graciela agrees. I decide to have my hair straightened. I know Eric likes it that way. After consulting with the stylists, Graciela decides on a cut that makes her look more youthful. The result is amazing.

Every time Graciela makes a change, I'm more perplexed. This young woman is terribly attractive and should be doing more with her assets.

When we leave the beauty shop, we're immediately complimented by two men on the street.

"What are two stars doing flying so low to the ground?" says one of them.

What a hoot!

We both laugh.

"It's the first time in years a man has had anything to say to me," says Graciela.

"Mamacita . . . *que sabrosas!*" says another passerby.

We both laugh again. "These guys can't keep their mouths shut," says Graciela.

"Listen, Graciela," I say as I pull her over to a window so she can see her reflection, "have you taken a good look at yourself?"

She can't believe what she sees.

"Thank you, Judith. Thank you so much for spending the day with me like this."

I give her a big kiss on the cheek and take her arm.

"You're welcome, beautiful. With this new look, you're going to get all kinds of comments. And get ready, because when we get back, Dexter is going to be left speechless."

"You think?"

"Uh-huh." I'm grinning. "I promise he's going to be stunned. But you also have to play your part so he'll notice you. You go on and act the way you always have with him, very proper, and let others compliment you. You're young, gorgeous, single, and this trip you're going to make with us may help clear many things up for you. I think Dexter is like Eric in many ways, and, if he's interested, he'll make his move very quickly."

We laugh together again.

"Now are you sure you want to hook up with him?"

"Totally sure, Judith."

"Very well then. Do you have dinner with Dexter every night?"

"Yes, when he doesn't go out, we have dinner together."

"Well, tonight you're not going to have dinner with him or us."

"No?" she says disconcerted. I shake my head.

"Call a friend and make plans for dinner or to go to the movies. Can you do that?"

"I don't have a lot of friends, to be honest. I've spent four years focused on Dexter and lost a lot of friends along the way."

I'm not surprised by this.

"There isn't anyone you can call to just go get a cup of coffee?"

"Well . . . there is a couple I see every once in a while."

I can tell by the look on her face the kind of relationship she has with the couple.

"Look, girl, enjoy yourself if the occasion comes up, just like Dexter does. In any case, you look splendid today, and you'll have a doubly good time."

She blushes again.

"We'll tell Dexter we ran into a friend of yours while shopping and that you're having dinner with him. If it bothers him, we'll be able to tell. What do you think of the idea?"

Graciela is enjoying this as much as if she were a teenager.

"I promise I'll tell you tomorrow if Dexter misses you at dinner."

I laugh. I'm so bad! But she laughs too.

Graciela calls the couple and makes her plans. We head toward the parking lot and the car.

"Get ready, Graciela. You're going to knock Dexter for a loop today."

At seven that evening, after an entire day of shopping, we arrive at Dexter's house wearing our new boots. The men, who'd been sitting in the living room, turn to look at us. My eyes find my Iceman, and I smile.

Graciela and I walk confidently up to Eric, Juan Alberto, and Dexter.

"Look at these two beauties!" says Dexter, and I almost crack up. He looks over at Graciela. "Tell me right now who you are and what have you done to Graciela."

With a kind of an indifferent wave, like I've taught her, Graciela grins. "I'm the same as always, just wearing new clothes."

Dexter is quite surprised by this incredible change.

"Graciela, do you have plans for dinner?" asks Juan Alberto.

Wow! This is getting interesting!

I knew this girl had potential.

She is, of course, blushing a brilliant bright red.

C'mon, Graciela, respond . . . respond.

"Of course she has plans," says Dexter. "She's having dinner with us."

Graciela looks over at me. Poor girl; this isn't easy for her.

I still remember how much Eric would pressure me, and so I wink at her, letting her know the moment has arrived.

"I'm sorry, Dexter, but I'm not having dinner here tonight. I made plans with a friend."

Good. Very good!

I have to hold myself back from clapping when I see his face.

"Since you have company for dinner, I didn't think you'd care if I was here," she adds.

I want to shout "Olé, Graciela!" as I look at my watch. "We ran into a friend of Graciela's while shopping. Anyway, you should go, or you're not going to make your date on time."

Nervous, she glances down at her own watch.

She's as disconcerted as Dexter, and, to try and help her out, I let go of Eric and give her two kisses.

"Go on. Have a good time and don't come home too late. We're going to Spain tomorrow."

"Wait for me, Graciela," says Juan Alberto. "I'm going too."

Dexter rolls his wheelchair next to her. "I'll tell the driver to take you."

"No, thank you. I don't need a driver."

She turns around in her impressive boots and disappears alongside Juan Alberto.

Once the two of them are gone, Dexter is still pretty shocked, and Eric looks over at me. I wink at my Iceman, and he hugs me and touches my hair.

"You're beautiful with your hair like that," he whispers, "and I love your boots."

"Thank you."

"I sense you're planning something, sweetheart," says my one and only love as soon as Dexter disappears. I laugh. Eric does too.

That night, the three of us have dinner together. The typically talkative Dexter is quieter than usual. On occasion, I even catch him checking the time. Look at that . . .

5

At breakfast the next day, I don't see Graciela. Where is she?

I have cramps, and my belly aches. My damned period is a drag at the beginning and at the end. A real joy.

When I get fussy, Eric furrows his brow, but he knows I'm not feeling well and respects my silence. He's learned to do so for his own good.

We're the first to arrive on our private jet. I spread out on one of the more comfortable seats and take something to help with my cramps. I need this to go away.

I don't talk. If I do, it'll just get worse.

Eric sits by my side and touches my head.

"I hate that you're in pain, and I can't do anything about it."

"I hate it even more," I say.

Poor guy. What a look on his face.

"Don't worry about it, my love," I whisper as I snuggle up to him. "It will soon pass, and I won't be in pain again until next month."

My blond boy hugs me, and, still crampy, I fall fast asleep.

When I wake up, we're flying, and I'm alone in my seat. Eric is with Dexter and Juan Alberto, but as soon as he hears me move, he's at my side.

"Hello, sweetheart. How are you feeling?"

I blink a few times and realize my pain is gone.

"Right this instant, perfect. I'm pain-free."

"That was a nice little nap you took."

"How long was I sleeping?"

"Three hours," he says, caressing my hair and kissing my forehead.

"Three hours!"

"Yes, my love." He laughs.

I'm surprised I slept that long.

"Do you want something to eat?"

I nod. I've slept like a polar bear, and now I'm ravenous.

At that moment, Graciela emerges from the bathroom. When she sees me, her eyes sparkle, and she comes quickly to sit by my side.

"I'll tell the flight attendant to bring you two something to eat," Eric says.

"Dexter asked me where I was last night," she whispers conspiratorially.

"And what did you tell him?"

"That I had dinner with a friend."

"Did you have a good time with your friends?" I ask, remembering she was meeting a couple.

"They were floored with my new look, and we had a very good time," says a smiling Graciela.

We both laugh aloud, which draws the attention of the men. Eric grins, but Dexter is very serious.

"Wow . . . somebody is not very happy."

"Dexter wanted to know my friend's name, and, when I wouldn't tell him, he got really pissed," she says in a low voice.

I smile at that.

"He barely said a word at dinner last night and spent the whole meal checking the time. When Eric and I went to bed, he stayed up by himself."

"When I came back at three in the morning, he was right there, awake."

"What?"

"Yes," she says, laughing. "He was in the living room, reading. When I came in, he didn't say a word, and I went straight to my room. A few minutes later, I heard him go to his room."

I look over and see Dexter watching us. I'm a little surprised that this seems to have worked so well.

"Let me see if I understand, Graciela. When you've flirted with Dexter in the past, he's never responded?"

"Never."

"But what did he say?"

The flight attendant brings us a pair of trays with a smorgasbord of treats.

"The last time I tried, which must've been about a year ago, he told me not to do it again because he couldn't give me any of the things I wanted, and he didn't want to disappoint me."

"I see . . ."

"I remember I was really hurt, and I didn't talk to him for almost a month. In fact, I looked for another job, and, when he realized what I was doing, he was furious. He didn't want me to work for anyone else. And then, incredibly, he doubled my salary the next month. When I told him I hadn't asked for a raise, he said that since he couldn't give me what I wanted, he could at least try to make me happy financially so that I wouldn't work for anyone else."

Well, well . . . there's a lot going on here!

"Mother of God, Graciela," I say, "what you just told me confirms that he likes you, and a whole lot."

"No . . ."

"Then why would he give you a raise without you asking?"

"I don't know. Dexter is very loose with money."

"Could it be he's very loose with it when it comes to you because he likes you?"

"I don't think so."

"Well, that's what I think. No boss doubles a salary just because."

"You think?"

I nod. I still remember when Eric suggested I go with him on that trip to all the German branches and told me to name my own salary.

"I'm telling you, Graciela, that man is drooling for you."

"Oh God," she says, blushing a deep red.

Dexter's watching us again. I wink at him. Poor man, if only he knew what we were talking about. He smiles and looks away.

"Oh, Graciela, people say women are strange, but men are so strange too." We both laugh. "I'm telling you, Dexter likes you as much as you like him. He's overreacting to what you did last night, making it clear that he's interested."

"Oh, Judith . . . don't say that; it makes me nervous."

We laugh again. "It's only going to get worse when we get to Jerez and my friends start flirting with you left and right."

Our arrival in Jerez is a very big deal.

My father wants to get us at the airport, but Eric has already made arrangements. We're greeted by a man who hands us the keys to an eight-seat Mitsubishi Montero, the exact copy of what we drive in Germany.

"I bought this so we could have it at our disposal when we come to Jerez," Eric says when he sees the surprise on my face. "Is that OK by you?"

I nod and smile. Eric likes to be in control.

We all laugh and have a good time on the way to Jerez. When we arrive at the house Eric bought me, I see a new sign that says "Sweetheart Villa." I crack up, as does my husband.

I give him a kiss. I'm grinning like a fool as he takes the remote out of the glove compartment to open the black gate. I love his surprises, and when I see the house is so well taken care of, I get emotional. He tells me he asked my dad to contract with somebody to keep up the place even when we're not here. As soon as the car stops, I'm the first to jump out.

"Welcome to our home in Jerez," I tell our guests.

As soon as I'm in the house, I call my dad to let him know we'll be over at his place in an hour. He's made dinner and is happily waiting for us with my sister and the kids.

As the hostess of Sweetheart Villa, I quickly figure out who is sleeping where. There are enough bedrooms for everyone, and, after we've all had a chance to shower and change, we climb back into the Mitsubishi and head over to my father's house.

I can't wait to see him.

When we park the car, I see Flyn and Luz come running toward us. These beautiful children!

They throw themselves on me, and I hug them back. "Auntie . . . Auntie," says an excited Luz, "what did you bring me?"

"What did you bring me?" asks Flyn.

"A bunch of gifts, don't worry. Now come and say hi."

But Flyn is already hugging his uncle Eric, and I'm moved, like always, when I see how much they love each other. All of a sudden, my niece, who can sometimes be dumber than a rock, launches herself on them, and Eric loses his balance, and the three end up splattered on the ground.

Dexter and our other guests laugh. "Jude, help me!" Eric calls out to me.

He stretches his hand to me, but when I take it, he yanks me down, and I end up on the ground with him and the kids. Love and laughter, that's what he makes me feel.

When we finally get up, my father is there, his arms outstretched.

"And how is my little sweetheart?"

I rush over and hug him.

I love my father so much.

"I'm doing great, Papá," I say. "I'm happy and crazy in love with Mr. Bullheaded."

Eric shakes my father's hand and hugs him and introduces him to Dexter, Juan Alberto, and Graciela. Before we go in the house, we have to greet the neighbors, who have all come out to say hello.

"Papá, where is Raquel?"

"She's finishing up giving Lucía a bath, my love. She's in your room."

I run back to my old room, and there's my crazy sister, toweling down her baby, who's now a little more than a month old, on the changing table. I smell her perfume and hug her from the back.

"Hello."

"Cuchu!" she responds.

We hug and kiss. We have so many things to talk about that we both talk all over each other until baby Lucía makes a noise, and the two of us instantly turn to her.

"My God, I can't believe how big she's gotten!"

Raquel nods and starts babbling as she touches the baby's cheeks. "She's so big, so fat, isn't that right, you pretty little thing?"

I give the baby a kiss, sniff her sweetness, and pick up where my sister left off.

"Hello, you little cutie. I could eat you up . . . Oh, I could eat this pretty little girl up from head to toe."

"Say hi to your auntie," insists my sister as she takes the baby's hand and waves at me. "Hello, Auntie. I'm Lucía."

"Hello, little love."

And then we are lost in our jabber.

And then the baby closes her eyes. I'm sure if she could talk, she'd tell us to stop acting like such idiots.

Lucía sneezes, and my sister responds by finishing dressing her immediately.

"I made you what you wanted, and it's in the kitchen."

"You made me a chocolate cake?"

"Yes." She grins.

"You have no idea what it took to make it behind the kids' back, but I did it. Anything for my brother-in-law. It's in Tupperware in the back of the fridge, behind the Cokes."

Tomorrow is our one-month wedding anniversary, and I want to surprise my husband.

"Cuchufleta, go on with your guests, Lucía and I will join you soon."

I kiss her and run out to the garden where everyone has settled around the table to drink beer. Dexter and my father are talking about planting roses. They're beautiful. They're the most beautiful roses I've ever seen in my whole life. Eric and Flyn are trading stories, and Graciela and Juan Alberto listen in.

"Auntie, Uncle Eric says you should give us our gifts," Luz says as soon as she sees me.

"What I said was that you bought them, and you—"

"No way, my love," I say. "We bought these gifts together, and we will give them out together."

The kids can't stop staring at the suitcase full of gifts. Eric finally lifts it up on the table and opens it, and we pass the gifts out for the kids and for my father.

The kids are tearing into their packages when, all of a sudden, as if there was an earthquake, my sister comes down, her hair gathered on her head, the baby in one arm, and her cell in the other hand. Without so much as blinking, she drops Lucía in the arms of a very disconcerted Juan Alberto, who has no idea what to do with an infant.

"Look, that's a no," she says into the phone. "It doesn't work for me this weekend. I have other plans."

Everyone's staring at her. There's no point in saying anything to her when she's like that. I look over at my father, who shakes his head as a salty Raquel walks over to the pool and then comes to a dead stop. "I said no. I don't want to see you, Jesús. Forget about me. Go ahead and talk to your lawyer, but do me a favor and pay the monthly child support for the girls because I need it. Did you hear me? I need it!"

But my ex-brother-in-law, that idiot, must've said something because she takes it up a serious notch.

"Fuck you and your father and your mother and every living creature in your family! I could give three shits about your situation! And do you know why?" Everyone is staring, and you could hear a pin drop. "Because I've got two girls I've got to support, and I need the money. So, just save the money you would have used on the trip because I don't want to see you. And whatever you save, you can deposit in the bank, because the girls need to eat and a thousand other things. What? You're a shameless asshole with a Peter Pan complex. Grow up . . . you idiot, grow up! And don't ask me again if we can see each other tomorrow because, I swear, if I say yes, it'll be only so I can slap you hard across the face."

Amazed by what I'm hearing, I don't know what to do. My God, my sister can really give it back. Suddenly, I realize Luz is hearing the same thing I am, and my blood starts to boil. Eric and I exchange looks.

"Look, Luz, did you see the SpongeBob SquarePants camera I got you?" Eric asks her.

Just hearing the name SpongeBob SquarePants makes my niece turn around and forget all about her mom's conversation.

"Wow, Uncle Eric!"

Mercifully, the yellow digital camera with SpongeBob is the only thing that matters in that moment. I'm so glad Eric responded so quickly.

Eric gives Flyn another camera, but this one has *Mortal Kombat* characters; the two of them go nuts. Graciela springs into action and distracts them by pulling them away from the phone conversation. My sister is really giving it to her ex!

Anguished, my father goes to her to try to calm her down. Poor man, he really has his hands full with Raquel and me. And seeing Juan Alberto disconcerted with the baby in his arms, I rush over to take her from him.

I think if he'd had the baby one more second, he wouldn't have been able to breathe. He literally sighs when he hands her to me. He is so relieved!

"Hi, Cucurucucu . . . I'm gonna eat your cheeks. Yes, I am!" I say, holding her close to my face.

The baby stares at me. She surely thinks I'm some kind of fool.

"You look good with a baby in your arms, Judith," says Dexter.

I turn to him and see all three men have their eyes on me. But my husband's face gets a special mention. His expression is beatific and soft, and he's wearing a radiant smile.

"You look beautiful with a baby," he says.

Uff . . . my neck is starting to itch!

No, I don't want to talk about babies or any other such nonsense.

I start to look for someone to hand the baby to, and Eric comes over with open arms. I deliver her to him as if she were a delicate package.

"Hello . . . Hello, beautiful . . . I'm your uncle Eric. How's my gorgeous girl?"

Eric sits next to Dexter, and the two of them babble at her. I glance over at my father. I can read his lips as he is asking Raquel to take it easy. Suddenly, she slams her cell phone down on a table. She's furious, and when my sister is furious there's no stopping her.

She finally looks over at me, and when I'm about to say something, she suddenly changes expression as if she were the greatest actor in Hollywood.

"Hello, brother-in-law," she says, turning to Eric, "how's it going?"

"Good. And you?"

Raquel shrugs. "Like my father says, screwed but happy."

She and Eric exchange a couple of quick cheek kisses.

"Are you sure you're all right?" he asks.

Raquel nods, and Dexter takes ahold of her hands. "What's going on with this handsome Spanish girl?" he asks.

My sister sighs and looks around, and, when she sees Luz is nowhere near, tries to explain. "My ex is trying to drive me crazy, but I'll have him committed first!"

Eric's eyes widen.

"Raquel," I say quickly, "let me introduce you to Juan Alberto. He's Dexter's cousin and will be in Spain for a few days."

"Charmed," she says, barely looking at him.

I notice he can't take his eyes off her.

"Man, what a woman," he whispers to Dexter.

Graciela brings Luz and Flyn back, and they take pictures of us with their new cameras. A half hour later, my father presents us with a sumptuous meal in which there is no lack of delicious ham, shrimp, roasted meats, and tomato soup.

The next morning, my alarm clock goes off at six thirty in the morning. I quickly put a stop to it.

I'm so sleepy! But I want to get up and surprise Eric.

It's our wedding anniversary. One month! And I want to make him breakfast in bed.

He's sleeping, and, like always, I feel a tremendous desire to cuddle him. Of course, if I cuddle him, I'll wake him, and I won't be able to give him his surprise.

I get up stealthily, go to the bathroom, and close the door. I quickly take off my pj's, wash, put on the T-shirt I bought Eric, and comb my hair. My period is over. Yay!

I look at myself in the mirror, smile approvingly, and sneak out of the room. When I get to the kitchen, I look behind the Cokes in the fridge like my sister told me, and there's the pink Tupperware.

Raquel is an artist when it comes to cakes.

I quickly grab a tray and prepare a couple of café con leches. I get little plates, spoons, and napkins and place the beautiful cake in the middle and a knife to cut it with by its side.

This looks great!

I take a picture of it with my cell phone. It is, after all, our first month of married life.

Happy to be surprising my man, I go back to the bedroom, come up to the bed, and put the cake on my side of the bed as I sing a little song I made up. I carefully set the tray down on the side table.

Happy . . . happy . . . onemonthofmarriedlife.
German guy who hooked up with a Spanish girl,
I hope you are happy at my side
And that there will be many, many more.

Eric opens his eyes and smiles when he hears me. Usually, it's the other way around, and he is waking me up. He grins when he sees the T-shirt I'm wearing.

"Happy one-month anniversary, my treasure! We've been married thirty days."

He hugs me and throws me on top of him, then tries to imitate a Mexican accent to read my T-shirt. "Viva la morenita!"

We both laugh.

"They've been the best thirty days of my life," he says. "Now I want to go for much more."

His mouth searches for mine and kisses me. Incredible. His breath is sweet even when he first wakes up.

He licks my upper lip . . . then my lower lip, and finally he does that little marvelous nibble thing . . . oh yes.

I love it when he does that!

His breathing picks up, and the way he's holding me becomes more intense. He pulls off my T-shirt, which falls to the floor.

I let myself be carried away by the passion of the moment when Eric suddenly lifts me up in the air and rolls with me back down on the bed. We both hear the same terrible sound.

He's stunned and stares at me.

"That was not what you think," I say, trying to explain. Eric arches his brow. "What you just heard was the cake I brought you, which is now smashed under my ass."

I see his eyes scan down to my butt, confirming the flattened chocolate cake. He falls back on the bed, laughing. I can't move. If I do, I'll make a mess of this cake all over the bed. I watch him rolling around and laughing. And, finally, I join him.

"Well, the cake is history, but at least our coffees are alive and well," I say.

Eric stretches his arm, picks up a cup, and takes a long swallow.

"What are you doing?"

"Having breakfast."

"Breakfast?"

He nods. "And now I want my cake."

When I see where he's going, I shake my head. "Don't even think about it."

"I want my cake," he insists.

"I said don't even think about it."

But when I see how determined he is, I laugh and put up no resistance when he flips me over on the bed.

"Eric, no!"

But it doesn't matter what I say. My crazy love is licking my butt cheeks.

"Hmm . . . this is the best cake I've ever had in my life."

"Eric!" I protest, but he just keeps on licking and sucking his cake. I'm laughing much too hard.

"This is quite a banquet."

"It was supposed to be a gift."

"Great! Remind me later to give you your gift."

"You have a gift for me?"

"Did you have any doubts? Like you said, it's our one-month anniversary!"

I'm laughing when he flips me over again.

"I love you, sweetheart."

I grab a piece of the squashed cake and smear some on my breasts, then down on my navel and my mound.

I decide to smear it all over him as well, and I grab another piece and smash it against his belly and his shoulder.

Dessert is served!

Eric is playful and throws himself on top of me and kisses me. That cake is completely destroyed and all over the two of us on the bed at this point.

"You've always seemed sweet to me, sweetheart, but never more than today."

Eric sucks my breasts as I breathe in the smell of chocolate. He follows the trail I've left him and goes down to my navel, and, when he gets to my mound, he inhales my scent and dives directly for me. He opens my legs, and his tongue goes right inside me.

I twist when I feel vibrations all over my body as he, like a hungry wolf, pushes my thighs down for better access.

"Oh yes . . . yes . . . ," I say.

He does this over and over, running his tongue on my wetness. His playful fingers quickly find me, and he penetrates me with two of them as his tongue plays and plays with me, and I cry out with delight.

The bed moves, and I grab the sheets and try not to scream. I don't want everyone else to wake up. I push down with my feet on the mattress until my head falls off the side of the bed.

Eric holds me and centers me on the bed, and now I can't move. I see him biting his lower lip as he gets up on his knees, grabs me by the waist, and turns me over.

I love how he handles me in bed. I love his possessiveness. And since I know what he wants, I get up a little bit so I'm on all fours. He brings me his hard cock and slowly glides into me.

"More," I demand.

"You want more?"

"Yes . . ."

"You're eager," he says, teasing.

"I like being eager," I say. "Go deeper."

He slaps my ass and grabs my hips and gives me what I want, burying himself in me as I groan. I bite the sheets.

"Shh . . . Don't scream or you'll wake everybody up," he whispers in my ear.

He goes in and out of me again and again while I bite the sheets to drown my screams. I love what he does. I like our wild side, and, trying to keep him going, I arch my hips and push back on him.

The two of us pant even harder.

He stops abruptly. He takes his stiff erection out of me and turns me around again. Our eyes meet. He starts to penetrate me again.

"Look at me," he says.

I stare right at him. He's my king, my sun, and then it's me who jerks my pelvis up and surprises him. He smiles slyly at me.

Wow . . . the Iceman awakens!

He puts a hand under me to keep me from moving, and, pressing against me, he kisses me while he continues to fuck me, and all our panting and moaning drowns in our mouths.

Pleasure . . .

Heat . . .

Desire . . .

And love . . .

It's everything I feel as he thrusts in and out of me, and I open up to receive him until I spasm and come. An instant later, he impales me one final time, and after a long groan, he falls limp on top of me.

I won't let him go. I'm trembling as his body presses against me. He is wet from sweat, and I hug him even tighter.

Two minutes later, Eric rolls over on the bed and takes me with him so I'm on top of him. He loves doing that. He loves having me on top.

My hair is full of cake and chocolate, and we're both still covered in the stuff.

"When my sister asks you if you liked the cake, say yes, or she'll kill me," I tell him.

"Don't worry about that, sweetheart," Eric says, still trying to catch his breath. "I'm completely convinced it's the best cake I've ever had in my life."

We both laugh. Five minutes later, the sugar begins to glue us together, and we get up and go straight to the shower. Passion overtakes us once more as we wash, and I get to make love with my German once again.

6

That afternoon, everyone except Juan Alberto, who went to see a potential client, is gathered at Pachuca's restaurant. Eric has invited them to celebrate our one-month anniversary.

Before going to the restaurant, he gives me my gift. It's in an envelope. Eric and his envelopes. I laugh and open it.

"Good for one complete motocross crew."

He's happy. His face, his eyes, his smile tell me everything is all right, and I am the happiest woman in the world. I cover him in kisses.

I am astonished we haven't had a single argument since we got married. I have been thinking about calling the editors at the *Guinness Book of World Records*. Like our song says, if he says white, I say black, but we've been so happy so far. We're in complete harmony, and I hope this lasts a long, long time.

My father is beaming because he has us all here, and I love seeing him happy. I've always thought he's the best father in the world, and I feel confirmed in this with every passing day. He's getting an express ticket to heaven just for putting up with my sister and me.

He and Eric get along marvelously, and I love that. I love seeing their complicity, and, even though it won't always be in my favor, I don't care. That ease between them is something my father never had with that pig of an ex-son-in-law.

Eric listens to him and doesn't try to be clever with him, which pleases my father and pleases me even more.

It's very clear they come from different social classes, but they both try to adapt to the circumstances, and that's what I think I love about each of them: that they know how to be.

As we all sit at the table, I see Dexter eyeing some young men who've just come into the restaurant. Graciela's just back from the bathroom when they whistle at her.

I love the way Dexter tries to look like a tough guy. I don't know what's going to happen between them, but something is going to happen. Dexter just needs a little time.

My sister seems more relaxed. After talking to her and hearing that my foolish ex-brother-in-law wants to get back together with her, I'm relieved when Raquel makes it clear that's never going to happen. He's already taken enough advantage of her, and she's not going to give him another chance.

In addition, my father has convinced her to stay and live with him in Jerez, at least during baby Lucía's first year. It sets back returning to Madrid and looking for work, but I think it's an excellent idea. With my father, Raquel will live like a queen, even though they may want to strangle each other now and again.

Flyn and Luz have become very good friends during this vacation, and when I hear about some of their adventures, I can't help but laugh. Every time someone mentions that we're going back to Germany in a few days, they get sad, although they understand the school year will start up again shortly and that we all have to go back to our regular lives.

"Did you like the cake this morning?" my sister asks Eric as Pachuca brings out her cake.

Eric grins foolishly.

"It was the best cake I've ever had in my life," he says.

Raquel is delighted with the compliment. "Well, whenever you like, let me know, and I'll make you a lemon cake, which is also quite delicious," she offers.

"Lemon?" whispers Eric. "How refreshing!"

I can't help it and just crack up; Eric does too. We kiss.

"Oh, Cuchu, love is so beautiful when it's mutual," says my sister, rocking baby Lucía in her arms.

But that comment, said with just a trace of longing, saddens me. I'd really love it if Raquel would meet somebody and start her life over again. She needs to. She is the kind of woman who really needs a man by her side to love her and make her happy. And that man is not my father.

The days pass, and we have a splendid time in Jerez. Juan Alberto has meetings with various companies in Andalusia and happily reports that he sees possibilities for his business in the region. During this time, I notice how he looks at my sister. He's clearly interested, and I've also picked up that he's getting along very well with my niece. Frankly, it's hard not to get along with Luz; she's so easygoing that the minute you pay attention to her and play her games, she loves you for the rest of your life.

Obviously, Raquel knows exactly what's going on, and I'm surprised when the days go by and she doesn't mention it. But, as I always say, my sister is my sister, and she finally opens up one afternoon when just she and I are sunbathing by the pool at my father's house.

"Juan Alberto is handsome, isn't he?" she asks.

"Yes."

I wait . . . If she wants to talk about it, I'm ready, but she takes her time.

"He seems well educated, don't you think?" she says after a few minutes.

"Yes."

I smile. She looks at me sideways.

"What do you think of him as a man?"

"He's good-looking."

"Do you know what he said to me the other day when we were all going out to dinner?"

"No."

"Do you want to know?"

"Of course . . . tell me."

Graciela joins us at exactly that moment, and I imagine my sister's going to shut up, but, to my surprise, she goes on.

"The other night, after we'd had a few drinks and were on our way over to your house, he looked me in the eye and said, 'You're like a delicious cappuccino: sweet, hot, and you make me nervous.'"

"He said that?" I ask, surprised.

"Yes, that's an exact quote."

"Well . . . that's kind of sweet, don't you think?"

Raquel nods. "Yes, it's rather elegant actually, like him."

We're quiet, but I know her, this peace won't last long. In less than two minutes, she sits back up.

"Now every time he sees me, he says, 'Sabrosa!'"

"Sabrosa?" asks Graciela as she sits up too. "In Mexico, that's like saying you're really hot, or I'd eat you up right here and now."

"Seriously?" asks Raquel, who's now blushing. Graciela nods.

I try not to laugh. My sister is trying to keep it together—that's new. Suddenly, she punches me on the arm.

"All right, enough! I can't keep pretending I don't like that handsome Mexican. He's got the face and voice of a soap opera star, and whenever he says 'sabrosa' . . . oh, Cuchu, I feel it all over my body. And now that I know what it means . . . oh God, that's hot!"

I burst out laughing.

"Cuchu, please don't laugh. I'm worried."

"Worried?"

She leans in toward Graciela and me.

"I've had some very sexy dreams about him, and now the one who's all shaky without having had a cappuccino is me."

I'm still laughing. My sister is hilarious. But she really does look worried.

"So, let's see, you like Juan Alberto?"

My sister picks up her orange Fanta and takes a long swallow.

"I like him more than eating crawfish with my hands."

The three of us roar with laughter.

"I'd like to know more about him, Cuchu. He's a very nice guy, and I like his personality."

"He's not right for you, Raquel."

"Why?"

"Because he's going back to Mexico and—"

"Why would I care about that?"

That throws me off. Of course she's going to care about that.

"I'm not looking for him to swear eternal love or anything like that," she says. "I want to be a modern woman for once in my life and know what it's like to have a little fling."

"What?" I ask, stunned.

"Cuchufleta, I just want to have a good time. Forget my problems. To feel pretty and desired. I just don't want to mess around with him and later find out he's married. I don't want to be the cause of another woman's suffering."

My sister is the most conventional person on the face of the earth, but now she wants to have a little fling? I'm totally flabbergasted.

It's clear she wants me to tell her something about her possible fling, but I just look over at Graciela. She knows Juan Alberto better than I do.

"A fling?"

She smiles. She's so pretty when she does.

"Oh, Cuchu, I must be very desperate for attention because, when I'm with him or he says 'sabrosa,' all I want to do is grab him by the neck, throw him in my room, and do things to him," she says. "I mean, he just really revs me up!"

Revs her up?

My sister just said Juan Alberto revs her up?

I'm dying here. My God! Raquel desperately needs sex and really wants me to give her any info at all about this guy.

"Graciela, you know Juan Alberto better than I do, so, please, help my sister out and tell her something about him," I say.

"Well, he's divorced and—"

"Divorced?"

"Uh-huh . . ."

My sister actually likes that. She quickly takes another swallow of her orange Fanta.

"His full name is Juan Alberto Riquelme de San Juan Bolívares."

"See? He has a soap opera name," whispers Raquel.

"Yes, I can see," I say, teasing.

"He's forty years old, and he's Dexter's cousin on his mother's side. He doesn't have kids. His ex-wife, Jazmina, who's a viper to be avoided, never wanted kids in the six years they were married, but now that she's divorced, she's pregnant with her new partner."

"There are women like that," says my sister.

"Yes," I say, thinking I don't want kids either.

"Juanal owns a very successful security firm in Mexico, and he's trying to expand his business to Europe with this trip. He's a guy who likes being home, who's very loving and a very good friend to his friends."

I watch my sister process the information Graciela is providing.

"I figured out about his not having kids. You only had to take one look at him with Lucía to realize he'd never had a baby in his arms his whole life."

"Well, Eric doesn't have kids either and—"

"But he's different," affirms Raquel.

"Different how?" I ask.

"Because he has raised his nephew by himself, and I'm sure when Flyn was a baby, he was super loving with him. You just have to see how he takes care of him, how he spoils Luz and how he falls apart with Lucía. And, anyway, speaking of kids—"

"No," I say, cutting her off. "We haven't talked about having them yet, so we don't have to go there."

But as soon as I say that, I realize how both my sister and Graciela are looking at me.

"Oh, Cuchufleta," says Raquel as she drops back down, "and to think of how pretty those kids are going to be!"

Why does everyone insist I have kids?

In the end, and since I don't want to talk about this, I just lie back down, deciding to simply enjoy the Andalusian sun.

That night, when we all gather at my father's house for dinner, I watch Juan Alberto and my sister more carefully. They don't make a bad couple.

After dinner, when Raquel gets off her cell after talking to her ex, I watch as Juan Alberto calms her down. Every time my ex-brother-in-law calls, my sister goes out of her mind.

My father looks over at me, and I arch my brows and suddenly realize he's smiling and nodding toward Juan Alberto. I can imagine what he's thinking.

Papá, I know you all too well!

The days pass, and we need to go back to Germany. Vacation is over. Eric has to get back to work, Flyn's school is starting, and our lives need to get back on track.

After one last meal at Pachuca's restaurant, in which Flyn and I almost drown in her tomato soup, we decide to go out for drinks on our final night.

My father excuses himself. He prefers to stay home and take care of the kids.

At eight in the evening, when Juan Alberto gets back from a trip to Málaga, we go by my father's house to pick up Raquel.

When we get to Sergio and Elena's bar, always the most popular in Jerez, my friends are there to greet me. They congratulate me on the wedding, and Eric buys drinks for everyone. My friend Rocío is delighted. She sees I'm happy, and that's good enough for her. The music is playing, and when she hears a particular song, she takes me by the hand and pulls me toward the dance floor as we both sing.

We laugh. We have so many memories from crazy summers singing that Jimmy Somerville song at the top of our lungs.

When it's over, we race to the bathroom, which is really a gossip center, and I answer every single one of her questions. We talk and talk and talk. We go up to dance again, and then we're thirsty and head straight to the bar to get drinks.

"Hello, beautiful," a voice says in my ear as a pair of hands grab me by the waist.

I know that voice . . .

I quickly turn around and see David Guepardo, my friend from the motocross meets. He gives me a couple of kisses and hugs me. I'm sure Eric wouldn't like the way he's holding me, so I wiggle away from him.

"How are you? What are you doing around these parts?"

David is hot by any measure, and he looks my body up and down and takes another step toward me that leaves me smack against the bar.

"I just got in yesterday," he says. "And I came out to see if I could find you."

Rocío looks over at me. I look back, but before she can say anything, I see my German, my Iceman, looking furious behind David.

"Could you please step back so my wife can breathe?" he hisses.

David turns around.

"You again," he says before I have a chance to interrupt him. "Look, my friend, she's not your wife, and, from what I can see, never will be. So, why don't you take a little stroll and leave us in peace?"

Oh Mother of God, the Iceman's face. His nostrils are flaring.

"David," I say, "you have to—"

But I don't get to finish. Eric grabs him by the arm with his giant hands and pulls him away from me.

"You're the one who's going to take a little stroll," he says, inches from his face. "If you ever get that close to my wife again, you're going to have a problem with me, do you understand?"

David freezes. I raise my hand to show him my wedding ring.

"David, Eric is my husband. We're married."

David's face completely transforms. Deep down, he's a good guy, and he raises his hands in surrender.

"I'm so sorry, dude. I thought everything was the same as last time."

Eric's face relaxes. His anger dissipates. He takes me by the hand and pulls me to him as we exit.

"Well, now you know," he says. "Try not to make the same mistake twice."

Rocío looks at me from the bar, and I smile at her as Eric and I walk away. Although I don't approve of his jealousy, I have to admit this possessive little episode really turned me on. He's so sexy when he looks at me like that.

We leave the place without saying another word and suddenly run into Fernando. We both grin.

He's holding hands with the same lovely girl he brought to my wedding in Germany, and, as we come close, Eric lets me go, and Fernando and I hug tightly.

"Hi there, Jerez girl."

He reaches over to shake Eric's hand. "How's it going?"

"Really well, buddy, really well."

They understand each other now. After everything that went down between the three of us, we've managed to normalize our relationships and be friends. I love that. Fernando is one of the most wonderful people I know, and I'm happy to see he and Eric are finally getting along.

We greet his girlfriend, whose name is Aurora, and go have a drink together, the four of us.

After a while, Fernando takes a quick look at his watch. "We have to go. We're meeting some friends."

We say goodbye, and Eric slips his arm around my waist.

"Are you happy, sweetheart?"

"So happy, big guy," I say, giving him a kiss.

We join the rest of our group, chat for hours, and enjoy ourselves. What I love about hanging out with my people is the joy, the fun, the joking around.

I find myself amused by the attention Graciela provokes. This sweet-voiced girl really knocks out the men of Jerez; Dexter watches and sighs. He knows how to control himself. This is going to take more than I had originally imagined.

"Oh, Cuchu . . . ," says my sister, sitting by my side and looking annoyed.

"What's up?"

"I just saw Jesús park his car," she whispers, a worried look on her face.

My blood instantly boils. If my idiot of an ex-brother-in-law so much as comes close, I swear I'm going to slap him so hard, he won't need a car to get back to Madrid. Eric notices the change in me immediately.

"What's going on?" he asks.

"That imbecile Jesús is here."

He stiffens. "It's OK, sweetheart. We're adults; we're civilized people."

His words make me laugh when I think about what happened with David, but in order to calm myself down—I just want to punch this guy who has made my sister suffer so much—I take a drink. Raquel gets up. Where is she going?

I move to grab her by the arm so she won't go near Jesús, but she gets away from me. She walks up to Juan Alberto, who's talking to Dexter, puts her arm around his neck, sits on his lap, and kisses him on the mouth. I'm speechless.

Wow!

I choke on my drink.

Eric takes my hand.

Dexter looks over at me, but all I can see is my sister smooching like a teenager in front of everybody.

"Raquel!" screams my ex-brother-in-law when he stumbles on the scene.

But she just goes on with her devastating kiss with Juan Alberto. Of course, she's dragging it out, the vixen. I can practically hear her saying "sabroso!"

But things don't end there. Totally in the moment, Juan Alberto puts his arms around my sister's waist and passionately kisses her back as one of his hands wanders down and squeezes her butt.

For the love of God, what are they doing?

Time seems to pass in slow motion as they continue kissing until, finally, their lips part.

"Raquel, do you believe in love at first sight," says Juan Alberto, "or do I have to kiss you again?"

Wow, I can't believe this!

That is some melodrama, live and in person!

An ex-husband, a new lover, and the protagonist of the show who is none other than my sister.

My mouth is agape, but Eric, who's by my side, watches everything very calmly. Sometimes it's like he has ice in his veins. And then, with a sly look on her face that leaves me totally stunned, my sister finally recognizes her ex-husband's presence.

"And what do you want?" she asks.

He's speechless. His chin is trembling. I want to shout, "Take that!"

Jesús manages to compose himself after a moment.

"Raquel, I'm not going to hold this against you, but we need to talk," he says.

He's not going to hold it against her?

I want to get up and kick his head in. What kind of an asshole is he?

Eric sees me shifting around in my seat, and, not letting go of my hand, he looks at me. That look alone tells me to be cool.

"Look, Jesús," Raquel responds, surprising me, "please hold it against me, because I plan to do it again as many times as I wish. We're separated! And before you start with your speech, the answer is no!"

"But . . . but . . ."

"But nothing!" she exclaims.

Jesús looks at her like he doesn't know her, and I'm not in the least bit surprised—I don't think I know her either!

Suddenly Juan Alberto stuns us all by standing up, and, with my sister still in his arms, stares down my ex-brother-in-law.

"Listen, dude, this beautiful woman has nothing to say to you," he says. "From now on, every time you call her cell, you're going to have to deal with me because we're sick of your calls and your insistence. She has no desire to see you, to dine with you, to talk to you. First of all, because she doesn't want to, and second of all, because this beautiful woman is with me. And I'm very possessive. What's mine is mine, and I don't let anyone else near it. Pay your alimony and support, which is your responsibility because you're the father. As far as my queen here is concerned, I'll take care of the rest. So, run along and get out of my sight, got it?"

I'm flabbergasted.

Totally floored.

"You heard him, Jesús," says my sister, holding on to Juan Alberto and looking at her ex with incredible satisfaction. "Goodbye!"

"But what about the girls?"

"You'll see the girls whenever it's your turn," says Raquel. "Don't ever worry about that."

The poor man processes what's happened and turns around and slinks away. Once he's gone, I look over at my sister, still amazed, and see she can't believe it either. She's looking scared and babbling at Juan Alberto.

"Thanks . . . Thanks for your help."

He lets go of her and sits back down, and, as he does, his gaze runs over Raquel's body. "You're something else," he says.

"Man alive," Eric says and laughs.

How can he laugh at a moment like this?

I realize my sister is completely traumatized by what just happened, and I go into action immediately. I take her hand and pull her away from everyone. We go to the bathroom, where she pours water on her neck. I don't know what to say.

"Oh, Cuchufleta . . ."

"I know."

"Oh, I'm so hot, Cuchu."

"Not surprising."

"Did I just do what I think I did?" my sister asks, astonished.

"Yes."

"Seriously?"

"I witnessed it all. You did it."

"I just made out with . . . with . . . Juan Alberto?"

"Yes." She doesn't respond. "You just made out like a teenager with your little roll in the hay. The only thing you didn't do is say 'sabroso'!"

My sister blinks.

"Mother of God . . . did you see how that man kisses?"

I nod. I saw, along with half of Jerez.

"I just threw myself at him and . . . and . . . he squeezed me and . . . and . . . then he grabbed my ass, the pig! And he shoved his tongue down my throat. Oh God . . . I'm so hot! And then he said that thing about love at first sight or—"

"Or he'd kiss you again. Yes, it was very much like a scene in a soap opera," I say.

I try to fan her and she swoons, because she loves being dramatic.

She pours some more water on her neck and pants. She still can't believe what she did. Poor woman.

"I think today you got rid of Jesús for the rest of your life," I say. "Juan Alberto made that very clear to him, dude."

"Oh, Cuchu, don't laugh."

"I can't help it, Raquel."

"That man must think I'm out of my mind," she says, touching her face.

"But didn't you say you wanted to be fresh and modern?"

"Yes, but not slutty," she says, blushing now.

"Look, Raquel, let him think whatever he wants to think," I say. "Did you like kissing him?"

She has no hesitation. "Yes . . . I'm not going to deny it."

"So, that's that. Be positive and think about these two things. First, you got rid of Jesús. Second, this man you like has kissed you like they do on the soap operas and completely knocked you out."

She finally laughs. I do too.

"My God, Cuchu," she says.

7

I've never liked farewells, and I like them even less when I'm saying goodbye to my family. Leaving them breaks my heart, but Eric is right there to make me smile and promises I can see them again whenever I want.

The jet is waiting for us at the Jerez airport. My niece insists on climbing in. She wants chocolates, and the flight attendant gives her some. But time is passing, and we have to go, so there is no choice but to finally say goodbye.

"Listen, sweetheart," says my father as he hugs me, "you're very happy. I can tell. I always liked Eric from the first minute; you know that, right?"

I nod.

"Then smile and enjoy your life, and that way I'll enjoy mine too."

"Papá, it's just that I miss you so much. And not knowing when I'm going to see you again kills me."

My father smiles and puts a finger on my lips.

"I promised Eric we will all spend next Christmas in Germany. That guy loves you, and he didn't stop asking until I finally said yes."

"Seriously?"

Now I'm really smiling, and I hug my father back. While still in his arms, I look over his shoulder at Eric, who is saying goodbye to my sister. I never imagined a man like him would take such good care of me. But there he is, my somber German who managed to make me fall in love with him.

After I let go of my father, I turn to hug my sister.

"You haven't left yet, and I already miss you so much," she says.

"Oh, my sister," I say, laughing, "I love you so much! Be nice to Juan Alberto. And, though you want to be fresh and modern, try to think through things before doing them, OK?"

My crazy sister whispers in my ear, "He asked me to go with him to Madrid."

"Seriously?" I ask.

Raquel nods.

"When?"

"In three weeks. He's going to Barcelona tomorrow, and I promised to go with him when he gets back. Listen, deep down, I know it's good for me, and I'll be able to pick up some of Luz's things. Anyway, don't worry, I'm not going to sleep with him. I'm not that desperate! I told Papá about the trip last night, and he thought it sounded good. He also said he likes Juan Alberto. That he seems like a good man."

That makes me laugh. My father and his good men.

It's the same thing he told me about Eric when he met him. It's like certain men have a special code that we women don't know, but he sees in Juan Alberto the seriousness he saw in Eric.

"Listen, Raquel, are you sure about what you're doing?"

She looks over at Juan Alberto and the rest of the group.

"No, Cuchu, but I need to do something crazy. I've never been spontaneous, and I like the idea of doing something different with this man. What we have will only last while he's in Spain but—"

"Raquel, you're going to suffer when he leaves. I know you!"

My sister nods with a seriousness that surprises me.

"I know, Cuchu . . . but I want to enjoy myself while he's here. I'm well aware of my situation and that I have two girls, so there aren't a lot of crazy things I can do in my life. That's why I'm determined to enjoy those two days!"

I smile, but I feel bad that she thinks like this. She's too young to think she won't have big emotions yet in her life.

"Girls, I hate to interrupt your moment, but the pilot says we need to go," says Eric as he puts his hands on my waist.

As my sister says goodbye to Eric, Juan Alberto comes over to say goodbye to me.

"I know; don't worry," he says. "I'll take care of her and make sure everyone's OK. I already told Eric, but I wanted to thank you as well for letting me stay at Sweetheart Villa."

I can't reproach him about anything.

I playfully smack him on the chest with my hand.

"You already know, dude, how I get when I don't like something, you know what I mean?" I say, warning him.

Raquel's little roll in the hay grins and gives me a pair of kisses. When I pull away from him, I hug my father and my sister, I kiss Luz, who's sniffling because Flyn is leaving—can you believe it?—and then babble something at little Lucía.

"Just remember, sweetheart, that I want more grandchildren," says my father, "and if it's a boy, even better!"

"I'd rather have a little girl," says my husband.

I have nothing to say.

I'm sure my face says it all.

They both grin, and I roll my eyes as I scratch my neck. Men!

8

We arrive at Franz Josef Strauss International Airport in Munich on time and without complications. As we deplane, Eric chats with the pilot, and I see Norbert has come to pick us up. Flyn runs toward him when he sees him and gives him a hug. I love seeing how Norbert blushes with happiness over the boy's attentions.

As soon as Flyn's in the car with Graciela and Dexter, I hug Norbert too. As always, he's stiff as a board, but I don't care and hug him anyway.

"How wonderful to have you back home again, missus," he says, betraying his emotions.

I've gone from Miss Judith to missus.

"Norbert, didn't we agree you would call me by my name?"

He nods and shakes Eric's hand heartily.

"It's my wife's idea, missus. She's so looking forward to having you home again."

Norbert stuffs the luggage in the trunk while Eric hugs me and gives me a kiss.

"You're on my turf again, sweetheart."

"Sorry to tell you, handsome, but this is my turf now too."

We climb in the car and head home. Our home. On the way, Graciela looks out the window, and the men joke around with Flyn. I tell her about some of the things she's seeing.

Eric looks happy to see how much I know about Munich, and I wink at him.

When we get back, Norbert opens the gate. As soon as we cross the beautiful garden, I see Simona with Susto and Calamar at the front door. She smiles radiantly and runs toward the car with the dogs chasing behind her.

I jump out of the car before it's come to a full stop, and Susto and Calamar leap all over me. I kiss them as they bark up a storm. Then I see Simona—my Simona!—and I give her a very warm hug.

Suddenly, I realize Eric is pulling on my arm, his brow wrinkled. What's wrong with him?

"Are you out of your mind?"

I'm surprised by his solemnness and his tone of voice. Why? What's happened?

"Aunt Jude, you can't open the door of a car until it's come to a full stop," says Flyn, who's now hugging Simona. "It's dangerous."

I realize what he's saying is true. My impulsiveness got the better of me. I'm not being the best role model for Flyn. My German is mad at me.

"I'm so sorry, Eric," I say as Susto leaps about, wanting me to play with him. "It's just that I saw Simona and . . ."

Eric's face relaxes, and he touches my face. "I know, love, but, please, be more careful, OK?"

I hold on to him and sigh.

"I promise, but please smile."

He does. His expression is completely transformed, and he gives me a kiss on the lips.

"You're still gonna pay for it as soon as we're alone."

"Wow . . . this suddenly got interesting," I say, feeling naughty.

Eric laughs and plays with Susto and Calamar.

When I see Eric and Flyn squat to hug them, I feel like my heart is going to burst. Neither one of them would have believed this scene a year ago. But, there they are, uncle and nephew, showering our two pets with cascades of love. Flyn runs off to a side yard, and the dogs chase after him. Norbert pulls our luggage from the car, and Eric gets Dexter's wheelchair.

"Judith, I'm so happy to see you," says Simona.

"I'm so happy to see you too, Simona! I missed you."

As soon as Graciela gets out of the car, I introduce them.

"Simona, this is Graciela."

"Happy to meet you, Miss Graciela."

"Please, Simona," the young woman says in German. "I'd feel more comfortable if you would just call me by my first name, the way you do Judith." Here we go again.

It's obvious that with us middle-class girls, this business of "miss" is unsettling.

"You can drop the 'miss' altogether," I tell her.

"There's no need for it, OK?" Graciela says, seconding me.

"Oh my God, you talk just like the star of *Emerald Madness*!" says Simona, surprised at Graciela's Mexican accent.

"You watch *Emerald Madness* in Germany?"

Simona and I nod.

"Seriously?"

"Dead serious, Graciela," I respond.

I'm laughing like a fool.

I still don't know how I got so hooked on this soap opera.

"You wouldn't believe how addicted we are to *Emerald Madness* and Luis Alfredo Quiñones. I couldn't believe they shot him in the last episode. He won't die, will he?"

Graciela shakes her head, and Simona and I sigh with gratitude. Thank God!

"Simona, how are you, beautiful?" says Dexter, joining us.

"Stupendous, Mr. Ramírez, and welcome!" Simona says and nods toward Graciela. "And your fiancé—your wife?—is wonderful."

Oh my God!

When he hears that, Dexter freezes. Graciela blushes, and I decide not to say anything and see where this goes.

"You've chosen very well, sir."

Eric grins, but Dexter decides to clear up what we've chosen not to.

"Thank you, but I have to tell you that Graciela is just my personal assistant."

Simona stares at him for a minute and then at Graciela and brings her hands together, embarrassed. "My apologies, sir. I was out of line."

"It's fine, Simona," says Dexter with a smile.

We all go in the house, and I hear Simona talking to Graciela. "You're single?"

"Yes."

"Well, I can assure you you'll have many admirers in Germany," she says, winking at me.

"Brunettes are very popular around these parts."

I can't look at Dexter's face when she says that because I'm afraid I'm going to laugh. He's going to have to deal with Graciela sooner or later.

Later that afternoon, Sonia, Eric's mother; Marta, his sister; and her boyfriend, Arthur, come over for a while. Flyn gives them big hugs when he sees them. I can tell Sonia loves having that kind of physical contact with her grandson. Marta spins him around in her arms. They've never been apart from the boy for so long, and they're emotional at his return.

Like Simona, they both think Graciela is Dexter's girlfriend or his wife, and he's forced to explain once more.

I ask Sonia about Trevor. "We broke up," she whispers to me. "I don't want commitments at my age!"

I laugh. My mother-in-law never ceases to amaze me.

For several hours, we all sit around the table and talk and drink, and Eric and I show photos of our honeymoon.

Not all of them. Some we keep to ourselves. They're just too intimate.

When Marta realizes Graciela is single, she quickly invites her out for a night on the town, and I agree to join them. I'm dying to go to Guantanamera to see my friends, dance salsa, and shout azúcar. I can see in Eric's eyes he's not in the least amused by this, but I'm not going to stop going out with my friends just because I'm now Mrs. Zimmerman. No way!

Getting back into our routine means establishing everything all over again. The whirlwind of the wedding and honeymoon is one thing, and the day-to-day is another. Although I adore my husband, and he adores me, I know we're on a collision course. And I know it because of the way he's looking at me right now.

9

The next day we have a date for dinner with Björn, Frida, and Andrés at Jokers, Björn's father's restaurant. Dexter, Graciela, Eric, and I say hi to the delightful Klaus and go directly to the table he's reserved for us. We order beers and chat.

"Oh God, I love this beer," says Graciela.

"Löwenbräu?" Eric asks.

"Many years ago, when I lived in Chile, I had a neighbor whose father was German, and he would bring the beer from Germany," says Graciela after a sip. "It's so good!"

"Would you like another?" Dexter says, smiling because she's so happy.

"I'd love it."

They clearly like each other, but neither will make the first move. Well, Graciela tried, and now it's Dexter's turn. I'm sure he wants to, but his disability inhibits him. What I don't understand is how he can be so foolish. He knows she's aware of his limitations, and she's still interested. Honestly, I don't get it.

They bring us another round of beers, and we make toasts and laugh and enjoy each other's company, like always. Then we see Björn, who is with a woman. Who could it be?

He hasn't seen us yet so I can check her out as much as I want. As might be expected, she's a looker. Tall, sexy, blonde, wearing heels, and beautiful—very beautiful.

When his father lets him know we're waiting and Björn turns our way, I give him a wink.

He's such a great friend!

"Eric, your friend is here," I tell him in a low voice.

Eric gets up, and then the two titans I love so much come together in a long and meaningful hug. They adore each other. Afterward, Björn hugs me.

"Welcome home, Mrs. Zimmerman," he whispers in my ear.

His date is not exactly giving me a kindly look. I can see she's not thrilled to be at this dinner. Björn continues his greetings and shakes Dexter's hand as he's introduced to Graciela. "Frida and Andrés aren't here yet?"

"We're here!" says Frida, as they come up to the table. I leap up and run toward her. My crazy friend jumps up and down and hugs me.

"How's everything going?"

"Fantastic," I say. "We haven't killed each other yet."

Frida smiles and then Andrés hugs and squeezes me. Everyone is so sweet to me, I can't help but grin. I see they know Graciela from their visits to Mexico.

I look over at Björn's date, who's looking at us askance. "Please be a gentleman and introduce us to your date," I tell him.

"Agneta, let me introduce my friends. This is Eric and his wife, Judith; Andrés and his wife, Frida; and Dexter and his girlfriend, Graciela."

Uh-oh.

I can't help but laugh.

But before Dexter can say anything, Graciela looks up at the handsome Björn and says, "I'm not his girlfriend. I'm just his personal assistant."

Björn looks at Dexter, surprised, and then at Graciela and responds in Spanish so Agneta won't understand him. "Well then, I think you and I will have a date later."

I crack up. Björn never misses an opportunity.

"I'd be delighted," says Graciela with a poise that surprises us all. You go, girl.

I can't look at Dexter!

Poor man!

But in the end, I can't help it. I see him squaring his jaw as he pushes his hair back from his face. He doesn't say a word and takes another sip of his beer. I feel a little sorry for him.

After the introductions, we all sit and chat. Björn's father brings us all kinds of delicious things to eat. I try to explain what everything is to Graciela.

I'm so hungry!

"Do you know who she is?" Frida whispers.

"Who?" Then I see she means Björn's date.

"She works at CNN here in Germany. She's a TV anchor."

"Well," I whisper back, now intrigued.

"This is delicious!" says Graciela, who, like me, loves to eat. She's trying one of the meatballs.

They're to die for. I serve her a Brezn.

"Try this savory pastry," I say. "Dip it in that sauce, and you'll see."

"These are spectacular," says Frida as she picks one up.

All three of us dip our pastries and take a bite, and our dramatic expressions say it all. Delicious!

The men chat while we eat until I suddenly realize Agneta is not joining us.

"You don't eat?"

She shakes her head and wrinkles her nose. "Too much fat for me."

"Well then, more for us!" Graciela says in Spanish, and I have to stop myself from laughing. I think the beers are getting to her.

"But you must eat something," says Frida.

"I've ordered a radish and cheese salad," says Agneta.

"That's all you're going to have?"

She lifts her chin.

"Everything you're eating is in your mouth for one second but six months on your hips. I can't do that to my audience."

She's right.

But, hey, that second in the mouth is something else! As to the other thing she said, I'd rather not respond. This one is not the brightest bulb.

For several minutes, we just eat and eat, and, all of a sudden, I stop. I remember who Agneta's face reminds me of!

She's the same as a poodle named Fosqui, which Pachuca used to have when I was little. I laugh again. I can't help it, and Eric leans over and kisses my neck.

"What's so funny?"

I can't tell him the truth. "It's Graciela. Have you seen how happy she is?"

Eric looks over at her. "I don't think she should have any more Löwenbräu," he says.

I give him a little kiss on the tip of his nose.

"I love you, Mr. Zimmerman."

Eric grins and pushes a strand of hair behind my ear. "You know what?"

"What?"

"It's been a long time since we've fought and since you've called me names."

I burst out laughing, and, when I realize what he's actually referring to, I nod.

"I will only call you that when you deserve it, and you don't deserve it right now. So, no! I refuse to give you that pleasure."

"But it drives me crazy when you call me that."

"I know." I laugh.

"C'mon, say it," he says, tickling my waist.

"No."

"Say it."

"I said no . . . You don't deserve it right now."

He kisses me over and over, and I finally give in. "Dickhead."

Eric laughs. We kiss again. My God . . . I love how he kisses me.

And then, out of nowhere, we hear a strident voice.

"This is not the salad I ordered."

Eric and I come back to reality and see Agneta, her face angry. "I asked for a cheese salad and—"

"And this is a cheese and radish salad," says Björn, cutting her off.

The CNN star looks at her plate and transforms her expression into something sweeter.

"OK . . . if you say so, then I believe it."

"If I say so?"

"Yes, if you say so," says the blonde, who has hypnotized Björn.

Frida and I exchange a look, and I suspect we think the same thing. She's dumb, but not that dumb.

She has such a lousy personality . . . What does Björn see in her?

Well, we all know he's a beautiful guy, and, having a good sense of his taste, I'm assuming the girl must be a beast in the sack. But, wow, he needs to consider a muzzle for her when they go out.

We all keep eating, and the conversation stabilizes. Being German like Agneta, Frida tries to include her in the conversation, but Agneta is not interested in making an effort.

After the dessert and the laughter, we hear Graciela placing an order with the waiter. "Ten Löwenbräus to go."

We all laugh, except Dexter.

"No way . . . No way."

"Why not?" Graciela responds, holding her chin with her hand as she leans an arm on the table. "Why shouldn't I take some beer with me?"

"You're going to get sick, believe me," Dexter says tenderly.

Graciela laughs. For a little while now I've noticed her shyness has been completely absent.

"I'm tired of you not wanting me," she says, "when it could be amazing to play together in your pleasure dome."

Wow, Graciela has dropped the bomb! "What did you just say?" he asks, totally stunned.

"I know you like me, and our friend Judith here has noticed it too. Don't pretend, dude."

Here we go!

Frida looks at me. I look back at her.

Eric looks at me. I look back at him.

Björn looks at me. I look back at him.

They all look at me.

"Look, what Graciela means is . . ."

Then Dexter looks at me.

I can't finish.

Graciela takes him by the chin and, in front of everybody, gives him a kiss that leaves us all with mouths agape.

There goes another one, just like my sister. So much for the shy ones!

"This is what I'm talking about, my handsome boy," she says, just inches from Dexter's face. "I want to stop playing with others so I can play with you."

Mother of God . . .

I'm completely thrown. Graciela keeps looking at Dexter, but he turns to me.

"What does she mean by 'play'?"

I arch my brows, and Dexter suddenly understands.

"For the love of God, who do you play with?" he asks, staring at her.

"With my friends."

"What?" he says, a little too loudly.

"Since you don't want to do anything with me, I've had to find my own way," says Graciela.

Nobody moves.

No one knows what to do until Eric gets up and takes control of the situation.

"It's late," he says, "and it's probably best if we all go home."

We all get up. I stand near Graciela and see that Dexter is the first to move away from the table.

"What are you doing, crazy girl?"

She shrugs.

"I just wanted to tell him the truth once and for all. I think the beers helped me."

"I'll let you know later if they helped you. Just go home now," I say.

Once outside the restaurant, Dexter settles into the car, and Eric folds his wheelchair.

Frida and Andrés go home. Agneta, who's quite a diva, climbs into Björn's sports car without saying goodbye. She's so rude.

Björn waits for Eric to finish his task, then looks over at me and grins, well aware that Dexter can hear him. Like my father says, he's more clever than a red rat.

"It's been a pleasure," he says directly to Graciela, "and that dinner invitation is still on. We'll talk tomorrow."

What a scoundrel! We didn't even ask for his help, but he's already joined the team to push Dexter along. He kisses Graciela and me good night and runs off to his car. We get in Eric's car, and the four of us drive home in silence.

Once home, an angry Dexter hurries to the first-floor room where he's staying, and Graciela goes to hers.

"Why are you such a troublemaker, sweetheart?" asks Eric.

"Me?"

"Yes, you."

"Why are you saying that?"

"What's all this about Graciela playing and that you know Dexter's attracted to her?"

"First of all, she told me everything without my even asking," I say, enjoying myself now.

"So many secrets all at once," he says, kissing my neck.

"And second of all: it's obvious! All you have to do is look at Dexter whenever another man is anywhere near Graciela to realize that it bothers him when other men notice her."

"What do you think if you and I play for a little while and forget all about these first and second of alls?" Eric whispers as he takes me in his arms and gives me a warm kiss.

He pushes me against the wall.

"I'd love that, Mr. Zimmerman," I say and kiss him back.

10

Two days later, Marta, my sister-in-law, calls me, and we decide to go out on the town together.

I'm really looking forward to it!

Initially, Graciela and I were the only ones joining Marta, but, in the end, the guys decided to come along. They don't want us to go alone, and, when we get to Guantanamera, I look over at Eric's face and realize he doesn't really want to be here.

Once in the club, we spy Anita, Marta and Arthur, and a few other friends already out on the dance floor. My German sister-in-law really knows how to dance. Eric watches her. He's never seen her move like that, and he's very surprised.

"Why is my sister making those faces?"

I'm about to say something when Marta sees us and rushes over to us, dragging her boyfriend behind her.

Back on the dance floor, I notice the guy dancing with Anita. Where did this piece of candy come from?

"Impressive, right?" says Marta when she sees where my eyes are going.

I nod, amazed by this incredibly sensual, dark man.

"We've decided to call him Mr. Perfect Torso."

"I'll say," I murmur.

"His name is Máximo," Marta whispers back.

"Who is he?"

"A friend of Reinaldo's."

"Is he Cuban?"

"No, Argentinian, and he's to die for, right?"

"I'll let you know."

But it's obvious that denying it would be one of the biggest lies ever told.

We're just kind of stunned, watching Anita dance salsa with this Argentine, when I feel Eric by my side.

"Your drink, Jude."

When I take the drink, I realize he's overheard the conversation, and he's not happy.

Oh, my baby, he gets so jealous.

I smile. He doesn't smile back.

I kiss him.

"I only like you."

"And Máximo," he says.

In the end, after I just keep kissing him, I manage to get him to smile and kiss me back. As we all chat, I realize Dexter and Eric communicate with a look whenever a woman they find attractive goes by. I laugh. I can't get mad. I have eyes too.

I begin to move slowly and gently to the beat of the music and watch as my husband scans me with his blue eyes. He likes the very short dress I'm wearing; he bought it for me on our honeymoon, and I know it tempts him.

"C'mon," I say, "let's dance."

He arches his brow and shakes his head.

The only thing missing is him saying "No way!"

We're back in Germany, and all the easy ways from our honeymoon seem to have vanished. I'm sorry about that. I like uninhibited Eric very much.

He looks at me with a serious expression.

"You go dance," he says when he realizes I won't stop moving.

I want to dance and sing along to the song by Orishas that's playing, so I go out to the dance floor with my friends. We move languidly and seductively. The music invades our bodies as we dance along.

The dance floor is jammed. We're all dancing and singing along at full volume. Eric won't take his eyes off me.

My friend Reinaldo comes over.

He sees Eric and goes to say hi. My guy introduces him to Dexter and Graciela and points me out to him. Grinning that giant Cuban grin, Reinaldo comes running out to the dance floor, takes me by the waist, and begins to dance to the hot little song.

I watch Eric and realize he doesn't like this at all. I quickly get loose, and everyone starts jumping up and down as we sing.

The entire place is dancing, drunk with the song, and, when it's over, the DJ changes the beat. I go back with my husband. I'm thirsty and take a long swallow of my mojito.

"You won't dance, my love?"

Eric just stares at me as I sweat, and he pulls a stray hair off my face.

"Since when do I like to dance?"

His response is provocative, but since I don't want to argue and I don't want to remind him that during our honeymoon he danced all he wanted and more, I let it go and wrap my arms around his neck.

"OK. Then kiss me. You like doing that, right?"

He finally smiles!

He kisses and kisses me, but then Marta pulls on my arm and drags me to the dance floor, and we dance to "Bemba Colorá."

Eric's face darkens again. It's becoming very clear he doesn't like Guantanamera at all.

I wave Graciela over to join us. She doesn't hesitate and comes out shaking her hips. Dexter and Eric look at each other and both sigh.

Those two!

Reinaldo, Anita, Arthur, a couple of other Cuban friends, and Mr. Perfect Torso quickly join us.

Mother of God, up close the Argentinian is even hotter.

Since I've been to this club before, I know how to dance here. We make a little circle, and each couple takes a turn in the middle, showing off their dance moves. Marta and I gyrate like a couple of crazy women and shout, "Azúcar!"

I go back to Eric's side the minute the song is over.

"Is it going to be like this all night?" Eric asks, clearly irritated.

I notice Dexter is saying something to Graciela, and she rolls her eyes. I take a long swallow of my delicious mojito and gaze back at my non-Latino lover.

"Don't you like to have a good time and enjoy yourself out with our friends?"

Eric—or, I should say, Iceman—looks all around the club. "No, not at all," he says with his brutal honesty. "But you do?"

I finish my mojito. "You know the answer to that, my love," I say. His nostrils flare.

"You get me going like a Ducati when you get so possessive," I whisper.

I rub up against him. Even in heels, I only come up to his nose. Eric doesn't move. He just looks at me, and so I begin to move my body to the beat of the music. I notice his erection and kiss him.

"You want to go home?"

He nods enthusiastically, and I chuckle.

When we get home, it's two fifteen in the morning. After we say good night to Dexter and Graciela, we go to our room. Eric is still scowling.

"Listen, my love," I start to say, but I'm a little bit worse for the wear because of the mojitos, and I can't finish.

My Iceman grabs me by the arms, and, with a passion that leaves me speechless, he kisses me and devours me. He pushes me against the wall and tears my panties off.

"I don't like it when you dance with other people," he says as he unbuttons his pants.

He hammers me against the wall with a single thrust.

"I don't want you to go back to that place, do you understand?"

His lust drives me crazy, but I'm no fool. I hold on to his shoulders. "My friends go there," I say without losing it. "I don't see a problem."

Eric's face turns dark again. He grabs me by the hips and pulls me against him until I moan. I love how deep he goes.

"I don't like that place," he hisses.

I kiss him. "But I do," I say as I pull my lips back from his. "I have a good time, and it's harmless fun."

"It hurts me," he says, impaling me again.

I need air, but I like our hot little game, and I want more.

"No, my love, I would never hurt you." He penetrates me again.

"There are too many men staring at you," Eric says as he pants.

"But I'm yours, only yours."

His mouth takes mine again. His hands descend to my ass. He holds me tight and pushes into me again. He's tireless. I open for him. I'm thrilled by his possessiveness. So much passion, and soon my body can't take any more, and I squeeze against him and release all this intense and addictive pleasure.

When he realizes what's going on, Eric picks up speed. He loses himself in me without pause until he reaches his limit and grunts, coming right along with me.

We stay wrapped up and against the wall, still breathing heavily.

"It seems that Guantanamera got you excited."

When he sees my smile, he smiles too. "You excite me, sweetheart. Just you," he says, holding me closer.

He doesn't say anything more about what I can and cannot do. He knows he shouldn't. But now I know exactly what he thinks about Guantanamera.

That night, after making love once more like savages while in the shower, we sleep holding each other and are very, very much in love.

The days pass and Dexter and Graciela are going nowhere. Björn calls to make a dinner date with Graciela. She accepts, and Dexter doesn't say a word. Doesn't this man have blood in his veins?

The next day, I ask Graciela about her date, and she tells me delightedly that Björn was a perfect gentleman the entire night. Zero sex.

Honestly, I'm not surprised. If there's anything I know about Björn, other than that he's so very handsome, it's that he is a real gentleman and loyal to his friends.

Flyn goes back to school. He's excited about the first day. On the ride there, Norbert and I are glad to see him so happy. He has a gift he made himself for his special friend, Laura, in his backpack, and he's eager to give it to her. But when we go pick him up later that afternoon, he's sad and his eyes are downcast.

"What happened?" I ask.

His eyes moisten, and my little man looks at me while still holding the wrapped gift in his hands.

"Laura isn't at this school anymore."

"Why?"

"Ariadna told me her parents moved out of the city."

Oh, my poor little guy, his first heartbreak.

What a shame. Why is love always so difficult?

I hug him, and he lets himself be hugged as Norbert drives us home. I kiss his dark little head and try to imagine the kind of words my father would say in a situation like this.

"Listen, Flyn, I know you're sad because of Laura, but you have to be positive and imagine that, though she's no longer at this school, she's doing well. You don't want her to be doing badly, right?"

He shakes his head. "But I won't get to see her again."

"Well, you don't know about that. Life is full of twists and turns, and perhaps you'll run into her again someday."

He doesn't respond.

"What do you say we go shopping for Eric?" I propose. "Saturday is his birthday."

He nods. I give Norbert directions to a jewelry shop where I know there's a watch my husband likes. It costs a mint, but, hey, we can afford it!

They don't know me at the jewelry shop, but they know Flyn and Norbert, and, when I say I'm Mrs. Zimmerman, they practically roll out a red carpet and throw rose petals on it for me.

This is so intense. What a difference it is to have money.

After we buy the watch and a black leather bracelet Flyn has picked out for his uncle, I have them gift wrap everything. My nephew is still sad. I don't like it when he gets like this, especially when he's been so happy this last month.

"Do you know I'm going to be in a motocross race with Jurgen in a couple of weeks?" I say as we get back in the car.

"Really?"

I nod. "Do you want to be my assistant?"

He nods, but he's still not smiling.

"What do you say we start your apprenticeship with the motorcycle this coming weekend?"

His expression changes, and his eyes sparkle.

The boy has been wanting to learn how to ride a motorcycle since before our wedding, which is why I asked my father to teach him how to ride a bicycle this past summer. That will make my task much easier.

I know this is going to be hard on Eric. I know this apprenticeship is going to cause me more than just a headache, but I also know that, in the end, Eric will accept things. He has promised to change his attitude, and now he needs to prove it.

Flyn is asking me questions about the motorcycle, and I respond as best I can. "Uncle Eric is going to be mad, isn't he?"

"Don't worry about it," I say, trying not to give it too much importance. I kiss him on the head. "I promise I'll convince him."

But Flyn's right. Later that evening, after Dexter and Graciela leave to take care of some business matters, I discuss it with Eric, and he blows up.

"Why did you have to bring the subject back up?" he asks, sitting at his desk in his office.

"Listen, Eric," I respond, looking over the shelves that hold his gun collection. "Flyn was devastated by the loss of his mother, and I was thinking that . . ."

"That he can replace her with a motorcycle?"

I just stare at him. He stares back. It's a standoff, like always.

"Before the wedding, you promised him he could learn to ride a motorcycle," I remind him.

"I know I promised. I just don't know why you had to bring it back up."

I know I'm very impulsive and I don't think things through sometimes, but I'm not backing down on this one. "He would've asked me about it eventually, and I have a race with Jurgen in two weeks and—"

"You have a what?"

Uh-oh . . .

His brows freeze, and his body tenses up.

"I told you about this. You've known about it for a month. I told you Jurgen told me about the race, and you said you thought it would be fun if I took part. You even had my motorcycle brought over on your plane."

"I did?" he says, surprised.

"Yes, you did, and if you can't remember, that's not my problem! But, look, the important thing now is to deal with Flyn."

"He's starting school, and I don't want him to get distracted. Let's wait until spring for motocross lessons."

"What?"

"For the love of God, Jude, Flyn doesn't care if he learns now or later."

"What I promised—"

"Your promises are your business," he says, cutting me off dryly. "And, in any case, both your and Hannah's motorcycles are too big for him. We'd have to buy one that's the right size for him."

"Well . . ."

I learned on my father's motorcycle, and here I am, not a scratch on me!

"Look, Jude, I understand he's going to learn how to ride a motorcycle, but this is not the moment."

"Yes, it is."

"Jude . . . ," he hisses.

"Eric . . . ," I retort.

It's been a little while since I felt this. He stares at me with his frosty Iceman gaze, and I feel my stomach jump. God, he really knows how to make me nervous. Just as I'm about to tell him I don't want to argue, the phone rings. Eric picks up and gives me a sign to let me know it's work.

I wait five minutes to see if we can finish our conversation, but when I see this is going to take a while, I step out of the office and go get a drink in the kitchen. Flyn is there, looking sad. He's still holding the gift he made for Laura.

"I don't want you and my uncle to argue."

"Don't worry about it, love."

"But I heard my uncle get mad."

107

"He's mad because I reminded him I'm going to be in a motorcycle race, not because you're going to learn how to ride a motorcycle," I say, lying to his face. "Believe me, love, there's nothing to worry about."

"Yes, yes, there is. He'll get mad, and then you'll leave again."

My grumpy little boy loves me and that touches me. I sit down next to him and make him look at me.

"Listen, Flyn, your uncle and I love each other very much, but we're different in so many ways that it's going to be very hard for us not to argue. And even if we argue, that doesn't mean I'm going to leave. Because for me to leave him and you, it would have to be over something very, very serious, and I'm not going to let that happen, OK?"

He nods. I gather him in my lap. I'm still surprised we can be this close, and he hugs me and leans his head on my shoulder.

"Did you know I love your hugs?"

I feel him smile, and we just hug for a few more minutes.

"I love that you live with us."

We both laugh, and then he surprises me again.

"Now that Laura has moved away, I want this gift to be for you," he says.

"Are you sure?"

He nods and I accept the gift.

I open it and see there's a little handmade bracelet. It's made from my niece's Bratz game pieces and, surprisingly, in lilac, my favorite color.

"It's beautiful—I love it!"

"You really like it?"

"Of course I really like it." I put it on and extend my arm so he can see it on my wrist. "What do you think?"

"It looks really good on you, and it's your favorite color."

"How did you know?"

"Luz told me, and I remember my uncle mentioning it once too."

"Thank you, love," I say, and give him a kiss. "I love it."

"Don't argue with my uncle over me."

"Flyn . . ."

"Promise," he insists.

I want him to feel better, so I put my thumb up against his and swear. "I promise."

He hugs me tightly, so tightly that it hurts my shoulders, but I don't say anything because I want him to be happy.

"I'm going to bury you in kisses," I say, tickling him.

He laughs and then I laugh and then we're both aware Eric's standing at the door. He's looking at us, and his look, like always, has an effect on me.

"First of all," he says—and this makes me smile—"Jude is not going to ever leave us, OK?" The boy nods. "Second of all, we will buy a motorcycle appropriate to your age so you can start your lessons with Jude. And, third of all, what do you say that we go shopping so Jude can be the most beautiful woman during Oktoberfest?"

Flyn gives his uncle a hug and goes running out of the kitchen. I don't quite understand what's going on.

And, suddenly, my crazy love is kneeling before me. "It would have to be something very, very, very, very serious for me to let you go, OK, sweetheart?"

"You overheard our whole conversation, didn't you?"

"I heard enough to know my nephew and I are crazy about you, and we don't know how to live without you anymore," he says in a low voice as he brings his mouth closer to mine.

He completely unravels me . . .

His words destroy all my defenses . . .

We kiss, and I want him desperately, but Eric stops me.

"Even though what I want most in the world is to undress you and make you mine a thousand times, I can't right now."

I protest.

"Flyn is going to come back any minute so we can go shopping."

"Where are we going shopping?"

My man kisses me over and over, and when I've just about lost all my senses, he gives me a little pat on the butt.

"C'mon, we need to buy you something pretty for the big celebration in Munich."

Hours later, we meet up with Dexter and Graciela while shopping. Together, we have a fun time buying some traditional Bavarian costumes. We're going to celebrate!

11

Oktoberfest, the most important beer festival in the world, begins. Eric has agreed to meet friends and family there.

I'm wearing a dirndl and look like a typical German peasant. I am wearing a long skirt, an apron, a bodice, and a white blouse. I start to put my hair in braids, convinced Eric's going to love this look.

There's a knock on my door, and Flyn comes in. He's incredibly handsome in his short brown leather pants, suspenders, grayish jacket, and little green hat.

"Are you ready?"

"You look fantastic, Flyn."

I get up and take a spin. "Do I look German dressed like this?"

"You look really good, but you're like me. Neither one of us has a German face."

We both laugh, and I go back to braiding my hair. "Please tell your uncle I'll be down in five minutes."

Flyn leaves, and I finish doing my hair and spin again, only to find Eric watching me from the door.

"I don't know how you do it, but you always look gorgeous."

My mouth goes dry. What a husband I have.

He's the beautiful one, the handsome one, the impressive and alluring one!

He's wearing long brown leather pants, a beige shirt, and a pair of really dramatic tall brown leather boots. I never imagined a Bavarian Eric could be so sexy.

Turns out I like how he looks in leather. I should ask him to buy himself something in leather.

I repeat what I did with Flyn. I spin around so he can see me, but, before I know it, his hands are on my waist, and he's kissing me with a certain air of possessiveness. Oh yes . . . I adore his intensity.

I put my arms around his neck and leap up to encircle him with my legs.

"If you keep kissing me like that, I'm going to close the door and lock it, and the festival is going to be in this room."

"I like that idea, sweetheart." More kisses . . .

"What are you doing?" says Flyn, surprising us. "Stop kissing and let's go. Everyone's waiting for us."

"We're not done," says Eric as he untangles from me when he sees that Flyn, his arms akimbo, isn't going to leave without us.

Dexter and Graciela are waiting and looking adorable in their Bavarian costumes. We all get in the car and say goodbye to Simona, who refuses to join us.

Norbert drops us off as close as possible to the Theresienwiese Esplanade, where the festivities are taking place.

The place is jammed.

"Can you believe this? It reminds me of the April festival in Seville," I say. "I almost feel like shouting 'olé!'"

Eric is in a great mood and kisses me on the forehead as hundreds of Germans and tourists dressed in all sorts of ways continue with their fun, listening to music and drinking beer after beer.

Eric grips my hand firmly and holds on to Flyn with his other hand. He doesn't want to lose us in the tumult.

"Follow me," he says to Dexter and Graciela.

As we walk, I notice all the stands are named after beer brands. At one of the larger tents, the bouncer at the door lets us in when he sees Eric. There's music. People sing, dance, and drink. Everyone's having a good time. Eric pauses, looks around, and finally locates what he's looking for.

"This place is about to overflow," I shout.

Eric nods. "Don't worry," he says, "we have a reserved spot every year."

In the back, amid all the partying, I see Frida and Sonia with little Glen in her arms as Marta and Andrés dance.

"Look who's here!" says Sonia once she sees her grandson.

Flyn gives her a hug and goes immediately to make faces at Glen, who laughs.

"Girl, you look good no matter what you have on," says Frida when she sees me in my Bavarian drag.

"Thank you; just make sure and tell my husband," I say slyly. "Have you seen how handsome he looks?"

"Yes, it's true; your husband looks very good," she says as she scans Eric up and down. "But my Andrés is also very handsome today and, well, well, look at how handsome his friend is!"

My eyes follow the direction of her pointing finger, and I see Björn in all his splendor, accompanied by Fosqui the poodle and yet another blonde. People stare at them. Agneta is well known because of her TV work, and she's soon surrounded by fans asking for her autograph. As they get closer, I realize the other blonde is Diana. Björn manages to get his girlfriend away from the claws of her fans, and, after I give him a kiss, I try to be friendly to her.

"Hi, Agneta."

She looks at me and blinks.

"I'm sorry. I don't remember your name."

"Judith."

"Oh yes, that's right." And then she turns to her friend and introduces us. "This is Judith."

Diana nods. We already know each other. "Wonderful to see you again, Judith."

I get butterflies in my stomach remembering what this woman did to me that night at the swingers' party.

"It's wonderful to see you too," I say and blush.

And then I hear the screech of the poodle. "Eric! What a delight to see you again. Let me introduce you to Diana."

Mother of God, she remembers his name but not mine?

I didn't like her much before, and now I like her even less.

But my handsome husband knows exactly what I'm thinking. He says hello to them and immediately comes to be by my side. He takes me in his arms and lifts me up.

"My friends, this is my beautiful wife's first Oktoberfest in Germany, and I would like us all to toast to her."

And then all these Germans around us, friends and strangers, lift their giant beer mugs and, shouting their war cry, toast to me. I grin and Eric kisses me.

No more bad mood!

Flyn wants to go on the rides, and Marta and I offer to go with him. I do need a little air. When we leave the tent, the mob engulfs us. Marta looks back at me, a little worried, but I let her know I'm right behind her. Flyn immediately finds his way onto one of the rides while Marta and I wait.

"Oh man, those people are goners," I say, pointing out some guys who are drunk off their asses.

"They look like Brits," Marta says. "You know, they probably tried to drink alongside some German and don't realize that the beer at these festivals is much stronger than usual."

I laugh.

"I mean, if the smallest mug is the size of a book, what can you expect?" says Marta.

We go with Flyn from ride to ride. When we get back to the tent, Eric winks at me, and Frida takes me by the hand and makes me climb up on one of the tables to sing a typical German song. Amazingly, I know this tune, and Eric and his mother beam up at me.

As I start to come down off the table, a man comes up to help me.

"Do you know you're a very pretty woman?" he says, taking me by the waist and helping me down. I thank him and walk back to my group, but, as I get nearer, I stop and feel the fury rising within me when I realize Amanda is standing right in front of Eric. What is Amanda doing here?

I hate that woman!

My neck itches. I scratch and curse in Spanish so no one will understand me. Suddenly, she notices me. When Eric sees her discomfort, he follows her gaze and lands on me. Annoyed, I turn around and run right into the man who was flirting with me seconds before. I realize he's drunk as a skunk.

"Hello again, beautiful."

I don't respond.

"Let me buy you a beer."

"No, thank you."

I turn again. I'm pissed. Very pissed. And then someone grabs me by the waist again. Goddamned drunk. I lean away and launch my elbow back with all my might. I hear a grunt and turn back to see Eric, hunched over.

"What's wrong with you?"

Oh my God, I'm so stupid. I've hurt him!

I'm stunned. He recovers, takes me forcefully by the hand, and drags me to the side of the tent.

"What was that about?"

I'm about to respond, but he doesn't let me.

"If this is about Amanda, she hasn't done anything. She hasn't tried to flirt with me or in any way embarrass herself, because she likes her job and knows I don't want her to be a problem. She finally gets it. Do you?"

I have no plans to respond. I'm still pissed. Eric waits . . . and waits . . . and waits . . . and I see he's getting frustrated.

"Fine, I get it," I finally say.

His face relaxes, and he touches my hair. "Sweetheart, you're the only thing that's important to me."

He's about to kiss me, but I pull back.

"Did you just pull the cobra on me, Mrs. Zimmerman?" The look on his face, his voice, and laughter finally relax me.

"Be careful or next time, I'll pull the viper on you. Understood?"

Eric cracks up and hugs me. We go back to our friends, and I'm amazed to find Graciela sitting on Dexter's lap as he holds and kisses her. It looks like beer helped these two find their nerve.

"Everybody kisses everybody here except me," says Eric.

This amuses me, and I grab him by the neck.

"Kiss me, silly boy."

I don't have to beg. He kisses me in front of the whole world, and his mother is the first to offer a toast and take a swallow of her beer. I don't see Amanda again. She's slithered away.

The party goes on into the night. Björn leaves with his girlfriends, and Marta takes off with Arthur. Frida and Andrés take a tired Glen home, and Dexter and Graciela want to head back too. They're in a hurry, and I can't help but smile at the expression on Graciela's face. Eric calls Norbert to have him pick us up at the same place he dropped us off. Five minutes later, Dexter, Graciela, Sonia, and Flyn are gone, and it's just Eric and me.

"I think someone's going to have a very good time at our house tonight," says Eric.

Finally, Dexter and Graciela are going to enjoy each other, and, if everything goes well, maybe they'll take a chance.

Eric and I have fun for about an hour until his cell buzzes. He looks at the text.

"It's Björn."

We look at each other.

"He's at a swinger's club called Sensations, and he wants to know if we might be interested in joining him."

My body immediately heats up.

"We'll go only if you want to," says my guy as a smile sneaks up on his face. Oh, the heat!

I'm already warmed up from all the beer, so this just makes me burn.

I take another sip of my beer. I'm a little bit nervous.

"Will both the women who were with him be there?"

Eric knows the poodle and I are completely incompatible. "Just Diana."

I like the idea that the poodle won't be there and that three predators want to play with me: Eric, Björn, and Diana.

My heart beats faster.

"I want to offer you," Eric whispers when he sees how hot I'm getting. "I want to fuck you, and I want to watch."

I nod.

"I want to do this, Eric," I say, desire evident in my voice. "I want to do this so much."

Eric quickly types back on his cell.

"Let's go."

I would follow him to the ends of the earth.

12

When we leave the tent, Eric puts his arm around my shoulders and tries to make sure no one bumps into me. I like it when he tries to be protective. I like his possessiveness. He doesn't like it at all when men look at me or touch me, but, in our intimate moments, it arouses him to offer me to other men.

At the beginning of our relationship, I didn't understand it. It seemed crazy. But after months of having sex with him, I can tell the difference. Everyday life and respect is one thing, and sexual fantasy, when we agree, is another.

I also don't like it when another woman looks at him or flirts with him. It makes me furious. But when we play, I like to watch him enjoy himself. I know our relationship, especially our sexual relationship, is sometimes hard for other people to understand. My sister would surely freak out and call me a degenerate or a pig or even worse, and my father couldn't even imagine it. But it's our relationship, with our own norms, and it works, and I don't want it to change. No way. Eric has helped me discover a world of kink and pleasure I didn't know existed, and I feel terribly drawn to it. I like to be watched when I'm having sex. I like it when someone enjoys my body because my partner has opened my legs to them.

And I like watching my partner have a good time.

I'm lost in my own thoughts as Eric makes our way through the mob. When we emerge on the other side, he calls a taxi, and we're off.

"You're very quiet. What are you thinking about?"

I want to be honest.

"I'm thinking about what's going to happen."

"And what would you like to happen?" he whispers in my ear so the driver can't hear it.

"What do you want?"

He leans his head on the car seat and sighs.

"I want to watch, I want to fuck you, and I want you to get fucked," he whispers in Spanish. "I'm dying to kiss you as you moan. I want everything, absolutely everything, you're willing to give me."

I nod like one of those bobbleheads, and my stomach flips.

I love to hear him say "fuck." It gets me so hot. I'm wet just from thinking about it. "I'll give you everything you want," I respond.

"Right now just give me your panties."

I laugh aloud. Eric and his thing for my underwear.

I discreetly take off my underwear so the driver can't see what I'm doing; otherwise I might die of embarrassment. Eric brings my panties to his nose and then shoves them in his pants pocket.

Twenty minutes later, I'm commando as we're dropped off on a busy street. Eric takes me by the waist, and we walk to a bar with a lighted sign that says "Sensations." The bouncer looks us over. Even though we are wearing our Bavarian costumes, he recognizes what we're here for and lets us through.

Inside, I see a lot of couples dressed like us. We head toward the back. Eric opens a door, and we're in another place altogether. The music isn't as loud, and everyone looks at us. Because we're new, we attract attention.

Eric guides me to the bar, where two men and a woman are groping each other. I'm not surprised, and I smile as I watch their kinky game. Eric gets us a couple of drinks.

"Why are you laughing?" my husband asks me.

I sit on one of the stools, nod toward the trio, and circle his neck with my arms.

"I was remembering that time in Barcelona when you took me to that swinger's bar and made me sit on a stool and opened my legs so others could see me."

Eric grins at the memory.

"That night you got me hot for nothing."

"I was punishing you for leaving the hotel without telling me, sweetheart," he says as he kisses my neck. "That got you very aroused."

"Yes."

My breathing gets harder when Eric, my Eric, my love, begins to raise my long skirt until it's up near my thighs. He's so playful!

"There's a man to your right who can't stop watching us, and it would really get me going if he could see more of my wife. Is that OK?"

His hands go up the inside of my thighs until they arrive at the very core of my desire. He touches me.

"Yes, of course," I say.

He doesn't wait another moment. He kisses me and turns my stool toward the man. The guy, who's in his fifties and very attractive, watches us. Eric stands behind me and opens my legs and I see the stranger's eyes dilate and sparkle.

Now excited, I help him lift my skirt even more.

"He's dying for us to invite him between your legs. Just look at him. His eyes already possess you. Do you see that?"

I nod as I get wetter, and my breathing gets even heavier. Eric knows all this and puts a hand on my chest, then cradles my breast with it.

"You're delicious, my love. Very, very delicious." The older man can't take his eyes off us. "Have you ever had sex with a man that age?"

I shake my head.

"No, you're the oldest man I've ever been with."

"How would you like to have sex with him?" Eric asks, leaning his head on my shoulder.

"Sure," I say, not thinking.

At a moment like this, when I'm so hot, all I want is to be satisfied. I imagine things and turn back to him.

"Why are you smiling, sweetheart?"

I pin my gaze on him. I lick my lower lip. "Tonight I want to play with you too."

Eric gets it. I can see it in his eyes. But he doesn't smile.

"I want to see another man give you a blow job."

He looks down at the floor. "You liked watching that much?" he asks, arching his brow.

"Yes."

"And you're not afraid I might like that more than other things?"

I burst out laughing. If there's anything I know for sure, it's that he'll always like women best.

"You like seeing me with other women, don't you?"

"Yes."

"And you're not afraid I might like that more than everything else?"

He knows what I'm saying.

"All right, sweetheart," he says. "We'll both play. But just a blow job."

A loud exclamation brings us out of our warm little bubble.

"Eric, it's been so long since we've seen you here!" My love and the stranger shake hands.

Knowing Eric's willing to play my game excites me even more. So much more.

"Hi, Roger," says Eric. "This is my wife, Judith."

I can barely speak, I'm so aroused.

"Have you seen Björn?"

The man nods as he winks at a woman who walks past us. "He's in private room number 10."

Oh my . . . our friend doesn't waste any time. I close my legs and lower my skirt. Eric kisses my forehead. During the twenty minutes or so the three of us talk, I see the older man who was staring at me has found another partner and disappears with her behind the red curtain to have a good time. But I also note that Roger hasn't stopped looking at my breasts.

"Your wife is beautiful."

My husband nods.

"Her breasts would drive you crazy."

"Call me," says Roger, taking one quick look at them as he steps away.

But the whole conversation strikes me as odd.

"Why were you talking about my breasts?"

"Roger loves breasts. He loves to suck nipples."

I'm quite intrigued by that, but I can't ask any more questions because Eric has me get down from the stool and follow him behind the red curtain, where we saw the older man and his partner and other couples disappear.

As soon as we cross the threshold, I hear moaning. Lots of moaning and little cries of pleasure. I look around and see there are many reserved spaces separated by colorful curtains. Eric opens several of these so we can see what's going on. In these little cubicles, there are people having all kinds of sex.

"What do you think?" asks Eric as we stand before one of the spaces. I peek inside and see a man with two women. "It looks like they're having a good time."

We step away and open another one. This one features a couple and several men. They play with the woman and among themselves and enjoy their time together. The attractive older man who was staring at us in the bar sees us and stops. He gets up as the others continue their little game.

"Lie down, Jude," says Eric as the older man looks me over.

I don't question it and do as he says. I get totally fired up when he orders me around with that tone of voice. The bed is moving because of the way the others are fucking, and I get even hotter watching them.

The woman looks at me, and I realize she doesn't mind our presence at all. She smiles at me, and I smile back.

"I want you to be touched for my pleasure, is that OK?" whispers Eric as he leans over me.

"I want something else first," I say from the bed.

"You know what I want, don't you?"

He's hesitant, but I'm determined to get my wish.

He nods, so I turn to the older man.

"Kneel before him."

Instantly, the stranger does what I ask. He kneels in front of Eric. I unbutton his pants.

"Give him some pleasure," I say to the man.

He puts his hands on Eric's pants, and that startles him, but he doesn't move away. The man gently lowers my love's pants and boxers, leaving them midthigh.

Eric's cock is stiff and hard, and I sigh when the man kneeling before my husband touches it. He loves it. He runs his hands over Eric's dick and his balls, making him even harder.

Then the older man brings his mouth to the very tip of Eric's cock, touches it with his tongue, and envelops it. Eric closes his eyes, and I shiver.

This is so amazing!

I realize the stranger is expert at this. He covers every inch of Eric's member with his tongue, slowly and gently, until he finally takes the whole thing in his mouth all at once.

Wow! His hands squeeze Eric's balls tenderly, and, when he finally lets his cock out of his mouth, he kisses and sucks them.

Eric is panting. His body is vibrating, and his head is thrown back. So much heat!

My love's breathing gets heavier—and mine does too. Watching this feels kinky, naughty, and hot, especially when I see how much my love is enjoying it and how the veins in his neck throb. Combustion!

Everything in this room is kinky. Right beside me, three men are giving one woman pleasure, and a stranger is servicing my crazy love as I watch this spectacle I've arranged. I'm wet. I'm drenched.

Just then, the stranger moves one of his hands to Eric's ass, squeezes it, and separates his cheeks. But just as he's going to put a finger up his ass, my husband stops him. The man doesn't insist and focuses back on his enormous erection. He gets the message. His tongue lashing picks up speed, and I hear Eric groaning again.

Eric uses his right hand to forcefully push the stranger's head down so he'll take his whole cock in his mouth again. The older man goes nuts at that demand.

I do too.

He leans into Eric, and, squeezing his ass over and over, he repeats his actions until my love, my marvelous love, can't take it anymore and roars and comes.

As soon as they're through, the stranger goes to shower. I get up from the bed, pick up one of the little jars of water, and carefully wash my husband's penis. Then I dry it.

"Everything OK?"

Eric nods. "Are you hot?"

"So hot."

An instant later, the older man joins us again. I lie back down on the bed without Eric having to say anything. Without a word, the stranger lifts my skirt up to my waist, and I find I'm nervous. He runs his hands on my thighs and pushes my legs apart a little bit so he can wash my sex. He reads my tattoo and grins.

I appreciate the water and being able to cool down. I close my eyes.

"Open your legs and let him have you," Eric whispers.

I do as he says. It excites me just to do it, and I feel the man's breath on my moist thigh. His hands are on my labia, and one of his fingers slides inside me . . . He's playing . . .

Squeezing . . .

I open my eyes.

"That's it . . . Let him in," says Eric. "Just like that."

This moment . . .

His voice . . .

His requests . . .

Everything makes me feel exalted as everyone around us engages in their own passion.

The stranger pushes his finger in and out of me as his tongue plays with my clitoris, and my breathing quickens. I don't know how long we're like that, only that I'm enjoying every single moment.

Suddenly, the man stands up, rolls on a condom, and lays himself on top of me.

"Her mouth is exclusively mine," Eric tells him.

The stranger nods and grabs my ass so hard, he lifts me up. Demanding and impatient, he penetrates me. Oh yes . . . this is what I need.

"Look at me," Eric pleads.

I do as he says. In the meantime, this man with whom I haven't exchanged a single word, whose name I don't know, slams in and out of me, and all I want is more depth. I need more, and I swing my legs up to his shoulders. I can tell this excites him. He grabs my hips and impales me, and I almost suffocate when Eric brings his mouth to mine.

"Give me all your moans and cries, my love. Give them to me."

I need air, but I kiss my love, and I give him what he wants. I'm panting under his mouth. He bites my lips and drinks up every sound I make. This really turns him on, it drives him crazy, as the stranger continues his dance inside me, and I surrender completely. Then, suddenly, the man can't take it anymore, and, after one final thrust that makes me scream, he climaxes.

The stranger pulls out of me and washes my sex with fresh water once more. That feels so good!

He dries me with a clean cloth. After a few seconds, my heartbeat slows down, and Eric takes my hand.

"Get up, my love."

My skirt drops, and, without looking back or exchanging a word with the stranger, we leave the room. Eric's in a hurry.

When we get out to the hallway—where we can hear a thousand moans, cries, and sighs—my love, my husband, takes me in his arms, pushes me against the wall, and kisses me. His kiss is demanding, wild, devastating. I respond in kind. He lifts my skirt, unbuttons his pants, and drives himself inside me.

Oh yes . . . that is the touch and the depth I need.

Eric!

Without a word, my demanding husband goes in and out of me, and I mold myself to his body, holding on to his shoulders so I can better receive him.

Eric moves me around in his arms as if I were a doll. "I'm sorry, sweetheart," Eric says, "but I'm going to come."

He's too excited because of what he's seen, and his penetration is searching for relief, searching for the release he needs and I want to give him. My body contracts; Eric grits his teeth and lets himself go. "I'm sorry this was so quick," he whispers, holding me tight.

"Don't be sorry, my love," I say with a naughty tone. "I'm going to ask much more of you now."

Eric kisses me and lets me down. I feel his cum running down my legs. "I need a shower."

We start down the moan-filled hall. He comes to an abrupt stop and opens one of the curtains, and we see Björn and Diana. Each one of them is with two women. They look like they're having a great time. Björn sees us.

"We'll see you later in the hall of mirrors," he says. "It's reserved."

"I see you know this place very well," I say as we walk away.

"I've been here before, my love," Eric says, giving me a kiss.

When we get to a particular door, Eric leads me inside. It's dark, but when he turns on the light, I'm surprised to see the walls, the ceiling, and the floor are all mirrors. The light suddenly turns violet.

"Your favorite color," he says.

I kiss him. I love his delicious lips. He squeezes my ass.

"Let's go take a shower."

We laugh and head to the bathroom, where we take off our Bavarian costumes and get under the water. "Everything OK, my love?"

I nod. I had missed his asking.

"You're getting me to do things I never thought possible," Eric says as the water runs over our bodies.

"I love to see your face when a man gives you pleasure." We laugh and kiss.

As soon as we get out of the shower, the Jacuzzi calls to us. It's huge, and the water changes color. Eric takes me in his arms, and we get in.

We kiss and cuddle, enjoying touching each other.

Everything between us feels amazing, and then the door opens, and there's Björn, accompanied by Diana. They're both nude, but they each have bags in their hands that they drop on the bed. When they see us in the Jacuzzi, they go straight to the shower. Then Björn climbs into the Jacuzzi with us, and Diana takes some CDs out of her bag. She chooses one and leaves the rest on a chair. An instant later, I hear Duffy singing "Mercy."

"I love this woman," Diana says as she gets into the Jacuzzi and hears me singing. For a while, the four of us just talk. Our conversation revolves around what we've done that night, and I'm surprised I'm as honest as they are. I talk about sex casually and enjoy the conversation.

"You really haven't tried S and M?" asks Diana.

Eric and Björn smile. "No, I'm not into pain," I respond. "I prefer a different kind of enjoyment."

"Jude, I get you don't like S and M. But I've noticed you're submissive and like taking orders from me. Have you noticed that too?" Eric asks.

"But I like it when you obey me too," I say.

"I'm your master and you're mine," Eric says.

I sit on his lap and feel his cock being playful under the water.

"I'm yours and you're mine," I whisper. "Don't forget that, love."

"Your games are getting more daring by the day. First, you got into vibrators, then threesomes, then swinging, and then that day that we were with Dexter, I realized how much you like obeying and giving pleasure."

"Dexter likes S and M," says Björn. "There are certain things he very much enjoys."

"There are certain things he'll never do with Jude because she'd slice his throat first," says Eric.

We all laugh. But pain will never be a part of my pleasure. I refuse.
"I hope one day to meet a woman who surprises me and to have sex and live my life like you two," says Björn, startling us as he takes a sip of champagne. "I realize I envy you."

"Something good in my life," says Eric, kissing me. "It's about time, don't you think?"

Björn nods and toasts to his friend.

"As my father would say, your other half is surely out there. You just need to find her," I add.

Eric looks at me in a very special way. "If I order you to do something tonight, as if I were your owner, would you obey?"

"That depends."

He likes my response.

"I would never ask you to do anything you don't want, my love."

"Then I'm at your service, my master."

Our hot little game begins again, and his look arouses me. His mouth drives me crazy, and I know I'm going to like his orders. Eric is right: I like to obey and to give him everything he wants.

"Judith likes it when we talk to her as we fuck her, right?" says Björn as insightful as ever.

"Yes, my friend."

"What's driving me insane is the tattoo, 'Tell me what you want.' That tattoo makes my desire blossom and makes me want to do and ask you for many things, Judith," says Diana, who hasn't said a word until now.

"Well, what are you waiting for?" says Eric with a twisted smile. "Let's play."

They all look at me. I don't know what to say.

"I promise to be a very loving master," says Diana, and that leaves me breathless.

I'm not sure I'm going to like this game of masters though, and I furrow my brow.

"Jude, as your master, I want you to get out of the Jacuzzi and get in bed so Diana can have her way with you. Once she's satisfied, come back to the Jacuzzi, and sit between Björn and me. I have plans for you tonight, and you will obey."

Oh my God, I have such butterflies in my stomach.

I leave the Jacuzzi to enter the game. But when I reach for a towel, Eric stops me.

"Jude, I didn't tell you that you could dry yourself. Drop the towel and lie down on the bed."

I do as he says and see Diana leave the Jacuzzi too. Eric and Björn watch us in silence. Diana doesn't dry herself either. She comes straight to me, touches the tattoo she likes so much, and kisses it.

"Turn around," she says.

She doesn't need to say it again. I do as she says, and, when I'm facedown, she lays on top of me and touches me. I feel her mound all over my body.

"Get up."

I pose on all fours on the bed. Diana plays with my wet breasts. Her fingers squeeze my nipples, and I like how that feels. She presses her mound against my ass. It makes me hot.

The mirrored room gives me a good view of everything, and I can't help but smile when I see the look on Eric's face, which speaks for itself.

"Lie down," says Diana. I comply.

She picks up one of the bags she and Björn dropped down on the bed and pulls something out of it. She shows it to Eric, who nods. I don't know what it is.

"Give me your breasts."

I see she's holding a pair of clamps. I relax. She fastens them onto my nipples and pulls on the little chain.

"Your master has given you to me, and now I am your master," she says. I purr. I look over at Eric, and he nods.

In an instant, Diana cups my face with one hand and slaps me with the other.

"Don't look at him," she hisses, looking me straight in the eye. "Look only at me."

The situation excites me, and I look at her. She watches my mouth, comes toward me, and stops just as she's about to kiss me.

"I'm going to respect your mouth because I know it's only his. But I'll take from the rest of you as if it were mine because I want to possess you for my own pleasure."

I'm disconcerted. Her voice is sibilant and her gestures aggressive. But even so, I'm turned on, I don't move, and I let her take control of the situation and wait.

Once she has me how she wants me, she delights in what she sees and pulls on the clamps that stretch my nipples. "I want to taste you. Give me what I want," she says, staring at my tattoo.

I part my legs and lift my hips to show her my surrender. Wanting to savor what I offer, Diana lets go of the little chain, takes my ass in her hands, and brings her mouth down to my sex.

She kisses me, nibbles me, and then opens me with her fingers and goes directly to my clitoris. She licks it and sucks on it. I feel a tremendous pleasure. She sucks me eagerly, and I go mad and part my legs even more, wanting her to go on and on.

The demanding way she touches and sucks me always excites me. Diana has the gentleness of a woman but the eagerness of a man. She lays siege to my body, and I'm breathless. "C'mon, beautiful . . . c'mon . . . give me what I want . . ."

Tongue lashing after tongue lashing, she gets what she wants, and the wild beast in me surrenders to her. I get wetter and wetter. She manages to get one devastating cry after another out of me.

"Like that . . . Like that . . . Come like that."

I shiver. Diana stands up and I protest.

"Get on your knees and part your legs."

I'm dizzy when I try to sit up, but I recover immediately. I get on my knees on the bed, like her, and before I can turn to look at Eric, she grabs me by the waist and presses me completely against her, launching two fingers into my wetness.

"Like that . . . Let's go . . . Moan for me. Let me know how much you like it."

Her fingers come in and out of me. My God, this woman knows what she's doing.

"Move . . . C'mon . . . Move," she whispers into my mouth as I pant. "Like that . . . Just like that . . . I want you to come, I want you to come like a tsunami so I can open your legs and drink it all up."

I'm going crazy just listening to the sloshing of my juices in her hand as it goes up and down. I want to feel her mouth between my legs. I want her tongue on my clitoris; I want her licking me. I'm breathing like a locomotive, and she speeds up, gets more intense, and fucks me harder.

I can't believe it. This woman is unstoppable and takes me from one orgasm to another. I'm soaked. I'm wet everywhere, and then pleasure infuses every inch of my being, and I scream and fall back.

Diana quickly dives between my thighs and takes up what she most loves about me again. She sucks and licks, and I surrender yet again. I am hers completely, as long as she doesn't stop.

Just when I think she's had enough of me, she snaps off the clamps and takes my nipples in her mouth. The softness of her tongue is comforting, even more so when she blows air on them, and I feel a warm tingling. I love this.

I think about Eric. And his eyes. And how he must be looking at me just then, and I imagine how hard and excited he must be.

"Diana, use the inflatable double harness," I hear him say.

She rustles around in the bag and pulls out a harness I've never seen before. It's a leather thing with clasps, a ball, and two dildos. One goes outside the harness and the other inside the harness.

"Put this on me," she says. My nipples are hard as rocks as she hands me the harness. I don't know what to do with one of these.

"Slide the inside dildo into me and then tie the harness to my waist so I can fuck you," she explains.

She gets on her knees, parts her legs, and slaps my ass. "Do it."

When I put my hands between her legs, I feel her heat. Usually I don't touch the women I'm with. I prefer they touch me. And despite how much I want to do that now, I stick to what she's asked of me.

I part her labia, which are soft and wet, and slowly introduce the dildo. I like this feeling of control.

Would I like to be a master?

Once the harness has conformed to her body, I tighten the belts.

"Lie down and open your legs. Once I'm inside you, put your legs around my waist and go with me, OK?"

I nod and lie down. On her knees and with the harness on, Diana watches me, and, when I open my legs, she falls right on me. She very slowly penetrates me with the other dildo.

"Put your legs around me."

I obey. She squeezes the ball that hangs off the harness with her hands.

"I'm inflating the dildo inside you. I'm going to stretch you."

Second by second, my vagina gets fuller and fuller. I've never had anything so thick inside me, and, at one point, I think I'm going to explode. She stops. "Give me your hands," she says.

I do as she says, and she raises them above my head and squeezes me hard against the bed, moving her hips as we both breathe harder and harder.

"Do you like it?"

"Yes."

She presses against me again, and we both cry out. It is a profound sensation. I am totally full, and I notice how my vagina tries to mold itself to the dildo. Over and over, it goes in and out of me.

"Go deeper, Diana," I hear Eric say. "Jude likes it that way."

She places my legs on her shoulders and does as Eric has suggested. I'm now screaming from joy.

Oh yes . . . I like it.

Absolutely out of my mind, I make Diana lean over so I can take her breasts in my mouth, and, as I bite her nipple and see that she loves it, she continues to pound into me without pity. I scratch her back and moan with her nipples in my mouth.

"Yes . . . yes . . . Don't stop . . . Don't stop."

She doesn't stop.

She obeys me. She gives me what I've asked for.

I'm very hot . . .

I'm burning up . . . sizzling.

When the ardor overtakes us both, Diana falls on me, and I scream when I feel her climax.

Exhausted, sweaty, but satisfied, I look at the mirrors on the ceiling and see Eric and Björn. "Look at me," Diana demands.

I do. She takes me by the shoulders and makes me scream again. I bite her nipple in response. That makes her react, and, as if possessed, she pushes her pelvis against mine, and we both moan again.

A few minutes later, my breathing returns to normal. I don't move. I don't know yet if Diana has had enough of me. She commands and I obey. That's the game and I like it. I like it a lot.

When she pulls out from inside me, it feels like I'm deflating.

"I'd continue making you mine for the rest of the night, but I don't want to be selfish. Now it's their turn," she says, and turns to my husband. "Eric, I'm done for the moment." I like that "for the moment"!

I want to do it with Diana again. She knows how to make me feel very sexual.

"Jude, come over to the Jacuzzi," says Eric. My legs shake when I get up. My juices run down my thighs, but I make it over there anyway.

As soon as I get into the Jacuzzi, I remember Eric saying I should sit between the two of them when I came back. I do so, and sigh when I feel the water on my flesh.

How wonderful! Eric searches for my hand under the water. I squeeze his hand, aware of what he's asking me with this gesture.

For a few minutes, no one says anything; no one moves. I close my eyes and enjoy the moment. I know they're waiting for me to recharge.

I hear a sound, open my eyes, and see Diana in the shower.

"Jerk us off," says Eric.

He takes my hand to his cock. It's stiff and erect. I caress it, and, without pause, take Björn's with my other hand. They're both rock hard.

They're ready for me. And, though I would make different use of their equipment right now, I have to obey. I jerk them off.

My movements are rhythmic. Both my hands go up and down at the same time until their movements throw me off. I look in the mirror in front of me and see they both have their eyes closed and are enjoying themselves.

In a bit, my shoulders hurt. This is tiring, but I don't stop. I don't want to disappoint them.

"Diana, condoms please," says Eric in a husky voice.

She grabs a pair out of the bag and gives them to Björn. We look at each other, I let go of his dick, and he stands up. It's huge, and my mouth waters. Björn is so sexy.

"Diana, change the CD. Put on the blue one."

She does as he says, and then we hear the first notes of Michael Bublé's "Cry Me a River" and we both grin.

"This little song always reminds me of you."

Eric moves. His dick jumps out of the water, and I forget all about Björn. My husband's the max.

I want him.

I want him inside me now, urgently.

He pulls himself over to the side of the Jacuzzi where he can recline.

"C'mon, sweetheart, get on top of me."

I go over to him and kiss him. Our tongues tangle. We play; we touch each other. He grabs me and, slowly, introduces himself into me. I gasp.

"You make me insane, sweetheart."

He puts his arms around me. "Your surrender excites me more every day."

"I know."

I move my hips to find my pleasure.

"I like what we do, and I like that you order me around."

He looks me in the eye and nods and thrusts hard into me.

"I know you're having a good time. I could tell from your cries."

"Yes, a very good time."

"Now you'll have an even better time," he says, and then over my shoulder to Björn, he adds, "We're waiting for you."

I feel the water moving, and then our friend is behind me.

"I love your little ass, beautiful."

I think I know what's going to happen.

"Right now it's all for you, my friend," Eric says to him. "Let's delight in my wife and drive her crazy."

Björn kisses my neck and takes my bruised nipples in his hands from behind.

"I'm dying to do it."

Four hands are touching me underwater as Michael Bublé sings.

Eric parts my cheeks, and Björn guides his cock to my ass. I don't need a lubricant, and, in a matter of seconds, I'm being fucked by two men in the Jacuzzi while Diana watches and drinks from her cup of wine.

"Like that, my love. Like that . . . Tell me you like it."

"I like it . . . yes."

"How much do you like it?" Björn asks from behind me.

"A lot . . . a lot," I respond.

"I want you to have a good time with us, my love."

"I do . . . I do," I murmur.

They make me theirs without pause.

I go crazy with my two favorite men. I love Eric madly, and my life would make no sense without him now. And I love Björn like a friend and a playmate. Our threesome is always hot and kinky. The three of us have acclimated to each other, and we always have such a good time.

Suddenly, Eric sits up a little bit. "Double," he tells Björn.

"You sure?" he asks.

"Yes."

I don't know what they're talking about, but I feel when Björn pulls out of me, gets up, pulls off the condom, and puts on another one. He comes back into the Jacuzzi and finds where Eric's cock is penetrating me with one of his fingers.

"Mmm . . . I love how tight this is."

That makes me a little tense. Are they talking about a double vaginal penetration? I look down at Eric. He's calm, sure about everything. But I'm afraid of the pain. He can see it in my face.

"Don't worry, sweetheart. Diana stretched you out." He kisses me. "I would never let you suffer."

I savor his comforting kiss as I feel Björn's fingers next to Eric's cock inside me. After one finger, there's two, and then my husband stops his movements.

Björn brings the tip of his cock to my vagina; pulls out his fingers; and after a couple of thrusts, his very hard member is totally up against that of my love.

"Just like that, sweetheart . . . Just like that . . . Enjoy it."

"Oh my God, Judith, this is marvelous," says Björn as he presses against me.

I pant and pant and pant. My vagina is completely stretched out now. Two penises together, almost fused, come in and out of me, and all I can do is moan and open up for them.

Oh yes. I'm doing this. I'm being doubly penetrated.

"Is everything all right, my love?" Eric asks, super aroused, as he holds me by the waist.

All I can do is nod and enjoy.

Excited, Björn is moving behind me. His hands part my cheeks. He squeezes them. "Tell me what you're feeling."

But I can't speak. I can only pant.

"Tell us what you feel, or we'll stop," says Eric.

"No . . . Please don't stop . . . Don't stop . . . I like it," I babble. I'm so hot.

The heat rises all through my body. I feel like I'm burning up, and when the heat reaches my head, I scream and let myself fall on Eric while they continue penetrating me in search of their own pleasure. Oh my God, what a sensation. I push the button on the Jacuzzi, and the waters swirl up. I'm here, between my two titans. They touch me; they nibble at me; they make demands on me; they penetrate me.

Their hard cocks, one against the other, come in and out of me while pleasure envelops me, and I scream, squeezing them both.

We get home at around five in the morning, and I'm exhausted. It's cool when the taxi drops us off at the front gate. It's already chilly in September in Germany.

Eric takes my hand, and we walk quietly toward the house. Susto and Calamar come to welcome us. Eric and I kiss and cuddle them, and they run around us until they tire of it and disappear.

I like my life. I still can't believe everything I did tonight, but what I'm sure of is that I want to do it again.

It turns out I'm quite the little sex machine. Who would've thunk?

"I love you, and I adore everything we do together," I say, pulling on Eric's arm when we get to the door.

"Now and always, my love," he whispers with his mouth close to my mouth. We kiss.

We love each other . . .

We adore each other . . .

As our kiss comes to an end, we open the door and see there's a light on in the kitchen. We're surprised and head that way to find Graciela and Dexter making out.

"Ahem . . . Ahem."

The two turtledoves look up.

"What are you two still doing up at this hour?" I ask.

Graciela's sitting on Dexter's lap.

"We were thirsty and decided to come get something to drink."

There's a bottle with a pink label on the table.

"Good choice!" exclaims Eric.

"Absolutely, dude. This pink Moët and Chandon is fabulous," says Dexter.

"To die for," I add.

We laugh and sit down to have a glass with them, and at one point while Eric and Dexter are talking, Graciela leans my way.

"I liked this guy before, but now I'm absolutely crazy about him."

"So, everything's good between you?"

"Better than good—colossally great!"

Sometimes, love can be great, the greatest.

Fifteen minutes later, my love and I excuse ourselves to go up to our room. We're beyond exhausted, and when we undress and get in bed, Eric caresses my head the way he knows I like.

"Sweet dreams, sweetheart."

I snuggle into his arms, and, feeling happy and lucky, I fall fast asleep.

13

Two days later, I find myself feeling out of sorts.

My belly hurts, and I assume I'm getting my period.

When I get to the bathroom, I realize I already have it. I take something to ease the pain. Between that and my music, I can try and relax. I grab my iPod, put on my headphones, and let Pablo Alborán's voice relax me to sleep.

Soft, sweet kisses awaken me, and I take off my headphones.

"Hi, sweetheart, how are you?"

"Not great."

He looks alarmed.

"I got my period."

"There's a very good German remedy so it won't hurt so much."

"What's that?" I ask, hopeful.

I'll do anything so I won't be in such misery.

"Get pregnant, and you don't have to worry about it for almost a year."

I'm not amused.

"You don't think it's a good solution?"

"No."

"A little dark-eyed girl . . . with your little nose . . . your little mouth . . ."

"You see her quite clearly," I grumble.

Eric kisses me.

"She'd be beautiful. I know it."

"Then you have her . . . smart-ass."

"If I could, I would."

I scratch my neck.

"Look what you're doing to my neck. Will you please stop?"

He laughs. Goddamn it. I hit him on the head with one of the pillows.

If he keeps laughing, I'm going to strangle him. In fact, he laughs even harder.

"Could you please be so kind as to leave me alone until these cramps go away?"

"Don't get mad, my love."

But I know my ability to tolerate this kind of stuff at times like this is pretty much zero.

"Then please leave and shut your trap."

He gives me a kiss on the head and leaves. I close my eyes, put my headphones back on, and try to relax again, this time with Alejandro Sanz's raspy voice.

That Friday, Juan Alberto, Dexter's cousin, shows up in Munich.

I'm surprised to see him. Nobody had said anything about his coming.

"How did you leave my sister?"

He grins. "As beautiful as ever."

But that isn't enough for me.

"I mean, how does she feel about you leaving?"

"She's fine, just fine. I promised to go by Jerez on my way back to Mexico. And she gave me this to give to you."

He hands me a sealed envelope. I fold it and put it in my jeans pocket. Ten minutes later, I can't wait any longer to see what my sister has to say. I sneak away to my room, sit on my bed, and open the letter.

Hello, Cuchufleta:

Everything's great here. Papá is fabulous, Luz is happy with her school, and Lucía is growing and getting fat. I'm writing to tell you I'm fine even though Juan Alberto's departure crushed me. You warned me. But I wanted to be a more modern woman, and, in spite of how sad I feel, I'm happy for having made this effort.

Just for the record: I didn't sleep with him! I'm not quite that modern, even though it was more than just sweet and tender kisses between us. He's a marvelous man, warm and charming. What's certain is I've finally gotten the sour aftertaste of Jesús out of my mouth. Anyway, when you see Juan Alberto, be nice to him because he deserves it, OK?

I love you, Cuchu, and I promise I'll call one of these days.

Raquel

I get all weepy.

My poor sister, heartbroken and afraid I'm going to take it out on Juan Alberto. Damn it, I can be so stupid sometimes. I immediately dial the house in Jerez. I want to talk with her. One ring . . .

Two rings . . . I finally hear her voice after the third ring.

"Are you OK, Raquel?"

I hear one of her teary sighs.

"Yes, I'm fine in spite of everything."

"I told you, Raquel. I told you he was going back to Mexico."

"I know, Cuchu, I know . . ."

After a somewhat meaningful silence, she surprises me. "You know what? I'd do it again. It's been totally worth it to spend time with him. Juan Alberto is completely different from Jesús, and, even though I'm crying my heart out now, I realized he helped raise my self-esteem, and I see myself in a better light now. Is he OK?"

"Yes, I just saw him. He's downstairs with Eric and Dexter and—"

"Well, give him a kiss for me, will you?"

"Of course."

We talk for a few more minutes until Lucía starts to cry. When I go back downstairs, I see Graciela reading a magazine, and the men have disappeared. "They're in the office," she tells me.

I head to the kitchen. I'm thirsty.

Talking to my sister makes me sad, but knowing Juan Alberto has raised her self-esteem makes me feel better. Every cloud has a silver lining.

I open the fridge, grab a Coke, and lean on the counter to drink it when I hear Simona whispering in the mudroom off the kitchen.

"Why does she have to come here?"

Norbert responds. "Laila is coming to Germany because of work."

"Doesn't she realize she makes us uncomfortable?"

"Simona, listen," Norbert says. "What happened is in the past. She's my niece."

"Your niece, precisely. A stupid girl who—"

"Simona . . ."

"When did she say she's arriving? My God!"

"Simona, please!" Norbert says, scolding her.

And then I hear Simona's even more angry response. "And, of course, since your niece is so well mannered, she calls Mr. Zimmerman instead of you and stays the night in this house instead of ours, right? Don't you remember what almost happened if not for Björn?"

"I do remember. Don't worry, that's not going to happen again."

I hear the back door open and see Simona through the kitchen window heading back to her house with Norbert trailing behind her. What's going on?

I follow them with my gaze. It's the first time I've ever seen them disagree about anything, and it worries me. But I'm even more concerned about knowing who this Laila is, why she calls Eric instead of her uncle, and what happened the last time. I should talk to Simona as soon as I can.

That night, when Eric and I are finally in our room, I say to him, "I bet you can't guess what ringtone I've assigned to you."

He calls me on his phone and cracks up when he hears "Si Nos Dejan."

We hug and kiss.

"Can I ask you something?" I say after he lets me go.

"Of course, my love. You can ask me anything."

"Would you consider giving me a job?"

He grins and hugs me.

"I told you that you have a lifetime contract with me, sweetheart."

I laugh, remembering he told me that the day he sent flowers to my office.

"I'm talking about working at Müller."

"A real job? Why?"

"Because once Dexter and Graciela leave, I'm going to get bored. I'm used to working, and a life of leisure isn't going to be good for me."

"My love, I work for both of us."

"But I want to do my part. I know you have a lot of money but—"

"We have, sweetheart," he says, correcting me, "we have. And before you go on, there's no need for you to work because I can support us both easily. I'm not willing to have my wife be subject to work hours that have nothing to do with mine and be without you because you have other responsibilities to deal with. Therefore, end of story."

End of story? I don't think so. "We'll leave the subject alone for now, but I want to be very clear, Mr. Macho, that we'll talk about it again. Understood?" Eric sighs, nods, and disappears into the bathroom.

"I need to ask you something else," I say once he's back. He sits on the edge of the bed.

"Go ahead."

I want to ask him about Laila, but I don't know how. Knowing she's called him and he hasn't said a word bothers me. Finally, I just go straight to the point.

"Who is Laila? Why haven't you said anything about her call? And why is she staying at our house?"

He's taken aback.

"How do you know all this?"

Oh God, I feel my jealousy rising.

I narrow my eyes. "The real question is, why haven't you said anything about the fact that a woman I don't know has called you and is arriving tomorrow to stay with us? Go ahead, get mad, but be assured I'm much madder because you didn't tell me about this."

"She's arriving tomorrow?" he asks, surprised.

I can tell by the look on his face that this is an honest reaction. He hadn't remembered.

"Yes, if I hadn't found out on my own, I might not have known about her until she was sitting at the table with us."

Eric gets my point.

"My love, I've been so busy recently, I completely forgot to tell you. Forgive me," he says. "She's Norbert and Simona's niece, and she was my sister Hannah's best friend. She called, and, when I found out she had a work trip to Germany, I invited her to stay with us."

"Why?"

"Hannah was very fond of her."

"Have you ever been with her?"

"Of course not," he says, taken aback. "Laila is an enchanting woman, but there's never been anything between us, Jude. Why do you ask?"

"What about with Björn?"

He's stunned by my line of questioning, and a little annoyed too.

"Not that I know of. But let's say they had. I couldn't care less, and I think you shouldn't care either. Should I worry that now you care who Björn has been with?"

"For God's sake, c'mon, Eric. Don't be ridiculous!"

"Then don't ask those questions."

I go silent. I don't want to tell him I heard what Simona said, but I'm determined to find out what she meant when she said, "Don't you remember what happened last time?"

"Are you jealous of Laila?"

To such a direct question, a direct answer. "Yes, in terms of you. And, yes, I'll forgive you for not telling me."

He smiles; I don't.

He leans toward me, but I don't move.

He hugs me, but I don't hug him back.

I'm feeling quite small. He takes me by the chin and makes me look up at him.

"You're still not convinced the only woman I need, want, and adore in my bed and my life is you?" he asks. "I told you and I'm going to tell you a thousand times that I'm going to love you my whole life."

Well, he's managed to destroy all my defenses with that.

And now he's made me smile!

"I know you love me as much as I love you, because the 'now and forever' on our rings is sincere," I say, waving my ring finger. "But it bothers me that you didn't tell me about the call, especially when it concerns a strange woman I don't know who's going to spend the night at our house."

Eric pulls me toward him, and, when he has me right up at his face, he brings his mouth to mine. He licks my upper lip, then my lower lip, and then finally gives me a little love bite.

"Silly, jealous girl, give me a kiss." I'm thinking of pulling the cobra on him, but, in the end, I give him a kiss, I give him twenty-one kisses, and we end up out of bed and fucking against the wall, which is how we like it.

The next day, when I get up and go downstairs, Juan Alberto has already left for Belgium. Last night, before we all went to bed, I gave him the kiss my sister asked me to. What a strange little fling those two have going on.

I try to find Simona to talk to her, but she's gone shopping.

Dexter and Eric are spending the morning out of the house, dealing with business matters, and Graciela and I are going shopping. They're going back to Mexico next week, and she wants a lot of souvenirs.

That afternoon, when we get home, Simona's in the kitchen. I give her a hug. I always need that contact when Eric's not around. She knows it, and she hugs me back.

I sit down at the little kitchen table, and she goes on with her many tasks.

"You're very serious today. What's going on?"

"Nothing."

"You sure, Simona?"

"Yes, Judith."

We stay quiet a few minutes. I'm about to say something when she suddenly announces, "C'mon, it's time. *Emerald Madness* is starting." I leap up to join her. In the living room, Graciela is reading. After greeting her, we settle on the couch and turn on the TV.

"*Emerald Madness* is starting," I say to Graciela.

She smiles but doesn't say anything.

As soon as the opening song begins, Simona and I sing along.

Graciela cracks up, and Simona and I do too.

We must sound ridiculous singing that syrupy little song in German. I'm turning into some kind of freak.

With our hearts in our throats, we turn to see the destiny of our beloved Luis Alfredo. He's been shot, and Esmeralda Mendoza runs to aid him as another very handsome man comes out of nowhere to help them. The episode ends with Esmeralda crying in the hospital. She worries about the life of her lover, Luis Alfredo. What's bad is not that she's crying, but that Simona, Graciela, and I are also crying.

When the episode finally ends, we're all really sad, and then we just burst out laughing. We run to the kitchen for drinks to replenish our tears. Just then, Norbert opens the door, and there's a young, fairly attractive woman behind him. "Hi, Aunt Simona," she says.

I watch as the stranger throws herself into my dear Simona's arms. Simona wraps them around her so as to not leave her hanging.

"Laila, how wonderful to see you."

Norbert puts the bags down, then turns and leaves. He's disconcerted and clearly getting out of the way.

"Laila, let me introduce you to Mrs. Zimmerman," says Simona once Laila pulls back from her.

"You can call me Judith," I say, extending my hand to the young woman, who smiles gladly.

"Delighted, Judith."

"And this is Graciela; she's a good friend," I say.

"Delighted."

"The same," says Laila.

"Where would you like me to have her stay, Judith?" asks Simona once we're through with the introductions.

"Wherever you want, Simona."

"You're calling her by her name!" Laila says, amused.

"Yes, now follow me," Simona says before I have a chance to say anything.

"Auntie, just take the bags up wherever, and you can tell me what room I'm in later," Laila tells her aunt with a tone I don't particularly like. "I'm already familiar with this house." Then she turns to me. "Thank you so much for letting me stay in your new home."

First of all, she should be carrying the bags to her room, not Simona.

Second of all, that bit about "I already know this house" doesn't go down well with me.

Third of all, she just crossed a line.

I'm about to say something as Eric steps into the kitchen, and when she sees him, she exclaims, "Eric!"

"Hello, Laila."

"Congratulations on your wedding. My aunt and uncle just introduced me to your wife, and she's charming."

He gives her a pair of kisses and looks over at me.

"Thanks for the congrats. You could say this is the best time of my life."

Everybody grins, and then Dexter comes to get him so they can get back to work in his office. The girl winks at me.

"I hope you'll be very happy, Judith."

Simona takes the bags, and Laila sits with Graciela and me at the kitchen table, where I submit her to an interrogation.

Goddamn it . . . I'm more like my sister Raquel with every passing day.

When Flyn gets home from school, Laila stands to hug him. He's glad to see his mother's friend.

That night, we have dinner an hour later than usual. I invite Simona and Norbert to join us, but Simona refuses. I don't insist. I've noticed how much Laila bothers her, and I've decided to talk to her tomorrow morning.

When I wake up, like always, I'm alone in bed.

I stretch and suddenly realize something of tremendous importance: it's Eric's birthday. I brush my teeth, take a shower, and get dressed. I quickly grab the gift I hid under the stairway and go down four steps at a time to wish him a happy birthday.

Eric and Dexter are sitting together in the living room. I want to surprise him so I run and leap up over the back of the couch to land in his arms. Unfortunately, I get a little too much lift and end up crashing on the other side of the couch, and the gift rolls away from me on the floor.

I may have hurt myself. I may have damaged my wrist.

Eric shoots up immediately, and Dexter comes over. They look at me very surprised, not sure what just happened, and I don't know if I'm more hurt physically or ego-wise.

How embarrassing.

Eric sits me down on the couch. "Where did you hurt yourself, my love?" he asks.

I give him my left hand, and, when he moves it, I groan. "Oh, c'mon, that hurts, that hurts. I think I sprained my wrist."

Eric goes blank; he doesn't quite understand what I mean because I used a Spanish phrase he doesn't know.

"My love, I twisted my hand." I move it to show him. "Don't worry, it'll be fine with a bandage."

The color comes back to his face.

"What happened?" asks Graciela as she and Laila come into the room.

"Got me, my love," says Dexter. "All I know is I suddenly saw Judith flying over the back of the couch and hitting herself hard against the floor."

Graciela, who's also a nurse, quickly goes into action.

"I'm fine, but my wrist hurts."

"OK, let's go. I'll take you to the hospital so they can do an X-ray or two," says Eric.

"Don't be silly," I say, laughing. "Graciela will fix this with a bandage, right?"

She checks out my hand and nods.

"I don't think there's a fracture. Take it easy, Eric."

But of course, Eric insists.

"I'm going to feel better if they do an X-ray."

"I agree with you," says Laila. "It's best to make sure everything is OK."

"Listen, my love, my hand is OK," I say. "I just need a bandage, and everything will be fine."

"Are you sure?"

"Absolutely."

"I'll go get the medical kit from the kitchen," says Laila.

Graciela and Dexter follow.

"Happy birthday, Mr. Zimmerman," I say, finally smiling.

Eric smiles back. Finally!

"Thank you, my love."

We kiss tenderly.

"This is the one-year anniversary of that free dinner I had with my friend Nacho at Moroccio when I pretended I was your wife. You came to my house later that night with a sour face and an angry voice and asked, incredulous, 'Mrs. Zimmerman?'!"

He busts out laughing.

"Do you remember?"

"Yes . . . little panda bear," he responds.

Oh, he's so cute!

I laugh. It amuses me that he remembers my black eye that day. I can't believe it's been a year. How time flies!

Happily bringing back those memories, I search for my gift and find it under the table.

"I hope you like it and, above all, that it works after all the abuse it just took."

He opens the package, sees the watch, looks at me, takes it out of the box, and puts it on.

"How did you know I like this watch?"

"I have eyes to see, my love, and I saw how you admired it every time you got your monthly catalog from that jewelry store. Also, you should know the owners opened an account for me even though I said no."

"Of course; you're my wife. Whenever you want something pretty and original, Sven, the jeweler, can make it for you."

I smile. I'm more the flea market and costume jewelry type.

Graciela comes back with the bandage and sits on Dexter's lap.

"C'mon, Judith. Let me wrap your wrist."

Suddenly, I realize I haven't seen Flyn.

"Where's Flyn?"

"Marta picked him up a while ago," Eric responds. "We'll see him at dinner."

"Oh, you're not having dinner here?" Laila asks.

"No, not tonight. I've invited everyone to dinner for my birthday," Eric replies, watching what Graciela's doing.

"Oh . . . then I guess I'll have dinner alone," Laila murmurs.

I look at her. I see her sad expression, and I feel sorry for her.

My eyes meet Eric's. We communicate in silence, and, when he agrees, I turn to Laila.

"Do you want to come with us?"

The young woman blinks. "I'd love to," she responds.

Everyone's happy to include her, and I go looking for Norbert. He's in the garage with my Ducati. When I lay eyes on it, I get an adrenaline rush.

"Need any help?" I ask.

"No, ma'am, don't worry. The bike is perfect, all ready for the race. You'll see. Do you want to give it a spin?"

Without hesitation, I climb on.

How could I resist my Ducati?

I ride off, screaming along to its powerful roar.

Norbert grins as I whoosh past him.

Without pads or helmet, I take a little blitz around our property. Susto and Calamar sprint behind me. The bike is amazing, as always! What a piece of machinery my father bought me!

When I pass one of the living room windows, I see Eric watching. I do a wheelie, but seeing his tense expression, I laugh and drop. When I come down, my wrist hurts.

Ten minutes later, I'm back in the garage, where Norbert's waiting for me, and I drop off the motorcycle.

"What do you think, ma'am? Everything in order?"

I nod and touch my wrist. It hurts, but I'm not worried. I'm sure in a week it'll be better.

Eric takes us to dinner at a wonderful restaurant. His mother, his cousin Jurgen, Marta, her boyfriend, and Flyn are there, waiting. We bring Dexter, Graciela, and Laila with us. Flyn rushes to hug us as soon as he catches sight of us, and Eric goes up to his mother, who kisses him.

"Happy birthday, my darling," she whispers to him.

With laughter and good vibes, we wait for those still not here. Jurgen sits between Laila and me, and we talk about the race. I'm excited. I can't wait to jump and race my bike. Eric doesn't say anything; he only listens. When I write down where the race will be on a piece of paper, Jurgen smiles.

Frida, Andrés, and an unaccompanied Björn finally arrive. I notice a certain discomfort when he sees Laila, but he greets her as if she's just someone he doesn't know well. Then he sits as far as he can from her. That makes me think. Laila is a very cute girl, and it's odd for Björn, the great predator, to move away in such a situation. Something happened, and I have to figure out what.

One by one, they give Eric their gifts, and he smiles gratefully. How happy my guy is on his thirty-third birthday. When I put candles on the cake and make him blow them out, I know he wants to kill me! I laugh and sing "Happy Birthday." Finally, he smiles and keeps on smiling.

"I think you have something to tell me, don't you?" Frida whispers in my ear.

When I see her face, I know exactly what she's talking about.

"If you mean where we ended up the night of Oktoberfest, I'll just tell you it was hot!"

Frida smiles and nods.

"Björn told me you had a great time."

I nod.

"Diana is tremendous, right?"

I nod again.

"And how are those two?" she asks, looking over at Graciela and Dexter. "Have you played with them yet?"

"To answer your first question, from what I sense, they're fine. And in reference to your second, no, we haven't played with them yet."

Half an hour later, Sonia gets a call from her current boyfriend. Marta and Arthur offer to give her a ride and leave. Laila is talking to Jurgen.

"What do you think of Laila?" I ask.

"She's very nice. She was Hannah's best friend." When she sees me frown, she asks, "What is it that really worries you about her?"

I don't want to reveal what I heard from Simona and the perception that Björn doesn't want anything to do with her. "Has she ever played with Eric or you?"

"Never. I think our thing is not her thing. Why do you ask?"

I'm glad to know Eric hasn't lied to me. That calms me down.

"Just curious."

14

Two days later, Sonia and Marta invite us to their graduation from parachuting school.

Eric goes, but reluctantly. Since I'm forcing the issue, in the end he doesn't have much choice but to be present and support his sister and mother. During graduation, he tries to keep his composure in spite of how nervous he is. But when his sister and mother and the other students disappear into the plane and it ascends into the sky, he leans my way.

"I can't look."

"What do you mean you can't look?"

"I said I can't look. Just let me know when they're back on terra firma, OK?"

I feel for the guy. He's making herculean efforts to try and understand us all.

Excited by the feats his grandmother and aunt are about to perform, Flyn applauds wildly. And when one of the monitors tells me the two dropping to the right are Sonia and Marta, I tell him, and the little boy cries out with Arthur, who has him perched on his shoulders.

"Amazing! They're one on top of the other!"

Eric curses. He's heard his nephew, and now he's in a tizzy.

Stuck together like glue, Graciela and Dexter can't seem to stop kissing. They're not bothering to watch the show at all. Their kisses and caresses are enough for them. That makes me laugh. It took them forever to decide, but now they can't let go of each other for a single minute. I can't even begin to imagine the bacchanal in their room. Their level of togetherness is so intense, Flyn now calls them the Limpets.

I look up at the sky and watch as various dots come rushing toward us. The parachutes open, and they begin to slowly drop. Eric's white as a sheet. I'm worried. "My love, are you OK?"

He shakes his head while staring at the ground. "Have they landed yet?"

"No, my love . . . they're still coming down."

"God, Jude, don't tell me that!"

Trying to understand the effort he's making to be there, I run my fingers through his hair to try and calm him. "They're here, my love. They've touched down safely," I say as soon as Sonia and Marta are on the ground.

Eric's breathing changes, he looks where everyone's looking, and claps so his mother and sister can see him.

What an actor!

As the days go by, I notice Laila is charming with Graciela and me but considerably less so with Simona. What is going on?

One afternoon when we're at the pool, Eric and Björn come by after work. They look so handsome in their suits.

"C'mon, dudes, take a dip with us," says Dexter, who's in the water with us.

Eric and Björn vanish, then come back about ten minutes later in their swimsuits and dive into the water.

Eric immediately swims toward me and encircles me in his arms.

"Hello, beautiful," he says after giving me an adoring kiss.

I return his kiss, and two seconds later we're playing in the water like a couple of kids. Simona leaves us a tray poolside with various goodies. Without hesitation, Laila goes to the tray, fills a glass with orange juice, and brings it over to the edge of the pool for my German.

"Here, Eric, freshly squeezed. Just like you like it."

Eric happily takes it, but I am somewhat astonished. She doesn't look at me; she only has eyes for Eric. And then suddenly, she adds, "And this Coke with double the ice is for Judith, which I know she loves."

That gets my attention. She's quite observant.

"Thank you, Laila."

"Thank you for always being so kind to me."

Twenty minutes later, we're all sitting on the edge of the pool, and Björn playfully shoves me in the water. Quickly, Eric pushes him, and he falls in too.

"Let's race," he challenges me.

I don't answer but start to swim with all my might toward the other end of the pool. When I've practically reached my goal, Björn grabs my feet and pulls me back.

When I manage to get my head out of the water, he grabs me by the waist, and pulls me to where I can stand.

"You're a cheater, you know that?" I say as he lets me go.

"I'm like you. I don't like to lose."

We both laugh, and, when I think I've found the right moment, I ask, "What's going on between you and Laila?"

"Nothing."

But his gaze is tense, and I can tell he wants to know what I know. We look at each other for a moment and understand one another perfectly.

"Something has happened between you two, I know it."

"You're too nosy."

"And you're a terrible actor."

"Shut up!"

"Oh my God—it wasn't hard to see that you barely talk to her, and you won't go near her. That's strange in a predator like you. She's very cute, and the logical thing would be that you'd be throwing everything at her."

Björn smiles. I've surprised him. "All I will say is that I'll be happy when she leaves."

"Does Eric know you can't stand her?"

He shakes his head. "No."

"Will you tell me what happened?"

"Yes, but not now. Another time."

I nod. I'm sure he will, so I go back to playing. I shove him, and he shoves me back. When I get out of the pool, Eric hands me a towel.

"It's so nice to see how well you and Björn get along," says Laila.

"He's a good friend," I respond.

"The best," Eric says.

Björn looks over and smiles.

"Well, you can't deny he's very handsome," adds Laila.

"Thank you, Laila," says Björn, but the expression on his face is telling her to shut up.

"Yup, Björn is very handsome and sexy," I say.

Eric looks over at me. I grin and give him a kiss.

"But there's no one like you, my love!" We all laugh. But then Laila decides to take it up a notch.

"If you hadn't met Eric, would you have been interested in Björn?"

Her question strikes me as funny, and so I respond honestly, like always. "Of course. I've always liked dark-haired men more than blond ones."

"Seriously?" says Graciela, laughing.

I nod, and then Eric grabs me by the waist and lifts me up.

"Well, you've married a blond man who doesn't plan to let you go."

"I don't want you to let me go," I say as I kiss him.

My crazy love throws me over his shoulder like a caveman. "Hey, everybody . . . we'll be right back."

"Let me go!" I say, laughing.

"No, my love . . . I'm getting payback for what you said."

"Go on and make her pay for the nerve of liking dark-haired men, my friend," says Dexter.

Without pause, Eric takes me all the way up to our room and throws me on the bed as if I were some bundle. "Get that off," he says as he drops his trunks.

I'm grinning ear to ear as I strip off my bikini. Eric throws himself on me and touches the cleft of my sex.

"You have me going a thousand miles an hour, sweetheart," he says.

We give in to our wild side and make love as if possessed.

15

I wake up at seven in the morning. It's Sunday, and I'm going to be competing in a motocross race. I leap out of bed and go straight to the shower. I dress in a pair of jeans and go down for breakfast. I find just Dexter in the kitchen.

"Good morning, my queen."

I get some coffee and sit at the table with him. He offers me a madeleine, and I give it a nibble.

"Eric is pretty anxious," Dexter says as I devour everything in sight. "He barely slept knowing you are going to be in that race today."

"How do you know that?"

"Because when I came down to get a glass of water at four in the morning, he was sitting in that very chair."

"And what were you doing awake at four in the morning?" I ask.

Dexter smiles. "I couldn't sleep. Too many headaches."

I take a sip of my coffee. "Do those headaches begin with G-R-A and end with C-I-E-L-A?"

Dexter leans back in his wheelchair. "I'm confused. I'm not sure being with her is fair."

"From what I know, she's thrilled, Dexter."

He nods, but something's seriously bothering him. "When I had my accident, my life did a one-eighty. I stopped being a desirable man, someone whose cell never stopped ringing, and became a man with desires but whose cell never rang. There was a time I struggled to accept what had happened, and I managed to get over it when I stopped having romantic feelings toward women. Everything was under control until Graciela—"

"But you like Graciela, right?"

"Yes, so much."

"And you're especially surprised because of what you and I know, right?"

Dexter nods. "I'm afraid I'll hurt her or that she'll hurt me. I'm well aware of my limitations and—"

"She knows about them too, and I can assure you she doesn't care," I say, cutting him off. "Maybe if you were a more typical couple, that would be important and worrisome to you, but you're not, and I think you both walk the same sexual path. I wouldn't worry."

"And what about kids? Shouldn't that worry me? She's a woman, and, sooner or later, she's going to want a baby, and I can't give her that."

Talking about kids is the last thing I want to do. "What do you mean you can't?" I ask.

Dexter looks at me with amazement. I think he thinks I've gone crazy.

"There are many kids in this world in search of a family," I say. "I don't think a baby has to come from you for you to love it, care for it, and protect it. I'm sure that, if and when the moment comes, you and Graciela can have your child if you both want one. You just need to talk about it. For the moment, enjoy it. Enjoy Graciela and let her enjoy you. Now is the time for the two of you to love each other, to have a good time, to get to know each other and not let anyone or anything get in the way."

"I understand my friend more and more each day," Dexter says as he takes a sip of his coffee. "You're a beautiful woman, not just on the outside, but on the inside too. May God grant you many years, my dear Judith."

"Thank you, handsome," I reply.

"Wow, trying to make it with my wife behind my back?" teases Eric as he bursts into the kitchen.

"Dude, my hope came alive again after she said she liked dark-haired men!" Dexter says.

We all laugh. Nobody would understand our particular friendship, but we do, and that's all that matters. When we finish with breakfast, it's time to go. I see Simona—with so many people in the house and so much activity, we've barely talked.

"Everything OK, Simona?"

She nods, but I know she's not OK.

"I know there's something going on with Laila."

She looks up at me, surprised.

"When I get back this afternoon we'll talk, all right?"

Simona says yes. I hug and kiss her.

"I'll see you later," I whisper in her ear.

"Good luck!" she responds, smiling.

At ten thirty, we arrive at the address Jurgen gave me. Dexter, Graciela, Laila, Norbert, and Flyn are with us, and I'm restless and dying to get on my motorcycle. Eric is having an anxiety attack. Marta and Arthur are waiting for us. Sonia apparently can't come.

I haven't been able to do jumps on a motorcycle since days before my wedding, and, though I drove several Jet Skis on my honeymoon, it's not the same, and I can't wait to mount my Ducati.

We park the car, and Norbert and I go register while Eric brings the motorcycle out of the trailer.

"Number sixty-nine. Pretty sexy, huh?" I say to Eric.

My crazy love smiles, but it's not a very relaxed smile. I know he's tense, but he has to chill, and he's the only one who can help himself with that. Jurgen and I hug. He's as excited about the race as I am. He gives me a map of the circuit, and, like my father back in Jerez, he tells me about the jumps and on what curves I need to be extra careful so I won't fall. Eric listens in and memorizes everything Jurgen says.

Jurgen marches off with Laila.

"Remember, be careful on curve number ten, and try to take it easy on fifteen," Eric says, pointing at the map.

"Yes, sir," I say and he grins.

Flyn is nervous and delighted with so many motorcycles around. He and Marta accompany me to the dressing rooms and help me put on my jumpsuit.

"Fantastic!" he says when I'm fully equipped for my motocross.

"Jude is our very own superhero," says Marta as she winks and takes her nephew's hand.

"You look incredible," says Laila when we go back to the group.

"Thank you." I smile.

"Judith, are you sure about this?" whispers Graciela.

With my helmet under my arm, I nod. "Absolutely."

Eric looks at me but he doesn't smile. He's afraid. I'm not.

The race is divided by gender. I accept it, but I prefer when it's mixed. They tell me I'm in the third round. I watch the first two as I listen to Guns N' Roses on my iPod.

Music like that always gets my adrenaline going, and to compete and win, I need to be at my peak. I've never raced on this particular circuit, and I need to see how the competition works in order to get a handle on my own race. Eric's beside me, watching and not saying a word. He lets me concentrate, but, every time someone falls, I can see that he's horrified.

When they call the third round, I give him a quick kiss and put on my helmet. "I'll be right back; wait for me!" I take off.

I know he's a mess, but I can't say goodbye as if I'm going to war. I'm simply running a race that lasts barely seven minutes. Once at the starting line with the other racers, I look for my guy and quickly spot him next to Flyn and Marta. I adjust my helmet and goggles.

I focus on the track. I visualize the circuit I went over with Jurgen and plan to lean to the right on the first curve, which is on the left.

We start our motors. My nerves are on edge when I finally hear a clang, and the hooks that keep our motorcycles in place are released. I take off like a bullet.

I accelerate and grin happily when I take the first curve exactly how I wanted to. As soon as I leave the curve behind, I skid and make the bike jump, and when I hit the ground, I notice my wrist hurts. But I'm not leaving this race because of some silly ache.

The rough patch almost kills me though, and I scream with pain and give the bike gas so I can get out of there as soon as possible. When I get to the next curve, I almost eat it. I can't go that fast, or I'll end up falling.

When I can, I keep myself in the first few slots, and, when the round is over and I'm in third place, I smile and sigh with relief. I now qualify for the next round.

When I leave the track and head toward my people, they all applaud, and Flyn jumps up and down with joy.

"I'm here, my love," I say, loud and clear so my handsome Mr. Zimmerman can relax. I take off my goggles and helmet and wink at my husband.

He hugs me and kisses me without worrying about the dust and the dirt. I hug him and kiss him back.

The next two rounds are a challenge because of the damned pain in my wrist, but I refuse to give in and manage to qualify for the final race.

It hurts like hell, but I know I need to shut up, or my husband will pull me out of here. I grit my teeth, but, when there are still ten minutes to the women's final, I turn to Graciela.

"I need you to change my bandage and make it as tight as you can."

"But that's not good, Judith. It'll cut your circulation."

"It doesn't matter. Do it."

She can tell it hurts me more than I'm saying.

"Judith, if it hurts that much you shouldn't—"

"Do it. I need it."

Without another word, she does as I say, and, when I put on my glove, my hand is practically rigid. That takes care of the pain, but it limits my movements and is very uncomfortable.

"Hey, put a smile on that face, my love," I say to Eric as he comes up to me. "This is my last race." He nods. "You should buy a big display case for my trophies. I'm hoping to come in first place here."

My confidence relaxes him, and he gives me a kiss.

"Get out there, champ. Get out there and show them who you are."

His positivity motivates me. All right, Zimmerman!

I'm at the starting line again.

It's the last of the women's races, and there will be three winners. Jurgen, Marta, Eric, and our whole group scream and cheer me on. I smile at them. I look all around me. The other racers are good, but I want to win. I really want to.

When the race begins, my adrenaline hits infinity and beyond.

Out of the corner of my eye, I see one of the other girls is trying to get ahead of me. She's good, very good, but I have confidence in myself, and I want to be better. When we get to curve number fifteen, I take it easy, but that makes me lose time, and another racer gets ahead of me. That enrages me, but there are two laps left so I still have time to beat her. I manage it and take the lead. There you go! But when we get to the rough patch again, my hand works against me, and they get ahead of me once more.

Shit! Now I'm in fourth place.

There's only one lap left, and I decide to risk it all and forget about the pain in my hand. When I approach curve number fifteen again, I sense that if I go inside instead of outside, I'll be able to win by a few seconds. There may be a problem coming out of it if my wrist fails, and I can't control the bike. But I've dealt with tougher things in my life, and I decide to chance it.

I grit my teeth as I come into the curve. The other women make room for me, I reduce my speed and go for it. I take the curve exactly as I planned and . . . all right! My wrist responds well, and I control the bike. Yes! Three more curves, and I'm taking home a trophy.

Suddenly, one of the other racers jumps, and her back wheel skids. She loses control, and her bike glances off my front wheel. Unable to avoid it, I go flying off and over my bike.

Everything goes dark.

16

I hear a constant and annoying sound.

Goddamned alarm clock!

I try to move to turn it off, but I can't. I'm so tired!

Noise. Voices. What a racket.

Someone calls me. Eric calls me.

I try to open my eyes. I can't. Darkness.

I don't know how much time passes until I hear the alarm again.

This time I can open my eyes, and I blink. I move my neck very carefully and sigh. My head hurts. What did I drink? When I open my eyes, I see a television anchored to the wall. Where am I? Someone is holding my hand, and I see Eric's head leaning on it.

What's going on?

Like a flash, everything rushes back: Race. Curve number fifteen. Flying over my motorcycle. I sigh.

Mother of God, I must have given myself a beating. I breathe. My body hurts, but I don't care about that. I just want to make sure Eric's OK. I know him, and I'm sure he's depressed and scared.

I look at his blond hair. He doesn't move, but when I gesture with my hand, he quickly raises his head and looks at me. I feel like my heart just stopped beating.

"Hello, handsome."

Eric sits up and comes closer to me. "Sweetheart, how are you?"

His eyes are red, terribly red.

"What happened to you, my love?" I ask.

And then he does something that leaves me completely speechless: his face, his beautiful face, tenses, and he sobs.

"Don't you ever scare me like that again, understand?"

I want to hug him and console him. I pull on him and make him hold me. Tears come rolling down my face when I realize how desperately he responds and how much he's crying. My Iceman—my serious, grumpy, and stubborn German—cries like a baby in my arms while I caress and kiss him.

We're like that for a few minutes until his breathing stabilizes, and he pulls back.

"I'm sorry, my love. Forgive me," he says, embarrassed.

I've never been so in love with him.

"There's nothing to forgive, baby."

"I was so scared . . . I . . ."

"You're human, and we humans have feelings, my love."

He moves his head and tries to smile and ends up giving me a kiss on the tip of my nose.

"What happened?"

He pushes the hair off my face and tries to explain.

"There was an accident. You flew off the motorcycle, lost consciousness, and didn't regain it until we got to the hospital. That scared me to death, Jude."

"Darling . . ."

"I thought I had lost you."

His despair makes me shiver.

"But I'm OK, right?"

Eric nods, but he's still very emotional.

"Yes, my love, you're OK. You have a very slight concussion." He swallows a knot of emotions. "But you're OK. You don't have a single break. Just a hairline fracture on your left wrist."

"You didn't call my father, did you?"

Eric shakes his head.

"I figured I would call him when you woke up."

"Don't call him. I'm all right, and there's no need to scare him."

He kisses my hand. "We have to call him, Jude. If you want, we can wait until tomorrow when they release you."

I protest.

"Tomorrow? And why not now?"

"Because they want to keep you for twenty-four hours of observation."

"But I'm OK. Can't you see?"

He finally grins. "Your stubbornness tells me you are, in fact, all right, and you have no idea how happy that makes me. But I want you to stay in the hospital as well. It'll ease my mind. I'll stay with you. I won't move from your side."

I like that. If I have to be here, he's the best company I could have. Just then, the door opens and in comes Marta with an anguished Sonia.

"Oh, my girl, are you all right?"

"Yes, it's OK, Sonia. I'm fine. It's just a bump."

"A bump? You mean a hell of a crash!" exclaims Marta. "You have to see the shape that motorcycle is in to fully understand what happened."

Eric moves so his mother can hug and kiss me. He touches her shoulder to reassure her.

"It's OK, Mamá. Judith's fine."

But now I'm the sad one. "What happened to my motorcycle?"

When no one responds, my eyes fill with tears, and my neck itches. "Please tell me my bike is OK," I say, which leaves them all aghast.

"My dear," says Sonia, "don't get anxious."

Eric scolds his mother with a look.

"Listen, my love, don't worry about the bike now. The only thing that's important is you."

But that doesn't convince me. I scratch my neck.

I adore my bike. My father sacrificed a lot to buy it for me many years ago.

"At least tell me if it can be fixed."

"It can be fixed," says Eric, now back at my side and blowing on my neck.

That helps. My bike is very important to me. It's my connection to my past, to my family, to Spain.

Eric's phone rings, and he goes out in the hallway to answer.

"Oh, my dear," whispers Sonia, "you have no idea how terrified I was when I got the call from Marta!"

I smile and try to calm her.

"But nobody was as scared as my son. I thought Eric wouldn't be able to deal with it. You have no idea how hysterical he got. Marta practically had to slap him so he'd let you go and let the paramedics attend to you."

"He must have been reliving Hannah's accident, poor man," I say, horrified.

We all know that's exactly what happened. He was present for that accident too.

Knowing Eric has gone through such a terrible thing hurts my soul.

"I know he's been crying," Sonia says.

"Don't say a word about it, Mamá. You know how he is."

"Simona and Norbert send kisses. I told them they didn't have to come, that you'd be home tomorrow," Eric says when he comes back.

Those poor souls; they must be so upset.

"Are you all right, my son?"

Eric knows what she's really asking.

"Yes, now that I know Jude's OK."

That makes me want to smile. He is definitely still my Iceman, but today he's shown me another side, one I didn't know. I can really see now how much he loves me and needs me.

A few hours later, the room is jammed with visitors. Dexter, Graciela, and Laila bring Flyn, who hugs me when he sees me, takes my hand, and refuses to let anyone get between us. Frida, Andrés, and

Björn arrive later. They bring me a beautiful bouquet of orange lilies, for which I am grateful.

Everyone is talking all around me, and then Björn settles next to me with a worried look.

"Quite the scare you gave us, you crazy girl."

"I know. It wasn't my intention."

"Are you OK?"

I nod. Eric leans into us. "Do you need anything?"

I say no and smile. Björn puts a hand on his friend's shoulder.

"Do you need me to get anything from the house?"

"We could use some clothes for Jude. All we have here is the jumpsuit, and I don't think she wants to leave the hospital in that tomorrow," says Eric.

"I'll stop by your house later. Simona will get that stuff ready, and I'll bring it by tonight," says Björn.

"You don't have to come back tonight, Björn. If we have it tomorrow, that's fine," says Eric as he kisses my forehead.

"I can bring it," says Laila. "There's no need for Björn to stop by the house."

"It's not a bother," insists our friend.

Eric isn't picking up on anything. "What if Björn picks you up, and you come together?"

"Ah, no . . . I can't," says Laila after a quick glance at Björn. "I just realized I have a meeting in the morning."

Björn nods, looks over at me, and I smile back. Problem solved.

17

As the days go by, I get better. On Thursday, we say goodbye to Graciela and Dexter. They're going back to Mexico, but we promise we'll see them again here or there.

I miss Graciela's company right away. She's such a good person, it's impossible not to miss her. Laila's still at the house. The truth is, she's charming. I haven't had a chance to talk to Simona yet, but, with me at least, she's very kind and good.

Eric has to see his doctors. They have to make an adjustment because of his vision problem. Marta lets me go in with him when they run tests, and I get a chance to see what he has to go through. Later, the three of us conference in Marta's office.

"Have you had headaches lately?" asks the doctor.

"A few."

I immediately protest. "Why didn't you tell me?"

"Because I didn't want you to worry," responds Eric.

I sigh. Marta gives me a look that tells me to calm down.

"Eric, everything's OK right now, but if your head hurts again, tell me, please."

He nods.

"If you smile, I'll smile," my German whispers to me as we leave the hospital.

Days later, when I feel a thousand times better after my accident, I call my father and tell him what happened. He gets scared and irritated because I'm telling him so many days after the fact, but, like always, he forgives me. He's a love.

I tell my sister too, but she's a whole different story. Raquel gets pissed and tells me I'm out of my mind for continuing to ride my motorcycle. I listen . . . and listen . . . and listen until I'm at the point of telling her to go to hell, and then I remember how much I love her and keep on listening.

When she finally has nothing else to say, I ask her about Juan Alberto. Eric told me that, after his trip to Belgium, he went back through Spain, so I'm not surprised when she says he visited Jerez. He's back in Mexico now, but he calls her every two or three days.

She sounds calm and seems serene, but I know she's suffering. She doesn't say anything, so I won't say anything either.

When I hang up, I lean back on the bed and fall asleep. I wake up about ten minutes later, and Simona's in my room with a glass of water and some pills. It's time to take them.

"Do you want to see *Emerald Madness* up here? It'll be on in ten minutes," she says.

I say yes and tell her to get up on the bed with me. I lean back on the pillows.

"What's going on with Laila?"

"Why do you think there's something going on?"

"I heard you arguing with Norbert about her visit. I've also noticed it's tense between you two and between her and Björn, but you all pretend otherwise. Are you going to tell me what happened?"

Simona touches my arm. "She's not my niece; she's Norbert's. And the dislike is mutual. According to that little monster's mother, that we work as servants is my fault, and that's why they always treat us with disdain. But you know what? I'd rather be a servant than someone as deplorable as that girl, no matter how educated she might be."

"What do you mean?"

"It's a shady story, Judith," she says, and lowers her voice. "I had another fight with Norbert yesterday because of that shameless girl. She puts things in his head and—"

"Like what?"

"Laila's mother lives in London and wants us to move there when we retire. But I'm not going to London or anywhere else. I refuse."

"I heard you say something about what happened with Björn," I say. "Can you tell me what that was about?"

"She did something very ugly, and I'm not going to talk about it. I would rather Björn tell you what happened. But that horrible girl is a bad seed . . . a very bad seed."

We remain on the bed and watch how Luis Alfredo Quiñones recovers from the gunshot to his chest but suffers amnesia and can't remember anything, not even that Esmeralda Mendoza's his lover and that he's the father of a beautiful boy. She suffers. We suffer.

Mother of God, what a melodrama!

Soon, my accident is forgotten. Eric and everyone else have taken very good care of me, everything's going very well, and I sometimes have a terrible fear of being too happy.

Eric and I argue a few times about my going back to work. He thinks if I do, it'll take time away from us and cause problems.

I want to work and can't stand to have limits imposed on my life so every time we talk about it, one of us ends up storming out of the room and slamming the door.

Also during this time, Eric, Flyn, and Laila go to the shooting range a couple of Sunday mornings. I refuse. I don't like guns and prefer to keep them out of my life.

One morning, Eric calls me from work and asks me to go to Björn's office to sign some papers. When I ask him what they are, he tells me the documents are our wills, and that leaves me cold.

After a few minutes of reasoning through it, I realize it's for the best. I know it will avoid problems for my family if something should happen to me.

At the office, everyone greets me affably. I'm Mrs. Zimmerman, and they're a little surprised to see me here, except Helga, who greets me warmly. I blush a little when I remember what she and I did together at that hotel so many months back.

Oh . . . the heat!

When I get to Björn's office, the memories make me sweat. The last time I was here, I ended up on the desk, nude, with my legs wide open. When Björn sees me, he stands and kisses me on each cheek.

He very professionally shows me the docs Eric has already signed, and I discover our friend is not only a lawyer but also a notary.

Handsome, good-hearted, elegant, a lawyer, and a notary . . . excellent! He tells me Eric has named my father, sister, and nieces as beneficiaries. That moves me. My husband thinks of everything.

Afterward, Björn suggests we have lunch together. I accept. I want to know about Laila. It's killing me!

We walk arm in arm to the restaurant. Björn is constantly joking around, and I can't stop laughing. We order wine and toast to the many years Eric and I still have to live. We're laughing but just about ready to really start talking when some friends of his show up and sit with us. We have to put off our talk. I set aside the wine and order a Coke.

One afternoon when I'm bored at home, Sonia calls. She wants me to come over. I have nothing better to do, so I say yes. Norbert drives me. Once I arrive, my mother-in-law receives me as warmly as ever. We're chatting when, suddenly, Earth, Wind & Fire's "September" comes on the radio.

"Do you know that every time I hear this song, I remember the first time I saw you dancing like a crazy woman at that hotel in Madrid?" says Sonia.

"Seriously?"

She nods.

"I love that song."

"Me too!"

We both laugh.

"Well then, let's dance," she says.

My mother-in-law is the best! She raises the volume, and we begin to dance and sing.

Marta comes in, sees us, and quickly joins the party.

When the song ends, we're still laughing. Sonia's housekeeper brings us some beverages, and I quickly claim a Coke. I'm so thirsty.

"All right, Mamá, now that we're past the moment of euphoria, what's going on?"

That gets my attention. There's something going on? Mother and daughter quickly look at each other; then Sonia turns to me. "I need your help." Now it's Marta and I who take a quick glance at one another.

"You know I broke up with Trevor Gerver a few months back, right?"

We both nod.

"Well, the night before last, when I was having dinner with a friend at a restaurant, I saw him with a very pretty young woman on his arm."

"So what, Mamá?"

"Well, that young woman couldn't have been more than thirty years old."

"And?" I ask.

"It enraged me to see him so well accompanied," mutters Sonia.

I blink, not quite sure I understand what's going on. I know my mother-in-law was really into that guy . . .

"Were you jealous?" asks Marta.

"No."

"Then what?"

"It angered me that his companion was younger than mine."

I want to laugh. I can't help it. Sonia never stops surprising me. Marta protests.

"Mamá, please, what are you saying?"

I'm still laughing.

"When Trevor saw me, he came over and invited me to a party at his house tomorrow."

"So?" asks Marta.

"Well, that's a problem."

"Then don't go," I say. "If it doesn't appeal to you, don't go—problem solved."

She glances at me and sighs. I'm even more lost than before.

"I want to go to that party, but not with a man my age. What I want is to go with a handsome and attractive young man. You know the kind. Scandalous. I want that snot Trevor Gerver to realize a woman like me can ignite passions in younger men."

Well, well, well . . .

"Mamá, are you saying you want to hire a gigolo?"

"No."

"Then what is it you want, Sonia?" I ask.

She looks at us a little desperately, takes a swallow of her drink, screams, and raises her hands. "A piece of arm candy, that's what I want!" Marta and I burst out laughing. I think I'm going to die, I'm laughing so much!

"So much for your help!" Sonia says as she watches us practically rolling on the floor.

"Mamá . . . Mamá . . . but . . ."

Marta can't even finish her sentence. Sonia just sits back and watches.

"Mamá, how do you want us to help you?" Marta finally manages to say.

"I think what she wants is for us to find her a dream boy from Guantanamera. Am I right?"

"Mamá!"

"That's right, girls. I need a delicious dark-skinned man who's also a good person and who'll leave Trevor Gerver and his date in the dust," says Sonia, clapping.

"Mamá!"

"If it wasn't important to me, I wouldn't ask," Sonia says after revealing her wish. "Surely you know a decent young man who can go with me."

"Let's see if I understand, Mamá. What you want is a young man who'll go with you to the party, respect you, and make you look like a queen in front of everyone else?"

"Exactly! I don't want an escort or a rent boy. Just a handsome young man who's decent and fun who would want to escort this poor elderly woman."

"Oh, now comes the melodrama," I tease and Sonia laughs.

"OK, OK," she says, laughing. "Bottom line: I need a piece of arm candy I can trust."

"We can ask Reinaldo," I say.

"No," says Marta. "Reinaldo was at your wedding, and Trevor might recognize him."

We both give it some thought until we both suddenly come to the same conclusion. "Mr. Perfect Torso!"

"Who's that?" asks Sonia.

"Our friend, Máximo," says Marta. "He came to Germany six months ago, and he's a great guy. He's a dance teacher, and he's in a relationship with Anita."

"Really?" I say and Marta nods.

"Anita is your friend who owns the boutique, right?" asks Sonia.

"Yes, Mamá."

"Máximo is definitely arm candy," I explain, "and he's Argentinian."

"*Che*, perfect!" says Sonia, clapping again. "I love Argentinians."

Marta immediately calls Anita and tells her what's going on. She agrees to talk to Máximo and says she'll call back.

"One thing, my dear, sweet daughter-in-law," says Sonia, "do not mention a word of this to Eric, or he will never speak to me again for the rest of my life."

"No worries! Because if he finds out I had a hand in any of this, he won't speak to me for the rest of my life either."

We all laugh. Marta's cell rings. It's Máximo. We all agree to meet in one hour at Anita's store.

The situation strikes me as surreal, but funny. One more of Sonia's eccentricities. When we get to the boutique, Máximo isn't there yet, and so we chat with Anita. She thinks the whole thing is funny too.

When Máximo shows up, Sonia's face gives her away. She's thrilled!

The Argentinian is impressive, not only because he's such a dreamboat but also because he's so nice too. He greets us all with kisses, turns to Sonia, and takes her by the arm.

"You and I are going to be the king and queen of that party," he says.

My mother-in-law nods, and we all laugh. Half an hour later, they've finalized the details.

"My dear mother-in-law, you're going to have a great time!" I say in the car on the way home.

"Oh yes, have no doubt!"

"Mamá, Jude and I can only tell you one more thing," says Marta, who's driving.

"What, my dears?"

We glance at each other and shout in unison, "Azúcar!"

Two days later, when I call Sonia to see how it all went, she's so happy. Máximo behaved like a gentleman, and Trevor Gerver and all those attending the party were speechless at the Argentinian's gallantry and the rhythm of his hips.

The days pass, and my wrist is perfect. Eric and I love each other more every day, despite our continued arguments about work. Flyn's happy at school. It's a good year for him.

The only thing souring my existence is my beloved motorcycle. The day I confront the harsh reality, it makes me so sad, I just sob. My beautiful 2007 Ducati Vox MX 530 is in terrible shape.

When we get home, I don't even want to talk about motorcycles. Eric tries to help make me forget and calls Marta and suggests she and Laila take me out to cheer me up.

So, a few nights later, I go party with them, and we end up at Guantanamera. Why do we always go there?

I'm sure when Eric finds out, he'll get his boxers in a knot. He doesn't like it because, according to him, people only come here to hook up.

Seeing us, Reinaldo greets me with affection, and I'm happily dancing to "Quimbara" with him in minutes.

The guy is a great dancer and makes me look good too. I'm not an expert, but, hey, I know how to move very well!

When Anita and Máximo arrive, he tells us about Sonia and what a great time he had with her. He asks me to dance later, and I accept. Máximo is like Reinaldo; he has a rhythm that can't be stopped!

It's hot, and I drink several mojitos. They are deadly, and I love them. I smoke a few cigarettes with Marta, and, for a few hours, I forget my motorbike and the arguments about work, and I smile again.

Around midnight, beautiful Björn unexpectedly shows up with Fosqui, the constipated poodle. We're surprised to see them, and I watch as Laila quickly goes off to dance with some guy.

Björn gives me a couple of kisses on the cheek and asks, "What are you doing here?"

"Dancing, drinking, shouting 'Azúcar!'," I say, several mojitos over the top.

He laughs. The poodle doesn't. "Is Eric here?"

"No . . . he doesn't like this den of perversion."

"If you were my wife, I wouldn't like it either," my friend whispers as he looks around.

I laugh. Another bore, just like his friend!

When the next song begins, I grab him by the hand and pull him to the dance floor. Wow . . . wow . . . this German keeps a decent beat.

The intensity of the song rises and, with it, our steps and our laughter.

The poodle dances with a friend of Reinaldo's.

Then Björn leans into my ear. "It's not a good idea for you to be out with Laila."

"Why?"

"She's not a good person."

Hearing that, I remember we have a pending conversation. I yank on his arm again and pull him to the bar; I don't care about the poodle barking. I order two mojitos.

"Tell me what happened between you and Laila."

My handsome friend nods, takes a sip of his drink, touches his chin, and centers his blue eyes on me.

"Do you know Leonard Guztle?"

"No."

"He's the man who was living with Hannah and Flyn when—"

"Oh, I do know him! Yes, a few months ago, I was walking Susto when I saw a man whose car wasn't working," I explained. "I took a look at it, and the trouble turned out to be a fuse. I changed it for him. Eric showed up, and it got really tense. When the guy left, Eric told me it was Leonard Guztle, Hannah's boyfriend, who didn't want anything to do with Flyn after she died. Same guy, right?"

Björn nods.

"Well, now that you know what Eric thinks of that imbecile, what would you say if I told you I spied Laila with him in Eric's car just one week after Hannah's death?"

I'm stunned.

"So, I saw an antique Mercedes of Eric's parked in my building's garage. Imagine my surprise when I find those two fucking like rabbits in the backseat. Hannah had just died and—"

"Mother of God, if Eric ever finds out . . ."

"Exactly. If Eric ever finds out! But he didn't. I made sure he didn't have to swallow that bitter pill. And I told that idiot girl to get away from Eric, or I'd tell him the truth."

"Thanks, Björn," I say. I'm grateful he's told me this. "But why were they in your parking garage?"

"After Hannah died, Leonard rented an apartment in my building. For me the real problem is that that brainless twit told her aunt and uncle her dress got torn because I'd made a pass at her."

"What?"

"Yes, my friend, you heard right. But Simona is very clever. She asked me about it, and I set her straight."

I blink. I can't believe this. What a little bitch, that Laila!

"Lucky for me and not so much for Laila, there are security cameras in my building, and I was able to show Simona and Norbert the tapes. They confirmed she was with Leonard, and he ripped her dress. After that, Laila went off to London to live with her mother."

I'm speechless.

I look over at Laila. She looks back, and I imagine she knows what Björn is telling me. I foresee trouble with that one.

"Therefore, my very dear Jude, the greater the distance between that woman and us, the better. She's a wolf in sheep's clothing."

Laila's staring at us.

She's not dancing anymore. She talks to the poodle, and the two seem to come to an understanding. Suddenly, I have a terrible notion.

"You said you have security cameras at your place?"

"Yes."

My face must have given me away. He knows what I'm thinking.

"Don't worry; when you and Eric visit, I turn them off," he says.

"Promise?"

He nods.

"Of course. Don't ever doubt my friendship. I value you both too much."

Marta comes over and leans on Björn.

"So, this is where this delicious piece of candy has been hanging out, mmm!"

Björn puts his hands around her waist. "Hello, beautiful. You're having quite a good time tonight. Where's Arthur?"

"Working," she says.

She shakes her hips and dances around.

"Honestly, I think I was Cuban in another life. I like this so much."

All of us laugh. She takes a sip of my mojito and says, "Azúcar!"

Still shaking her hips, she shimmies to the dance floor to salsa with Máximo. I order another drink.

"How many have you had?"

"A few."

"Be careful or you'll really feel it tomorrow."

"No worries," I say, grinning when the bartender brings me my drink. I take a sip. "And please stop treating me as if you were Eric or my father."

We both look over at the dance floor, where my sister-in-law is dancing up a storm.

"Marta is so much fun."

I watch the poodle as she dances with Reinaldo, and I can't help myself.

"How can you be with somebody so . . . so obnoxious?"

"Because all the delightful and entertaining girls are already taken," Björn responds.

That makes me laugh. He always sneaks in a compliment. They don't bother me. I know they're totally innocent. I watch as a pair of women position themselves near us just so they can get a look at him.

"You've never had a serious relationship?"

Björn grins, winks at the women behind me, and shakes his head.

"No, I'm too demanding."

"Demanding?"

I can't help but laugh and look back at the poodle.

"Agneta is a beast in bed," Björn whispers.

I knew it! That's what I'd figured, but, God, men can be so elementary!

"So, if it's not too much, can you tell me what kind of women you like?"

"Like you. Smart, beautiful, sexy, tempting, easygoing, a little crazy, and disconcerting. Plus, I love to be surprised."

"I'm all that?"

"Yes, beautiful, you are! But this is no declaration of love or anything like that. I respect you, and I respect my best friend. You're both too important to me. That said, if I'd met you first, you wouldn't have gotten away."

We both laugh.

"Now that we've cleared the air, if you know a woman who's single and has those qualities, tell me because I'd love to meet her."

"C'mon, this is so much fun," says Reinaldo in his peculiar Cuban Spanish, asking me to dance as "Guantanamera" starts to play.

Björn is confused. "What did he say?"

I laugh. "He wants me to dance."

"C'mon, love, let's party!" says Reinaldo as he pulls on my arm.

I shake my hips and dance with him as if I were going to unravel. Björn goes back to the poodle's side and squeezes her.

We all have great fun for a few hours. I dance with many different people, and then one guy crosses the line. When they see what happened, Björn and Reinaldo come to my rescue, but I stop them with just one look. I twist the guy's arm behind his back, and his face hits a table.

"Touch my ass one more time, I'll cut your hand off," I tell him.

Reinaldo and Björn are terribly amused. Minutes later, while I'm having a drink at the bar, Laila positions herself next to me.

"What were you talking about with Björn?"

Should I tell her to go fuck herself?

"You know what we were talking about," I say, not wanting much to do with her. "If Eric ever finds out, you'll never set foot in the house again."

Her eyes give her away. She's furious, enraged. Without a word, she turns and goes. I see her leave the bar.

Many mojitos later, Björn says goodbye to Marta and me. An hour later, we decide to leave too, and when I get home in the wee hours, happy as a clam, Eric is waiting up. As I come in, he takes a peek at his watch.

It's three thirty in the morning. "Guantanamera, right?"

"Yes."

I'm not going to lie to him. That's where my friends go.

Eric sighs. "Why didn't you come back with Laila?"

"Because I was having a good time," I say, giving him a kiss.

He's nervous about something.

"And I was having such a good time, time just flew. You know how it is, my love!" That last bit, I toss out with a Cuban accent.

"You're about to cross a line, sweetheart."

I can't help it, and I start giggling.

Goddamn those mojitos!

When I get up the next day, my head is pounding.

I don't remember drinking that much, but I know I danced nonstop.

Eric is at the office, and, when I see I don't have any messages from him on my cell, I imagine he's probably not very happy. I remember how he looked at me the night before while I giggled.

I call his cell. I need to hear his voice.

"Yes, Jude."

"Hello, my love, how are you?"

"Fine."

Silence. He doesn't say anything. He knows how to torture me.

"Listen, love, about last night—"

"I don't want to talk about it now. I'm busy. If you want to, we can talk about it when I get home."

"OK," I say with a sigh. "I love you."

I hear his breathing as he makes me wait a few seconds that seem eternal to me.

"I love you too."

When I hang up the phone, my stomach isn't happy and my throat is burning, and I run to the bathroom thinking I had way too many mojitos.

I have a terrible day. I feel like crap, and I decide to stay in bed and sleep. That evening, when I hear Eric's car, I feel better and get up. I don't run because I don't want to upset my stomach again, but, when I leave our room, I hear the front door open from the top of the stairs as Laila greets my husband.

"Jude is resting," she says. "She's not well."

"What happened?" I hear Eric ask.

Peeping over the landing, I watch them and listen to the young woman explain.

"Her head hurts; she didn't want to eat anything. She drank too much last night."

"Did you drink too much too?"

Laila nods. "Between you and me, I'm not surprised her head hurts; she and Marta smoked like fiends, and I lost track of the number of mojitos they had while dancing."

I'm blown away.

And as I'm dealing with my shock, she continues. "By the way, Björn was at Guantanamera too."

"Björn?"

I don't like the face Laila wears when she nods.

"He came with a woman and had a good time with her, but also with Judith. Well, you know how your friend is. He doesn't waste an opportunity when it comes to a woman alone."

I'll kill her. I will kill her.

I'll tear out her eyes and wear them as pendants.

I can't see Eric's face. From my vantage point, I can only see his back, and I notice it's stiff. This is bad!

"Thanks for the information, Laila," he says without further ado, then heads to his office.

He opens the door and, leaving her at the threshold, closes it in her face.

Damned girl. It's clear the goodwill between us is over.

I'm about to go downstairs and cut off her ears, but at that moment Simona comes in with Calamar in her arms.

"C'mon, let go of that monster and go prepare my bath," Laila says.

On hearing that, Simona stares at her.

"The only monster I see here is you. Prepare your own bath."

Olé and olé and olé, my Simona! I'm about to jump in, but I shut up. Björn is right. The girl is a wolf in sheep's clothing, and it's best to handle this carefully.

At night, Eric is not very communicative. I try to talk to him, but in the end, I give up. When it gets this bad, it's better to leave it.

When we go to bed, he turns his back to me. He's clearly still angry. I breathe while waiting for him to say something. But, nothing.

In the end, I put my mouth to his ear.

"I still love you even if you don't want to talk to me."

Afterward, I turn around in the bed. A good while later, when I'm almost asleep, I feel Eric move and hug me. I smile and fall asleep.

By November, I've had it with Laila.

Every day I find it harder to keep her close. Since she knows I know her secret, she's declared war on me. Of course, whenever Eric is with us, we are two great actresses.

Flyn's on a field trip with his school, and tonight he'll sleep elsewhere. My grumpy Smurf grows older.

"Flyn comes back tomorrow," I say at dinner. "I'm sure he's having a great time."

Eric nods and smiles. Thinking about my nephew always has that effect.

"By the way, my work ends next week, and I have to leave," says Laila.

Mother of God, that's great news!

"Oh, what a pity!" I say, lying like a scoundrel.

Laila looks at me, and I blink.

Eric knows me and raises an eyebrow. "When are you going?" he asks her.

"I want to look at tickets for November seventh."

"I have to go to London for a few days for work next week," he says. "If you want to come on the jet with me, I'd be delighted."

"Cool!" she replies.

Stop!

Eric is going to London?

How has he not even told me?

I decide to shut up and wait. When we're alone, I'll ask.

Once dinner's over, we watch TV for a while. Because she's insuffer-able, Laila sits right next to us. But I'm restless, and I want to talk to Eric.

"Honey, I have to talk to you," I say.

Hearing that, Laila surprises me and quickly gets up.

"I'll leave you two alone," she says with an angelic tone. "Tonight I want to read anyway."

Once he and I are alone in the living room, I can see Eric knows I'm upset about the trip, and, eager to placate me, he goes to play something on the stereo.

"You like this song a lot," he says, giving me a wink. "C'mon, dance with me."

Surprised he wants to dance, I get up to join him.

I don't want to miss this!

And then "Si Nos Dejan," that wonderful ranchera, starts to play, and I hug him.

"I love this song," I whisper.

Eric smiles and squeezes me against his body.

"I know, sweetheart . . . I know."

We dance in an embrace to the beautiful music and smile as we both sing along.

Being in his arms is the balm for my doubts.

Being in his arms makes me feel loved and safe.

Once the song is over, I let him guide me, and we sit very close together in the armchair. I love his kisses, and, when our mouths part, he's looking very satisfied.

"Listen," he says, "I wasn't fooled by that 'oh, what a pity' about Laila's departure. What's your problem with her?"

"What's this about you going to London?"

"Work, sweetheart."

"How many days?"

"Three. Four at the most."

"And when were you going to tell me?"

"Well, a few days beforehand." He knows this is upsetting. "You know—"

"Amanda's there. Is that it?"

Eric looks at me, and I hold his gaze.

As always when she comes up, the tension rises between us.

"When are you going to trust me?" he asks. "I think I've already shown you that—"

"It's Amanda . . . ," I say, cutting him off. "How can you expect me to trust her?"

He shakes his head and closes his eyes.

"Sweetheart, if you are so suspicious, come with me. Accompany me. I don't have anything to hide. I'm just going to work. I'm the head of the family, and I'm expected to do these things."

I understand. And it's not him but Amanda . . . Laila . . . these women make me distrust them.

Eric gets up and, without taking his eyes off me, serves himself a whisky while Luis Miguel sings "Te extraño." Then he comes back to the armchair and sits next to me.

"Sit back."

I'm surprised.

"I'm waiting," he says.

I do what he asks. The lust in his gaze has already hit me. When I lie back, he sneaks his hands under my comfortable cotton dress and pulls on my panties, taking them off. Luckily, he didn't rip them this time.

Overheated, I watch the way his eyes roam all over me.

"Bend your legs and part them."

"Eric, Laila could come in at any minute and—"

"Do as I say," he demands.

Spellbound by his look and very excited by his command, I obey. He puts a cushion under my butt, and, when he has my pelvis at the height he wants, he takes his whisky and splashes some on my sex.

"Sweetheart, as the song says, I only want these moments with you. I just want to drink from you."

Then he puts his mouth on my hot, wet sex, and I gasp. His licking makes me crazy, and, when his tongue imprisons my clit and nibbles it, a moan emerges from me.

I abandon myself to him.

Oh yes, yes!

I let his hands open my thighs while his demanding mouth sucks, licks, nibbles, and makes me vibrate. He takes me to seventh heaven, to the eighth, and to whichever one he wants. I adore him.

My hands clutch the chair, my legs tremble, and I fall apart as his tongue plays inside me. He owns me with his mouth, and I open myself like a flower.

The heat rises, and, crazed, I let go of the chair and grab him forcefully by the hair. I press him against the center of my desire, desperate for that intense pleasure to never end . . . never . . . never . . .

But before I can surrender, my love pulls away from me. With a fiery look that would singe the North Pole, he undoes the drawstrings on his sweatpants.

"Sit up. Turn around and put your hands on the back of the chair."

Without delay, I do as he asks. But Eric is impatient, and, before I can position myself, he grabs me by the waist, and his penis is inside me.

I fall against the back of the chair.

"Sweetheart, I just want . . . I want . . . I long to possess you."

His voice is full of desire, and the way he goes in and out of me— so hot, so possessive—drives me crazy. He's so forceful, and, as always happens to us, our wild sides come out, and we surrender to pure pleasure.

Again and again, Eric rams me and I open myself to him.

Again and again, faster and faster, stronger and stronger.

Again and again, my gasps and his gasps fuse.

Without pause, Eric squeezes me against the back of the chair, and his thrusts are deep and precise.

"Oh yes . . . yes . . . ," I murmur, possessed.

Our grunts increase in intensity and, together, we climax. He falls on me. I love his weight, his smell. I adore him. Only him.

For several seconds, I feel him on my back until he finally retreats.

"Sweetheart, I'm yours, and you're mine. Don't doubt me," he whispers.

18

The days pass, and there's a party at Flyn's school. He's made new friends this year, and he wants Eric and me to go with him. We promise we will.

Flyn brings home a flyer asking parents to prepare a dish for the event. Delighted, I accept the challenge and decide to cook Spanish-style potato omelets. I want them to eat a real potato omelet made by a Spaniard. Simona offers to make a carrot cake.

The party is held on a Saturday morning so parents can attend. Flyn has a cold, but he doesn't want to miss the party, so we go anyway.

"I don't like being here," Eric murmurs after we park the car next to the school.

My man is gorgeous, with a pair of jeans matching his denim shirt. I give him a slap on his tight little ass.

"You're accompanying your nephew to his party! Cheer up!"

Carrying Simona's cake, Flyn runs out in front of us. He's spotted one of his friends and happily goes up to chat.

"Look at him," I whisper proudly. "Don't you love to see him getting along so well?"

Eric agrees with his typical seriousness. "Of course I'm happy for him, but I just don't like coming here."

"Why?"

"Because I always hated this school."

"You went here?"

"Yes."

"But if you studied here and hated it so much, why are you sending Flyn here?" I say, surprised by the revelation.

He shrugs.

"Because Hannah wanted it; she wanted him to study here."

I get it.

"And in the last few years, the only time I've come here has been to hear about Flyn's bad behavior."

"Well, it's about time you came for another reason."

He's not very convinced so I bump hips with him.

"C'mon, be happy. After all, Flyn's very excited we're both here."

In the end, he smiles, and I do too.

It's so nice when he smiles like that!

Inside, the noise is deafening. Flyn guides us to his class. When we enter, the other parents look at us. They don't know us so I greet them with a smile and place the omelets next to the cake. Flyn takes me by the hand to show me some of his work. We're appraising it when I hear Eric snort.

"I hate that they're looking at me like that."

I scan the room and see what he's talking about. The mothers are staring and smiling at him. Sigh. I get that his presence discombobu-lates them, and, instead of getting jealous, I take him by the arm.

"Honey, most of them have not seen a man like you in their whole life," I say. "It's normal for them to stare at you. You're really hot! And if you weren't my husband, I'd also be looking at you like that. Moreover, I think I would try to hook up with you."

Surprised by my response, Eric goes to kiss me, but I stop him.

"No way. Behave, Mr. Zimmerman. We're surrounded by children."

Seeing him grin fills my soul.

"Will the parents who brought food please take it to the gym?" asks a teacher.

I take the omelets, Eric picks up the cake, and the herd of parents and I follow the teacher.

The place is busy!

This is one hell of an impressive gym. Nothing at all like the gyms in my neighborhood.

"Eric Zimmerman!"

Eric and I turn around, and he laughs.

"Joshua Kaufmann."

Joshua is a former schoolmate of Eric's, and he introduces us to his wife, a very well cared for German beauty. She looks me up and down while our husbands talk delightedly, and I realize this cockatoo and I are never going to be friends.

Suddenly, Flyn sidles up to us.

"Are you OK, honey?" I ask.

He nods. I caress his head, then bring my lips to his forehead, as my mother used to do and my father still does. Seeing that he doesn't have a fever, I breathe easy.

As soon as I can, I slip away from Eric, Joshua, and the cockatoo. I can't stand another second.

"Jude, you want a Coke?" Flyn asks and I accept.

He fills up a glass, and, as he hands it to me, a friend of his comes for him, and they run off, leaving me. But my solitude is short-lived, because soon the cockatoo and two friends of the same species find me.

"The little Chinese boy is yours?"

I'm trying to work up a poker face, like Flyn does, but I can't really pull it off.

"Yes, he's ours, and he's German."

"Is he adopted?"

Option one: I tell her to go fuck herself.

Option two: I slap her.

Option three: I explain to the cockatoos that Flyn is German and not Chinese and try to act like a lady.

I decide on option three. I think Eric would be upset by options one and two.

"Flyn isn't adopted. And, he's not Chinese; he's Korean German," I say and take a sip of my Coke.

The woman blinks.

"But is he your son or your husband's? It's clear he can't be both of yours because neither of you is Chinese."

Mother of God.

As my father would say, if she were any stupider, she wouldn't have been born!

I give her an Iceman look, and, just when I'm going to hit her with one of my zingers, Flyn takes my hand and makes me go with him.

All right! He just saved me from a real scene.

We go back to where the food is, and a woman my age, a platinum blonde, says hello.

"I'm María."

I respond in my perfect German. "Delighted. I'm Judith."

"The potato omelet is yours?"

"Yes," I say. "The ones with the black olive in the middle also have onion. The other two don't."

"Are you Spanish?"

Well . . . well . . . I have not heard that little question in a long time.

I tell her yes. As I sit down and wait to hear that "olé . . . torero . . . paella" crap, the stranger shouts, as excited as if I were Beyoncé herself.

"I'm Spanish too. From Salamanca!"

Now the one shouting as if she'd seen Paul Walker come back to life is me, and I give her a huge hug. A dishwater-blond man at our side smiles. When we stop hugging each other as if we were sisters, María turns to him.

"Let me introduce you to Alger, my husband."

I'm about to give him two kisses when I stop myself. Germans are not that much into kissing or Latin-style touching, so I just hold out my hand.

"Please, give me those two Spanish kisses, which I like so much better," he says.

I laugh and land two kisses like two suns on his cheeks.

"I love your perpetual joy."

Suddenly, my private German appears next to me. I'm sure he's seen me kiss the blond and he's come quick to see who it is. Oh, my jealous guy.

"My love, let me introduce you to María, who is Spanish too, and Alger, her husband," I say as I put my arms around his waist.

My sweetheart, who knows the Latin way, gives her two kisses and offers him his hand. The two Germans smile.

"What good choices we made," he says to Eric as he appraises us.

"The best."

I talk to María for a long while. She tells me she fell in love with Alger one summer in Salamanca, and that the German didn't stop courting her until he got her to marry him.

I see people devour my omelet in a matter of minutes. That gives me great satisfaction.

Drinking so many Cokes makes me want to pee so I urgently search for the bathroom. When I return to the gym, I find the cockatoos surrounding Flyn.

What are they doing to that child?

I approach stealthily and hear Flyn say, "The omelets were made by Judith, who's Spanish."

Wow, they're getting info out of him. And then I hear their next questions: Who's your mom or dad? Are you related to him or to her?

What?

My blood boils.

I have a Latin temper that my father says I need to learn to control.

My God, give me the patience to know how to deal with this, or I'll eat them alive!

How can they ask a child such a question?

Flyn is silent. He doesn't know what to say, but I'm ready so I go up like a wolf in defense of her pup and lean toward Flyn, who gives me a strange look.

"What's going on here, honey?" I ask.

The cockatoos are silent; then the queen comes out swinging.

"We asked who his biological parent is, if it's you or your husband."

Option one: Do I smack her, yes or yes?

Option two: I tear off her head and bury it somewhere deep and dark.

Option three: there is no option three.

Flyn, who knows me, sees my face and winces.

"Don't worry, honey. I've got this," I say. Without moving from his side, I ask, "Will you please go get me a Coke? I'm going to need it."

I give him a gentle push, and, when he walks away, I turn to them, feeling murderous.

"Aren't you ashamed to ask a child something like that? How would you like to have your children cornered by a gang of gossips?" They're uncomfortable. They know I'm right. "Not that it's your business, but I'll tell you I'm Flyn's mother, and my husband is his father, OK?" The women nod their heads. Before leaving, I ask, "Any more indiscreet questions?"

They don't say a word. They don't move.

Suddenly, I feel a hand grab mine and squeeze.

Flyn!

Oh God . . . he heard what I said. He hands me a Coke, and we walk away while I think about what to say. Poor Flyn. He drinks and looks at me with a strange expression.

C'mon, Jude . . . C'mon . . . Think . . . think!

His penetrating gaze is killing me. I put the Coke on the table and decide to face up to what I've done.

"You and I know Hannah is and will always be your mom for your whole life, right?"

Flyn nods.

"Well, now that that's clear, I want you to know that, from this moment on, and especially as far as those cockatoos are concerned, especially those really rude ones whose beaks I haven't torn out of respect for you, Eric and I are your parents, understood?"

He nods again as the newly named dad comes up.

"What's going on?"

I snort.

"I just officially declared you Flyn's dad and named myself as his mom."

Eric looks at the boy and then at me.

Then at him again and at me again.

I raise my hands. "Don't look at me like that; it feels like you're going to tear me apart."

"Jude," asks Flyn, "do I have to call you Mom?"

Oh God . . . oh God . . . Why am I such a loudmouth?

The boy's mother may be in heaven, but he has one, and I just stuck my foot in it.

Eric doesn't react.

"Flyn, you can call me whatever you want." Then I point to the women, who haven't stopped staring, and I speak in perfect Spanish so Eric and Flyn understand me. "But starting today, if those witches want something from you, let them first come talk to your mom or dad, understood? Because if I find out again they're asking you any indiscreet questions, as my sister Raquel would say, I swear by the blessed glory of my mother in heaven that I'll go for my father's ham knife and cut off their heads."

I take a sip of my Coke.

"OK, but don't get mad, Aunt-Mom Jude."

Eric surprises me and smiles and strokes the boy's head.

"Flyn has always known I'm his dad for whatever he needs, right?"

The kid nods and hugs me around the waist.

"And now I know Aunt Jude is my mom."

My eyes fill with tears. I'm such a softie!

Eric hugs and kisses me on the lips.

"I'll tell you again: you're the best thing I've ever had in my life," he says.

19

Three days later, I'm not feeling so great again.

I must be catching the cold Flyn has had.

My head hurts, and I just want to sleep, sleep, and sleep.

But I can't. Frida called yesterday because she wants to see us. She and Andrés have something to tell us, and, because of her tone, I think it must be something very exciting. She told me she had also invited Björn to come over. I take an acetaminophen and wait for them.

Laila's in the kitchen when I take the pill.

"Are you not feeling well?"

My relationship with her isn't cold but frozen.

"No."

She nods.

"By the way, some friends are coming over this afternoon and—"

"Oh, who?"

Her interest bothers me. What does she care?

"Friends of mine and Eric's," I say, hoping she'll take the hint. "I'd appreciate it if you gave us some privacy while they're here."

Could I be any clearer?

She doesn't like what I said.

"I'll go pick up Flyn," she volunteers.

"No, please," I say. "Norbert will go."

"Then I'll go with him."

An hour later, the first to arrive is Björn, as handsome as ever. We give each other a hug, and, grabbing him by the arm, I pull him into the living room. Out of the corner of my eye, I notice Laila watching us from the kitchen.

I close the sliding door.

"You OK? You don't look so good."

"I think Flyn gave me his cold."

"You should be in bed, beautiful," says Björn, smiling.

"I know, but I want to know what Frida and Andrés have to tell us."

"If they don't get here soon, I'll put you in bed myself, understood?"

I smile again and give him a punch on the shoulder.

Ten minutes later, Frida and Andrés arrive with little Glen, who's already running around and is a mess. The last to arrive is Eric who, seeing us all together, smiles and kisses me.

"Are you OK, sweetheart?"

"I'm somewhat congested. I think Flyn gave me his cold."

After eyeing me with concern, he greets his friends and takes Glen in his arms to kiss his neck. The boy starts laughing, and I get itchy when my husband looks up meaningfully. I get the message; I get it.

Twenty minutes later, Flyn comes home from school. Seeing him, Björn hugs him tight, and, as with Glen, we all make him the focus of our attention for a while. The kid loves that.

When Simona brings us a pitcher of lemonade and beers, she insists on taking Glen and Flyn to give them a snack. She disappears with the two kids, and we all sit on the couch. Björn keeps getting text messages.

"Well, what is it that you have to tell us?" I ask.

Frida and Andrés look at each other and grin.

"Don't tell me you're expecting another baby," I say.

"Congratulations!" says Eric. "We're next!"

"Sure, Iceman," I laugh, amused.

Frida and Andrés let out a laugh and shake their heads.

"We're moving to Switzerland," says Frida.

"What?"

Frida takes my hands. "It's a good opportunity for Andrés," she explains.

"Is that the offer you've been waiting for?" Eric asks.

Andrés nods.

"That's fantastic," says Björn. "Congratulations."

While they congratulate him, Frida tells me she and Andrés are excited about this new challenge in their lives. I nod like a bobblehead, despite the sadness I feel.

"Thank you, my friends," Andrés says with a laugh. "I'd forgotten about it, until a week ago, when they called and made the offer. After I discussed it with Frida, we decided to accept."

Everyone is happy.

And, suddenly, my eyes fill with tears.

Frida is my great friend, and I don't want them to leave.

"Are you all right?" she asks me.

I nod, but the tears keep falling. I can't control them.

What's wrong with me? Why am I crying like this?

Seeing me in such a state, Eric takes me in his arms.

"Sweetheart, what's the matter?"

I don't answer. I can't do it. I'll look like a chimpanzee and even more ridiculous. Touched by the hiccups that are now assaulting me, Björn gives me a squeeze.

"Incredible . . . You cry too."

That makes me laugh. But I keep crying even as I laugh.

"I'm glad Björn makes you smile," Eric says.

"Learn, my friend!" Björn says in jest.

Frida hugs me. She understands what's happening to me.

"We'll see you a lot, silly girl. You'll see. And, in any case, we're not leaving until the beginning of the year. There is still a bit of time left."

I nod, but I can't speak. Once more, someone I love will be far from me. I know I'll miss her very much.

Time passes and the long-awaited day of Laila's departure arrives, although that means Eric is also leaving.

I don't like that he's going to London, but I've decided to put jealousy aside and trust him. Eric deserves it. He shows me his love in such a way that, honestly, who am I to distrust him?

I go with them to the airport. Norbert takes us, and I hug my husband all the way there. I love his smell, I love his touch, and, as we get closer to our destination, I become anguished. Four days without seeing him is an eternity for me.

When we arrive, Eric gets out of the car first.

"It's been a pleasure to meet you," Laila tells me.

"I can't say the same," I reply. "And, if possible, please avoid coming back to our home at all costs, or I'll have to tell Eric you're not so good or so charming."

"Björn is a loudmouth."

"And you're a bitch."

There, I told her!

What a distinct pleasure!

Without answering, she gets out of the car and walks toward her uncle. It'll be a relief to have her out of my sight. She says goodbye to Norbert, and I notice she gets on the plane without looking back. After greeting the pilot, Eric returns to the car and embraces me.

"In four days at most, I'll be back at your side, OK?"

I nod. I convince myself and kiss him. I devour him as he presses against me.

"If you keep kissing me like that, you're not going anywhere."

Eric lets go and winks at me before heading up the stairs to the plane.

"Be good, sweetheart," he says.

"You too, big guy."

Twenty minutes later, I'm sitting with Norbert as we watch the plane take off. Eric disappears from view.

On the way home, I'm sad; I miss him already.

"Ma'am, Mr. Zimmerman asked me to give you this when we got home," Norbert says, handing me an envelope.

I quickly tear it open.

> *Sweetheart,*
> > *It'll only be a few days. Trust me, OK?*
> > *I love you.*
> > *Eric*

I smile immediately. I love these little gestures.

After dinner that night, Flyn takes Calamar to bed. I stay in the living room, watching TV with Susto at my feet. I'm hit by a wave of melancholia and—I can't help it—my eyes begin to tear up. I really miss him.

Finally, I decide to call. I need to hear his voice. He picks up on the fourth ring.

"Yes, Jude."

"I miss you."

I hear him excusing himself.

"Love, I'm at a business dinner."

"But I miss you."

His warm laugh when he hears me makes me feel good.

"Go to bed and read something, or play with something in your special drawer and think of me," he says.

"I'm still going to miss you," I say.

Eric laughs again.

"I have to hang up, sweetheart. But in an hour, I'll call you on Skype from my hotel room, and, if you want . . . we can play."

Oooh, webcam sex?

How intense!

I've never experienced that.

"I'll wait anxiously for your call," I say, excited. "In the meantime, I'll read."

Knowing I'm going to talk to him soon lifts my spirits. When I hang up, it's quarter to ten.

I turn off the television, give Susto a kiss on the head, and am about to go to my room when I stop to check in on Flyn. He's asleep with Calamar at his feet. They're beautiful!

I lock the door to my room.

I'm waiting for a hot, sexy, and kinky call. I brush my teeth, put on a suggestive nightgown, and get into the huge bed. It's so expansive when Eric's not here. Suddenly, I can smell him. The sheets. Wonderful!

I let myself fall on the side where my love sleeps, and I enjoy being surrounded by his aroma.

After I get my fill, I open my laptop and go on Facebook. I talk to my friends, the Warriors, until Skype lets me know I have a call. I say goodbye to them and accept the call. The camera connects, and I see my love.

"Hi, honey."

"Hello, beautiful."

It's so strange to see Eric on a screen. I want him by my side.

"How are you, sweetheart?"

"All right, now that I can see you."

We both smile.

"I'm naked and willing to play," he says as he leans back on the bed. "C'mon, undress for me."

Laughing, I take off my nightgown.

"Close your eyes. Don't look at the screen and imagine that two other men and I are looking at you. We're standing around the bed, and we want to possess you, although we want to look at you first. Do you like the idea?"

"Yes."

He knows I'll get wet just thinking about it.

"Touch your nipples. We like that. Pinch them for us."

I pinch myself as he asks, while my imagination flies and flies, and I feel a pleasant and strange pain. Imagining being the focus of three men provokes me. I want them to want me; I want them to play with me. Hearing Eric's breathing, I open my eyes.

"Touch yourself, Eric. Stroke your cock as if it were me who was doing it."

He does as I say. I watch. His penis is hard and smooth, just as I like it.

"Are you enjoying how those men are looking at me?"

"Yes."

"Do you like how I open my legs for them?"

I hear him gasp.

"I love it, baby . . . Open them a little more and flex them."

I do, and, excited to hear the noises coming from the screen, I focus on his pleasure.

"Touch yourself. Close your eyes and imagine you're offering me to one of those men. Do you like the idea?"

"Yes. Yes . . ."

I take a breath while my blond boy plays.

"He fucks me . . . And I gasp. He penetrates me while you kiss me; then you bite my lips the way you like, and I moan."

"Yes, Jude . . . Go on . . . Go on."

"The man lies down on the bed and asks me to get on top of him. He takes my nipples in his mouth and spanks me so I'll squeeze up against him. Then you spank me too." We both huff. "Now his fingers play inside me. You put yours inside me too, and I'm yours all over again."

"Yes, sweetheart . . . Yes."

"He brings his fingers out, opens my legs urgently, and rams into me. I scream. You stand behind me, grab me by the waist, and move me . . . begging me not to stop fucking and not to stop screaming."

For a while we dedicate ourselves to getting as hot as we can. I use my words to bring him to orgasm. Hearing his gruff groan drives me crazy. I want to kiss him, touch him, but I'm frustrated because I can't.

"My love, is everything OK?"

Eric moves on the bed and mutters while cleaning himself with a tissue.

"Have you ever done this before?" he asks.

I laugh.

"It's my first time. I think you're my first in many things."

We both laugh and continue our game.

"Open the nightstand drawer," says Eric. "Put our toys on the bed and show them to me."

I do what he asks.

"Let's play with the green gel dildo with the suction cup. Stick it on the small table in front of the fireplace. Then come back to bed."

Excited, I do as he asks. I get up, lick the suction cup, and press it on the side of the table. It sticks right out in front of me. I go back to bed and tell him it's ready.

"Now I want you to get the violet dildo for your clitoris."

"I've got it."

"Great . . . Now open your legs." His tone gets more intimate and low. "More . . . more . . . A little more . . . Like that."

"Close your eyes and touch yourself for me. Give me everything, sweetheart. Put that violet dildo on the tip of your clitoris and go gently, so your clitoris swells up like I like."

I do as he instructs, and, with my legs apart, I carefully place the device on my clitoris. My body responds immediately.

"Enjoy it . . . Like that . . . Like that . . . Now up the speed once, then again . . ."

The feeling and my breathing both get so intense.

My love, my German, my husband, knows what I like and what I need even thousands of miles away.

"Turn it up a little higher, Jude," he says.

I scream. I'm drenched. My clitoris is swollen, and I want more.

"Don't close your legs . . . No . . . no, sweetheart," he murmurs. "Squeeze the dildo against you and enjoy it . . . I want to see your wetness . . . C'mon, let me see you come."

My body tenses. I want to close my legs, but I obey. I want him to see how I come and how wet I get. The violet dildo at top speed is fantastic, and my clitoris blooms second by second. A bolt of heat runs through my body and goes to my head.

"Sweetheart . . . don't close your legs. Good . . . good . . . Hold on a bit more."

I convulse and my legs close as pleasure runs through me. In that moment, my love demands I keep going without rest.

"Now I want you to fuck me, Jude. Get up and fuck me."

I know what he wants. I get up urgently, my eyes glazed with lust, pick up the laptop, and take it to the green gel penis. I put the laptop on the little table and check the perspective I'm offering him. Then I impale myself on the dildo.

"I'm on top of you."

"Yes, sweetheart . . . Yes . . ."

"Like that? You like it like that?" I whisper, while the gel penis goes in and out of me.

"Yes," he answers as he jerks off. "I feel you, sweetheart . . . Do you feel me?"

I watch him.

"Yes . . ."

"Press down more and hold on to the edge of the table."

I moan the more I squeeze against the dildo while my love encourages me.

"C'mon, darling. Fuck me; enjoy it."

Clutching the table, I bite my lower lip while my hips rise and fall on the green gel dick. I close my eyes and feel my Iceman's gaze. His hands encircle my waist and help me up and down. Again and again I push myself up and down while Eric tells me how much he likes it . . . how much he's enjoying it.

"Oh yes, yes . . ."

My fluids soak the gel. I'm breathing like a locomotive. I'm drenched and pant and pant until I can't take it anymore. After one last penetration that reaches my deepest core, I finally come.

I'm still trembling when I hear my love tell me a hundred wonderful things. I feel his breath on my mouth. I want him. I adore him. I love everything I do with him, and I want to keep learning.

"Everything OK?" Eric asks after our breathing stabilizes.

"Yes."

I giggle.

"All right, sweetheart; let's go to bed."

I take the still wet dildo from inside me, pick up the laptop, and throw myself in bed.

"Thank you, love."

Eric laughs.

"There's nothing to thank me for, sweetheart."

"Rest, darling. It's late."

"OK."

"We'll talk tomorrow?"

"I love you."

"I love you more, sweetheart."

"Nope, me more."

"Me," he insists, chuckling.

"All right, say good night."

"You say good night first," he says, grinning.

After five minutes of laughter during which we behave like two teenagers, we finally say good night and sign off at the same time.

I'm exhausted, satisfied, and wet. Our toys are scattered all around the bed, but I decide to put an end to the orgy. I get up and put away those I didn't use. I go to the little table and pull the dildo. Wow, I enjoyed that. I take it and the violet dildo to the bathroom and wash them. When everything is clean, I put them away.

So tired, I unlock the door, lie down, and fall asleep on Eric's pillow. It smells like him.

20

The next morning, I open my eyes and feel an irrepressible urge to vomit.

I run to the bathroom just in time. I've definitely caught Flyn's bug.

With a sour stomach and a sore throat, I go back to bed. I sleep like a log.

"Judith, aren't you going to get up today?" I hear Simona asking.

I raise my head.

"What time is it?"

"Are you OK?"

I nod. I don't want to scare her or for her to call Eric. I look at the clock: eleven thirty in the morning.

Crap.

Simona won't take her eyes off me.

"I stayed up reading last night, and now I can't seem to stay awake."

"C'mon, sleepyhead. I made churros for you, but they'll be cold."

When the door closes, my stomach contracts, and I run back to the bathroom. I'm in there a good while, and then I go right back to bed. Suddenly, I think about the churros, and I get nauseous. The mere thought of them makes me want to die. I get up. Since when do churros disgust me?

I'm dizzy.

I look in the mirror, and, out of nowhere, I remember that when my sister was pregnant, she was also disgusted by churros. My stomach flips over again, and I bring my hands to my head.

"No . . . no . . . no . . . It can't be."

My mind is blocked, my stomach goes nuts again, and I run to the bathroom.

Ten minutes later, I'm lying on the floor, my feet resting on the sink. Everything is spinning around me. I just realized I haven't had my period in longer than I would like.

I need air.

I think I'm going to have a heart attack.

When I finally get my head to stop spinning, I put my feet on the floor and sit up. I look at myself in the mirror.

"Please . . . please . . . I can't be pregnant," I moan pitifully.

My neck itches.

My God, I have a rash!

I scratch and scratch, but I have to stop. I can't help myself, and I scratch again!

I go back to bed. I open the drawer on my nightstand and check my pillbox. I'm horrified to realize it's been several days since I took the last one. I remember my last period was barely there. I was surprised, but I know I was taking the pill.

Oh God . . . oh God!

I curse and throw a little tantrum. I've been so busy with everything lately, I didn't realize what was happening. I open the pill leaflet and read that the margin of error is 0.001 percent.

I'm so unlucky that I'm going to be that tiny percentage?

I lie back on the bed and close my eyes. Eric's smell comes to me, and I love it. When I finally pull myself together, I get dressed and decide to go to a pharmacy. This is urgent!

"Don't eat the cold churros, Judith," Simona says when she sees I'm downstairs. "Wait and I'll get you some food. By the way, *Emerald Madness* starts in fifteen minutes. I'm going to leave these shirts for Mr. Zimmerman in your room. Then we can watch it together, OK?"

I nod and walk right past her.

"Is something the matter, Judith?"

"Nothing. Why?"

"You're pale," she says.

Oh Mother of God, if she only knew!

"I stayed up reading until four in the morning. I missed Eric."

Simona smiles. "Don't worry, Judith. He'll be back the day after tomorrow at the latest."

As soon as she disappears up the stairs, I go to the kitchen. The churros are on the table.

To prove to myself they don't disgust me, I throw myself at them. I gobble away, and my stomach keeps still. That relaxes me for an instant. But I'm a wreck, and I shove seven churros down my throat until my stomach rebels and I have to rush out of the kitchen.

I run into Simona on the way, and she follows me. Easy and sanguine, she does what my mother did so many times when I was little. She holds my head while my body expels absolutely everything.

I'm so disgusted with myself!

When I finally relax, I'm covered by a horrible cold sweat. I let Simona guide me by the hand to the kitchen.

"You're pale . . . very pale," she says.

I don't say a thing. I can't.

I don't want to talk about what's happening to me but, suddenly, Simona fixes her eyes on the plate of churros.

"How are you not going to throw up with all the churros you've eaten?"

I nod.

I don't want to explain anything.

"I was so hungry, I ate them in a rush, and I think my stomach got angry at me."

She prepares some tea and asks me to drink it so my stomach will calm down.

Gross!

I hate tea.

But Simona insists, and I listen to her. Otherwise she'll call Eric. Ten minutes later, I'm feeling like me again, and color returns to my face.

I turn on the TV and we watch *Emerald Madness*. But I'm not following it. My thoughts are elsewhere. And Simona is oblivious.

"Poor little Esmeralda," she says when the episode concludes. "All her life suffering and now her love doesn't recognize her and falls in love with the hospital nurse. How sad . . . How sad."

When she leaves, and I'm alone in the kitchen, I decide to go to the pharmacy. I tell Simona I'm not going to be home for lunch. I need to go out and get some air. I grab my red anorak, go to the garage, and get in the Mitsubishi. Eric's scent is all over me again.

"If I'm pregnant, I'm going to kill you, Mr. Zimmerman."

I start to drive aimlessly while the music plays in the car, but I can't even sing.

I can't believe this is happening to me. I'm a disaster as a person; how can I have a child?

I park the car near Bogenhausen and decide to take a walk through the English Garden. It's cold. In Munich it gets cold as hell in November. As I think and walk, I pass a beer bike, the city's star attraction. I notice the driver is drinking beer and having fun while pedaling. My stomach turns. Gross!

I continue my walk and stroll past several mothers and their babies.

I don't know how long I've been walking when I realize I'm totally frozen. My anorak isn't warm enough, and, if I go on like this, I'll get pneumonia. As I leave the English Garden, I see a tobacco shop. I head straight to it and buy a pack of cigarettes and a lighter. I light a cigarette, inhale, and enjoy.

I can't be pregnant. It must be a mistake.

I keep walking until I see a pharmacy.

I stare at it from a distance, and, when I finish my smoke, I go in and wait in line. "I want a pregnancy test, please," I say when it's my turn.

"Digital or not digital?" the clerk asks.

"I don't care," I respond.

She opens a drawer and takes out several long, colored boxes.

"Any of these can be taken at any time of the day. This is digital; this is ultrasensitive . . ."

For a few minutes, the woman talks and talks, and I just want her to shut up and give me a fucking pregnancy test.

"Although you can take these anytime, I'd recommend you do it with your first morning urine."

I finally look at the packages. What am I doing?

"Which would you like? It's up to you."

I don't know what to say.

"I'll take these," I say, randomly choosing four.

"All of them?"

"All of them," I say.

The clerk smiles, stops asking questions, and puts them in a plastic bag. I give her my card, and, once paid, I leave.

When I get to the car, I open the bag and take out the tests. I read the instructions on all of them; they're all basically the same. I have to pee on the wand—they're 99 percent reliable.

Fuck the percentages.

When I get home, Simona scolds me because I only wore my anorak and for being gone so long. I suddenly realize it's three in the afternoon. The morning has vanished, and I hadn't even noticed.

Simona tells me a worried Eric has called about twenty times, and that he'll call again. I suddenly realize I'm so overwhelmed, I left the house without my cell.

"You didn't tell him what happened to me this morning, did you?"

She shakes her head.

"No, Judith. He was worried enough about not being able to get in touch with you. Besides, I know him, and that would distress him. I didn't tell him anything."

"Thank you," I whisper, and hug her.

Once Simona returns to her chores, I pick up my cell, put it in my pants pocket, and hurry to my room. I lock myself in the bathroom, sit on the toilet, and stare at the package I've placed on the bidet. For several minutes, I tell myself this can't be happening.

I can't be pregnant!

Summoning all my strength, I take out one of the tests.

I unbutton my jeans and lower them and my underwear. I sit back down on the toilet. With trembling hands, I remove the cap on one of the tests. When I finally manage to pee on it (as well as my hand), I cover it back up and place it horizontally on the bathroom countertop.

Once I'm ready and buckled back up, I light a cigarette. But after two drags, I get dizzy. I sit on the floor, then lie down and raise my legs up on the sink.

Mother of God . . . I'm so afraid.

Me, with a baby?

No fucking way!

Ugh . . . I'm so dizzy!

When I think back to Raquel's delivery, I get nauseous. What unbelievable stress!

It's been two minutes and thirty-seven seconds . . . thirty-eight . . . thirty-nine.

I try to sing. That always relaxes me, and our song is the first thing that comes to mind.

I stop singing to myself and look at my watch. Five minutes. I have to look at the results, but I don't have the courage!

I can't open the cap.

I light another cigarette, even at the risk of getting dizzy. I need it. My neck itches.

I can't even sing anymore.

I bring my legs down off the sink.

I grab the package again and reread it for the umpteenth time. If it's two lines, it's positive, and if it's only one, negative.

I want a negative as big as a truck. Please, please . . .

I extinguish the cigarette and try to drum up my courage. I pick up the test and, without thinking about it one more second, look.

"Two lines," I whisper.

I drop the test and pick up the package again. It's right there: two lines, positive. One, negative.

I'm so dizzy . . .

I reread it. Two lines, positive. One, negative.

I lie on the bathroom floor and mutter with my eyes closed. "It can't be; it can't be . . ."

I decide to repeat the test when I remember there's a 1 percent chance of an error. If the contraceptive failed, why can't the pregnancy test fail as well?

I carry out the same operation as before. Again I hope and pray, this time without a cigarette. Five minutes later, I check again.

"Nooooooo."

I do a third test. A fourth. The result is the same: positive.

My heart is going a thousand beats a minute. I'm going to have a heart attack, and, when Eric comes back, I'll be stiffer than a piece of tuna jerky on the bathroom floor.

I think about the margin of error on these tests. But it seems that after four of them, there's little room for doubt.

I'm getting dizzy again . . .

Everything's spinning . . .

I lie on the floor and put my feet up on the sink again.

"Why? Why does this have to happen to me?"

Suddenly, my cell rings. I take it out of my jeans pocket and see it's Eric. The baby's father!

Ugh . . . my nerves.

I'm so warm and I fan myself with my hand.

I don't want him to think I sound strange so, after six rings, I greet him as cheerfully as I can.

"Hi, my love."

"How could you leave the house without your cell? Are you nuts?" he asks in a tense voice.

I'm not up for this.

"First: don't scream at me. Second: I forgot. And third: if you're going to call me just to be a jerk, be prepared because I can be one too."

Silence.

"Where have you been, Jude?"

"I went to buy some sundries, and then I took a walk because—"

"A very long walk, don't you think?" he asks, cutting me off. "Alone or with company?"

"Where's that coming from?"

"Alone or with company?" His voice is even edgier.

What's going on? But before I can ask, the call drops.

I stare at the phone like a fool.

Did he hang up on me?

Did that dickhead hang up on me?

Furious, I dial his number. Now he's going to find out what it means to raise your voice. But as soon as it rings, he hangs up without picking up. That enrages me. I try three more times, but the result is the same.

I'm hysterical, nervous, and—to make matters worse—pregnant!

If I could get my hands on Eric right now, I'd kill him!

I don't know what to do and decide to swim a few laps. I need to do something.

I put on my swimsuit, and, when I reach the edge of the pool, my stomach flips over, and I run to the bathroom.

When Flyn comes home, I'm sitting at the edge of the water, totally out of my mind. The boy hugs me from behind and kisses me on the cheek. Delighted by that display of affection, I close my eyes.

"Thanks, sweetie. I needed that."

The kid, who is very smart, sits next to me.

"What did you talk about with my uncle?"

"Nothing, sweetie. He's in London, and it's hard to have a discussion at such a distance."

The boy looks at me and nods but doesn't say anything. He's drawing his own conclusions. Suddenly, my stomach gurgles.

"What do you have in there, an alien?"

I laugh and can't stop.

Everything is surreal again.

I'm pregnant, and Eric, the man who should be by my side, kissing me like crazy because he's going to be a father, is angry.

"Let's have dinner, or I'll have to eat you up right now," I say.

When Flyn goes to bed, I'm alone again in the huge living room, accompanied only by Susto. I gesture for him to climb on the couch. Now that Eric isn't here, he takes advantage of me.

I call Eric. He doesn't pick up. Why is he so angry? I turn on the TV, but, after a while, I have a need to tell someone what's wrong. I touch Susto and he raises his head.

"I'm pregnant, Susto. We're going to have a little Zimmerman Flores."

He seems to understand and lies down again, covering his eyes with one of his paws. That makes me laugh. Even he knows this is crazy.

At eleven o'clock, seeing that Eric isn't calling me back, I decide to go up to our room. I drag myself up the stairs. In the bathroom, I brush my teeth and see the pack of cigarettes. I throw it in the trash at the exact moment my cell rings. Eric at last!

"Hi, honey," I say, without the slightest urge to argue.

There's a lot of background noise where he's at.

"When were you going to tell me?"

Surprised, I sit on the toilet. I look around for the hidden camera. Does he know I'm pregnant?

"What?"

"You know very well what I'm talking about."

"No, I don't . . ."

"Yes, you do!" he shouts.

I'm disconcerted. If he was talking about my pregnancy, he wouldn't be so angry. Eric's drunk. It's the first time he's been drunk since we've been together and that worries me.

"Where are you, Eric?"

"Out drinking."

"Are you with Amanda?"

He laughs. I don't like this laugh.

"No, I'm not with Amanda. I'm alone."

"Eric," I say, not raising my voice, "can you tell me what's going on? I don't understand a thing and—"

"Have you seen Björn today?"

"What?"

"Don't play innocent, sweetheart. I know you."

"What is *wrong* with you?" I cry, desperate now.

"I don't know how I didn't figure it out before." He raises his voice. "My best friend and my wife, shacking up!"

Has he gone mad?

Besides drunk, he's out of his mind! Once more, the communication is cut off.

I don't understand anything and call him back. He won't pick up. My nerves are making my stomach queasy, and, in the end, what happens, happens. Goodbye, dinner.

I don't sleep. I just want to know he's OK. I've never heard him so drunk. I'm worried something will happen to him, but no matter how many times I call, he won't pick up. I send several emails. I know he'll see them. But he doesn't answer them either.

I think about Björn. Should I call him and tell him what happened? I ultimately decide not to. It's five o'clock in the morning, and I don't think it's the time for that.

At six thirty, after a horrible night unable to get through to Eric, I'm in the kitchen. Simona comes in and is surprised to see me.

"What are you doing up so early?"

My face falls, and I begin to cry. She's completely thrown off. She sits next to me, and, like a mother, wipes my tears with a napkin while I talk and talk, but Simona doesn't understand any of it.

I keep the pregnancy to myself but explain clearly what happened with Eric. She's puzzled. She knows I love and adore my German like few people in the world, and that Björn is just a great friend to the two of us.

At eight o'clock, she goes to wake Flyn, and at half past eight, when the kid comes down and sees my deplorable state, he sits next to me.

"You argued with my uncle, right?"

This time I nod. I can't deny it.

"Whatever it is, I'm sure my uncle is in the wrong," he says, surprising both Simona and me.

"Flyn . . ."

"You are a very good mom," he insists.

I burst into tears again. He called me Mom. There is no stopping me anymore.

After Simona serves Flyn breakfast, and Norbert comes to take him to school, I decide to go with them. The air will be good for me. On the way, my little man grabs my hand and doesn't let go. As always, that gives me strength. It amuses me when he kisses me before getting out of the car so no one can see him. When he finally goes on his way, I ask Norbert to wait a second so I can get out of the vehicle.

I need air.

I take a small card from my pocket, and, after staring at it, make the decision to call. The doctor gives me the number for a private gynecologist. I immediately get an appointment for the next day. The good thing about having money is that everything is at your disposal. It's the same as Social Security in Spain. When María, my new Spanish friend, sees me, she notices the dark circles under my eyes.

"Are you OK, Judith?"

I nod and smile.

I'm not the kind of person to go telling my sorrows to everyone. But then I notice something strange in her eyes.

"What's going on?" I ask.

She sighs. She hesitates, but finally confesses.

"I'm not comfortable telling you what I'm going to tell you, but if I don't, I won't be able to sleep." She points at the cockatoos a few yards from us. "Your friends, those who claim to appreciate you so much, are doing a number on you. They're saying terrible things about you."

"About me? But they don't know me!"

María nods.

"What happened? Tell me."

"They say you're involved with your husband's friend, a guy named Björn."

The earth trembles under my feet, and a phrase suddenly comes to mind from a song by Alejandro Sanz that I like so much: "You see, there are no two without three."

What the hell is going on?

I'm pregnant, Eric thinks I'm involved with Björn, and now they're talking about it at Flyn's school.

I'm shaking . . .

"Besides that," María continues, "they're making fun of you because you were Eric's secretary, and, well, you can imagine."

I'm utterly aghast.

"Actually, I worked for Eric's company, but . . . but I'm not cheating on my husband, not with Björn or anyone else. I just got married about four months ago. I love Eric, I'm happy and . . . and . . ."

María hugs me and I close my eyes. My nerves are at a peak when I notice the cockatoos staring at us and smiling. What a bunch of bitches. And then my blood boils, and I recover as quickly as a tsunami.

"Since when is that rumor circulating?"

"I heard it yesterday for the first time."

"And it came from those cockatoos, right?"

María nods. I raise my chin, and, not thinking twice, I head directly toward them. I thought I had made things clear, but since they don't seem to get it, I'm going to have to repeat myself.

I don't care if I come off like a slut.

I don't care if they think I'm the worst.

Nothing matters to me except that they stop telling lies about me.

"I don't like you, and you don't like me. We both know that, right?" I say to the lead cockatoo. She doesn't move; she's cowering. "Well, I want you to know I like you spreading rumors about me even less. Therefore, if you don't want to have a serious problem with me, tell me who's the goddamn person talking shit about me, or I swear you're going to lose some teeth today," I hiss right into the lead cockatoo's face—Joshua's wife, I believe. My face is right up to hers when I see Norbert exit the car out of the corner of my eye.

"Judith," whispers María. She's embarrassed.

The lead cockatoo turns as red as a tomato. Her little friends step back. They're leaving her on her own. Now that's friendship!

Seeing she's been left with no support, she tries to get away from me, but I won't allow it. I grab her arm forcefully.

"I told you to tell me who's telling you those lies."

She's scared and trembling. "The . . . the young woman who sometimes comes to pick up the little Chinese boy."

I close my eyes: Laila!

My blood boils, and I suddenly understand everything. Laila has been poisoning Eric in London. I open my eyes.

"My son has a name. It's Flyn." I let her go. "And, for the last time, he is not Chinese! And, yes, I worked for my husband's company, and, of course, I'm not involved with Björn. For your own good, I hope that rumor dies, or I swear I'm going to make your life impossible. Understood?"

"Mrs. Zimmerman, what's wrong?" Norbert asks.

The cockatoos quickly move away in terror.

Poor María is on the verge of fainting.

"Thank you for telling me, María. I'll see you another time."

Norbert's disconcerted because he knows I'm about to collapse.

"Take me home, please," I tell him. "I don't feel well."

21

When I get home, I throw up.

Between crying and vomiting, I can't catch a break!

Worried about me, Simona offers one of her infusions, but I reject it. The smell alone makes it worse. She should call Eric so at least I'll know what's going on with him.

My head explodes, and she makes me lie down. Exhausted, I fall asleep. When I wake up a couple of hours later, I'm angry, very angry, and I call Eric. He picks up on the third ring.

Hallelujah!

"Talk to me."

"No, you'd better talk to me, dickhead!"

"It's been so long since I've heard that sweet word out of your mouth," he says, dripping with sarcasm. "It's a pity not to be able to see it live and in person."

He's drunk again. But I want to stay focused.

"How can you be such a dickhead that you believe Laila?"

I notice his breathing changes. He must be tired.

"And how do you know Laila said anything?"

"Because news flies faster than you think," I reply coldly.

Silence.

A tense silence.

It's killing me.

"I haven't talked to my good friend Björn yet. I'll wait to chat with him face to face, but—"

"You don't have to talk to him about any of this, because nothing has ever happened between us. Björn is your best friend and a great guy. I don't know how you can distrust him, how you can believe there's anything between him and me other than friendship."

I quickly identify the bar sounds behind him.

"Oh, Judith, how you defend him. How tender," Eric says.

"I defend him because you don't know what you're talking about."

"Maybe I know too much."

"What do you know? Tell me!" I cry. "Because, as far as I know, he and I have only been together with your consent and, more than anything else, under your supervision."

"Are you sure, Judith?" he asks in a tone that baffles me.

"I'm sure, Eric. Very sure."

You can cut the tension with a knife.

"Where are you?"

"Out drinking. It's the best thing I can do to forget."

"Eric . . ."

"What a disappointment. I thought you were unique and unrepeatable, but—"

"Don't tell me again what you once told me that caused our breakup," I exclaim. "Hold your tongue, you damned dickhead, or I swear to you—"

"Or you swear what?"

His voice, his tone, tell me he's beside himself.

"I don't understand how you can believe such a thing," I say, trying to calm him. "You know I love you."

"I have evidence," he says furiously. "I have evidence, and neither of you will be able to deny it."

I understand less with each passing minute. "Proof? What possible proof could you have?" I scream at him.

"I don't want to talk to you right now, Judith."

"You can't just accuse me and—"

"Not now." He cuts me off again. "And, by the way, my trip is going to take longer. I won't be going home this week. I don't want to see you."

Then he hangs up. He hangs up on me again.

I'm about to scream, but instead, I throw myself on the bed and cry.

I don't have the strength for anything else. When I calm down, I take a shower. Then I go to the kitchen, but there's nobody there. I see a note from Simona.

We're at the supermarket.

Susto and Calamar come and beg for cuddles. They're very intuitive and seem to understand how I'm feeling; they follow me for a moment. In the living room, I head to the music corner and look through several CDs. I put on the one I know is going to hurt me the most. I'm that masochistic, and, when "Si Nos Dejan" begins to play, I cry all over again, remembering that, just a few days ago, I danced to this song with Eric.

When it's over, I play it again. I walk toward the window with my face wet and my heart aching. It's raining outside, and I wipe my tears while my heart breaks.

Hours later, when Simona returns, I'm calmer, and I'm not crying anymore. I must have used up all the tears for this year.

Oblivious to what's going on with me, she makes lunch, and, when ready, she calls me to the table, but I barely eat. I'm not hungry.

But Simona's smart and knows I'm suffering. She tries to talk to me, but I don't want to talk. I can't. Eventually, she gives up.

When Flyn comes home from school in the afternoon, I try to welcome him with a big smile. He doesn't deserve to live with the anguish of seeing me depressed all the time.

I try to make the best of it. I help with his homework and have dinner with him. We talk about video games. After he goes to bed, I stay in the living room and am tempted to play some of our songs. There are so many, I know any one will make me cry again. Suddenly, Norbert and Simona burst in.

"I don't believe anything my niece Laila said at school," says Norbert, "and I assure you this will be cleared up. I'm very sorry for everything, ma'am."

I get up and hug him. He remains stiff as a stick whenever I show him love, but, this time, he hugs me back.

"I will do everything possible to set things straight," he whispers in my ear.

I nod and sigh.

"That girl is a liar, and I'm going to rip her head off if she doesn't set the record straight with everyone," says an angry Simona as she rubs her hands.

I hug her too.

I'd typically be furious at a moment like this, but I'm in such bad shape, so dizzy, so upset and bewildered, I can only nod and hug.

That night, Eric doesn't call, nor do I call him.

I don't want to think he's still drinking or imagine he ends up in Amanda's bed, but I'm a masochist and torture myself thinking about it and suffer like a fool.

Why am I so stupid?

I don't call Björn either. That he doesn't call me is a good sign. It means Eric hasn't unleashed his fury on him yet. Poor thing; this is so unfair!

The next day, I'm shredded, but I decide to visit my gynecologist anyway. After tricking Norbert so he won't go with me, I take a cab. In the waiting room, I watch the girls next to me.

My neck itches, my guts are churning, and I want to run out of there.

But I don't. I control my impulses and wait, watching several pregnant women hugging their partners.

My God, how can I be pregnant?

When a girl says my name, I get up and follow her to the office. The doctor is a woman a little older than me. She smiles and invites me to sit down. After filling out the forms, I open my bag and drop the four pregnancy tests and their corresponding positive lines on the table.

She looks at me and chuckles. What's so funny?

"Could you tell me the date of your last menses?"

"I haven't gotten it this month. But I remembered I just stained last month. But . . . but . . . I just started taking the pill again a week ago . . . and . . . maybe that wasn't such a great idea . . . but I . . ."

The doctor sees how nervous I am.

"You'll be OK," she says.

I nod.

"Try to remember the date of that period when you only stained."

"I think it was September twenty-second."

She grabs a colored spinning wheel.

"Your due date would be June twenty-ninth."

Oh God . . . this is real!

I answer all her questions as best I can. Then she asks me to lie on a table to get an ultrasound. After lowering my pants, she puts gel on my belly and spreads it around.

I pray to all the saints that there's nothing inside me. But suddenly the doctor stops moving the ultrasound wand. "Here's the heartbeat, Judith, and, because of the size, I'd say you're almost two months along."

I direct my eyes to the screen and see something. Because of its irregular shape and movement, it reminds me of a jellyfish, a medusa.

I think I'm going to have a heart attack!

I can't speak . . .

I can't blink . . . God, I'm drained!

I can only look at that moving blob that seems to say "Danger!"

Since I'm not speaking, the doctor stops moving the wand, and, after pressing a few buttons, we get a piece of paper. When she hands it to me, I see it's a photo. I get excited in a way I never thought possible. I assume that jellyfish shape is a baby, and apparently, like it or not, I'm pregnant!

Before leaving, she makes an appointment for me for a month from now and gives me some pamphlets. I must take folic acid, among other things, and there are some tests I need to do next time.

22

Two days go by, and I still haven't heard a word from Eric.

I'm broken . . .

I whimper and whine and think about how happy Eric would feel if he knew.

I don't tell anyone else. I swallow the problem and try to draw strength from God knows where so I can deal with the painful and disconcerting emotions I'm going through. Of course, my neck is raw.

I take folic acid each morning, and I get scared the first day when I go to the bathroom and see something black, very black, coming out of me. But then I remember this is a possible side effect. For God's sake—disgusting!

I don't go out. I spend the day on the couch or in my bed, dozing like a bear, and when Simona comes in and tells me Björn's on the phone, I almost vomit.

She attributes my discomfort to what's happening with Eric and doesn't ask. Good thing, because I don't want to lie to her.

"Easy, everything will be OK," she says when she hands me the phone.

With a knot in the pit of my stomach that I'm sure, if undone, would loosen a Niagara Falls of tears, I greet him as cheerfully as I can. "Hello, Björn."

"Hello, beautiful, is the boss back yet?"

His tone of voice and the question tell me he doesn't know anything.

"Well, no, handsome," I say. "He called a few days ago and told me the trip is going to be a little longer. Why? Did you want something?"

"There's a private party this weekend at Nacht, and I wanted to know if you're going to go," Björn says with a charming laugh.

"Well, no, he won't be back by then. And you know I won't go alone."

"You'd better not go without your husband!"

Now the one who laughs bitterly is me. If he only knew what Eric's thinking!

We talk for a few more minutes, and, after saying goodbye, I hang up anguished because I'm hiding something from Björn, but I can't tell him. This is a bomb, and when it explodes, I want to be present. I don't want him and Eric to quarrel without me there to mediate. I'm afraid they'll break off their beautiful friendship because of Laila, that slut.

I think about what Björn told me about her and Leonard and how in all that time he kept the secret to not hurt Eric. Now I think it would've been better to hurt him at the time so Laila would've disappeared from our lives and not have caused all this.

What the girl wants is clear: to antagonize Björn and Eric and, in the process, take me down. I can't let her get away with that. But without seeing the evidence Eric says he has, I can't do anything but call her out.

Convinced I want to do that, I ask Simona for Laila's phone number in London. She gives it to me reluctantly, and, after two rings, I hear her voice.

"You're a bad person," I say. "How could you do what you've done?"

Laila lets out a laugh.

"Fuck you, dear Judith. Your perfect world is cracking."

If she were in front of me, I'd rip her head off!

"I hope you know there'll be consequences," I say.

I don't say anything more and hang up before my voice betrays me. And then I cry again. It's what I do best lately.

I haven't seen Eric in ten days, and I need him.

I long for his hugs, his kisses, his glances, and even his grunts. Above all, I need to tell him one of his dreams is going to come true.

He's going to be a dad!

I'm lying in my bed when the phone rings. I quickly answer.

"Hello, Cuchufleta!"

My sister.

I feel a crazy desire to cry, to tell her my secret, but no. I shut up and swallow my tears. I don't want anyone to know about the baby before Eric.

I quickly sit up. Talking to her is sure to make me happy.

"Hi, crazy girl. How are you?"

"Good, Cuchu."

"And the girls?"

"My great girls. Luz is more rebellious every day. Who's she taking after, huh? And Lucía is more clever every day. By the way, Papá says she seems more your daughter than mine. She looks a lot like you. And how are you?"

I think of my favorite German, his grief, and my sadness.

"Good. Flyn's at school and Eric's on a trip, but he'll be back soon."

"Well, well, I know somebody who'll have a great time at the reunion."

I laugh so as not to cry. If she only knew! But my sister brings me joy and good vibes and never more than when she's anxious to tell me something.

"What's up?" I ask.

"Guess!"

"Raquel, no riddles—just tell me!"

"Do you know who's in Spain staying at Sweetheart Villa?" But before I can answer, Raquel shouts it out: "My wild little roll in the hay!"

"No!" I exclaim, amused.

"Yes!" Raquel whispers. "He told me he couldn't stop thinking about me and that he's crazy about my bones."

I blink . . .

"Cuchu, are you there?"

I nod.

"Yes . . . yes . . . It's that you just left me speechless."

"I know. That's how I was yesterday when I opened the door and there was my Mexican paramour, so tall, so handsome, so gallant, with a nice bouquet of white roses in his hands and—"

"Wow, white roses . . . your favorite."

"Yeah, but wait, wait, I still haven't told you the best part. It turns out that when I opened the door, he tells me with all that Mexican heartthrob smoothness, 'Sweetie, if a star were to go out every time I think of you, soon there wouldn't be a single light in the sky.' Ohhhh . . . my God. My God. The only thing missing were the mariachis, but I almost peed my pants, I was so happy."

"Impressive!" I say, laughing like I haven't in days.

Those two!

"It's the most romantic thing that's happened to me, Cuchu. That man is . . . he's . . . different . . . very different, and when he's with me, he makes me feel like a fairy princess. He looks at me intensely, he kisses me with fervor, he touches me with delight, and . . ."

"Whoa, stop. TMI!"

I suddenly feel like I'm watching *Emerald Madness* with my sister and Juan Alberto as protagonists.

"And best of all," she continues in her soft, melodious voice, "when he came over, he went straight to Papá and said, 'Mr. Flores, I have come to formally ask you for your pretty daughter's hand.'"

"Wow, Raquel!"

"Yes!" My sister screams, and I have to pull the phone from my ear.

I have to laugh.

"Are you telling me you're engaged?"

"No."

"But you just told me he asked Papá for your hand."

"He asked Papá, but I took it upon myself to tell him no way."

"What?"

"Ah, Cuchu . . . you should've seen his face when I told him I don't give my hand to anyone, that I already gave it to someone once and now my hand is mine, only mine and no one else's."

I'm stunned. My sister's so weird.

"So, you're not engaged to him?"

"Well, no. I'm a modern woman, and I go out to dinner with who I want and when I want. Moreover, tonight I'm meeting up with Juanín, the guy from the appliance store next to the potato shop, and Juan Alberto is very offended."

"Of course, Raquel, if the poor man comes all the way from Mexico and tells you something romantic about the stars, accompanied by a bouquet of your favorite flowers, and then asks Papá for your hand, what do you expect?"

"Well, too bad if he thinks that just because he comes spouting his sweet words, I have to stop my life and go after him."

"But, Raquel—"

"No way."

"But didn't you say he's special and makes you feel . . ."

"Yes, but I don't ever want to suffer over a man again."

My sister is so right. Suffering over love is the worst.

"Juan Alberto is not Jesús. I'm convinced he wants something serious with you and—"

"I'm scared, OK? I'm scared!"

I understand.

She's gone through a lot, and now she doesn't want to suffer again. But even though I barely know Juan Alberto, I can already tell he's different from my ex-brother-in-law. Juan Alberto has also suffered because of love, and I'm convinced Raquel is what he needs and vice versa.

Still, it's my sister who has to decide.

"It's normal that you're afraid, but not all men are alike. If you're afraid, be careful. But if you don't want to lose Juan Alberto, also be careful what you do or you'll regret it later. Think about what you want and what's going to make you happiest."

"Oh, Cuchu . . . you just told me the same thing Papá told me," she says, then pauses. "Speaking of Papá, he wants to talk to you. Let's talk later. I'm going to the beauty shop to get pretty so I can go to dinner with Juanín."

"Goodbye, crazy girl, and behave yourself," I reply, amused.

Moments later, I hear my father's voice, and I get excited. The tears fall as I cover my mouth so he can't hear me crying. If he knew I was pregnant, he'd be so happy. But if he knew the situation I'm in with Eric, a great sadness would overwhelm him.

"How's my dark-haired girl?"

Fucked . . . very fucked, but I take a breath.

"Good—how are you, Papá?"

He lowers his voice.

"Oh, girl . . . your sister is driving me crazy. And now the Mexican is here too."

"I know, she just told me."

"What do you think?"

I dry my tears.

"Uff, Papá, I don't know what to tell you. It's Raquel who has to decide."

My father laughs.

"I know, but until she does, I'm trapped in crazy town. Although, to be honest, she's been so happy since that man showed up, I think she's already made up her mind."

"And you like her decision?"

"More than eating with my hands, girl," he says with a laugh. "But I'm not going to say squat so she can make up her own mind."

"Yes, Papá, that's best. That way, whether it's good or bad, it's just her decision, hers and hers alone."

We talk for a while longer.

"And Eric?" he asks.

"In London. He'll be back in a few days."

"Sweetheart, your voice is kind of sad. Are you all right?"

How smart is my father?

He could have been a fortune-teller but chose to be a mechanic.

Determined not to alarm him, I answer as calmly as possible.

"All right, Papá. I'm just here waiting for my favorite German's return."

"That's what I want to hear. I love it when my girls are happy." He laughs delightedly.

I laugh too, although my eyes are filled with tears.

"Tell Eric to call me so we can decide when he's going to send the plane to come get us. He told me not to buy tickets, that he'll send his jet so we can spend Christmas together."

"It'll be the first thing I do when I see him, Papá."

Suddenly, I hear a baby cry. It's my niece, Lucía, and my hair stands on end.

Good God, I'm pregnant, and soon I'll have a baby who cries like that too!

I know something nobody knows. For the first time in my life, I'm keeping a secret I only want to tell to the person I love with all my soul.

Once I say goodbye to my father and hang up the phone, I lie down on the bed again.

Suddenly, the bedroom door opens and Simona blurts out, "*Emerald Madness* is starting."

On the screen we see how Luis Alfredo Quiñones, Esmeralda's great love, kisses Lupita Santúñez, the hospital nurse, and Esmeralda watches, desperate, behind a column. Unable to avoid it, I cry. Poor little Esmeralda. So in love and always so many problems. Just like me!

Simona gives me a Kleenex. I soak it within seconds, when Esmeralda Mendoza, devastated by the loss of her love, tells her little son, "Papá loves you!" I cry and cry and can't stop.

When *Emerald Madness* ends and I'm alone in the room again, my cell phone rings. I don't recognize the number.

"Yes?"

"Hello, Judith. This is Amanda."

My jaw drops. Her!

Why is this woman calling me?

"Don't hang up, please. I have something to tell you."

"I don't have anything to say to you."

Just as I'm about to hang up, she says, "Eric's in the hospital."

My breathing stops.

My world is shattered, but I manage to ask in the thinnest voice, "What . . . what happened?"

"A few nights ago, he drank too much and got into a fight. God . . . God . . . I knew something was going to happen. I had never heard him so angry."

"But . . . but is he OK?" I babble.

"Yes, more or less. He has a broken leg and bruises all over his body. But . . ."

"What, Amanda?"

"He received a pretty severe blow to the head and has hemorrhages in both eyes."

My world is spinning.

His eyes . . .

When I recover from the shock, I breathe with difficulty.

"I appreciate your call, Amanda. Thank you very much. Now please, tell me what hospital is he in?"

"At St. Thomas' Hospital on Westminster Bridge Road, room 507."

I jot it down on a piece of paper. My hand trembles, and I think I'm going to throw up.

Two minutes after hanging up, tears, my great companions in the last days, quickly overcome me. Desperate, I sit on the bed and cry for my love.

Why didn't he call me? Why is he alone in a hospital? I want to see him.

I need to hug him and feel he's OK.

My stomach warns me, and I run to the bathroom.

I pick up my cell and speed dial. I hear two rings.

"Björn, I need you," I mutter when he picks up.

23

When Björn and I arrive at St. Thomas' Hospital, I'm a mess. I threw up several times on the plane, and the poor man doesn't know what to do to make me feel better. He attributes it to nerves and restlessness, and I don't go out of my way to correct him.

"Are you any better?" Björn asks once we're in the hospital lobby, holding me by the waist to reassure me.

I nod. It's a lie, but I don't want to say no.

"It's OK. Everything'll be fine; everything will be cleared up," he says with a sad smile.

I say yes in my head and thank heaven for a friend like him. When I called him, he was at the house in less than twenty minutes, ready to help me with whatever I needed. Even after I told him what had happened, he put aside his fury toward Laila and his friend's accusations and focused on comforting me and telling me everything was going to be all right.

I don't call either Eric's mother or sister. I want to see what I find first. But one thing I know for sure is that no one is going to touch his eyes without Marta knowing first.

I'm terrified when I think about his eyes. His beautiful eyes. How can something so precious always have so many problems?

When the elevator opens on the fifth floor, my heart beats faster.

Björn asks a nurse for Eric Zimmerman's room.

We walk in silence, and, without realizing it, I reach for Björn's hand again. He squeezes mine, giving me strength.

When we arrive at room 507, we look at each other for a more than significant silence.

"I want to go in alone," I say.

Björn nods.

"I'll give you three minutes. Then I'll come in."

With my pulse racing, I open the door and go in. It's silent. My heart suddenly jumps when I see Eric, his eyes closed. Is he asleep? I approach stealthily and just observe him. His face is bruised, his lip is split, and his leg is in a cast. He looks terrible. But I love him, and I don't care what he looks like.

I need to touch him . . .

I want to kiss him . . .

But I don't dare. I'm afraid he'll open his eyes and kick me out.

"What are you doing here?"

His husky voice makes me jump. Oh God . . . his eyes.

His beautiful eyes are filled with blood, and he looks atrocious. I can't help him, and my breathing accelerates.

"Who told you? What the hell are you doing here?"

I don't answer. I just look at him, and he screams.

"Out! I said get out of here!"

I'm panting, and, without a word, I turn around, leave the room, and run down the hall. Björn runs after me and stops me. When he sees the state I'm in, he tries to calm me down.

I want to throw up. I tell him, and he quickly hands me a garbage can.

"Don't go anywhere, understood?" says my friend with an unusual seriousness.

I nod. He heads to Eric's room.

He opens the door forcefully. I hear their voices. They argue. Several nurses come in to see what's going on, and, moments later, Björn leaves, looking annoyed and taking my arm.

"Let's go. We'll come back tomorrow."

I'm cold and scared, and I let him lead.

I don't want to leave, but I know there's nothing for me to do out in the hall.

We sleep at a London hotel that night. I can barely catch a wink. All I can think about is my love and his loneliness in that hospital room.

The next morning, Björn comes to get me. He's worried about my condition. I'm pale. When we get back to the hospital, my stomach churns. Eric will surely ask me to leave. This time I won't pay any attention to him. This time he'll have to listen to what I have to say.

When I arrive at room 507 again, I ask Björn once more for some privacy.

He shakes his head, not convinced by what I have to say, but, eventually, he gives in. With a trembling hand and tension as high as the clouds, I open the door. This time, Eric is awake, and, seeing me, his already sullen face cracks.

"Get out of here, for God's sake."

I go in anyway, and, having shed yesterday's impotence, I go right up to the edge of the bed.

"At least tell me you're OK."

He won't look at me.

"I was fine until you arrived."

His words hurt me—they kill me—but when he sees I'm not saying anything, he goes on the attack again.

"Get out of here. I haven't called you because I don't want to see you."

"But I want to see you. I care about you and—"

"You care about me?" he shouts, bloody eyes boring into me. "Come now, please . . . Go with your lover and get out of my life."

The room door flies open, and Björn comes in in a fury. Eric's face hardens even more.

"You two are too much. Get out of my room, both of you, right now."

No one moves.

"I want you to leave! Out!"

His voice, his hard voice, makes me react, and, forgetting how bad he looks, I stare at those eyes I barely recognize and let loose.

"I've come to tell you live and in person: you're a dickhead!"

My statement puzzles him.

"How can you be such an asshole?" Björn adds. "How can you think something like that about Jude and me?"

"You and I will talk when I feel better," Eric growls. "Now go away. I don't want to talk."

"Oh, we're going to talk," Björn replies. "Stop being an idiot and behave like the man I've always believed you to be."

"Björn . . . ," hisses Eric.

Björn looks at him and, with no change in his angry expression, declares, "I don't care about your condition, your leg, your bruised face, or your eyes. I'm not moving from here until I see that proof you say so gratuitously you have against us. Douchebag!"

To hear that from Björn's mouth in this moment of maximum tension makes me laugh, although there's nothing funny about any of this. There's a terrible tension.

Eric curses. He says hundreds of profanities in German, but we don't move. He doesn't scare us. We won't leave without clearing things up once and for all.

I'm exhausted all over again.

I look around for the bathroom. When I locate it, I quickly vomit. I don't feel well at all. I sit on the toilet until Björn comes in.

"If you're sick, we can leave."

I shake my head.

"I'm fine, don't worry about it. I just need Eric to believe us."

"He will, precious. I promise he will."

Minutes later, we're back with Eric. He glares at us. I sit in one of the chairs and watch silently as he and Björn get into an argument. They say everything, and I stand on the sidelines. I don't have the strength to speak.

Eric doesn't look at me. He keeps avoiding me.

A nurse comes in to see what's going on. Eric asks her to throw us out, but Björn, using all his charm, gets her out of the room by flirting and cajoling.

Eric and I are finally alone. I find my courage.

"I'm not going anywhere unless it's with you," I declare. "And right now, I'm going to call your mother and sister so they know what's happened to you."

"Damn it, Judith. Don't do that."

"I'm doing it because you're my husband, and I love you, got that?"

The Iceman is at his most sinister and devastating.

"Jude . . ."

Well . . . at least he called me Jude.

"When I was in the hospital, you stayed with me. You didn't leave me for a single minute and now . . ."

"Now you're going to leave," he says.

"That's not going to happen," I respond to the challenge in his eyes. I sit down again in the armchair next to his bed. I take my cell out of my bag. "If you want to, get up and throw me out. In the meantime, I'll just stay right here."

He just stares at me.

I stare right back.

He knows he can't do a thing and that I'm not going to leave. The door opens, and Björn comes in again.

"C'mon, buddy. I'm dying to see that proof. Show it to me," he says.

Eric's uncomfortable, but he points to his laptop. Björn hands it to him. He opens it, types, and turns it so we can see the screen.

"I want you out of my sight as soon as you see this."

Björn starts a video, and I immediately recognize the Guantanamera. Björn and I are at the bar, and you can hear us talking.

"So, if it's not too much, can you tell me what kind of women you like?"

"Like you. Smart, beautiful, sexy, tempting, easygoing, a little crazy, and disconcerting. Plus, I love to be surprised."

"Am I all that?"

"Yes, beautiful, you are!"

Stunned, Björn and I exchange glances. Seen isolated like that, it really looks bad.

In the next video, we're both dancing and having fun. After that, we see a series of photographs of the two of us walking down the street arm in arm or sitting in a restaurant, toasting with wine.

Incredulous, we turn to Eric, who's beyond irritated.

"Now what? Who's lying here?" he asks.

Fury, anger, and despair eat away at me.

"You dickhead!" I say, slapping shut the laptop.

I've closed it so forcefully that Eric cringes in pain when it hits his leg. He curses.

"Don't insult me again or—"

"Or what, you stubborn idiot?" Incensed, I throw my phone at his chest. "Or you'll kick me out of your life? Look, handsome, go fuck yourself!"

Björn stares at me. He tries to signal for me to calm down, but I'm like a hydra, and, grabbing my bag, I storm out of the room. I march to the elevator, and then Björn stops me.

"Where are you going?"

"Far from here. Far from him and far from . . . from . . ."

"Jude . . ."

I stop. What am I doing? Where am I going?

I hug Björn.

"We both know what happened and that there was nothing to it. Now we just have to explain it to your stubborn, deluded husband and my friend and make him understand Laila's dirty game."

I let myself be convinced, and, when I return to the room, Eric is more upset than before.

"Laila records us and makes a montage of the recordings, and you believe it? That's the confidence you have in me, in your wife?"

I place my bag on the bed, and I bump Eric without meaning to.

"You fuck," I say.

He huffs, and Björn, seeing we're about to fall into an argument, intervenes.

"The photos are from the day Jude came to the office to sign the papers you wanted her to sign. I invited her to lunch afterward, as I have done with you, with Frida, and with many of my friends. What makes you think it's anything else?"

Eric doesn't answer, and Björn gets annoyed.

"We've been friends for many years, and I've always trusted you one hundred percent. It hurts me that you think I, your friend, am going to play dirty with your wife. Do you think I'm going to spoil our friendship over a fuck with Judith?" His voice is angry. "I'll remind you, my friend, that it's you who offers me your wife and who enjoys what we three do. The three of us! And yes, I love it. I like Judith. I told you the first time you introduced her to me and every time you've ever brought it up. But I also told you that you're made for each other and shouldn't let anything or anyone get in your way. You're both very important to me. You, because you're like my brother, and her, because she's your love and a good person. I love you both, and it hurts me to know you doubt me."

Eric doesn't respond. But he listens.

"Our friendship is special. I've only touched your wife when you've allowed it. When have I failed you in something like that? When have you ever had to reproach me, or I you, for playing dirty? If before, when you weren't married, I always respected you, why would I not respect you now? Does what a stupid girl like Laila says matter more than what Jude or I say?"

Eric looks at him. His words hurt, but Björn keeps going.

"You're smart enough to know who loves you and who doesn't. If you decide Jude and I are lying, you're going to come out losing, my friend, because if anyone loves you and respects you in this world, it's her and me. And to clear up this mess, I want you to know Norbert is bringing Laila here, to the hospital. She'll be in a tizzy, but I want her to tell the truth in front of Jude, you, and me once and for all."

Then Björn turns to me.

"I'll be right outside."

He leaves us alone. The words came straight from his heart, and I know Eric knows. Sullen, he closes his eyes, and I see him shake his head.

"That's the truth. Laila played us all," I say.

Eric looks at me.

"You know Björn and I would never fail you. Why are you questioning it? Have you not realized I love you more than my life, and he does too?" Again, he keeps his silence. "I'll tell you something you don't know and that Laila surely hasn't told you. And then I'll leave and let you think about it. You trust her because she was Hannah's friend, right?"

He nods.

"Well, I want you to know that, while you suffered for what happened to your sister, that woman had a great time with Leonard."

"What?"

"Did you know Leonard lived in the same building as Björn?"

"Yes."

"Well, Björn caught them in the garage, entertaining themselves in the backseat of a Mercedes you had loaned her, just a week after Hannah died."

Eric is floored.

"When he caught them, he had strong words with her and told her she either disappeared from your life or he told you about it. Laila decided to disappear, but trying to get ahead of him, she told Simona and Norbert that Björn had tried to make a forceful pass at her and ripped her dress. Simona went to Björn to ask for an explanation, and, luckily for him, there are cameras in his garage. The whole scene was on tape so he could show Simona who was really with Laila and who'd ripped her dress."

"I . . . I didn't know that . . ."

"You didn't know because Norbert, Simona, and Björn decided to keep the secret. They didn't want you to suffer more than you were already suffering from Hannah's death. But now Laila wants to take revenge on Björn by recording him with me. He took her away from you, and so she tries to take us away from you."

He's speechless. At that moment, the door opens, and Björn, Norbert, and Laila come in.

When I see her, I walk right up to her and smack her across the face. She tries to smack me back, but Björn restrains her.

"Let's see whose beautiful life is falling apart now," I hiss.

Eric watches us from the bed. His expression is indecipherable. When Björn tries to put his good lawyerly skills to work to make her talk, she attempts to slip away, but, pressed and cornered, in the end she confesses to everything. Amazed, Eric listens, and, when Laila finally leaves with Björn and Norbert, he curses. He's bewildered, furious, and hurt.

Eager to hug him, I take a step forward, but he slows me down with a gesture. That baffles me. He doesn't want me near him. For a few minutes, I look at him in silence, waiting for a sign, a signal, anything! But he doesn't look at me.

Damned dickhead!

I wait and despair. Finally, I can't take it anymore.

"A few weeks ago, when I found out you were coming to London and I got jealous about Amanda, you made me see I shouldn't worry, because you loved and wanted only me. I believed you and trusted you. Now we just need you to believe us and, above all, trust me."

Silence . . .

Nothing . . .

He doesn't look at me. I'm nervous and sad, and I decide to risk everything.

"I have a tattoo that says 'Tell me what you want.' I did it for you. I have a ring on my finger that you gave me that says 'Tell me what you want, now and forever.'" But he still avoids my gaze. "I love you; I adore you. You know I'd turn the world upside down for you, but now I'm confused. You don't want to be hugged, and I feel terrible because you won't even look at me. I'm going to put everything on the line and say this just once: tell me what you want or leave me." My voice breaks when he says nothing. "I'm leaving. I'll let you think. If you want me back because you love and need me, you know my number."

I grab my bag, turn, and leave the room, not looking back.

Björn is outside, sitting in one of the chairs. Seeing the state I'm in, he gets up and hugs me.

I need air . . .

Tears flow again.

"Easy, Judith," Björn whispers.

"I can't. I can't . . ."

He nods. He tries to comfort me.

"And his eyes? Have you seen his eyes?"

"Yes," he responds, and I know he's worried too. He tries to distract me. "The leg, that's just a simple fracture. One of the nurses just explained it to me."

I cry and hiccup.

"No . . . no . . . He didn't let me hold him. He won't look at me. He hasn't said a word."

Björn curses.

"Eric isn't stupid, and he loves you."

I shake my head. What if he really doesn't love me?

Björn seems to read my thoughts. He holds my face with his hands.

"He loves you. I know that's the way it is. You just have to see how he looks at you to know my foolish friend can't live without you."

"He's a dickhead."

We both grin.

"A crazy dickhead who loves you madly. I hope someday I find a woman as crazy, loving, and fun as you to make me feel what you make him feel."

"You'll find her, Björn. You'll find her, and then you'll complain about her like Eric does about me." We both grin again. "Thank you for forcing Laila to clear everything up."

My good friend nods.

"Where's Norbert?"

"He went with his niece. He wanted to talk with her."

Poor man. This is all so awful for him.

"C'mon, let's get something to eat," Björn says. "You need it."

But I don't want to eat. My heart is broken.

"I want to go home."

"What?"

"I want to go back to Germany," I say. "I told him to decide what he wants to do with our relationship and to call me with whatever he decides."

"What are you saying?" says Björn. "Now you've gone crazy too? How are you going to leave?"

I swallow the knot of emotions in my throat.

"I laid everything out for him, Björn. I told him to tell me what he wants or let me go. Now I just need to wait. I don't want to overwhelm him. I want him to decide what he wants to do."

My good friend tries to convince me not to leave, but I refuse. I'm tired, very tired, and I'm not feeling well. The coldness of my husband and his rejection have touched my heart deeply.

In the end, Björn gives up, and we take the elevator. When we reach the lobby and are about to leave the hospital, we hear shouting and a fuss. When I turn to look, I'm speechless. I see Eric struggling with two nurses.

"Jude . . . wait. Jude!" he shouts.

My heart races.

The Iceman is in total pissed-off mode, dressed in that ridiculous hospital gown, letting loose with myriad expletives while trying to break free from two nurses who look like professional wrestlers.

I can't move.

"From what I can tell, Eric has decided what he wants," Björn says.

My crazy love suddenly sees me looking at him and, raising a hand, shouts at me not to move from where I am. Then he shakes off the nurses and drags himself, including the leg in the cast, over to us.

"I called you, darling," he says, showing me my cell. "I called you, but you'd left your phone in my room."

My heart is beating out of my chest.

Again my love, my Iceman, shows me he loves me.

"I'm sorry, sweetheart . . . I'm sorry."

I don't move . . . I can't speak . . .

Eric tenses up. He's nervous. He wants me to say something.

"I'm a dickhead," he says.

"You are, my friend. You are," says Björn.

My guy extends his hand to his good friend, and, moments later, they embrace.

"I'm sorry, Björn. I'm so sorry."

"You're forgiven, dickhead," says Björn.

They both smile.

They let go, and the nurses come to get Eric. They ask him to get back to his room. He shouldn't be there in the hallway in his condition.

Everyone in the hospital lobby is watching us. This is surreal. There's this guy wearing a hospital gown that reveals more than it covers struggling with the nurses and staring at me.

"I love you. Say something, sweetheart," he says, those fiery eyes on me.

But I can't and he insists.

"I'm not going to leave you, sweetheart. You're my life, the woman I want, and I need you to forgive me for having been—"

"Such a dickhead," I say, finishing his sentence.

Eric nods. I see in his eyes he needs me to embrace him. But I don't. I'm so paralyzed I can't even blink. Then he presses a button on my cell, and we hear a ringtone. "Si Nos Dejan."

"I promised you I'd take care of you all my life, and I intend to do that," he says.

It's almost like we're daring each other . . .

But eager to hug him because of what he's just done and said, I take a step forward.

"First, let it be clear to you that, for me to leave you and want to live without you, something very . . . very . . . very bad has to happen. Second, I still want you to take care of me, but never again doubt me or Björn. And third, what are you doing showing your ass to the whole hospital, my love?"

We all laugh.

When I throw myself in his arms and feel him hugging me, I close my eyes, and I'm happy. People clap, and Björn walks behind his friend and whispers.

"Let's go back to your room so you can stop showing off your ass."

My tears wet Eric's chest, and he squeezes me against him. "C'mon . . . Don't cry, sweetheart. Please don't cry."

But I'm so excited . . .

So happy . . .

And so worried about him . . .

I cry and laugh uncontrollably.

Five minutes later, accompanied by Björn and the nurses, we're back in his room. Eric had ripped off his IV, and they have to reconnect it. The nurses scold him. He won't stop looking at me and smiling.

I'm the only thing he cares about!

Seeing everything is in order, Björn goes down to the cafeteria for some food. He insists I have to eat something, and, quickly, Eric supports him. Those two!

When we're alone in the room, Eric asks me to lie beside him on the bed. I do. He hugs me.

"Are you OK?" I ask.

"I've been better, but I'll recover."

His eyes scare me. I can't stop looking at them.

"Don't worry. They'll heal."

"Does your head hurt?"

He nods.

"But everything is under control." He smiles and runs his hand down my chin.

"As you say, I love you more than life itself."

I go to kiss his mouth, and he winces in pain. "Oh, honey, I'm sorry. I'm sorry."

"I'm more sorry, sweetheart. Not being able to kiss you is torture."

He hugs me again.

"Despite how sinister those vampire eyes make you look, you're still the most handsome, sexy dickhead in the world. And now that half the hospital and beyond has seen your ass, I know I'm the most envied woman ever."

He smiles, and his smile fills my soul.

"God, sweetheart . . . Forgive me for not trusting you. I love you so much that when I saw those damned images, I lost my mind."

"You are forgiven. I hope it doesn't happen again."

"It won't. I promise."

"Ah, and by the way, it was Amanda who called me. You were right; she respects me."

Finally ready to tell him what I've been hiding from the rest of the world for several days, I try to sit up.

"I have something to tell you, but you have to let go first."

Eric looks at me and makes a fuss.

"Tell me later. Now I want to keep holding you."

I laugh and squirm.

"OK, but when I tell you, you'll regret not having known before."

"You sure about that?"

"Absolutely."

He's curious now and kisses my head.

"It's a good thing, right?"

"I think so, although given what we just went through, I don't know how you're going to take it!"

"Don't scare me."

"I'm not trying to scare you."

"Jude . . ."

I shrug. I love the warmth of his body. And his voice in my ear even more. He runs his fingers through my hair. Oh God, that feels so good! Two minutes later, he can't take it anymore and lets go.

"C'mon. I want to know."

I'm gentle with him, but I get up from the bed and go get my bag. My news is going to drive him crazy. I open my purse, take out a bulging envelope, and show it to him. Eric looks at it and raises an eyebrow. I tell him to wait and take off the handkerchief around my neck.

"Look."

Seeing my neck red and almost raw, he sits up in alarm.

"Sweetheart, what's happened to you?"

"My rash. My nerves have done me in."

Open-mouthed, he looks at me again and frowns.

"It's my fault."

"In part, yes." I nod. "You know what happens to me when I get nervous." I hand him the bulky envelope. "Open it."

When he does, the four pregnancy tests fall on the bed.

Surprised, and not knowing what to say, he looks at me. I show him the photo the gynecologist gave me.

"Congratulations, Mr. Zimmerman. You're going to be a dad."

He's stunned. He doesn't react.

"Yes, get ready because since I found out about Medusa—"

"Medusa?"

"That's what I call her," I reply, pointing to the image in the photo.

He doesn't quite follow and tries to get up. Where does he think he's going?

I stop him. He can't mess with the IV again, or the nurses will kill us.

"Since I've known about Medusa, I can't sleep, I can't eat, and I'm in such a terrible mood—you don't want to know. I'm scared. Very scared! I'm going to be a mom, and I'm not ready."

We look at each other. I smile and grab his arms again. He hugs me so tight.

"Baby . . . honey, you're suffocating me."

He lets go of me, kisses me, and cringes in pain. He hugs me again. He looks at me, then at the tests.

"We're going to have a baby?" he asks, his voice trembling.

"It seems so."

"A little dark-haired girl?"

"Or a blonde?"

He just stares at me again.

For a while, Eric doesn't let me go, and together we look at the ultrasound and rejoice.

"Sweetheart, are you OK?"

His joy is my joy.

"Well, actually I feel like shit," I say as honestly as I can. "I've been vomiting nonstop for days and crying, and I can't stop scratching my neck. I'm scared shitless of Medusa. And if you add that my husband suddenly didn't love me and accused me of betraying him with his best friend, how do you think I feel?" But before he can say anything, I add, "But . . . now, in this moment, this very moment here by your side, I'm fine, very . . . very fine."

Eric hugs me again.

He's so surprised by the news, he can hardly speak.

"For the record, and despite my pregnancy, you will still have your punishment for distrusting me," I whisper in a way I know drives him crazy.

When Björn comes back from the cafeteria, a beaming Eric asks him, "Hey, do you want to be my Medusa's godfather?"

24

The next day, Björn and Norbert return to Germany. Björn has a couple of court appearances he can't miss. I call Marta and Sonia and tell them what happened, which scares them. They quickly fly to London.

Seeing the state of her brother's eyes, Marta meets with the doctors at the hospital. In the end she decides to wait and see if time or the medication resolves it. If not, she'll schedule an appointment to drain the blood once we're back in Germany. After this point is clarified, the doctor tells us we can go home soon.

Sonia goes crazy once she knows she's having another grandchild, and Marta applauds. That the family grows gives them great joy. Frida and Andrés call to check on Eric and calm down when they talk to him directly—and it goes without saying how happy they are to know about my pregnancy.

When we call Flyn for him to talk to his uncle, we don't tell him or Simona about the pregnancy. Norbert keeps the secret until we're back.

Then one afternoon when I'm alone with Eric in the hospital room, Amanda comes by.

Her presence still bothers me, but I recognize what she did was a good thing. For an hour, she talks to Eric about work, and I decide to take the time to call my father. I want to break the news.

Excited and nervous at the same time, I leave the room and dial Jerez. After two rings, Luz greets me.

"Tita!"

"Hello, my dear Pokémon teacher. How are you?"

"Well, as Grandpa would say, screwed but happy."

"Luz, that mouth," I say, scolding her.

But it comes out of her so naturally, so authentically, I can't help but chuckle.

"Today the teacher, Miss Colines, gave me a four on homework that deserved at least a seven."

I laugh. I remember Miss Colines.

"Well, honey, maybe you have to try harder."

"That rat-faced witch has a thing for me. Tita, I try hard, but they're really nitpicky at this school."

"Well, honey, I think—"

But then she does that thing I know so well from my sister and changes the subject.

"How's my uncle? Is he better?"

"Yes, honey, he's getting his strength back. We'll be back in Germany in a few days."

"That's cool! And Flyn?"

"In Munich with Simona and Norbert. By the way, he's looking forward to seeing you again at Christmas."

"He's so complicated," she says, all sassy. "Tell him I'm going to bring my own Wii games, and he should get ready, because I'm going to whomp him, OK?"

"I'll pass it on."

"Tita, I'll let my mom talk to you now. She's bugging me! A big, big kiss."

"One for you too, my love."

My Luz is so beautiful!

"Cuchufleta, how's Eric?" my sister asks, worried.

When I called my father and her to tell them Eric was in the hospital, they wanted to come to London. I stopped them. I know so many people would have been overwhelming for Eric.

"All right. We go home the day after tomorrow. I'm exhausted."

"Oh, Cuchu . . . what a pity you're so far away. I would have loved to squeeze and comfort you."

"I know. I would have liked to have you near. How's Lucía?"

"Ferocious. This girl eats anything and everything. Any day now, she'll eat us."

We both laugh.

"I know something you don't know . . ."

"What?"

"Guess."

"You're coming to live in Spain?"

"Nooooooo."

"You dyed your hair blonde?"

"No."

"My delightful brother-in-law has given you a red Ferrari?"

"No."

"What is it, Cuchu?"

I laugh.

"I think someone will be calling you Tía Raquel very soon."

My sister's scream is deafening.

She starts to clap like crazy, and I hear her tell Luz. The two shout and applaud. I laugh, and then I hear my father.

"Is it true, sweetheart? Is it true you're going to give me another grandchild?"

"Yes, Papá, it's true."

"Oh, my dear girl, you've just so gladdened my life. Are you tired, my sweet girl?"

"Yes, Papá, a little."

His laughter and happiness, as always, swell my heart. I talk to him and Raquel at the same time. They both want to talk and show me their joy. Then my sister takes command of the phone.

"Cuchu . . . as soon as you get home, call me, and we'll talk. I have lots of Lucía's little things that can be useful for the first months. Oh God . . . oh God . . . you're pregnant. I can't believe it!"

"Neither can I, Raquel. Neither can I," I murmur.

There's another struggle for the phone. My father wins this time.

"Sweetheart, are you eating well?"

"Yes, Papá, don't worry."

"Have you already gone to the doctor?"

"Yes."

"Your sister wants to know if you're taking any kind of folk remedies."

I crack up.

"Yes, Papá. Tell her I take folic acid."

"Oh, I'm so happy. Another little grandchild!"

"Yes, Papá, another little grandchild."

"Maybe it'll be a boy."

"And what if it's a girl? Then what?"

My father laughs.

"Well, I'll have another woman to love and pamper in my life."

We both laugh again.

"Is Eric better?"

"Yes, Papá, much better. We'll be discharged in a couple of days."

"Well . . . hey, is he happy about the baby?"

Eric has hardly slept since he found out. He's constantly worrying about my eating and resting, and, when he sees me vomiting, he gets sick too.

"Eric is like you . . . happy."

We talk several more minutes, and, when I see Amanda leave the room, I quickly say goodbye to my family.

"I'll walk you out," I tell her.

We go to the elevator together. We know we have a pending conversation.

"Thank you for letting me know."

"Congratulations on the baby," she says.

"Thanks, Amanda."

"The only reason I didn't tell you earlier is because Eric forbade it. But on the third day, I ignored him. You had to know what was happening."

I'm grateful for this detail.

The tension between us is thick.

"Judith, I want you to know things have been very clear to me for a long time," she says. "Eric is a happily married man, and I won't go there."

"I'm glad to know that," I reply. That'll make our lives easier.

She smiles and points to a man in a suit in an impressive Audi A8.

"I have to go. He's waiting for me."

Moving quickly, I plant a kiss on each of her cheeks. We look at each other. Her telling me about Eric and my giving her two kisses means we're at peace.

I watch her from the hospital door, how she wiggles her hips for the man in the Audi, gets in, and kisses him.

When I return to Eric's room, he's working on his laptop and smiles when he sees me.

He's looking better, and I kiss him.

"I love you," I say.

Two days later, we're back in Munich.

Home sweet home!

Having all my things at hand, my bed, and my bathroom are what I need most.

When Flyn and Simona see Eric, their faces say it all.

They're horrified.

I understand their alarm; Eric's eyes look scary.

"Easy, although he looks like the evil vampire from *Twilight* with those eyes, I swear it's Eric! And he won't bite your necks."

My comment relaxes them a bit.

Flyn hugs his uncle.

"Are you going to get better, or is this the way you are now?" he asks.

"He'll be fine," I say.

"I hope so," Eric murmurs, his arm around his nephew.

I don't say more. I know that, even if he's not talking about it, my German is concerned. You just have to see how he looks at himself in the mirror. I just hope the medication manages to drain the blood and everything resolves by itself. My father always says, positivity calls forth positivity. Therefore, I'm positive!

That night, when we sit down for dinner, we ask Norbert and Simona to join us for dessert. We need to talk to them. When we tell them the good news about my pregnancy, Flyn shouts.

"I'm going to have a cousin! How cool!"

"You're going to be a big brother, and we'll need you to teach him many things," I say. Everyone looks at me. "Flyn is my child, and Medusa will be too."

"Medusa?" Simona and Flyn ask in unison.

Norbert smiles. Eric does too. I point to my flat belly.

"I'm calling it Medusa until I know if it's a girl or a boy." They nod, and, looking at Flyn, who can't take his eyes off me, I ask, "You want to be her big brother, right?"

He nods. "Of course, Mom!"

Sometimes he calls me Mom, sometimes Aunt, other times just Jude. He hasn't decided what to do yet, but it doesn't matter to me. All I want is for him to call me.

Very excited about everything, Simona takes Norbert's hand.

"What joy! Another child scampering about the house. Such delight!"

I love them so much. They don't have children. Months ago, Simona confessed they tried for years, but fate never granted them their wish. I know she's received the news with an open heart and that Medusa will be like a granddaughter to her.

"Then we shouldn't buy the bike for my classes, right?" Flyn asks.

I sigh. Flyn's motorcycle! I'd forgotten about it.

"Jude can't teach you now. She can't ride a motorcycle while she's pregnant, but if you want, we can buy it this weekend, and Jurgen can teach you."

Eric is right. I can't and shouldn't. But I think it's a fantastic solution, though I'm surprised by Flyn's response.

"No, that's OK. I want Jude to teach me."

"It's just that I can't ride a motorcycle or run after you right now," I explain.

"But you will after you have Medusa, right?"

I nod. It becomes clear that, for him, what's important is that I teach him. I look at Eric, who smiles, and then I kiss my boy on the head.

"We don't need to talk about it anymore. The lessons and the bike will wait until after Medusa is already sleeping in her crib."

That night, Eric and I are exhausted. He sits on the bed and very carefully puts the crutches aside. He's clearly happy to be home.

"Can I help you undress?" I ask.

With a smoldering smile, my guy nods, and I proceed.

First, I unbutton his shirt and take it off, and, with care, I caress his shoulders. God, I love him. After that, without touching the leg in the cast, I pull his black track pants down.

"Oh yes . . . just what I need," I murmur on seeing the prominent erection in his underwear.

Eric laughs.

"It's been too long without . . . and I want . . . I want . . . I want . . ."

Eager, I bring my mouth to his. We can kiss without worry now. His lip has healed, and we can finally devour each other with passion and delight. Immediately turned on by the closeness of this man with whom I'm madly in love, I very carefully straddle him.

"Is it OK if I sit like this?"

He nods.

"Well then, I'm not moving from here."

Eric kisses my lips and places his hot hands on my hips. "Of course you're not going to move."

I grin and nibble his lips.

"I'm going to move so much, they'll hear you moaning in Australia."

"How tempting," he purrs.

I'm so happy to have him back in my arms.

"Although, now that I think about it, I remember I told you I'd punish you later."

Eric stops and gives me a sad look.

"You behaved very badly toward me. You didn't trust me and—"

"I know, sweetheart. I'll never forgive myself."

I don't smile because I want him to believe I'm going to punish him.

"I need you, Jude . . . please. Punish me another day, I don't want to be without you today."

"You've punished me without you for many days, Eric. Have you ever thought about that?"

"Yes . . ." And he brings his mouth to me and implores, "Please, Jude . . ."

Listening to him beg is music to my ears.

He's at my mercy.

He needs me as much as I need him.

"The punishment must be in accordance with your crime."

He doesn't move. I know this is making him sore. He looks at me, waiting for instructions, but I can't continue torturing him like this.

"All right then, your punishment will be to satisfy me until I can't take it anymore."

Eric lets out a laugh, and I grin. That's one helluva punishment!

He tempts me with his mouth.

He runs his lips over mine, and, when I open my mouth, ready for him, he does what I like so much. He sticks out his tongue, sucks my upper lip, then the lower one. He nibbles it and finally kisses me. He eats me right up. It drives me crazy.

All this time, his hard cock beats against my body.

"Tear off my thong."

"Hmm . . . sweetheart, this is getting interesting."

He pulls on both sides of my hips, and the thong disintegrates. Yes!

Eager to have him inside me, I take my husband's tempting penis and direct it to the center of my desire, introducing it little by little.

"I missed you," I say.

Eric's hands go straight to my ass, and he gives me a spanking. Two. Three. And, without speaking, he demands I move. I obey, and he throws his head back and closes his eyes.

Oh yes . . . Enjoy . . . Enjoy, my love.

I grab his neck, and, biting his chin carefully, I move my hips back and forth and join in his gasps. I'm impaled again and again on my German's cock, and I can't breathe.

My body trembles with what he makes me feel.

My hormones, my body, and I ask for more. Aware of what I want, and even though he can't move his leg, Eric grabs me by the hips and stops my movements.

"Let me have my punishment, sweetheart."

That baffles me; I don't want to stop. Suddenly, he jerks my hips in a way that drives me down even more on him and makes me scream. He knows I like it, and he repeats the move. This time we both scream. He goes deeper into me. Seven, eight, nine times, he repeats it, and, when the ecstasy peaks after so many days of drought, we let ourselves go.

An hour later, I'm hugging him in bed and falling asleep.

"Jude," he whispers.

"What?"

"Fuck me."

I quickly open my eyes and turn to him.

"I'd fuck you, but my leg won't let me, and I want to finish my punishment."

I look at the clock: 12:45 a.m.

It's very late for my German.

"Are you feeling playful?"

My guy smiles and touches my hips.

"I've been wanting you these days, and I need to make up for lost time."

I quickly get on board. I open the drawer on my night table and pull out the toy bag.

"I'll take off my thong before you rip it. Two in one night is too many."

Eric laughs. "Don't turn on the light."

"Why not?"

"I want the darkness to help me fantasize."

I take off my thong, and I sit on him in bed. I pull his pajamas down and immediately see how far along things are, even in the dark.

"Well . . . well . . . well, Mr. Zimmerman. You are very, very needy indeed."

Eric smiles.

"Too many days without you, Mrs. Zimmerman."

"Oh yeah?" After sliding down on my husband's erect member, I bring my mouth close to his. "It's your fault for not trusting me."

Eric slaps my ass hard and loud. Then he squeezes my ass with his big hands. "Tell me what you want, sweetheart, but fuck me."

His voice . . . and the darkness of the room drives us both mad.

When he lies back on the bed, I have him at my mercy and eager to play. He wants to fantasize. Me too.

"There's a couple watching us," I tell him, "and they want to see us play."

"Yes," he murmurs.

"The woman likes to watch you suck my nipples, and he wants," I say as I put a toy in his hand, "for you to show him my ass and then place the anal ring inside me."

Eric's fully in it now. He loves it!

His breathing gets deeper, wheezier, as he sucks my nipples. Oh yes . . . they're so sensitive, and I love the mix of bliss and pain. Without letting go of my nipples, he separates my ass cheeks.

"Let the man look at your beautiful ass," he says.

"Yes," I whisper.

"He loves your butt, sweetheart. Look at how he's enjoying it. He wants it."

"Yes . . ."

"And he wants to see how hard I can penetrate you."

He jerks, which makes me gasp and bite his shoulder.

"The woman is dying to suck your pretty nipples. Her mouth is watering, and with her eyes she's asking me to let you go so she can have you."

"No, no, don't let me go. Keep enjoying yourself and then give me to her."

My breathing changes. What my guy says excites me as much as what he does. He gives me another slap on the butt, and I arch my back.

"This is how you like me to show it off."

"Arch a little more, sweetheart . . ."

My body shudders at our seductive game. Placing the anal ring in my mouth, Eric whispers, "Suck it, yes, let's go . . . suck it."

I do what he says, while my mind imagines two people watching us and enjoying our intimate moment. Eric sucks my hard and swollen nipples while I suck the anal ring. I lick it the way Eric licks me.

"Now I'm going to give you what you and they both want," he says.

Excited and maddened by our verbal play, I bend my body while Eric takes the ring out of my mouth and walks it slowly down my spine. He applies a handful of lube to my asshole.

"So, sweetheart, like this . . ."

I gasp as I feel the pressure, but my willing body accepts it. Once the ring's inside me, Eric moves it, and I moan while my hard nipples hit his chest.

"I'm going to fuck you, and then, after I'm satisfied, I'm going to give you to them. First to the woman and then to the man. I'll open your legs so they have access, and you'll give me your moans, OK?"

"Yes . . . yes . . . ," I say as he squeezes me against him, and I feel like he's going to split me in two.

"You won't close your legs at any time. You'll let her take from you what she wants, OK?"

"Yes, yes."

The tone of my voice, our fantasies and desire, create the ambience we both seek. I put my hands on his hard chest and fuck him again and again while Eric holds me by the waist and squeezes me hard to get more depth.

Our wild side surfaces again and again. We can't stop, we're possessed, and we give ourselves over and over until we reach our climax.

We're insatiable tonight, and, after one last time, we decide to rest and I drop in his arms.

"I want you to fulfill your punishment every night," I tell him.

Eric kisses me and touches my hair.

"Sleep, you sex goddess," he whispers.

25

When I wake up the next morning, my stomach contracts, and I have to run to the bathroom.

Eric, who's in bed with me, rushes behind me as fast as he can, dragging his cast. When he sees I'm vomiting, he holds my hair back.

The nausea passes, and I just sit in the bathroom.

"This is horrible . . . Medusa's killing me."

He has taken a towel and wet it, bringing it to my face with all the tenderness in the world.

"Easy, sweetheart. She'll be here soon enough."

"I . . . I'm not going to be able to do this . . . I can't."

"Yes, you can, honey. You'll have our precious baby and all this will be forgotten."

"Are you sure?"

"Absolutely sure. She's going to be a little brunette, like you. You'll see!"

"And she's going to give you a lot of trouble, like me."

He smiles and gives me a kiss on the tip of my nose.

"I'm sure I'll love every minute of it."

I nod and finally smile back. My husband is wonderful, and even at moments like this, he makes me forget how bad I feel.

I've read that vomiting usually lasts only the first three months, and that is my hope—let it end soon!

Once color returns to my face, Eric leaves me in the bathroom, and I decide to take a shower. I get naked, and, when I take off my thong, I blink. Blood!

Oh my God!

Nervous, I quickly call Eric.

In spite of his handicap, Eric's in the bathroom in zero seconds.

"There's blood."

"Get dressed, sweetheart. We'll go to the hospital."

Like an automaton, I leave the bathroom and quickly dress. Eric is ready before me, and he and Norbert wait for me downstairs.

"Don't worry," says Simona as she gives me a kiss. "Everything will be fine."

In the car, Eric takes my hands. They're cold. I'm scared. Blood isn't a good sign during a pregnancy.

What if I've lost Medusa?

When we arrive at the hospital, Marta's at the door with a wheelchair. They roll me to the emergency room at full speed. They don't let Eric in though. Marta stays with him while I go with the doctors.

I'm terrified.

They ask me hundreds of questions, and I answer, even though I don't understand what I'm saying half the time. I've never wanted to be pregnant, but Medusa suddenly means a lot to me. To Eric. To both of us.

They ask me if I've been nervous about something lately. I nod. I don't tell them about my life, but I know the stress I've been under may have caused this. They have me lie down, and they do an ultrasound. Silently and breathing heavily, I watch the two doctors' faces.

They stare at the monitor. I want everything to be OK. In the end, after assessing what they think is relevant, they turn back to me.

"Everything's fine. Your baby's fine."

I burst into tears.

Five minutes later, they let Eric in. He looks worried and very tense. When he sees me, he hugs me. I'm so excited I can't say anything, I just keep crying, and the doctors have to explain that everything's fine. Kissing me on the head, Eric cradles me.

"Quiet, champ. Our baby's fine."

I nod and reassure myself.

Before sending us home, one of the doctors gives us a report and tells us that, if I don't bleed anymore, I should just go to my regular gynecologist's appointment. He adds that, at the moment, I have to rest. Eric nods and I sigh. I don't even want to think how horrible it's about to get for me now that I'm under doctor's orders to rest.

As I imagined, as soon as I get home, Eric sends me to bed. I have no issue with that at the moment. After the fright we just had, I'm exhausted, and, when I put head to pillow, I go to sleep immediately.

When I wake up, Eric's by my side. He's working on his laptop. When he sees I'm awake, he quickly sets the computer aside.

"Are you OK, sweetheart?"

"Yes, perfectly."

"Frida and Andrés called. They send you kisses and rejoice that everything's well."

"How did they find out?"

"Björn," he says.

I go to the bathroom. Eric accompanies me, and, when I see I'm not bleeding anymore, I relax. When I go back to bed, he lies down beside me.

"I feel guilty about what happened," he says.

"Why?"

Eric shakes his head.

"I'm the culprit who caused the tension you suffered. Because of me, we almost lost our baby. Also, last night, I asked too much of you and—"

"Don't be ridiculous; cut it out," I respond. "The doctors said sometimes this happens. And, as for last night, don't martyr yourself please with something you don't know."

My Iceman nods, although I know him and know he'll always blame himself. I decide not to broach the subject.

I sleep for what feels like days, but when I try to get up, Eric insists I stay in bed. In the morning, I entertain myself as best as I can. I watch *Emerald Madness* with Simona, and I talk on Facebook with my friends, the Warriors, but I'm bored to death by the afternoon. When Flyn comes home from school, I get up. When Eric sees me in the kitchen, he's none too happy, but, before he can say anything, I declare my position.

"Rest is taking it easy, not being in bed for twenty-four hours. So, don't stress me out or make me nervous, understood?"

He doesn't say anything. He stays contained, and, an hour later, when he sees me running toward the bathroom, he comes over and takes me in his arms.

"To bed, sweetheart."

I protest and complain, but it doesn't matter. He takes me to bed.

The following days are more of the same. Rest, rest, and rest.

A week later, I'm drowning in rest.

Eric lets my family know what happened. Papá insists on coming to Germany to take care of me. As best I can, I try to convince him it's not necessary. I'm dying to see him and hug him, but I know he, Raquel, and Eric, the three of them together, can drive me crazy, and I don't want that.

In the end, Papá and Raquel call every day, and I know from their voices that it calms them down when they hear me laugh.

Dexter and Graciela call from Mexico, and I'm glad to hear their relationship is going well. According to Graciela, Dexter sleeps with her every night and has told everyone she's his fiancée. I can't even imagine the joy Dexter's mother must be feeling.

As the days go by, Eric seems to understand I'm bored out of my mind in bed, and he lets me spend time on the sofa in the living room. Big step!

According to him, until the gynecologist sees me again, he's not accepting any other change in my care. He even refuses to touch me beyond anything that's not a sweet caress or a kiss. At first, that made me laugh, but not anymore. I feel like I'm going to scream.

We talk a lot about Medusa. Will she be a brunette? Will she be blonde? It horrifies him that I call the baby Medusa, but in the end, he gives in, understanding that I do it with affection and that I can't call it anything else now.

Every night, in the privacy of our room, Eric kisses me and the baby, and that makes me feel a little silly. It's so nice though. Love just oozes through his pores, and I can only smile.

One night when we're both in bed, I hug him and murmur, "I want you."

Eric smiles and gives me a chaste kiss on the lips.

"And I love you, honey, but we can't."

I'm too turned on.

"You don't have to penetrate me . . ."

Getting up from the bed, he moves away from me.

"No, sweetie. We'd better not try our luck." But he can read my face. "When your doctor gives us the OK, everything will return to normal."

"But, Eric . . . there are still two weeks until I go to the gynecologist."

Amused by my insistence, he opens the bedroom door. "Less than that with every second. We just have to wait."

When I'm alone, I'm frustrated. My hormones are all stirred up and I want sex, but it's clear I'm not getting it tonight.

The days pass, and Eric's cast is removed. That makes me happy and him even more so. Being able to recover his mobility and independence is huge.

One afternoon after a three-hour nap, Eric wakes me with lots of kisses. I love that. I squeeze up against him and, when I go in for more, he stops me.

"No, sweetheart . . . We shouldn't."

That completely wakes me up; I growl.

Eric smiles. "C'mon," he says. "Flyn and I want to show you something."

He guides me down the stairs, but I'm in a bad mood. Not having sex is killing me. But when he opens the living room doors and I see what the two of them have done for me, I'm so incredibly moved.

"Surprise! It's Christmas, and my uncle and I have put up the wish tree," Flyn exclaims.

I drop to the floor and cover my mouth with my hands, and, unable to stop myself, I cry like a fool. Flyn's surprised by my response; he doesn't understand. Eric quickly helps me up to a chair.

Before me is the red Christmas tree that caused us so much angst last year. I want to say thank you and tell them it's beautiful, but my tears won't let me. "If you don't like it, we can buy another one," Flyn says.

That makes me cry even more. I cry, cry, and cry.

After kissing me on the head, Eric explains, "Jude doesn't want another one. She loves this one."

"Then why is she crying?"

"Because pregnancy makes her very sensitive."

The kid looks at me.

"Oh man . . ."

What they've done is so beautiful, so precious, so loving that I can't repress my tears. All I can do is picture my two boys, alone, decorating the tree for me.

Eric bends down and dries my tears with his hands.

"Flyn and I know it's your favorite time of year, and we wanted to give you this surprise. We know you prefer this tree to a fir, which takes a long time to grow." He points at a small sheet of paper on the table. "Now you have to write down your wishes so we can hang them up."

"And these other sheets," Flyn continues, "are so that when the family comes over, they can write down their wishes, and we can hang them on the tree too. Good idea, right?"

"It's a great idea, honey," I say, swallowing my tears.

The boy gives me a hug. Seeing us so close, Eric nods and mouths, "I love you."

The next day, we go to Marta's office at the hospital to review Eric's case. At first, he refuses to let me go, insisting I stay home and rest. But he gives in when I throw a shoe at his head and shout that either I'm going with him or alone in a taxi behind him.

His eyes are still bloody. They don't seem to improve with medication or with time. After assessing the situation with other colleagues, Marta decides to schedule surgery to drain the blood for December 16.

I'm scared, and I know Eric's scared. But neither of us says anything. I stay quiet so as not to worry him, and he does it so as not to worry me.

The day of the operation, I'm trembling. I insist on accompanying him, and he doesn't put up a fight. He needs me. Sonia comes with us too. When it's time to split up, Eric gives me a kiss.

"Don't worry, everything's going to be OK," he says.

I nod and smile. I want to look strong. But when he disappears from sight, Sonia hugs me, and I do what I do so well lately: I cry!

The surgery is a success, like we all hoped and wanted, and Marta insists Eric spend the night at the hospital. He refuses, but when I scold him, he gives in and even accepts that I'll stay and keep him company.

"I hope our baby doesn't inherit my eye problem," he says that night in the dark.

I'd never considered it, and it saddens me to know Eric's already worrying about that. As always, he thinks of everything.

"I'm sure not, honey. Don't concern yourself with that now."

"Jude . . . my eyes are always going to be a problem."

"I'm also always going to be a problem. And I don't need to tell you about Medusa. Wow, get ready, Zimmerman."

He laughs and that comforts me.

Eager to embrace him, I get up from my bed and lie down in his.

"You have a problem with your sight, honey, and we'll live with it forever, but I love you, you love me, and we're going to deal with that problem and every other problem that comes our way. I don't want you to get overwhelmed by it now, OK?"

"All right, sweetheart."

"And when Medusa's here, don't think you're going to get out of taking care of her because of your damned eyes. Oh no, don't even think about it! I plan on having you involved in every way from the day she's born until she goes to college or becomes a hippy and wants to live in a commune. Understood, champ?"

Eric smiles and kisses me on the head.

"Understood, champ."

After two days, his eyes slowly return to what they once were, and I'm happy because of that and because my family's coming to spend Christmas with us.

But despite my happiness, I feel like shit. I can't stop vomiting, I'm thinner than I've ever been in my whole life. My clothes are falling off me, I'm never hungry, and I know my mood just brings Eric down. I see it in his eyes. He suffers when he sees me run to the bathroom and even more when he holds my head.

My hormones are out of control, and as soon as I laugh, I cry. I don't recognize myself.

On December 21, we go to the airport to pick up my family. That they're here for Christmas with us fills me with joy. But when my father and my sister see me, their faces tell me everything. They don't say a word, but my niece goes right to the point.

"Tita, are you not feeling well?"

"No, honey, I'm not—why?"

"Because you look horrible."

"She's throwing up all the time," Flyn says. "And that has us worried."

"Do you take good care of her?" Luz asks.

"Yes, we all take good care of Mom."

My niece is surprised.

"My tita is your mom?"

He looks at me, and I wink at him.

"Yes, Aunt Jude is my mom," he replies.

"How wild is that!" Luz exclaims.

Children and their sincerity.

On December 24, we celebrate Christmas Eve together. My family's happy. They write their wishes and hang them on the tree. Eric smiles, and I love having them all here together.

But this pregnancy is taking its toll on me.

Because I can't keep anything down, I can't digest the rich ham my father brought. I eat it with delight, but it soon leaves me, like everything lately. Of course, when I recover, I shove more ham in my mouth.

I'm stubborn that way!

In her eagerness to reassure me, my sister confirms that the nausea will disappear after the first three months.

"I hope so, because Medusa—"

"Cuchufleta, don't call it that! It's a baby, and it'll be offended if you call it by that name."

I just shut up. It's for the best.

Then I watch my father and Eric play Wii tennis with Flyn and Luz. What a good time they're having!

"Oh, Cuchu, I still can't believe you're going to be a mom."

"Me neither," I reply.

Raquel yaks on about pregnancies, stretch marks, swollen feet, and skin spots, and I'm dying. Is all this going to happen to me? I listen to her. I process the information, and, when I can't do it anymore, I do what she does so well and change the subject.

"Well, aren't you going to tell me about your wild little fling?"

Raquel grins.

"When I got home the night I was with Juanín, the guy from the appliance store, Juan Alberto was waiting for me in the alley next to the house."

"And?"

"He was jealous, Cuchu."

"No surprise there!"

We talk, but in very low voices so no one can hear us.

"If you went out with another man, it's normal he'd be jealous. In his place I would have raised holy hell, especially after asking for your hand and having you deny it to me."

My crazy sister lets out a laugh. I can see the happiness in her face. I laugh too and watch my niece screaming when she wins on the Wii.

"I slept with him," says Raquel. "By the way, it's really uncomfortable in a car. Luckily we were able to go back to Sweetheart Villa."

I'm absolutely floored.

"He's such a gentleman," she says. "That man drives me crazy."

"You slept with him!"

"Yes."

"Seriously?"

"Yes, seriously."

"You?"

"What? Yes!" Raquel says. "Yes, of course, me. Do you think I'm an asexual clam or something? Hey, I have my needs, and I like Juan Alberto. Of course I slept with him. But I waited to tell you because I wanted to tell you in person."

"Is this a new you?"

My sister raises her eyebrow.

"Hey, I'm modern now."

We laugh.

"But wait—didn't you say you had an argument?"

"Yes, but when he got out of the car and cornered me, oh God . . . oh God, Cuchu, my body was electrified!"

I can imagine! I think about Eric and sigh.

"And then he kissed me and said, with that accent of his, 'I wouldn't mind being your slave if you were my mistress,' and I couldn't take it anymore. That's when I dragged him into the car and threw myself at him."

I'm going to die from laughing so hard.

My sister kills me.

"You threw yourself at him?"

"Oh yes . . . right there, in that very alley, it was the craziest thing I've ever done in my life. I skinned my left leg with the gear shift, but Mother of God! What a moment! It felt amazing. I hadn't had sex since the fourth month of being pregnant with Lucía and, Cuchu . . . it was incredible."

Eric looks over at me and grins. He likes to see me happy.

"When we finished, he didn't let me get out of the car and drove like a madman to your house," says my sister. "You know, Papá had left him the keys and, when we went in—"

"Tell me, tell me . . ."

God . . . I'm going crazy. My own lack of sex makes me want to know everything about my sister's adventures. She blushes, but she can't stop her confession. It just pours out of her.

"We made love everywhere. On the dining table, on the porch, in the shower, against the pantry wall, on the floor . . ."

"Wow, Raquel."

"Ah . . . and in bed too." When she sees the look of amazement on my face, she adds, "Oh, Cuchufleta, that man knows how to possess me in a way I never thought I would experience. When we're together, I literally become a she-wolf!"

My sister's earnestness is overwhelming, and just listening to her raises my libido.

"I'm so jealous of you," I tell her.

"Why?" But then she gets it. "When I got pregnant with Luz, Jesús didn't touch me for four months. He was afraid of hurting the baby."

Maybe what's happening with Eric isn't so strange.

"And when you had sex while pregnant, it was all right?"

"Hallucinatory. The desire is devastating, because your hormones are at peak levels, and that can be scary. Of course, when I got pregnant with Lucía, we separated, so I had a great time with Superman instead."

"Wait, who's Superman?"

"The dildo my foolish ex gave me. Thanks to him, I managed to get some relief."

I am increasingly shocked by the things my sister says.

"Oh, c'mon, it's not like I told you I participated in an orgy. How old are you?"

Her comment makes me laugh aloud. If she only knew.

Two days later, it's time for my visit with the gynecologist. Everyone wants to go with me, but I insist on just Eric. My father and sister understand and stay with the children at home.

I take all the test results my doctor requested on my first visit, along with the records from my visit to the emergency room. I'm nervous, expectant. The doctor looks over everything. When she does the ultrasound, she keeps an eye on Eric.

"The fetus is fine. The heartbeat is perfect and measures correctly. Just continue your normal life and take your vitamins, and I'll see you in two months," she says.

Eric and I look at each other and smile. Medusa is perfect!

When I clean the gel from my belly and return to the office, the doctor's typing on the computer.

"I'd like to ask you one thing," I say.

She stops typing.

"Yes?"

"The vomiting will eventually stop?"

"Usually, yes. At the end of the first trimester, the nausea typically disappears."

I'm about to clap. Eric smiles.

"And I can have sex? Sex with penetration?"

My husband's face is something now. He loves that I asked.

The doctor smiles knowingly.

"Of course. Just be careful, understood?"

When we leave the doctor's office, Eric is serious. Once in the car, I can't stand the tension anymore.

"You need to understand, darling, that I'm not made of stone, and you're a perpetual temptation. Your hands make me want you to touch me, your mouth makes me want your kiss, and your penis, oh God!" I say, touching it over his pants. "It makes me want you to play with me."

"Jude . . . stop."

I laugh. He smiles and gives me a kiss.

"I assure you that if I provoke you like that, I can't begin to tell you what you do to me."

"Hmm, this could get interesting."

"But—"

"I . . . I've never liked 'buts' . . ."

"We have to take it easy so we don't get freaked out again."

"You're absolutely right," I say, "but—"

"Oh, so you have a 'but' too!" Eric laughs.

"I just want to play with you!"

He doesn't answer. But he smiles. And that's a good sign.

26

I'm a little better the next day, and I decide to go shopping in Munich with Frida, Marta, and my sister. We have a great time. I insist on eating a burger and, when I dip my French fry in ketchup, I laugh.

"I love junk food," I say. "Medusa loves junk food."

My sister frowns when she hears me call my baby that name, and Frida notices.

"When Glen was in my belly, I called him Eidechse," she says.

Marta and I laugh.

"What does it mean?" Raquel asks.

I put another greasy fry in my mouth. "Lizard."

When we leave the burger place, we consider going for coffee, but then we wind up at the oldest brewery in Munich, the Hofbräuhaus, so my sister can experience it. I drink water.

Raquel is blown away. She looks as dazed as I was the first time I came here and then shows off her great talent for beer drinking. That surprises me. I didn't know that side of her. I notice Marta and Frida order a fourth round.

"Raquel, if you don't stop, I'm going to have to drag you home."

"Since you can't drink, I'm drinking for both of us," she says. "You know, you're now in the most delicious phase of pregnancy: heartburn, swollen ankles, sore tits, and wonderful morning nausea."

"Oh, you're funny, beautiful," I say, teasing.

"And from what you said, your libido is on high. How's that going?"

I can't answer. She's being so mean!

"I can tell you that, during my pregnancy, poor Andrés avoided me," Frida says. "I was a nightmare when it came to sex."

What's happening to me has happened to others, and they didn't lose their minds!

We all laugh when they bring the next round. Seeing a friend, Marta calls her over. "Tatianaaa!"

A young blonde greets my sister-in-law, who introduces her to us. The girl is charming and chats with us for a while. When she leaves, I can tell my sister has had a bit too much to drink.

"Cuchu . . . I'm very faint, or I haven't understood a thing," she says.

I'm horrified when I realize we've been talking in German the whole time.

"Oh, Raquel, honey, I'm so sorry," I say, and hug her. "We're just so used to it."

Finally, it's the last night of the year.

We still haven't had sex, but not because Eric doesn't want to, rather because I'm still feeling like crap, and now I'm the one who can't even imagine it. When Eric's mother and sister come over this afternoon, he disappears. He doesn't tell me where he's going, and that makes me angry. I'm getting very grumpy.

It's time for dinner, and Eric isn't back yet.

"Simona, we'll take everything to the table between all of us," I tell her. "But I want you seated next to Norbert, understood?"

She pretends she didn't hear me.

"I'm warning you: either you sit at the table and have dinner with everyone, or no one is having dinner."

"Oh, Simona," teases Marta, "please don't make us go without dinner."

"No chance of that," says Sonia. "Simona and Norbert will join everyone for dinner."

"My daughter is very stubborn," my father tells Simona as we carry the trays from the kitchen.

Simona winks at me.

"Yes, Manuel, I'm starting to know her." When she sees me wrinkling my nose at the coleslaw, she takes the tray from me. "I'll take this to the table. The farther away from you, the better."

"Thanks, Simona."

"Sit down, honey," says my father. "I'm done organizing the shrimp tray."

I do as he says. Today's not my best day. He sits next to me and gently moves the hair from my face.

"Why don't you go to bed, my love?"

I snort and roll my eyes.

"No, Papá. It's New Year's Eve, and I want to be with you."

"But, sweetheart, your face is telling us how drained you are. You feel terrible, don't you?"

I nod. It's my worst day by far.

"I think seeing and smelling all this food is not going to be good for you."

I look at the rich prawns, the sautéed marinade, the roast lamb, and the ham my father brought from Spain, all of it prepared with such love.

"Oh, Papá, but I love your sautéed marinade, roast lamb the way you make it, the prawns. I think eating all that would give me a sweet exhaustion."

He kisses me on the cheek. "You're like your mother even that way. She was also very disgusted by the marinade during her pregnancies. Of course, when it passed, she ate everything in sight."

The kitchen door opens, and Eric comes in.

"Sweetheart, why aren't you in bed?" he asks when he sees me with my father.

"That's what I'm saying, Eric, but you know how she is. Stubborn!"

I ignore them.

"Where have you been?" I ask Eric.

"I got an urgent call and had to deal with it."

"Cuchu, look who's here!" shouts my sister.

When I see Juan Alberto with little Lucía in his arms, I look at Eric and smile. That was the urgent matter!

Juan Alberto greets my father, who shakes his hand with a manly grip. Then he turns to me and gives me two kisses.

"How is the lovely new mom?"

"Bloated, but glad to have you here," I reply, happy for my sister.

"Dexter and Graciela send you many kisses and hope to come soon to meet the baby."

My niece comes running.

"Hey, dude, what are you doing here?"

"I came to see my pretty little lady and to challenge her to *Mario Brothers*."

Luz throws herself into his arms. It is clear this guy knows how to win over my family.

Once Luz runs off, Juan Alberto looks at my sister, who's in a daze, and kisses her on the lips.

"How is my queen?" he asks, right in front of my father.

Raquel kisses him back without hesitation.

"Very happy to see you."

My father winks at me. I know he's loving this.

"Sabrosa, tell me all about it."

My sister, totally undone, puts a finger to his mouth.

"I'd eat you up if I could."

Did she just say that in front of everyone?

Eric laughs. It's clear Juan Alberto likes this. It's clear that, after me, my father isn't surprised by much. He's such a good man!

287

When everyone finally leaves the room, the two most important men in my life hover around me, worried.

"I want to spend this special night with you, and I wouldn't miss it for anything in the world, understood?"

Half an hour later, we are all sitting around the table, and happiness has flooded my home despite my not feeling well.

This Christmas season is so different from last year, when we were just Eric, Flyn, Simona, Norbert, and me. Now my whole family is here, Eric's family, Susto, Calamar, and Juan Alberto. Wonderful!

When Sonia offers lentils to my niece and Flyn, they wrinkle their noses. That makes me smile. But I laugh when my father offers Flyn tomato soup. His eyes sparkle. I do my best to deal with dinner. Seeing so much food and, especially, smelling it, is killing me. But everyone's happiness makes this sacrifice worthwhile.

I squirm but tell myself I'm a champ and resist, barely eating, while everyone else stuffs themselves. My husband and Juan Alberto can't get enough of the ham.

Once dinner's over, we sit on the couch in front of the TV and explain to my family that we're going to see a traditional German comedy skit.

When *Dinner for One* begins, everyone laughs, and my sister, who's sitting on Juan Alberto's lap, doesn't understand a thing.

"Oh, Cuchu, Germans are so weird!"

Eric has his arms around me on the couch, just like last year. Once the skit ends, my father, Simona, and Sonia bring us glasses with grapes, and Eric does the same as he did last year: he sets up the international channel so we can see Puerta del Sol.

Oh, my Spain!

But unlike last year, this time I don't cry. My family's right here in the living room, and I feel completely happy. When midnight chimes, we all talk and ask for silence at the same time (that's a Spanish tradition). I look at Eric, who's gazing back at me, and we swallow grape after grape without looking away from each other. I want him to be the last thing I see this year and the first thing I see in the new year.

"Happy New Year!" Flyn and Luz shout as they finish their grapes.

This time nobody comes between us, and Eric, totally in love, hugs me, kisses me, and whispers in my mouth, "Happy New Year, sweetheart."

27

Spending the Epiphany with my family here is everything I wanted: laughter, noise, and gifts. We all give each other presents, and when I open my sister's and find a yellow onesie for Medusa, I'm so touched.

"Since we don't know if it's a boy or a girl, then yellow!"

Everyone laughs, and I cry, of course!

When I think there are no more gifts, Eric surprises me. He has more gifts for everyone! For my father, Juan Alberto, and Norbert, watches; for the girls, clothes and toys; and for my sister and Simona, beautiful white gold bracelets. Then he gives Flyn and me a pair of envelopes, which leave us speechless. Envelopes again?

Flyn and I look at each other, resigned. But when we open them our expression changes.

To see the gifts, go to the garage.

Laughing, we hold hands and rush to the garage. Everyone follows us, and, when we open the door, the two of us shriek. Motorcycles!

Two precious and shining Ducatis.

Flyn goes crazy with the notion of a motorcycle his own height, and I cry. My motorcycle is right here in front of me! My Ducati! I'd recognize it even among two hundred thousand others.

"I know how important it is to you," says Eric, seeing my reaction and holding me. "They tried to respect as much of the original as possible, but some things had to be replaced. Your father looked it over and said it's much better now."

I hug him and kiss him.

"Sweetheart, your bike was good before, but now it's great," says my father, who looks at us, delighted. "But I don't want you anywhere near it until you have the baby, understood?"

I nod, excited.

"No worries, Manuel," says Eric. "I'll make sure of that myself."

After a great Christmas holiday, my family and Juan Alberto return to Spain on Eric's plane. As always when I say goodbye to them, sadness overwhelms me, and this time it's double. Eric comforts me, but I don't make it easy for him, and I cry uncontrollably.

Two days later, we go back to the airport to say goodbye to Frida, Andrés, and little Glen.

"I'm going to miss you so much," I whimper.

My friend embraces me and gives me a charming smile.

"Me too. But take it easy, you know that as soon as Medusa is born, you'll have me here."

Andrés grabs me by the waist.

"Llorona, you have to come see us in Switzerland," he says. "Promise?"

"We'll try," Eric says.

At that moment, Björn is saying goodbye to Frida. "Oh . . . oh . . . another one crying. Are you pregnant too?"

I laugh, and Frida slaps him.

"Don't say that even in jest!"

After saying goodbye to our good friends and seeing them through security, Eric and Björn each take me by the arm, and we go straight to the car. I can't stop crying the whole way home. They laugh but I'm inconsolable.

"I hate my hormones!" I shout.

The next day, bored, I start to put away the Christmas decorations and see the little pieces of paper with our wishes. I smile as I remember when we read them the morning of Epiphany. I read them again now. I love Flyn's: "I want Jude to stop vomiting," "I want my uncle's eyes to heal," and "I want Simona to learn how to make *salmorejo*."

I never read the wishes he wrote last year, but I'm sure they weren't as wonderful as these. It's probably better not to have read them.

I feel good today. I haven't vomited. When I finish collecting the ornaments, I decide to take a walk in the countryside with Susto and Calamar. Seeing me grab the leashes, they jump like crazy.

How long since I've done this?

The field is beautiful. It snowed, and it's a wonderland all around me. For a long time, I just throw sticks. Susto and Calamar run after them. After spending a very pleasant time out in the fresh air, the three of us return home. It's the kind of cold that makes your skin peel, and my hands are frozen stiff and very wet.

In the afternoon, when Eric comes home, he gets upset when he finds out I went out alone with the dogs.

"I'm not angry because you went for a walk, Jude, but because you went alone."

"But what did you want me to do?" I argue. "Simona wasn't here, and I wanted to take a walk."

"And what if you'd suddenly not felt well, what then?"

We're facing off in his office when the door flies open and in come Flyn and Björn. We shut up, and the boy runs to me, hugs me, and looks accusingly at his uncle.

"Why are you always angry with my aunt?"

"What did you say?" Eric asks.

But Flyn's angry voice is equal to his uncle's.

"Don't you see she's not feeling well? Don't yell at her."

Eric looks at him, annoyed.

"Flyn, don't stick your nose where it doesn't belong, OK?"

"Then don't yell at Jude."

"Flyn . . . ," Eric says in warning.

The boy looks at me. I know him, and I know he's going to talk back, so I jump in before he has a chance to say anything else.

"OK, honey, go with Simona and let her know I want to have a snack with you today."

The boy nods, gives his uncle one of his icy looks, and leaves. Once the three of us are alone, Björn gives me an affectionate kiss on the cheek.

"Well, well, now I see what kind of support Jude has."

Eric smiles and nods.

"Flyn has decided to overprotect his aunt-mom Jude. And he really believes he has the last word. Moreover, I'm sure that right now he'd rather I leave than her."

"Don't doubt it," I say, teasing, but that just earns me an icy look from my love.

"If you're going to argue, I'm leaving," says Björn, laying a folder on Eric's desk.

"I'm the one who's leaving," I say. "I'm hungry, and I want a snack."

Eric's surprised. "You're hungry?"

It's the first time in a long time I can confirm that.

"God, eat everything and anything you want, sweetheart."

The double meaning I give to that makes me laugh, but I don't say anything. I leave the office for the kitchen. Simona's preparing a sandwich for Flyn.

"Is it true you want a snack?"

I nod and put the chocolate and vanilla plum cake she made on the table.

"I'm dying to eat this."

Simona and Flyn smile, and I stuff myself with the plum cake.

Days go by, and my nausea disappears. I'm so happy!

I've suddenly started to recover my strength, and everything that made me sick months ago now seems rich and wonderful. I listen to music and dance again.

Eric is thrilled on seeing this turn of events, and I can't even describe how I feel. I'm finally able to eat breakfast, and it feels so good. Day by day, I dare to eat more things, and suddenly I'm gobbling everything up. I'm a bottomless pit!

I get addicted to Simona's plum cake and ice cream. I want to eat them all the time, and Eric, to please me, fills the freezer with all kinds of flavors while Simona spends the whole day making plum cake after plum cake. They spoil me plenty.

In time, Eric and Flyn go back to their old ways too. If I'm careless, they'll throw themselves on the couch and play Wii for hours. That drives me crazy, even though I've convinced them to not have the game music on all the time.

While they play, I read the books I bought about babies and births. Sometimes I read things that give me goose bumps, but I have to be strong and continue. I must be informed. I'm going to be a mom!

One Saturday afternoon, after I convince them to take a walk in the countryside with the dogs, we're all frozen when we get back.

As usual, uncle and nephew take up the Wii and play. Of the two, I don't know who's the bigger kid. For more than an hour, I play with them, but when my fingers hurt from so much playing, I decide to give myself a bath in our beautiful Jacuzzi.

I go up to our room, drink a little juice, and prep the Jacuzzi. I light candles that smell like peach and put on music to relax. Perfect! When the Jacuzzi's full, I carefully step into it.

"Oh yes . . . ," I say. "This is the life."

I close my eyes and relax.

The music plays, and I notice how my body releases tensions second by second. I love these moments of peace. I deserve them. But then the bathroom door opens, and there's Flyn.

So much for peace!

He puts a hand over his eyes so he can't see my breasts.

"I'm going with Aunt Marta to her house."

"Oh, is Marta here?"

"Yes, here I am!" she says with Eric in tow.

My relaxing bath has gone to hell.

"What's going on? Did something happen?" I ask.

My sister-in-law smiles and winks at me.

"I was hanging out with my friend Tatiana, and, when we went by her house, she gave me that little dress you asked about a long time ago. You know, the blue one. So, I left it in your closet." I laugh when I think about the blue dress. "And since tomorrow I'm going riding in a hot-air balloon with Arthur, I thought maybe Flyn would like to join us."

"Yes, yes, yes, I want to go!" the boy exclaims.

I look at Eric. He's serious. Like always, he considers the pros and cons of balloon riding and when I see him hesitate, I know I have to say something.

"It seems perfect, Flyn. Have a good time, honey."

"Thanks, Mom."

Every time he calls me that, my heart leaps with joy.

Eric looks at me. I smile, and then the boy kisses me and runs to his uncle.

"I promise I'll pay attention to everything Aunt Marta says . . . Dad."

I laugh. My grumpy Smurf is pretty smart.

In the end, my Iceman defrosts. He smiles, hugs the boy, and kisses him on the head.

"Have fun," he says, then turns to his sister. "Please keep an eye on him; be careful. I don't want anything to happen."

Amused, Marta rolls her eyes.

"C'mon, Flyn. Let me put a collar and leash on you."

When everyone finally leaves the bathroom, I lie back in the Jacuzzi. I close my eyes again and try to relax.

A little music . . .

A little calm . . .

I'm almost there when the door opens again. Eric. Again. Before he can say anything, I try to reassure him.

"Nothing's going to happen, honey. Marta takes good care of Flyn."

My guy doesn't answer, but he comes up to the Jacuzzi. He's looking at my nipples. With my pregnancy, they've gotten dark and huge and tempting.

"Do you want to give me a little kiss here?" I ask as I point to my nipple.

Eric leans down, and I yank him, fully dressed, into the Jacuzzi. The water overflows, and the entire bathroom floods. I laugh, and he goes to protest, then cracks up too.

But he grimaces when he gets near one of the lit candles.

"Did you burn yourself?" I ask, concerned.

Eric examines his hand.

"No, sweetheart, but be careful with so many candles, or we'll end up with a visit from the fire department."

That makes me laugh. I finally manage to take off his clothes and leave him naked in the Jacuzzi despite his protests. I get out of the water, and, being careful not to slip on the wet floor, I throw down about two hundred towels and stomp all over them.

"I have a surprise for you."

"A surprise?"

I nod and open the door.

"Give me two minutes and don't move."

Happy to find myself feeling so much better, I go to the closet where Marta left the little blue dress! I'm going to surprise him!

I put on the firefighter's outfit, though it's a little big on me, and go back to the bathroom, where I see my favorite German's surprised face.

"Did the gentleman call the fire department?"

Eric laughs.

"Where did you get that?"

"A friend of your sister's left it for me."

"For what?"

Oh, how little imagination men have sometimes.

"For a striptease, silly boy."

"A striptease?" he asks, open-mouthed.

I say yes.

"I've never really performed one for you."

My guy raises his eyebrows, sprawls in the Jacuzzi, and nods delightedly.

I go change the CD. Moments later, music begins to play, and, recognizing it, Eric claps and laughs.

Start the show!

Tom Jones's sultry voice begins to sing "Sex Bomb" and, without an iota of shame, I wiggle to the beat of the music. I slide off my huge jacket and throw it aside. Eric whistles. After that comes the helmet. I toss my hair in the purest Hollywood way. Eric applauds and whistles again, and I cheer as I sing.

Piece by piece, I strip off the firefighter's outfit while my sweetheart gazes at me just the way I like: with desire. I know he's loving this. His expression and the intensity of his look give him away. I dance; I shimmy. When I'm finally naked, I get in the Jacuzzi. Eric kisses me.

"I love you, my little stripper." He reaches for my breasts. "These are the nicest ever."

That makes me laugh. Actually, pregnancy has made my breasts incredible. Every time I look at them in the mirror, I love them more, but I know that when Medusa comes, they'll disappear.

Excited by the show I've offered him, my love grabs me by the waist and sits me on top of him in the Jacuzzi. He penetrates me gently while he murmurs in my ear.

"You really are a sex bomb, sweetheart."

"Yes . . . and that bomb is about to explode."

Eric grins and, when I go to hold on to the Jacuzzi to better position myself on him, he stops me.

"Let me, sweetheart. I don't want to hurt you."

"You're not hurting me."

"Careful, sweetheart . . . slowly."

But I don't want care or slow. I want passion and force.

"Jude . . . ," he scolds me.

"Eric . . . ," I scold him back.

My German looks at me, stops, and spoils our beautiful moment.

"Jude, either you do it carefully so as not to hurt yourself, or we're not doing anything."

I have two options: I can get angry and send him out for a walk or accept his caution.

I decide on the second option. I want sex!

I let him set the pace. I let him limit himself and limit me, and although we have a good time, when we reach our climax, I know we both missed our wild side.

When we go to bed that night, he kisses me and tenderly hugs me.

"I love you, sex bomb."

In February I enter my fifth month, and my body has undergone many changes. The first is that now I notice how Medusa moves. The second is that my little belly is becoming a balloon. If it goes on like this, I'm not going to be able to walk. I'm going to roll!

Everything that thinned out the first months has fattened up in the blink of an eye.

"Judith," my gynecologist says when she weighs me, "you must begin to control your diet. In this last month you've gained almost eight pounds."

"OK," I say.

Eric intuits that I'm lying, and I make sure I speak before he does.

"Give me a diet, and I'll follow it," I tell the doctor.

She opens a folder, and, after looking at several sheets, she hands me one.

"This will be best for you."

Diets and I have never been friends.

We talk to the doctor about what my body needs, and she tells me this next month, the sixth, I should start prenatal classes. I listen to everything she has to say.

"And can I have sex?"

Eric looks at me. He knows why I'm asking.

"Of course, yes. Your sex life should be normal," the gynecologist says.

"Normal?" I insist.

"Totally normal," she says.

I'm about to ask if it can be more intense than normal, but Eric's eyes tell me to cool it. I back off. I don't want to irritate him with my direct questions.

When it's time to do the ultrasound, I can hardly look at the screen. Eric's face is so expressive that I feel like covering him with kisses right then and there.

"Look at your baby!" says the gynecologist.

I say "ohh!" in this cottony way that's reminiscent of my sister. I'm turning into a gushball.

"Incredible," Eric murmurs.

Eric and I stare at the 3-D ultrasound like two fools and grin.

"Can you see if it's a boy or a girl?" I ask.

The doctor moves the device, but we can't see anything. The baby's not cooperating.

"Sorry. Your baby's legs are crossed in a way that I can't tell."

"It doesn't matter," Eric says. "The important thing is the baby's well."

The doctor nods.

"It's going to be a pretty big baby."

Stop!

Did she say big?

How big?

That's terrifying. The bigger, the more painful to get that baby out of me.

But I don't want to screw up this moment, so I just shut up. For several minutes, the doctor lets us stare at the screen, and, when the session ends, Eric and I kiss each other. Everything's going well!

When we get home, excited about what the doctor has shown us, we let Flyn, Norbert, and Simona also see the images. We all watch like fools, playing the video several times.

That I'm back to my usual good mood pleases everyone. Laughter has returned to the house. I play jokes and am my usual crazy self.

That night, when we go up to our room, I sit on the bed next to Eric.

"Have you thought of a name for Medusa?" I ask him.

"If it's a girl, I would like her named Hannah, after my sister," he says.

I agree. I like the name, and it seems like a beautiful idea.

"What if it's a boy?" I ask.

My German kisses me.

"If it's a boy, you choose. What are you thinking?"

"I don't know. Maybe Manuel, like my father."

Eric nods. I snuggle up against him.

"I want you."

He lies back on the bed.

"And I want you, beautiful," he murmurs.

Oh yeah, oh yeah . . .

The months of drought and malaise are over.

I want my Iceman, and he wants me. Without stopping to kiss me, Eric takes off my panties, crawls between my legs, and, without preliminaries, slowly introduces his penis in me.

My God, I've been so long without this feeling.

I wrap my legs around his body, but Eric pulls back.

"No, sweetheart . . . I don't want to risk hurting the baby."

I stop and look at him.

"What did you say?"

He's still inside me.

"I don't want to put too much pressure on you. I don't want to hurt the baby."

I laugh. Oh, what a pisser!

He thinks he's going to hit Medusa on the head with his dick. When he sees me laughing, he frowns.

"I don't know what you think is so funny. I don't think I'm saying anything crazy."

Gripping his ass hard, I impale myself on him, and he gasps.

"This is what I need," I tell him. "Give it to me."

Eric resists, and I repeat the same operation. I force myself on him. This time we both gasp.

That depth is what I need, what I crave. Eric's breathing accelerates. He tries to fight against his animal instincts. I provoke him by rubbing against him, and in the end, I win.

Eric is so hot, so excited, that he puts my hands flat on the bed, and, without thinking, starts pumping inside me with passion and delight. I don't stop him. His thrusts make me feel alive. I need this. Oh yeah.

I rotate my hips to give him even more depth, and I scream. I bite him on the shoulder, and Eric grinds his teeth as he sinks into me again and again, and I go crazy.

Our animal instincts emerge, and we savor our hot encounter.

When we finish, we're both panting. We haven't done anything like that in a long time.

"I want to do it again," I say.

Eric leaps out of bed.

"No, sweetheart. We can't do it like that again."

I protest but he's adamant.

"Think about what happened last time."

"But, Eric . . ."

"I said no."

"But I need it. My hormones are out of control and—"

"No, sweetheart. That's enough for today."

I feel a heat rising.

My eyes fill, and I sit and sob on the bed. I've become such a crybaby. I cover my face with my hands.

"Sweetheart, sweetheart, don't cry. Get mad at me, yell at me, but don't cry."

He pulls my hands from my face, and, despite how horrible I am when I cry, I look at him and whimper.

"You don't like me anymore."

"Don't say that, my treasure."

"I don't turn you on at all anymore. I have big, dark nipples and . . . and . . . I'm fat . . . and ugly, and that's why you don't want to make love with me."

A patient Eric wipes away my tears.

"No, sweetheart. None of that is true."

"Yes, it is," I insist. "You're a sexually active man and . . . and . . . I'm just a cow!"

He smiles, sits next to me on the bed, and puts his arms around me.
"Listen, beautiful . . ."

But I don't listen and, between hiccups and the most ridiculous crying, I go on.

"I'm afraid you're not asking for what you want, and in the end, you'll get bored and leave me!"

Eric is surprised.

"Why would I leave you, sweetheart?"

"Because I've become so weepy, horrible, grumpy, and deformed, and you don't like it. You aren't looking for me anymore. You don't want to play with me. You don't throw me up against the wall to make love to me."

My guy hugs me. He cradles me until the hiccups go away.

"Kiss me," he says. "I'm asking for what I want. I want you to kiss me right now."

Hearing that makes me cry more. Why am I being so silly?

Am I really going crazy?

I sob and scratch my neck. Eric pushes me lovingly down on the bed. He takes my hand from my neck so I won't scratch anymore and kisses me.

"You are the most beautiful thing and what I want and desire most in the world. You're beautiful—the most beautiful woman on the face of the earth to me. You're so special that I'm afraid of hurting you. Don't you understand?"

"Why would you hurt me?"

He fixes his impressive eyes on me.

"Because you and I are savages when we make love." He's right about that—we are tremendous!

"But the doctor said we can continue doing it as usual. We'll be careful and . . ."

Eric smiles and kisses the tip of my nose.

"I know. But I don't want to hurt you. Your body is experiencing too many changes, and I'm afraid. Put yourself in my situation for a moment, please, sweetheart."

"I do, Eric, but my hormones are totally out of control, and I need you."

He smiles again. He gives me a kiss, two . . . more hot and kinky kisses.

"Now I'm going to sit you on me, and we'll do it again but carefully, OK?"

I nod and smile. I'm getting what I want.

Let's do it again!

I'm so spoiled.

When I sit on him, I let his cock enter me slowly, and I close my eyes. Oh yeah! His hands encircle my round waist.

"God . . . how I like having you like this," he says.

I open my eyes and look at him. His face is before me. I grab him by the neck and pull him up to suck one of my nipples. I'm ultrasensitive, but I love it.

"Oh yes . . . don't stop."

He doesn't. I'm pleased, and I move my hips in search of my pleasure. Yes . . . oh yes . . . I don't want him to stop.

Suddenly, I squeeze my hips against him, and I wince. Eric stops.

"It hurt, right?"

I don't want to lie, and I nod. His face breaks a little, and I kiss him. "Let's go."

"Sweet . . ."

"I need you," I whisper.

He pauses to consider the situation.

"Careful, OK?"

I nod. We move.

Being on top gives me more depth, and, when Eric can't take it anymore, he gets up with me still in his arms, puts me down on the bed, and, holding back our wilder impulses, we reach climax together.

That night, when we turn off the light and hug, he kisses me on the lips.

"I'm never going to leave you, crazy girl," he says. "I don't know how to live without you."

28

The days pass, and I'm still demanding sex. Eric only gives it to me in small doses.

I try to understand him, but my hormones don't make it easy for me.

Sometimes, to avoid the discussion, Eric works late in his office. I know that's why he does it, even if he denies it. He knows that when he makes it back to our room, I'll be sleeping like a log and won't wake up.

I start my prenatal classes. They're two hours each, two days a week. Eric goes with me. He doesn't skip a single one. Surrounded by other couples, we do everything the teacher tells us, on a mat and then on a huge ball. We have fun and learn to breathe for when the time comes. I crack up. Seeing Eric huffing and puffing like this is the best!

During these same days, I start to feel a slight pulling inside me. I consult with the gynecologist, and she tells me they're small contractions, but that I don't have anything to worry about. It's normal.

I worry anyway . . .

I get restless . . .

I'm scared to death . . .

Every time I feel one, even if it doesn't hurt, I totally freeze, and Eric blanches when he sees me. I don't know who's more scared, him or me.

Some afternoons I go pick up Flyn at school. I see my new friend María and have fun talking to her about Spain and our lives here in Germany.

The cockatoos haven't talked about me again, and I have that on good authority. One of them turned out to be María's friend, and she told me that, after what happened, the school sent a memo to each of them in which Laila denied what she'd said. It also had a clear warning that any new defamatory comment could be the basis for a lawsuit.

Surprised, I speak with Björn, and he confesses it was him who'd sent the letter.

And, hey, it worked. They may continue talking among themselves, but the rumors have died.

One afternoon, Eric surprises me when he comes home from work. After kissing me, he asks me to pretty up and invites me to dinner.

I look in the mirror, and I don't like what I see.

I'm not sexy. I'm as big as a tank. My ankles are swollen, and my belly's a huge ball. But there's nothing I can do about it. I can't hide it so I wear a trendy little maternity dress and my high boots, and when Eric and Flyn see me come down the stairs, they both exclaim, "Beautiful!"

I smile and figure they're just saying that to make me feel good. What dears!

The night has promise, and in the car, I sing along to a song on the radio called "Ja" from a German group I really like named Silbermond.

"I like to hear you sing in German."

I rest my head back.

"It's a very nice song."

"And romantic," he says.

When we arrive at the beautiful restaurant, Eric gets out of the car, comes around, and takes my hand to go in. The valet quickly takes our vehicle. The maître d' greets us and guides us to a nice table.

Dinner is wonderful, and with the appetite I now have, I eat everything on my plate, and, if Eric isn't careful, everything on his. We talk, we laugh, and we're the same as always when suddenly he asks me, "Why didn't you tell me about Máximo and my mother?"

I stare at him. Now we're in it!

How did he find out about that?

"What do you mean?"

Eric tilts his head.

"Did you think I wouldn't find out my mother went to a party with your little friend from Guantanamera?"

I laugh. He doesn't.

Just thinking about that great moment when Sonia asked us to find her a dark-skinned escort makes me laugh.

But damn it. And we were getting along so well.

My face must be giving me away. I drink some water.

"Look, Eric, your mother's a young, single woman who just wants to have fun."

"But does it have to be with Máximo?"

I get it. Máximo and my mother-in-law is a crazy combo. I decide to be honest.

"Honey, I confess! I knew about it. But before you get all bent out of shape and the Iceman returns, let me tell you it was your mother who called us, your sister and me. She wanted a date for the party who'd leave Trevor in the dust, and all we did was look for someone to go with her. Of course, Máximo was a gentleman. He didn't cross any lines; you can be sure of that. He escorted her to the party and then took her home. End of story."

Suddenly, he laughs. That unsettles me. Then he takes my hand and kisses it.

"The three of you are going to be the end of me."

I'm glad to see he's beginning to understand his mother's philosophy of life.

Unexpectedly, Medusa moves. I quickly put his hand on my belly. Eric notices the movement, and we kiss.

When we finish dinner, he surprises me again by asking if I want to go for a drink. I accept even though I can't have alcohol. I'm having too much fun to go home yet. And when we arrive at Sensations, the place with all the mirrors, I'm confused.

"We're only here for drinks, understood?"

I nod; my libido's on a break anyway. After so many threesomes and orgies, I only want Eric. Will there be hot sex for me when we get home tonight?

On entering the first room, I see Björn at the bar. When he spots us, he gives me a loving hug and greets Eric.

"What a delight to see you here. You look gorgeous today, my little chub."

Eric smiles, and I'm happy too.

Björn introduces me to some friends of his I don't know, but I notice Eric does know them. The two women are lovely and quickly inquire about my condition. One of them is a mom and smiles when she listens to me. For an hour or so, we all talk, and I'm aware of an occasional man looking at me, but Eric doesn't let me go. That excites me.

My mind is clouded, and I almost snort when I think about what Eric and Björn could make me feel in any of those reserved rooms. Suddenly, I see our friend greeting someone, and I'm stunned to see it's the constipated poodle.

When she comes over to me, Fosqui barks with her thin little voice.

"You look amazing, Judith. More beautiful than ever," she says, surprising me.

I know she's just saying that to look good in front of Björn, but I'll take it!

We talk for another hour or so, and the place fills up. I yawn without realizing it. Eric kisses me on the neck.

"We're going home, beautiful."

"We can stay a little more," I say. We haven't been out in a long time.

"Jude, we've only come for a drink," he says, seemingly reading my mind.

I know, but does he have to remind me? Does he think I'm asking for something else? I must look particularly bewildered because we catch Björn's attention.

"What's going on?"

"Jude and I are leaving," Eric says.

I look to Björn for help, but he doesn't offer any.

"Yes, it's better if you go now. It's late for her."

How is it late for me?

Who do these two think they are, my father?

I want to protest, but I don't. It won't do any good anyway.

Once we say goodbye to everyone, Eric and I leave the premises.

"I want to drive," I say when we get to the car.

Eric looks at me.

"You're tired, sweetheart. Let me."

"I'm not."

My response is so intense that he gives in without a word. I'm behind the wheel, driving in silence. I watch him out of the corner of my eye, looking at me.

"Sweetheart, we only went to have a drink."

I nod. I don't say a word. I drive.

Seeing my frown, Eric sighs. He knows me and knows my defenses are up. I watch him open the glove compartment, take out a CD, and put it on. Moments later, our song plays. "Black and White," by Malú. He's trying to placate me. But my hormones and my bad mood have come together, and I'm the worst of the worst.

His hand reaches for my hair.

"Better?"

I don't answer. The reminder that music tames the savage beasts makes me angrier.

"You're not going to answer me?"

I drive in silence while Malú's voice rings in the car. It's for the best. I know if I say anything, it'll be inappropriate, and I'll mess everything up.

Eric gives up. He rests his head back while the beautiful song continues. When it's over and Ricardo Montaner begins to sing "Convénceme," I hear Eric humming, and I don't know what happens to me.

I swerve to the right and stop the car.

"Get out of the car."

Eric looks at me. I look at him.

I turn up the song.

Suddenly, my German grins when he thinks he understands what that means.

I'm so bad!

He undoes his seatbelt, opens the door, and gets out of the car. I reach over, close the car door, and take off like a rocket.

Through the rearview mirror, I see Eric standing still. He wasn't expecting that. But the same fury that made me take off now makes me stop once he starts vanishing from sight.

What am I doing?

Once again, I've let myself be carried away by my impulses, and what I've just done is wrong. Very wrong. I look for traffic both ways and make a U-turn. I feel a contraction and curse. There's no question I brought this on myself. I'm going back for him. I see Eric walking down the sidewalk. He sees me and stops. His face is totally Iceman.

He looks scary!

I make another U-turn, and, when I'm at his side, his eyes pierce me. He walks to my door decisively and throws it open.

"Get out of the car!"

He's furious. I don't move.

"Get. Out. Of. The. Car," he says very slowly.

I do what he says, but when I try to kiss him to ask for forgiveness, he does the cobra. Not unexpected. At a time like this, I would do the same.

He's very angry.

It's cold as fuck, and I suspect he's going to pay me back by just driving away and leaving me here. I deserve it.

I don't move, just watch him get in the car, and, after huffing and slamming his hand on the steering wheel, he looks at me and hisses.

"What are you waiting for? Get in the car."

As I walk to the passenger door, I hope he takes off. But he doesn't. He waits until I get in the car, and, once I've put on my seatbelt, he turns off the car.

"Can you tell me why you just did that?" he asks.

"It's the hormones."

"Don't be ridiculous, Jude. I'm sick of your fucking hormones," he says, seething.

He's right. I can't blame everything on my hormones.

"I was furious."

Eric nods. "And since you were furious, you can make me get out of the car in the middle of the night and just leave, right?"

"I came back. I'm here, right?"

My eyes fill with tears. I've screwed up, and it's my doing, mine alone.

Eric looks at me again and finally moderates his tone of voice.

"Jude, I'm trying to have all the patience in the world with you. I understand your hormones are playing tricks on you. I understand you resent me for a thousand things every day, and that you'll get mad at absurd things. I understand that's all part of being pregnant. But now I want you to understand that my patience has begun to crack, and I'm afraid of losing my temper with you."

I don't answer. He has more right to respond that way than a saint. His patience with me has been infinite. I feel terrible.

"In your state, I don't want anyone to touch you," he says. "I want to take care of you. I need it! I enjoy sharing you other times, but not now. Now I only want you for me and—"

"Have you thought about what I want?"

The Iceman looks at me and cuts me with his eyes, and, understanding his frustration, I try to clarify.

"I don't need you to share me with anyone," I say. "I don't want to be with others. I just want you to make love to me like we like. Our way. I need you. I've been telling you for months and months, and you don't want to listen to me."

Eric curses and slams the steering wheel again.

"I've told you a thousand times I don't want to hurt you. Don't you hear me? Do you think I don't want to fuck you the way you want? That I don't want to have you in my arms and make love, balls to the wall like we like? Goddamn it, Jude! I want it with all my might, and I can't wait until we do it like that again."

"But—"

"I love you; you love me. Your pregnancy and our baby are what's important right now. That's all."

I love Medusa more every day, but I need him too.

Eric starts the car and drives silently to our house, while I feel that I need, as Alejandro Sanz says, "support for my heart."

The days pass, and our evening out did nothing but worsen our communications. The situation is so bad that, when Eric comes home, even Susto and Calamar get out of the way.

And sex between us is weird. I compare it to eating salt-free chips. You enjoy them because you like them, but you know they could be better with a little more spice.

Like every night, I wake up with an immediate urge to pee. I'm constantly peeing! I look at the clock: 2:12 a.m., and I'm surprised to see Eric's not in bed.

I go to the bathroom and then stealthily go looking for him and find him in his office. He's jerking off to the video he recorded with Frida that day at the hotel. I crawl back to bed and cry when I realize I'm not included in his game. Damned hormones!

I love my Medusa, but I don't want to get pregnant ever again!

When he comes back to our room, I pretend I'm asleep. Eric gets into bed, and, when he hugs me from behind and I feel his huge erection, I relax. Hmm, how delicious! But I contain myself. I'm not going to ask for anything. I'm tired of this.

Surprised, I notice he's kissing me on the shoulder, the neck, and around my head.

"I know you're not asleep, you cheater. I heard you going up the stairs."

My answer is to say nothing. But when I feel him taking off my panties, I let go. Hardly moving, I notice his hands on my sex. Oh yes . . . play with me. When he gets me all wet, he brings his cock close and slides it inside.

I moan.

"After you have the baby, I'm going to lock you up for a month, and I'm not going to stop fucking you against the wall, on the floor, on the table, everywhere."

His words excite me, my spine arches, and I feel his penis go deeper.

"I'll undress you; I'll fuck you; I'll offer you; I'll look at you, and you'll accept, right?"

"Yes," I gasp.

Carefully, Eric penetrates me again and again. His attacks increase in rhythm, and I join him in search of more. The sound of our bodies coming together is electrifying. Again and again, he pierces me with care until he can't take it anymore and lets himself go.

When it's over, he kisses my neck.

"I miss you, sweetheart."

"And I miss you," I reply.

For a few minutes, we don't move, until Eric pulls himself from inside me, and I turn toward him.

"I'm sorry, my love."

"For what?"

"For the other day, in the car."

The darkness doesn't let me see his eyes, but after kissing me on the lips, he hugs me tight.

"Don't worry about it. It was nothing; just don't do it again."

"I promise I won't."

I notice how his body moves when he smiles, and I look for his mouth and kiss him. I do what he does to me that I like so much. I suck his upper lip, then the lower one, and after giving him a little nibble, I kiss him passionately.

Eric accepts my kiss willingly. He devours it, and, moments later, he leaves me breathless, but it doesn't matter. I need that passion. I crave that. Kiss after kiss, our bodies are warm, and, when I feel his cock erect and playful again, I take it in my hands.

"Shall we do it again?"

Eric kisses me.

"No."

"Why not?"

"It's late, and I think we've had enough."

That's a blow to me. It's not enough, and I insist.

"Eric . . ."

315

He moves away from me, gets up, and turns on the light in the room. We look each other in the eye.

"Jude, please don't start."

He disappears into the bathroom and closes the door. I get up and head to the bathroom, but when I put my hand on the knob, I stop and go back to bed.

I'm angry and excited. How can he leave me like this?

I need sex. I open the drawer. I do like my sister in her time of drought and snag my own Superman. The lipstick Eric gave me months ago. I immediately bring it to my swollen, wet clit and masturbate.

Oh yeah!

This is what I need.

This gives me what I'm looking for. Love my toy!

I close my eyes and press it to me. I find my pleasure and let myself go while I gasp and vibrate in bed.

When I open my eyes, Eric's beside me, and he doesn't look happy. He's caught me!

We face each other like rivals. I gaze down his body and see his steely and erect cock. He knows my game and is even more excited. His look is wild and drives me crazy. I know what he wants to do with me this instant, and I want it too. I want it with all my soul.

My breathing is still ragged from my climax, but I open my legs for him. I show myself; I extend an invitation to keep playing. I tempt him to take me however he wants. But he isn't into it and turns around and goes back to the bathroom again, slamming the door.

I'm pissed now and curse. I squirm in bed, feeling rejected. I'm getting angrier and angrier by the moment. When he comes out of the bathroom ten minutes later, he's drenched. He took a shower. He's wearing boxers, and I notice his erection's gone. I imagine what happened in the bathroom, and, without speaking, I take my turn, lipstick vibrator in hand.

I slam the door, of course. How could it be otherwise?

I look in the mirror and see my crazy hair.

"Fuck you, Eric Zimmerman."

I wash. I wash the lipstick. I get back in bed, and under his watchful eye, I put on a pair of panties. I put the toy away in the drawer. I don't kiss him.

"Good night," I say.

He doesn't answer. I wrap myself in the blankets.

But my body is so hot that I take off the covers and sit up.

"I hate what you just did."

"And what am I supposed to do?" he answers. His voice is hard.

"You jerked off."

"Didn't you do the same?"

I want to smash the lamp on his head.

"The difference is that I did it because you didn't want anything to do with me."

I turn around and cover myself. I don't want to talk to him anymore.

29

When I wake up the next morning, I'm alone in bed like always. Eric's already at work. Down in the kitchen, Simona's preparing me breakfast.

"We have two episodes of *Emerald Madness* saved. Do you want to watch them?" she asks.

I nod and, once I've finished eating, we both head to the living room.

That day, we watch hopefully as Luis Alfredo Quiñones opens a small box and sees a pendant Esmeralda Mendoza gave him, then experiences a flashback and begins to remember things. Simona and I hold hands. This looks good. That morning, Esmeralda rides out with her son, and Luis Alfredo watches them from afar and has another flashback. His mind floods with memories, and Simona and I applaud when he's suddenly aware the woman in his life is Esmeralda and not Lupita Santúñez, the nurse.

When the two episodes finish, we're both worked up.

I propose we go for a walk. She refuses. It's snowing, and it's not a good time for a pregnant woman like me to go walking on those roads.

She's right. I go to my little room, although I can't sit on the soft carpet like I used to, or they'd have to use a crane to hoist me up. I sit on a chair, open my laptop, and connect to Facebook to chat with my friends, the Warriors. As always, talking to them lifts my spirits, and I end up grinning.

After a while, Simona brings me the phone. It's Eric.

"What's up?"

"Hi, dear. How are you today?"

"All right."

"Are you still upset about last night?"

"Yes."

"Listen, sweetheart, you have to—"

"No, you listen to me." I cut him off. I'm very angry. "What you did last night hurt me. Why are you so hard? Didn't you hear the doctor say we can have a full sex life?"

"Jude . . ."

"Don't 'Jude' me, please. Why are you such a . . . ?"

I stop myself. It's not fair to insult him.

"Just say it, sweetheart; you know you want to say it!"

"I don't. I refuse to give you the pleasure from saying it."

He shuts up. I consider the advantage I have of being at home while he's at the office.

"I have a basketball game this afternoon," he finally says, "and I forgot my gym bag. Would you please bring it to me at the sports center at five?"

I want to say no.

"Fine. Norbert will take it to you."

"I'd like you to bring it to me."

How nice, but the viper in me can't stop.

"I'd like other things, and, look, I'm dealing with it and putting up with it."

I hear Eric snort.

"I look forward to seeing you, sweetheart."

"Fine, fine. I'll bring it to you."

When I hang up, I realize I didn't even say goodbye. My God, what an asshole I am!

The truth is my Iceman deserves express entry to heaven. To put up with me when I get unbearable is unbearable. And lately I'm the worst. I call his cell back.

"I love you, grumpy," I say when he picks up.

I hear him laugh, a laugh I adore.

"And I love you more than my life, sweetheart."

It's snowing when we leave home in the afternoon, and it's very cold. Norbert takes me to the sports center, and I'm happy again. I'm all over the place with my hormones. When we arrive, I see my guy leaning on our car, waiting for me.

God, he's so handsome!

Once he spots us, Eric comes over to the car and kisses me on the lips.

"Hello, beautiful, how are you?"

"Happy, now that I'm with you."

We walk to the sports center and go directly to the locker rooms.

"You know where you have to go, right?"

I nod, and, when I think he's going to let go, he pulls me toward him again, sucks my upper lip, then the lower one, and kisses me after a little nibble.

Oh yeah, oh yeah . . .

I love that, and I don't care who sees us.

"I don't want to argue with you again, understood, sweetheart?"

I nod. It's clear the Zimmerman Effect knocks me completely out of combat. I smile, and he gives me a sweet little slap on the ass.

"I'll look for you in the bleachers. Wait for me," he says.

With a silly little smile on my face, I climb the stands. I see none of our friends are here yet, and I miss Frida. I look around and notice people have started coming in. My spirits sink when I see Björn's constipated poodle.

Fosqui comes up, wiggling her hips on her impressive heels. The TV diva is dressed in leopard pants and a semitransparent blouse of the most suggestive sort. I smile without realizing it. I'm wearing a down vest and snow boots. Glamorous to the nth degree.

"Hi, Judith," she says.

Surprised she remembers my name, I try to remember hers. What was it? I rack my brain but all that comes to me is "Fosqui" or "constipated poodle."

"Hello, how are you?" I say.

She looks at me curiously.

"Are you OK?"

Oh, what?

"I'm perfectly fine," I respond.

She nods, sits down next to me, and doesn't say a word to me again. Ten minutes later, when the boys come out on the court, I scream and wave at Eric and Björn. They wave back, and the game begins.

I'm committed to my team, so I shriek and groan when necessary, while the poodle sits quietly. She simply watches them play. In the end, Eric's team loses.

"Today's not been a good day," I say.

The poodle looks at me and blinks.

"But from this moment on, it will be, at least for me. Björn and I are staying with friends." She lowers her voice. "So we can play."

Why is she telling me this?

She seems to be gloating, but I'm not willing to let her.

"You do that. Play as much as you can."

Without looking at her, I walk to the locker room and feel one of my contractions. I touch my belly and calm down. Björn comes out of the locker room, kisses the poodle on the lips, and then greets me.

"Hi, chubs, how are you?"

"I roll more than I walk, but I'm good," I answer.

He hugs me and smiles, and then Eric emerges from the locker room. Björn and I are still wrapped around each other.

"Should I be worried about anything?" Eric asks, teasing.

"Yes!" we answer in unison.

We all laugh. Björn lets go of me, and Eric hugs me.

"Lunch the other day was fantastic, wasn't it?" asks the poodle.

Björn nods, and Eric does too. Lunch? What lunch?

"We have to do it again sometime. I'd be happy to go back to your house, Björn."

My face freezes.

What is this about Eric having lunch with Fosqui and Björn at his house?

A girl approaches the poodle to ask for an autograph, and they step away from us. Björn and Eric look at me, understanding what I've picked up.

"Jude, it was a work lunch," says Björn.

"At your house?"

Alarmed, Eric takes my wrist.

"Jude, don't draw any conclusions."

"Did you have lunch with Fosqui? With the constipated poodle?"

Björn lets out a laugh.

"Fosqui? You call her the constipated poodle?"

But Eric isn't laughing, especially when I start to walk toward the sports center exit.

"We didn't eat at his house," he says. "We ate at a restaurant, Jude."

"I know very well what you do at his house." And then I turn to Björn. "And you, you bad friend, how could you allow it?"

Stunned, Björn is about to respond when Eric interrupts.

"Sweetheart, will you calm down? Nothing happened. We went to the restaurant next to Björn's house. I wanted to ask Agneta for advertising contacts to put the company on TV."

It doesn't matter—he's already put me in a horrible mood. I'm furious.

"Dickheads! You are two dickheads!"

They look at each other. Björn's astonished.

"There goes our day," Eric mutters.

His comment makes me even angrier, and I start walking away again.

"Listen, chubs," says Björn, anticipating me. "Don't do this. Eric came to pick me up. Then Agneta arrived, and five minutes later, we went out and grabbed a bite at a restaurant while we talked about Müller's advertising. Why don't you believe us?"

When he goes to hold me, I slap his hands away.

"First, I'm letting you call me chubs because I'm pregnant, but once I stop being pregnant, if you ever say it again, I'll break your legs. Second, I don't give three shits what you do with your poodle, and, believe it or not, I know Eric hasn't done squat with that . . . that . . ." Then I turn to Eric. "Third, why didn't you just tell me you'd had a meal with her?"

"Fuck, you really are in a state," says Björn.

Eric exchanges glances with his friend.

"You were angry that day and didn't want to talk. That's why I didn't tell you. But, please, don't get it in your head that this woman, Björn, and I have anything going because it's not true, all right?"

I close my eyes. I know he's right, and, getting close to him, I put my head on his chest.

"Don't ever let me get pregnant again. I'm going crazy."

Eric smiles. He hugs me.

"I'm going home with Jude," he tells Björn. "Good luck with the poodle!"

30

I'm getting so big!

I can't see my feet anymore! Never mind all the other things that are lost from view.

I'm wearing panties that look like they're from the Victorian era. According to the salesclerks, they're panties for pregnant women, but, according to me, they're like turtlenecks for my groin. Is it possible to be sexy while pregnant? With these panties that come all the way up to my tits, the answer is a definite no.

When Eric sees them, he can't stop laughing until I throw a shoe at his head. Poor thing, I hit him smack on the noggin, and now he has a bump.

My contractions are more frequent and more intense. They don't hurt, but I know they're the prelude to the ordeal I'm going to have to go through. Mother of God, what intense pain. I don't even want to think about it!

I don't follow the doctor's diet nor her other instructions, and, on my next visit, the gynecologist reads me the riot act.

Why am I trying to deny it? It all goes in one ear and out the other. I've only gained twenty-six pounds in eight and a half months. My sister gained fifty-five. What's there to complain about?

Eric looks at me while the gynecologist scolds me. I tell him to please keep quiet, and he prudently does not open his mouth. I'm aware that in these last months, I've become a tyrant, and the poor guy just silently endures.

Once more, when they do the ultrasound, Medusa plays hide and seek. This baby's shy. Once we're finished, the doctor gives me an appointment for the following week. I have to come back in for monitoring.

When we leave the doctor's office, I call the painter who's going to do Medusa's room and tell him to do it in yellow.

Two days later, when the painter comes over to do the work I requested, I change my mind. Now I want him to paint two of the four walls in yellow, one in red, and one in blue.

A week later, Eric and I go to the hospital because I'm having contractions. He's nervous and I'm hysterical. The nurse makes me lie down, places a wide belt over my belly, connects it to a monitor, and explains that they're checking the parameters of the baby's heart rate and contractions of the uterus, among other things.

I'm scared, but on hearing Medusa's heart gallop, my fears evaporate. I'm awed! The nurse tells us everything is fine and that we should come back the following week.

When we leave the hospital, we're both excited. Our relationship is a roller coaster these days. Couples are supposed to bond and love each other during pregnancy. In our case, we love each other, and Eric puts up with me. I'm aware I have become a fat viper and am weeping, bingeing, and short-tempered.

One night I can't sleep. I look at the clock. It's 3:28 in the morning, and I decide to get up. I'm tired of tossing and turning in bed, and the contractions make me uncomfortable, so it's impossible to rest.

Quietly, I put on my robe, and, like a whale about to explode, tiptoe down the stairs. When Susto and Calamar see me, they come to greet me. Whatever, whenever, they're always there to give you a little

325

love. For several minutes, I dedicate myself to kissing them and paying attention to them, and when they're exhausted, they go off to sleep, and I head to the kitchen.

I open the freezer. I stare at the ice cream, and, after deciding on the vanilla with macadamia nuts, I grab the pint and a spoon and sit down to savor it. I watch the darkness outside. I love ice cream. It's great.

"What's the matter, darling?"

The voice startles me, and, seeing it's Eric, I put my hand over my pounding heart.

"Fuck, you scared me."

"Are you OK, sweetheart?"

We look at each other, and I finally say, "The fucking contractions won't let me sleep. But don't worry. There's nothing to be worried about."

Eric nods and says nothing. He sits across from me at the table and tries to cheer me up.

"It's almost over, beautiful. In about three weeks our baby will be here."

I nod, but I'm scared. Labor is approaching and my anxiety is sky-high.

"I love you, darling," he whispers.

I love him too, but instead of saying anything, I offer him a spoonful of ice cream.

"Listen, sweetheart, don't get upset with me about what I'm going to tell you, but if you keep eating ice cream, when the doctor weighs you—"

"Shut up," I say, cutting him off. "Don't start."

We're silent while I continue to devour the ice cream. I'm a machine. Once I finish the pint, I get up and throw it away while Eric, with grim countenance and biting his tongue, watches.

"Happy now?"

I nod.

"Extremely happy."

We leave the kitchen and go to bed. We look away from each other until I finally fall asleep.

The next day, it's very late when I wake up. Eleven in the morning.

When I get up, my stomach's upset, and I curse the relatives of whoever invented vanilla ice cream with macadamia nuts. I'm heavy and feel like I'm idling.

I'm brushing my teeth when I see Eric in his dark suit. He's so handsome. He comes in and gives me a kiss on the head.

"Get dressed; let's go."

"Aren't you going to the office today?"

"No, I have other plans," he replies.

After I get dressed, I go down to the kitchen and drink a glass of milk. Acidity and heaviness are killing me. We're alone. Flyn's at school, and I don't know where Simona and Norbert are off to. I don't ask.

When I get in the car, neither of us speaks. We don't play music either. Eric drives through the streets of Munich and eventually navigates into a parking lot.

After we park, we walk hand in hand. The fresh air helps clear my head, and, eventually, I'm smiling. He doesn't speak. He's imposing in his dark suit, and I'm proud to be with him. Suddenly, I realize where we are, and I'm surprised.

"Don't tell me this is where we're going."

Eric nods.

"That's the bridge you visited months ago, right?"

I nod.

Before us is the Kabelsteg bridge, from which hang hundreds of love locks.

We cross the street, and Eric hugs me.

"I remembered you told me you liked walking here, and that you saw many of these love locks, right?"

If we're here to do what I think, I'm going to drown him in kisses. He's serious, but he can't fool me: his mouth is cocked.

"Are we going to put a lock on this bridge?"

Surprising me again, Eric pulls a red-and-blue one from his jacket. He shows it to me; our names are engraved on it.

"Where do you want us to put it?"

I put my hand to my lips. I'm so excited. I have a contraction. Oh, that hurt! His expression changes.

"No . . . no . . . no . . . Don't cry now, darling."

But the floodgates are open, and I'm inconsolable. The passersby look at us, and Eric leads me to a bench. He quickly takes a handkerchief from his pocket and dries my tears.

"Eh . . . sweetheart, why are you crying now? Don't you like the idea of putting our lock on the bridge?"

I try to speak, but I can only babble.

Eric hugs me again. I squeeze him and try to calm down.

"I'm sorry, Eric . . . I'm sorry."

"For what?"

"For behaving so badly with you lately."

He smiles. He's a love.

"It's not your fault, darling. It's the hormones."

That makes me cry again. I have the hiccups now.

"The hormones . . . I have a lot of guilt around the hormones. I'm so angry lately about everything that—"

"Nothing happened, sweetheart. You're scared. I understand."

Eric kisses me. I kiss him.

Eric hugs me. I hug him.

I'm in love and crazy about my German. I point to one side of the bridge.

"That's where I want to put our lock."

We get up, holding hands, and walk to where I indicated. I open the padlock and give it a kiss. Eric gives it one too, and then we anchor it to the bridge. Afterward, he takes my hand and throws the key into the river, and we kiss again.

"So, where would you like me to take you to eat?"

I'm not very hungry. My body feels somewhat scrambled, but I don't want to seem difficult.

"I'm dying for one of Björn's father's *Brezns*, so I can dip it in their special sauce," I say with a big smile.

When we arrive at the restaurant, we see Björn all dressed up, like Eric, and talking to his father.

"Hey, what are you two doing here?" he asks.

"We came to eat," I answer.

"She's dying to eat one of your father's Brezns with sauce," explains Eric.

"I'm going to make one for you right now, beautiful," says Björn's father. "Please go to room 2. It's quieter there."

"Will you join us?" Eric asks his friend.

Björn nods, and, minutes later, I'm enjoying a rich Brezn. When we finish eating, we encourage Björn to come shopping with us. We have to buy the crib for Medusa. We left it until the last minute because we didn't know the baby's sex, but then we realized we couldn't wait anymore.

We go to a huge baby store. In all this time, Eric and I haven't done much shopping, and now we go wild. We buy the crib; Björn gives us a cute red stroller. We buy everything in sight. We give the store our address so they can deliver everything at home.

Three hours later, Björn and Eric can't take it anymore, but I want to keep shopping. I suggest they go for coffee or a drink at a bar in the mall, while I go to take a peek at some of the other stores.

They like my idea, and I leave after assuring Eric a thousand times that I have my phone with me.

As I leave the store where I bought the bottle warmer, I'm tired and feel a new contraction. This one's stronger than the others. I stop and breathe, and, when it passes, I continue on my way.

I try shopping at several more stores, but the contractions repeat. I tell myself they'll pass. I pull out my cell to call Eric, but I just put it back in my jacket pocket.

It's June 11, and I'm not due until June 29. I have to calm down. Everything's fine. I'm not going to alarm him.

I see the Disney Store on the mall's second floor. I rush to the elevator. I don't feel like climbing stairs. A girl goes up with me. I like her camouflage pants. I push the button for the second floor, and she pushes the one for four. The elevator doors close and, suddenly, as it goes up, the lights go out, and the elevator comes to an abrupt halt.

The girl and I look at each other and frown. I have yet another contraction. This one's the strongest and so painful that I drop my shopping bags. I grab the elevator handrail.

"Are you OK?"

I can't answer. I try to breathe . . . breathe . . . as I have been taught in prenatal classes. When the pain subsides, I look at the young woman with short dark hair, who looks at me from behind a pair of aviator glasses.

"Yeah, don't worry. I'm fine."

But as soon as I say that, I notice a liquid running down my legs.

God, did I just piss all over myself?

I try to contain it, but it's uncontrollable. My feet are soon soaked.

"Fuck . . . fuck . . . I can't believe this!"

"Are you Spanish?" the girl asks. I nod, but I can't talk.

My water just broke!

I start pressing all the buttons, but the elevator won't move. I'm panicking.

The young woman takes me by the hand and pulls me away from the elevator panel.

"It's OK. Don't worry," she says. "I'll get you out of here right away."

She presses the button for the elevator alarm.

I begin to shake, and she grabs me by the shoulders to steady me.

"My name is Melanie Parker, but you can call me Mel."

"Why do you speak Spanish?"

"Because I was born in Asturias."

"You're from Asturias with that name?"

The young woman smiles, takes off her aviator glasses, and shows me her blue eyes.

"My father is American, and my mother is from Asturias," she says. "I think that says it all."

I nod. But I'm not here for a chat. I take my cell out of my jacket.

"I have to call my husband," I tell her.

As I dial Eric's number, I see the girl keeps pressing the Help button, and my feet are wetter and wetter. One ring later, Eric answers.

"Hi, dear."

Controlling the desire to scream because of how frightened I am, I scratch my neck.

"Eric, don't be scared, but—"

"Don't be scared, me?" he asks, alarmed. "Where are you? What happened?"

I close my eyes. I imagine him losing it that instant. Poor, poor Eric. Then I get a contraction, and, leaning against the elevator wall, I slip to the floor. When the young woman sees me, she takes my phone from me.

"Hi, I'm Mel. I'm with your wife in the elevator at the back of the mall. The power has gone out, and it seems her water has broken. Call an ambulance, please!"

Eric must have said something because I hear her responding.

"She's quiet . . . Yes, I said quiet. I'm with her, and everything will be fine."

When she hangs up, she gives me back the phone and smiles.

"By the sound of your husband's voice, I don't think it'll take him long to get help."

I don't doubt it. I imagine him running through the mall like a crazy person. Luckily, he's with Björn. I pity anyone who gets in their way.

A new contraction makes me wince again. Why does this have to happen to me right now? This one's deathly painful, and I can't breathe. I feel like I'm drowning!

Mel watches me, utterly calm.

I'm surprised at her poise while I'm climbing the walls. But, of course, I'm the one in pain, not her.

With tremendous patience, she makes me look at her and breathe. The pain gives way, and she opens her cell phone and chats briefly.

"I've asked for reinforcements," she says. "If your husband doesn't get someone to get us out, my friends will."

Is it getting hot, or is it just me sweating?

My neck itches.

"What's your name?"

"Judith . . . Judith Flores."

"Where in Spain are you from?"

"I was born in Jerez, but my mother was Catalan. My father's from Jerez, and I lived in Madrid."

I can't say more. The pain is back. It overwhelms me. The young woman takes my hands.

"Very well, Judith . . . Look at me again. Let's breathe. C'mon! Do it."

I begin to breathe with Mel, and, when the pain passes again, I'm grateful.

"Thank you."

She smiles. The minutes pass, and the elevator doesn't move. I scratch myself. My cell rings. I guess it's Eric, worried. Mel answers. She calms him down, and, when she hangs up, she holds my hand.

"You're destroying your neck."

We hear noises, but the elevator doesn't go up or down. She fans me with a piece of paper she's taken out of her backpack.

"So, are you having a boy or a girl?"

"We don't know. Medusa won't let us see."

She smiles again; she understands the name.

"I told my daughter that, while I was pregnant, I called her Cookie. Whatever it is, it'll be beautiful."

"I hope so."

I'm hot. It's overwhelming and stifling, but Mel keeps her wits about her.

"I have a girl, and I know what you're going through," she says. "I can only tell you that you'll forget everything. When you have your baby in your arms, everything will be erased from your memory."

"That's supposed to reassure me?"

"I'm sure," she says with a laugh.

"How old is your daughter?"

"Fifteen months, and her name is Samantha."

We hear the noises again. Mel's phone rings. She picks up.

"We'll be out of here in two minutes," she says when she hangs up.

And she's right. Moments later, the lights of the elevator come on, and we resume the ascent. Mel quickly pushes the Stop button; then she presses the button for the ground floor. The elevator starts to descend, and, when the doors fly open, I see four huge guys dressed in camouflage pants like Mel's.

"Where's the ambulance?" she asks.

One of the guys is about to respond when a very pale Eric pushes through. "Sweetheart, are you OK?"

I nod, but it's a lie, I'm not good at all! He takes a glance at my neck and sees how red it is.

"Easy, easy," he says.

Worried in the midst of the chaos, Björn takes a step toward me, but Mel stops him.

"Don't overwhelm her now."

"What?" he asks, perplexed.

"You need air . . . baby," says Mel.

"Get out of my way . . . baby," Björn replies, his voice deep, car keys in his hand.

"Listen, James Bond, I said you need to get some fresh air," Mel insists.

"And I said to get out of my way," he hisses, pushing her away.

People swarm around us, and I experience a new contraction. I squeeze Eric's hand.

"Fuck, Eric . . ."

Mel pushes him and Björn aside and takes my hand.

"Look at me, Judith," she says in a commanding voice. "Let's breathe."

I do as she says, and the pain passes. Without letting go, she gives orders to those uniformed like her.

"Hernández, Fraser, clear this," she says.

Without hesitation, they do what Mel tells them. While I observe her leadership skills, Eric pulls back the bangs from my face.

"Tell me you're fine, sweetheart."

"I'm not, Eric . . . I think Medusa wants to come out."

Björn looks worried.

"I just spoke with Marta," he says. "They are waiting for us at the hospital."

"Oh my God . . . oh my God," I whisper.

There's no turning back. I'm in labor!

It hurts so much, so much!

Eric kisses me.

"Easy, sweetheart. It's OK. Everything will be fine."

Chaos becomes tangible. Everyone's looking at us.

"Where is the damned ambulance?" Mel asks. But nobody knows. "Fraser," she says to one of the men, "go get the car. I want it at the north gate in two minutes." Then she turns to Eric. "What hospital do you need to take her to?"

"To Frauenklinik München West," he replies.

She turns around and barks, "Hernández, give me route and time. Thomson, call Bryan to let him know about the situation. Tell him to wait for us where we agreed. I'll call Neill."

Seeing I'm a little better, Björn leans down to me.

"Where did Superwoman come from?" he asks.

I laugh. I don't know Mel, but I love her assertiveness. She'll just as soon speak English, Spanish, or German. Once she gets off her cell, she says something to one of her colleagues.

"Follow me," she tells Eric. "I'll have you at the hospital in twelve minutes."

"No need," says Björn, looking at her. "I'll take them."

"In twelve minutes?" she asks.

Feeling cocky, our friend pats down the dark suit he's wearing and touches the knot of his tie.

"In eight, Catwoman."

Eric and I look at each other. I laugh. This is a duel of titans. Then the young woman smiles, and, undaunted by a guy like Björn, she passes her bluish eyes over his body with a heck of a lot of bravado and puts on her aviator glasses.

"Don't make me laugh, James Bond." She turns to Eric and me. "You have three options. The first is me, the second is James Bond, and the third is to wait for the ambulance. You decide."

"I'll sign up for the first one," I say decisively.

Surprised, Björn protests, and she grins.

"Follow me," she tells Eric.

Eric looks at me, and I nod. I know it's more than forty minutes to the hospital but, strangely, I think that if Mel says we'll be there in twelve, we'll be there in twelve. Eric picks me up and runs through the mall. An impressive black Hummer awaits us. We climb in, and, when Björn tries to go with us, Mel stops him.

"It's better if you go in your Aston Martin."

She closes the door, and the Hummer goes full steam ahead.

"It's 4:15; we'll be there at 4:27," she says.

The pain is back. It's intense, but I can take it. Eric and Mel make me breathe, and I appreciate their attention. I notice how the car goes at full speed and doesn't slow down even once.

When we stop, Mel says, "We've arrived."

Eric shakes her hand and gives her a huge smile.

"Thanks, friend."

When I get out of the car, Marta is waiting for us with the wheelchair at the hospital door.

"Let maternity know Mrs. Zimmerman has arrived," she tells a nurse. Then she turns to me. "C'mon, champ. When you're ready, we're going to celebrate at Guantanamera."

"Marta, please!" Eric protests and I laugh.

"The time is 4:27. I promised you I'd bring you in twelve minutes, and I've fulfilled my promise," Mel says to me. "Nice to meet you, Judith. I hope everything goes well."

I grab her hand.

"Thank you for everything, Mel."

"If I have time tomorrow, I'll come by to meet Medusa, OK?"

"That'd be great," Eric replies, very grateful.

"Will you bring Samantha?" I ask.

Mel smiles and nods. Moments later, the young woman climbs into the Hummer and disappears. We go in the hospital, and they take me directly to a nice room in the maternity wing.

My gynecologist tells me not to worry. Everything's going well. Then she puts her hand inside me, and I see stars. I curse her entire family. Eric holds me, but all this makes him suffer. When the doctor takes her hand from between my legs, she snaps off the latex glove.

"You're four centimeters."

Everything hurts.

"Everything's all right, doctor?" Eric asks.

She says yes. "It's going like it's supposed to go." Then she gives me a reassuring pat on the leg. "Now relax and try to rest. I'll see you in a little while."

When she leaves, I look at Eric, and my chin trembles.

"No, no, no, don't cry, champ," he says.

He hugs me and, feeling the pain return, I protest.

"This hurts a lot."

I take Eric's hand and twist it with the same intensity with which I feel my gut, and, even though I know I'm hurting him, he doesn't say a word. He holds me tighter.

"I can't, Eric . . . I can't stand the pain," I murmur.

"You have to, sweetheart."

"Tell them to give me the epidural now. Get Medusa out of me; do something!"

"Take it easy, Jude."

"I don't want to!" I shout. "If you were in such pain, I would move heaven and earth to help you."

As I say that, I realize I'm being cruel. Eric doesn't deserve this. I pull him by the hand and make him come closer.

"I'm sorry . . . I'm sorry, honey. There's nobody in this world better than you to take care of me."

He doesn't need any of what I'm saying.

"Quiet, sweet—"

But my angelic and quiet moment doesn't last long. The pain attacks, and I twist his arm.

"God . . . God . . . This is really hurting again!"

Eric calls the nurse and asks for the epidural. She sees I'm hysterical, but says she can't give it to me until the doctor approves it. I curse everything. Absolutely everything. Yes, in Spanish so they don't understand me. The pain is getting more intense, and I can't stand it.

I'm a bad patient . . .

I have a potty mouth . . .

I'm the worst . . .

Eric tries to distract me with a thousand words of love. He makes me breathe like they taught us in the prenatal classes, but I can't. The pain makes me clench, and I don't know if I'm breathing, if I'll scream, or if I'll end up wanting to shit on the relatives of everyone in the hospital.

I'm sweating up a storm.

I'm shaking . . .

I feel a new contraction coming . . .

I squeeze Eric's hand, and he encourages me to breathe again. I breathe . . . breathe . . . breathe.

Once again, the pain stops. But it's increasingly more frequent, more intense, and more devastating.

"I shit on everyone!"

Eric hands me a fresh washcloth for my face.

"Fix your eyes on one point and breathe, sweetheart."

I do as he says, and the pain stops.

But then I foresee that it's going to start again, and he's going to tell me for the umpteenth time to fix my gaze . . . So, I grab him tightly by his tie and bring his face close to mine.

"If you tell me one more time to fix my sight on a single point, I swear by my father that I'm going to gouge your eyes out and nail them on that fucking point," I say.

He doesn't say anything. He just holds my hand while I squirm in bed, dying from pain.

God . . . God . . . It hurts!

Surely if men gave birth, they would've already invented having babies in a test tube.

The door opens, and I look at the doctor like the girl in *The Exorcist*. I'm feeling murderous . . . I swear I could kill her. Without flinching, she removes the sheet and puts a hand on me again.

"For a first-timer, you're dilating very quickly, Judith." She looks over at the nurse. "You're almost six centimeters. Let Ralf come and give you the epidural. I think this baby's in a hurry to get out."

Oh yes . . . the epidural!

Hearing this is better than an orgasm. Or two . . . Or twenty.

I want tons of epidural. Long live the epidural!

Eric dries the sweat on my brow.

I writhe with a new contraction.

"Eric?"

"Yes, sweetheart?"

"I don't want to get pregnant ever again. Can you promise that?"

The poor man agrees. No one would dare take the opposite position at a time like this.

I dry my sweat and say something when the door opens, and a man comes in, introducing himself as Ralf, the anesthesiologist. When I see the needle he's carrying, I get dizzy.

Where are they going to stick that?

Ralf asks me to sit up and lean forward. He explains that he needs me to be totally still so as not to damage my spine. I'm overwhelmed, but I'm 100 percent willing to cooperate, and I hardly even breathe.

Eric helps me. He does not pull away from me. I notice a small pinch when I least expect it.

"It's done," says the anesthesiologist. "You already have the epidural."

I'm surprised. That's fast!

I thought I'd get dizzy from the pain of the puncture but so far, nothing. He explains that he leaves a catheter in in case the doctor needs to administer more anesthesia. Then he picks up his gear and leaves. Eric and I stay behind in the room, alone. Eric kisses me.

"You're a champ."

This is so nice. He has so much patience with me and shows me so much love with his words and actions.

Ten minutes later, I notice the horrible pains have begun to subside and then disappear. I feel like the Queen of Sheba. It's me again. I can talk, smile, and communicate with Eric without looking like a seven-headed hydra.

We call Sonia and ask her to go by our house to pick up the bag with the Medusa stuff. She's out of her mind knowing we're at the hospital. I don't even want to imagine what my father and sister are going to be like.

Then I call Simona. I know how important it is for her that I call her myself and make her promise to come with Sonia to the hospital when she goes home to pick up the bag. Otherwise, she'll have doubts about my wanting her here now.

Then, after much consideration, I call my father. Eric thinks it's the fairest thing. But as I already assumed, on learning I'm in the hospital to give birth, the poor man goes into a real spiral. I notice it in his speech. When Papá gets nervous, he can't always be understood. He doesn't make sense.

He hands the phone to my sister. Another one with nerves on fire. Screaming and cheering is enough for Raquel. I finally give the phone to Eric, who tells them he'll send his plane to pick them up in Jerez.

When we hang up, he carefully kisses me on the lips.

"The day is here, sweetheart. We're going to be parents."

I'm scared but happy.

"You're going to be an excellent father, Mr. Zimmerman."

Eric kisses me again.

"So, Hannah if it's a girl. What if it's a boy?"

The door to the room opens, and Björn comes in, flushed.

"Man . . . James Bond is here," he says.

He looks at me. The joke isn't funny, so he reconsiders.

"How are you?"

"Perfect now. I had an epidural, I don't feel pain, and I'm OK."

Eric is calmer now too. He doesn't say anything, but I know he's had a hard time. My God, I love him so much! He and Björn talk for a little while, and I have to laugh when I hear Eric say, "Twelve minutes, buddy. It took her exactly twelve minutes."

Björn is stunned. It took him almost an hour. Traffic was horrible.

"How'd she get you here, flying?"

"No idea. I was watching Jude. But, wow, that Mel, what a character!"

"She must be unbearable," murmurs Björn. I laugh.

I'm chatting with them, calm and relaxed, when Sonia comes in with Flyn and Simona. Everyone kisses me, and I smile even though I can't feel my legs. This is so intense. They feel like cardboard. While everyone's talking, Flyn grabs my hand.

"We'll meet Medusa today?"

"I think so, honey."

"Wow!"

The door opens again for Norbert. When he sees me, he smiles, and I wink at him. Ten minutes later, a nurse comes in and says there are too many people in the room. As always, Björn takes care of everything without anyone telling him and leads the others to the cafeteria.

Flyn protests. He doesn't want to be separated from me. He wants to be the first to see Medusa. I finally convince him that it's OK to go.

"Flyn is going to be a great brother," Eric says when we're finally alone.

The door opens yet again, and the doctor comes in. I'm overwhelmed when I see she removes the sheets from round me. Fuck, she's going to stick her hand inside me again. That's so painful! But with the epidural, it doesn't hurt.

"The delivery room! Let's meet your baby."

She calls the nurses, and, when they take me, I don't want to let go of Eric.

"He comes with me," the doctor says. "He has to pretty up to go into the operating room."

I let go of his hand and blow him a kiss. My God, what a moment. When we get to the delivery room, my heart is going a thousand beats a minute. I'm terrified. I don't hurt right now, but the idea of meeting Medusa terrifies me. What if Medusa doesn't like me as a mother?

They transfer me from the wheelchair to the stretcher in the room, and the nurses leave. Two women wearing surgical masks connect me to several monitors and ask me to put my feet in the stirrups.

"Well, 'Tell me what you want.' What a most original tattoo."

I laugh.

"My husband loves it."

The three of us laugh. The doctor comes in with Eric by her side. He's wearing green pajamas and a most ridiculous hat. I laugh again.

She stands by me and explains how I'm supposed to push. Having the epidural, I won't feel the pain, so I have to push whenever she asks or when I see the monitor's red light come on and stop when she tells me to. I'm scared, but I'm sitting here, ready to do it right.

The doctor positions herself between my legs, and, when the red light on the monitor on my right blinks, she asks me to push. I take a breath like I was taught in my classes, and I push . . . and push . . . and push . . . and push.

Eric encourages me. Eric helps me. Eric doesn't move an inch from me. I repeat the same routine so many times that, despite not feeling pain, exhaustion begins to take its toll on me. Between pushes, a surprised Eric tells me I'm quite strong. I'm impressed with myself too. I realize I'm pushing like a beast.

The doctor explains that Medusa is pretty big and wedged in such a way that, despite my dilation and my pushing, it's still hard to come out.

The monitor light turns red again. I keep pushing. Time passes, and I just push and push. I hold it, hold it and hold it, and then, drained, I put my head down.

"Hey, Dad . . . don't miss the next contractions. Your baby is already here," the doctor tells Eric.

That perks me up, and my eyes fill with tears, especially when I see Eric's face full of excitement and disbelief. I push and push again and feel something coming out of me. Eric opens his eyes so wide.

"His head is out, Jude . . . his head!"

I want to see, but, of course, I can't!

Although it's better that way because seeing a head poking out of my vagina might be traumatic for me!

The doctor encourages me. "C'mon, Judith, one last push. As soon as the shoulders come out, the rest of that little body will follow."

Exhausted but exhilarated, I do it again when the light flashes red. I push . . . push . . . push and push until I notice a huge weight leaving my body.

"We got it!"

I can't see anything. I only see Eric.

His eyes fill with tears, and he grins. His look softens at that moment, and I think it's the most beautiful I've ever seen him. I'm so thrilled. I cry with happiness when, suddenly, Medusa's cry fills the room.

"It's a boy," says the doctor, "a beautiful boy!"

I'm this boy's mom!

Eric's breathing is so agitated.

"C'mon, Dad," says the doctor, "come here and cut the umbilical cord."

I cry. I want to see my child. What's he like?

Eric releases my hand, cuts the cord, and then comes back to me. He lowers his mouth to mine and kisses me.

"Thanks, sweetheart. He's beautiful. Beautiful!"

In that instant, they put my Medusa on my belly. My baby. My child. Amazed, I look at him, I touch him, and we both cry.

"Hello, little one. Hello, dear, I am your *mamá*."

Am I already babbling nonsense?

I never imagined I would experience a moment like this . . .

I never imagined I would feel what I feel . . .

I never imagined I would feel so complete . . .

Eric kisses me, and I touch my child. He's perfect, wonderful. And he's as blond as his dad and looks just like him.

Eric and I can't stop grinning. Then one of the nurses holds the baby while the doctor finishes caring for me and removes the placenta. Eric and I follow the nurse with our eyes. We see her test the baby several times and wash him as our little one cries. She puts a band around his wrist, dresses him, and weighs him.

"Seven point nine—almost eight pounds!"

"Almost eight pounds!" I say.

When the doctor finally finishes with me, the nurses bring him to my bed. They transfer me and put my baby in my arms.

My God, this is the most beautiful moment of my life!

I look at him with an incredible love. I watch him and fall in love with him. He's so handsome. Perfect. Eric doesn't blink and grins when he sees that the wristband says, "Zimmerman Hab.610."

Again a big, handsome blond Zimmerman has come into the world to make trouble.

"Let's name him after you, Eric Zimmerman," I say.

"After me?"

I nod and, with a smile I know will touch Eric's soul, I add, "In a few years, I want another Eric Zimmerman to fall madly in love with another woman and make her as happy as you make me."

Eric grins nonstop.

Without him telling me, I know it's the happiest day of his life. Mine too.

31

The first night in the hospital is pretty hectic.

After the pediatrician sees us and tells us the baby's perfect, he asks me if I'm going to breastfeed or bottle-feed him.

I don't intend to become a walking milk factory when I know that bottle-fed babies grow up wonderfully.

The day I spoke with Frida on the phone about it, she told me that didn't seem right to her. She said breast milk is ideal. It immunizes; it's the best. Sonia told me the same thing; she even told me about how breastfeeding and the maternal instinct interact. Well, my maternal instinct tells me to give him a bottle and that if anyone so much as touches my son, I'll kill them.

When I mention it to Eric, he tells me it's my decision. And since what I want from minute one is for my husband to be as much a part of this story as I am, I choose a bottle so it's a shared ball and chain. I don't give a shit what the rest of the world thinks!

When they bring a bottle with a little milk for our baby, I pass it to Eric.

"C'mon, Daddy, give him his first bottle," I say.

I watch how my love lifts the baby from the crib, sits on a chair, and feeds him. The little boy, who is ravenous, quickly throws himself at the nipple like a beast and gobbles what he's been crying for.

Once the feeding's over, he falls asleep like a little colt. I can't tell if I should clean the drool off the baby or his father first.

They're both so cute!

After the feeding, the nurses come to take little Eric to his crib. They want me to sleep and rest. But the little boy has tremendous lungs and likes to be noticed. He has quite a temper!

Knowing it's his son who's screaming, Eric keeps him in my room and takes care of him all night. He rocks him, cradles him, talks to him. I watch them in the dark, my heart pounding.

I'm tired—exhausted—but I can't sleep. My eyes don't want to stop looking at the beautiful show my two Erics are putting on for me.

"C'mon, go to sleep, sweetheart. Rest," my love whispers. "He's perfect, right?"

The little one wiggles in his arms.

"As perfect as you are, my beautiful love."

He touches my head, which is a balm for me. He knows that relaxes me, and, finally, I fall exhausted into Morpheus's arms.

When I wake up, I'm alone in the room. Light streaks in through the window, and, when I call the nurse, the door opens to Eric.

"Come on in, Grandfather. Your dark-haired daughter has finally woken up," he says with a radiant smile.

When I see my father, I grin from ear to ear.

He rushes to hug me. Raquel follows with Lucía and Luz.

"Congratulations, my love. You have a beautiful baby."

"A boy, Papá—what you wanted!" I exclaim.

My father nods. "I'm sorry, son. This time, I won the bet," he says to Eric.

"I'm as happy as you are, Manuel. Don't doubt it for a second."

"Wow!" My sister hugs me. "What a handsome boy."

"He looks just like Eric, right?"

"That's why I said handsome," my sister says, making me laugh.

Luz, my Luz, gets on the bed and hugs me and gives me a package.

"I have seen my cousin, and he is gorgeous, Tita."

I smile at this and open the package. There's a little Spanish national soccer team ensemble. I laugh.

"Do you want him to be kicked out of Germany?" I ask, and everyone laughs. "Where is my little guy, anyway?"

"They're doing some tests, sweetheart," says Eric. "Don't worry; they'll bring him back."

When my father, Lucía, Eric, and Luz go have a drink in the cafeteria, my sister sits next to me.

"Congratulations, Judith. You're a mom."

Raquel hugs me.

"This is for life, Cuchu. Little Eric is beautiful, and I'm sure he'll give you many joys. The bad thing is that they grow up, and one day they start going out with girls, looking at dirty magazines, and smoking joints."

"Raquel . . ."

We both laugh. It's impossible not to laugh with my sister.

"Well, tell me something new."

"Jesús and I, by mutual agreement, filed for divorce twenty days ago."

"Seriously?"

"He has a new girl, and, apparently, it's serious. And, taking advantage of the hurry he's in, I mentioned the express divorce."

"Wow, that's great. You'll be a single woman for your wild little tryst." I laugh. But when I see her face, I know something's not right.

"How's it going with your wild little fling?"

"Very badly."

"Very badly?"

"He wants us to go live in Mexico with him."

"Oh my God."

"That's right, Cuchu . . . and I said no. First, because I don't want to be away from Papá and you so much. Second, because Jesús won't agree to letting me take the girls so far, and, third, because if it were the other way around, I wouldn't want Jesús to take the girls so far away from me. And before you say anything, Jesús may have been an ass with me, but with the girls he's always tried to be a good father, and I'm not going to make him look like a fool. I know he loves them, and they, especially Luz, love him. It's one thing to get a divorce and another to take the girls from his side."

I consider what she's saying and understand completely.

"So, the guy—as Luz says—feels rejected and hasn't called me in ten long and stormy days."

"So, you call him."

"No way."

"Did you tell him about your divorce?"

"Not yet."

"You have to explain things to him the way you explained them to me."

"No."

"Why not?"

"Because Juan Alberto has not given me an option. When I said no to Mexico, he got very stubborn after getting angry and didn't let me explain. He literally said, 'Very well, my queen; you go have a beautiful life.'"

"He said that?"

Raquel nods.

"What did you say?"

"Well, look, girl, he's not going to do me like that! I wanted to say something terrible. You know how I get when I turn into a viper, but I thought to myself: restraint!"

I laugh and hug her.

"Then your wild little fling is over?"

"I think so but, girl . . . I still think about him."

"Raquel, if you love him and he loves you, why don't you explain everything to him and suggest that—"

"What? That he come live in Spain?" She snorts. "No . . . no . . . And then his company crashes, and he blames me. No way!"

We talk for a long time, but nothing comes of it. Raquel closes off, and it's impossible to reason with her. Everybody says the stubborn one in the family is me, but they just don't know my sister!

In a while, Eric comes back with Björn and my little one. Björn brings me a beautiful bouquet of roses. He says hello to my sister, then to me.

"Congratulations, Mom."

"Thanks, handsome."

My love puts our child in the crib.

"Everything OK?" I ask.

Eric nods.

"And my father?"

"He stayed with my mother and the children in the cafeteria. They'll be up in a bit."

"What do you think of our precious boy?" I ask Björn.

"He's beautiful, Judith. You two made a beautiful child."

"Do you want to hold him?"

Björn quickly steps back with a frightened look.

"No, I don't like little ones. I prefer them when they're Flyn's age, and I can communicate with them."

We all laugh.

"I hope he has Judith's personality because if he gets yours, my friend, we're in trouble," Björn says.

"Well, you're not exactly in the clear with my sister," Raquel says.

We're laughing when a knock on the door draws our attention. It's Mel, the girl from the elevator.

"May I come in?" she asks.

"Come in, Mel. Come in," I say, happy to see her.

I see she's pushing a stroller with a precious sleeping baby. She's also brought flowers, which she hands to me.

"She just fell asleep. I hope you can wait awhile!"

Eric greets her with two kisses.

"This baby's so handsome and chubby," she says looking at little Eric in the crib. "So, is Medusa a boy or a girl?"

"A lovely boy," I answer proudly.

She gives me a very affectionate hug.

"Congratulations, Judith."

When she separates from me, she collides with Björn.

"Ah . . . James Bond is here," she says, recognizing him.

Björn doesn't smile. He looks her up and down before responding.

"Man, the bossy Superwoman. What are you doing here?"

Eric and I look at each other, and, before we can say anything, she takes care of herself.

"So, how long did it take you to get here in your Aston Martin yesterday? Eight little minutes?"

As a rule, Björn is a born ladies' man, but not now. Instead of smiling and entering the game, he just wrinkles his brow.

"A little longer than that, smarty-pants."

Whoa, what is going on with Björn?

Does this woman baffle him because she doesn't fall at his feet?

Amazed, I watch as he stops acting like Don Juan.

"I'll be in the cafeteria with Manuel and Sonia," he tells Eric. "I'll come back later, when there are fewer people up here."

"I'll go with you," replies Eric.

When the two men leave, my sister looks at me, I look at Mel, and she shrugs, amused.

"Funny guy, Mr. Handsome, right?"

I don't answer and just laugh. It's clear my new friend and Björn are not going to get along.

When it's just the three of us, we talk about children, pregnancies, and deliveries. Suddenly, I realize I've joined the moms' club, and I talk about my delivery as something unique and amazing. Raquel and Mel do the same. I had never understood that commitment to talk about your delivery, but now that I've had my son, I like to talk about it and remember it.

Samantha wakes up, and, when Mel pulls her out of the stroller, my sister and I fall in love with her. She is a blonde doll with blue eyes like her mother. The girl smiles and makes all kinds of faces at us.

After an hour or so, Mel and the girl leave, but the room is full of people again.

Sonia and my father, little Eric's proud grandparents, want to be with him. Raquel goes down for a bite to eat with Lucía and the children and to hang with Björn and Eric. Shortly after, Marta, Arthur, and some friends from Guantanamera come by. When Sonia sees Máximo, they greet each other, and I can't help but smile. But I bust out laughing when Eric comes and sees the Argentine talking to his mother. He doesn't say a word and just pretends he doesn't know anything.

That night, after everyone leaves and the room is calm, I watch as Eric changes our son's diaper.

"Are you happy?"

He looks at me and puts our sleepy little boy in the crib.

"Like never before in my life, sweetheart."

The next day we are discharged from the hospital, and the whole family, plus one more, goes home.

32

Eric Junior is almost two months old.

He's a good boy, charming, with big blue eyes as captivating as his father's. He has us all drooling like fools over him.

After the first days, when everything is chaos, we acclimate to the new schedules. The little one is king of the house. He has total command, and we're all at his service.

He feeds every two hours, whether day or night. It's exhausting because, in addition to being an eating machine, he doesn't sleep much.

Eric takes care of him. He wants me to rest, but I see how drained he is. One day, after a whole night dealing with the baby's gas, he didn't get up until eleven o'clock in the morning. Even he was surprised by that!

Two nights later, I woke up startled and found Eric sitting on the side of the bed, swaying all by himself. He didn't have the baby in his arms, but they were still forming a cradle. I saw the baby asleep in his crib.

"Honey, lie down and go to sleep," I told him, suppressing a laugh.

He did, and he was asleep in seconds. When he curled up in my arms, I felt like the luckiest woman in the world.

Flyn is a wonderful brother. There's no jealousy, and he's more affectionate than ever. In the afternoon, after doing his homework, he wants to be with the little one. He's proud to be a big brother, and you can see it on his face.

We all talk baby gibberish!

Even Norbert!

I'm myself again. I'm back to being Judith, although I'm struggling with the last ten pounds of my baby weight. So much ice cream and plum cake. But it doesn't matter. The important thing is my baby's healthy.

The hormones have settled down, and I'm happy. I don't cry anymore, I no longer growl, and I don't have postpartum depression.

My father and sister have come a couple of times to see us in these two months. He's bursting with pride every time he sees his big boy, and Raquel is too. I do notice, though, that she's down because of the end of her wild little fling.

I try to talk to her, but she doesn't want to discuss it. I give up. When she wants to talk, she'll come to me. I know.

Little Eric is the most beautiful and wonderful thing that has ever happened to me, and now when I look at him, I'm sure I'd get pregnant a thousand times just to have him near me.

Like a fool, I'm watching him sleep when Eric comes in and kisses me.

"Let's go, sweetheart. We have to go."

Dressed in a wonderful evening gown and wearing the kind of heels that can cause a heart attack, I mutter, "I feel bad about leaving him."

Eric smiles and kisses me on the neck.

"It's our first night out. You and me alone."

His voice reanimates me. We've been planning this outing since the gynecologist told us we could resume our sex life. After Eric convinces me that life goes on and I have to get back to my routines, I get up. I give my precious baby a kiss and walk away, hand in hand with my love.

In the living room, Sonia is playing Monopoly on the Wii with Flyn. "Look how handsome you two look!" she exclaims.

"Ah, Jude, you're beautiful!" Flyn echoes.

I love hearing stuff like that. It's the first time I've managed to get dressed up since I gave birth. I take my usual little turn, and Flyn smiles and hugs me.

"You're in charge tonight; you're the big brother," I say.

Flyn nods and Sonia winks at me.

"No worries. I'll take care of both of them," she says.

I smile and kiss her.

"You have our cell phone numbers, right?"

"Yes, darling. Since forever. Go . . . Go and have a good time."

Eric kisses her.

"Thanks, Mamá." He hands her a note. "We'll be at this hotel, in case of anything. No matter what time it is, call us!"

"For God's sake, what's going to happen? Please leave!"

Laughing, we take off. Susto and Calamar come quickly, and we wave at them. Then we get into Eric's car, ready for fun.

When we arrive at the hotel and close the door to our room, we look at each other. It's our night. Tonight we'll finally be able to make love like we want and without interruptions. I see a bucket of champagne on the table.

"Well . . . and a pink label," I murmur and Eric smiles.

We look at each other . . .

We come close together . . .

I drop my bag on the floor.

Then my love grabs me by the waist and does what I like so much. He sucks my upper lip, then the lower one, and gives me a little nip.

"Do you want to have dinner?" he asks.

But I already know what I want.

"Let's go straight to dessert."

Eric smiles and whispers hoarsely, "Undress."

I turn around so he can unzip me. When my dress falls to the floor, he takes me in his arms and to bed.

After he drops me on the bed, I get to see how my man gets naked. Off with his shirt. Off with his pants. Off with his boxers.

Oh yes . . . what a wonderful view.

He makes my mouth water!

I have before me the sexiest man in the world, with a dangerous and provocative smile. He lies on top of me and kisses me. I taste his lips; I savor his ardent kiss. It's the first time we're going to do it after the birth of our son, and we know we have to be careful.

He runs his fingers down my thighs, which drives me crazy.

He whispers hot words in my ear that get me all worked up.

And when he pulls my thong and rips it to pieces, I go mad, and I'm glad I brought spares. The night will be long.

"I want to be inside you," he says.

"Do it," I whisper, my breath hot. "But ask me another way."

Eric smiles. He knows what I want.

"I want to fuck you."

I'm excited but scared.

Will sex hurt after having a baby?

Eric introduces himself to me a little at a time. His eyes search for the slightest sign of pain. I arch up, close my eyes, and take him in.

"Look at me," he demands.

I do. I look at him, and I get warmer, hotter.

Our breaths accelerate, and with all the care and caution in the world, my love, my Eric, my husband, touches my sex with his cock.

"Does it hurt?"

Oh no . . . it doesn't hurt. I like the feeling and bite my lower lip.

"No, sweetie . . . go on . . . go on."

"Yes, yes . . . yes."

Carefully, Eric moves the tip of his penis into my wet vagina. Mother of God . . . what a sensation.

He tempts me . . .

He drives me crazy . . .

"If I hurt you, tell me to stop, OK?"

I'm excited but scared.

"No, sweetie . . . go on . . . go on."

A little more . . .

A little more . . .

I feel my vagina opening completely, moistening, trembling.

I'm so horny, nothing at all hurts. I just feel pleasure. An intense pleasure, and, when I can't take it anymore, and my desire overflows, I grab his ass cheeks and squeeze him hard. We're both panting.

"I'm not pregnant anymore, so it doesn't hurt," I tell him. "Give me what I need, Zimmerman."

Eric's eyes shine. He grins. He gets goose bumps.

This is passion in its purest state.

Madness surrounds us, and we forget the world's existence—we only feel the touch of our own bodies while we kiss and make love our own way.

Five minutes later, we're both breathless on the bed.

"Wow!"

"Yes!"

"Amazing!"

Eric's breathing hard and lays a hand on my now almost-flat belly.

"As you would say, sweetheart, freaking amazing!"

We laugh and hug each other, and then we go right back to kisses.

"Shall we do it again?" I ask when I think we're both ready.

He's more than up for it. He gets out of bed and carries me with him.

"I'm not going to stop all night, sweetheart. Are you ready?" he asks.

I've been ready for months, and I bite his earlobe.

"I'm going to do something we both want," he murmurs.

I smile. I know what he's going to do, and then he pushes me up against the wall.

"You like it like that?" he asks.

Against the wall? Oh yeah! How I've wanted this moment.

"Yes."

Eric grinds and presses his hips against mine.

"Now, yes, sweetheart, now, yes."

And, without preamble, he sends his huge, hard, solid cock into me while we look into each other's eyes, and I moan, receive him, and gasp.

One, two . . .

A hundred times he comes and goes from inside me while wilder instincts take over us completely. We love it.

Everything between us is hot, scalding. I bite his shoulder. I savor the taste of his skin as he penetrates me. But suddenly he stops.

"Look at me," he says.

I do what he asks. His look is feline, and, pressing his hips against me to give me more depth, he asks in a choked voice when he feels how my vagina sucks him in, "Do you like it this way, sweetheart?"

I nod, and he gives me a pat on the ass.

"Yes . . . oh yes . . . don't stop."

He doesn't. He makes me crazy.

My wonderful and sweet love impales me again and again while we both go out of our minds until we climax and have no choice but to stop.

Our breaths are out of sync, and I suddenly start laughing.

"Honey, I missed you so much!"

Eric nods, sweaty from his efforts.

"Surely not as much as I missed you."

Without separating, we walk to the shower, where we make love again like two savages. The night is long, and we want to enjoy what we like most. What we like most about us.

At three in the morning, exhausted after five fiery assaults, we call room service. We're hungry. They bring us sandwiches and more drinks with pink stickers. We eat naked on the bed.

"Everything OK?" Eric asks.

I smile. I love when he asks me that.

We fill our glasses and toast while gazing into each other's eyes.

"Björn called yesterday. He says there's a little party at Sensations in two weeks. What do you think?"

Wow . . . Yes, our life is definitely back.

I raise an eyebrow and smile.

"A bit of a supplement never hurts, right?"

Eric laughs, leaves his sandwich on the tray, and embraces me.

"Tell me what you want."

Excited by that phrase that means so much to us, I also abandon my sandwich and open my legs for him.

"Give me pleasure."

We kiss. Eric begins to lower his mouth. Oh yeah. He kisses my navel, and I gasp, but then suddenly a buzzing sound interrupts us. My cell phone!

We look at each other. It's past three in the morning. A phone ringing at that time can't be good at all. We both immediately think of our baby. We jump out of bed, and Eric grabs the phone before I can.

I watch him, anguished, as he talks. He calms down. I'm trying to get his attention and gesture with my hand. Before he hangs up, I hear him say, "Don't move. We're coming to get you right now."

"What happened? Is Eric OK? Was it your mother?" I ask, my heart about to beat out of my chest.

He sits me on the bed. I'm about to cry.

"It's OK. It wasn't my mother."

Relief. My baby's fine. But suddenly fear strikes again. "Then who was it?"

"Your sister."

My sister? My heart races again. "What happened? Is my father all right?"

Eric nods. "Everyone's fine. C'mon, let's get dressed. We're going to pick up Raquel, who's at Munich airport, waiting for us."

"What?"

"C'mon, sweetheart," he urges me.

Stunned, I quickly dress. At five past four in the morning and dressed for an evening out, we both show up at the airport. I'm nervous. What's going on with my sister? Why is she at the airport?

Raquel is surprised to see us. "Are you coming from a party?"

Eric and I nod, and quickly bombard her with questions. "What happened? Are you OK? What are you doing here?"

She falls apart.

"Oh, Cuchu, I think I've messed up again."

Not having a clue what's going on, I look at her, then at Eric, who's watching us. "Don't scare me like this, Raquel."

My sister nods.

"Are Papá and the girls all right?"

She nods again.

"Papá doesn't know I'm here."

"What about the girls?" Eric asks, worried.

"With their father. He's taking them to Menorca for ten days."

Suddenly, I understand. I lay a hand on her shoulder. "I can't believe it."

"What?" Eric asks.

Raquel looks at me. I look at her.

"Don't tell me you've slept with Jesús, and you're stuck again with . . . that imbecile."

She starts crying, and I curse. I can't believe it!

Is my sister not playing with a full deck?

Eric calms me down, and when Raquel finally stops crying, she clarifies.

"Well, no, Cuchu. I haven't slept with Jesús, nor am I stuck with him. What kind of woman do you think I am?"

Now I'm lost, and, while I look at her for an explanation, she breaks down.

"I'm pregnant!"

Eric and I look at each other. Pregnant?

Raquel bellows in the middle of the Munich airport, and I don't know what to do. I look to my crazy love for help.

"I can't deal with more hormones, sweetheart. I really can't!"

I laugh. Poor thing, I made him go through so much during my pregnancy. I help my sister to a chair.

"Let's see, Raquel. If you didn't slept with Jesús, whose baby is it?"

"Who do you think?"

I blink.

"What do I know? According to you, you haven't been dating anyone."

Tears stream down her face.

"It's my wild little fling, c'mon."

"Juan Alberto?" Eric asks.

"Yes."

"What are you saying, Raquel?"

"Just that, Cuchufleta."

"But hadn't you broken up?" Eric asks.

My sister wipes her eyes.

"Yes, but we continued to see each other every time he came to Spain."

"Well, you didn't tell me," I say.

"There was nothing to tell."

"Fuck, well, considering there was nothing to tell, now you're going to have to do a lot of talking with Papá, your daughters, and Juan Alberto," I say.

Like a crazy woman, my sister gets up and screams in the middle of the airport. "I don't have to tell him anything! Absolutely nothing!"

"Calm down; calm down," Eric says.

"I don't want to calm down!" she yells.

Eric looks at me. He wants to kill her.

"Consider the hormones," I whisper his way.

"Fuck the hormones," he protests.

I take Raquel by the hand. She's trembling and freaked out.

"I don't ever want to see that guy again in my whole fucking life! I refuse!"

People look at us, and airport police officers approach us. They ask what's going on, and Eric, as best he can, explains there are family problems. They nod and leave.

My man and I glance at each other. We're baffled. Our beautiful night has ended at the airport, with my sister crying, pregnant and hormonal.

Eric decides to take charge of the situation. "C'mon, let's go home. You should rest," he tells her.

The three of us walk to the car. My sister doesn't have luggage or anything. On the way, she tells us she was in Madrid to bring the girls to their father and that Juan Alberto called her while she was asleep with Lucía. Luz picked up the phone and told her they were having dinner at her father's house and that both her parents were there. When Raquel went to talk to him, he went crazy, and, like a hydra, she told him to go fuck himself.

When we get home, Sonia has just given my baby a bottle and is very surprised to see us. But with one look at my sister, and after a few words with her son, she decides just to listen and keep quiet.

Raquel and I go see my little one, who sleeps like an angel. He's beautiful. My sister cries, and I help her settle into a guest room. I give her pajamas and make her lie down and join her. I don't want to leave her alone.

"Are you any better?" I ask in the darkness of the room.

"No, I'm terrible. I'm sorry I've ruined your and Eric's party."

"That doesn't matter, Raquel."

She moans pitifully.

"I've already gotten my express divorce."

"When did you find out?"

"The papers arrived two days ago. Legally, I'm a single woman again, Cuchu. And I . . . I . . ." She can't go on because her tears are back.

What a hard time she's having, my poor Raquel.

"What are you going to do?" I ask her once she calms down.

"With what?"

"With the baby. Are you going to tell Juan Alberto?"

"I thought about telling him when I told him about the divorce. I'd bought a ticket to Mexico, and I was going to surprise him, but now I don't want to see him. That guy accused me of being a bad woman. He must have thought he was fucking a cheeseball, like his ex-wife."

My sister's way of speaking always cracks me up. But it's no time to laugh. She's crying again. I try to comfort her, but it's hard. Suffering because of love while pregnant is crappy. It's the worst of the worst, and when she falls asleep, I get up stealthily and go back to our room. Eric is playing with our little boy.

"How'd it go?" he asks.

"It sucks, poor thing," I say.

"What should we do? Should we call Juan Alberto?"

I don't know what to do. Getting mixed up in other people's problems has never been my thing, and I decide against it. It's Raquel's problem, and she has to make the decisions. I hug Eric.

"I'm sorry this happened, honey," I say. "It seems the world won't leave us alone."

He smiles.

"We had a great time; that's what counts. We'll do it again."

The next morning, when my sister gets up, she still looks like hell. She has more dark circles under her eyes, if that's even possible. Seeing her, Simona's surprised, but when I tell her what happened, she feels for her.

Damned love!

Sonia takes Flyn home to get him out of the way, and Eric decides to escape from the hormones and locks himself in his office with the baby. He tells me not to worry, that he'll take care of little Eric while I deal with my sister.

I haven't seen *Emerald Madness* in days. Simona's taped it. We have three episodes pending, including the series finale. But before watching them, I take care of my sister and convince her to call our father and have some tea.

I hear her talking to Papá while she cries and tells him about the pregnancy. Raquel cries nonstop, and, when I can't take it anymore, I take the phone from her.

"Papá, I don't know what you said, but she can't stop crying."

I hear a snort on the other end of the line.

"Oh, sweetheart, there may only be two of you, but sometimes you seem like a hundred." That makes me smile. "I told her not to worry about a thing. If there's room for four, there's room for five. My new grandchild will be welcome in this house. I just told her not to be anxious and that she should talk to Juan Alberto."

Again, my father shows us what a good person he is. Though he knows my sister's new baby will be the source of much gossip in Jerez, he supports her. He supports us, always.

After talking to him for a while and telling him not to worry about anything, that I'll take care of Raquel, I send him a thousand kisses and hang up. I manage to get my sister back in her room after giving her another tea, and, when she falls asleep, I breathe a sigh of relief.

I leave the room to go to see my boys. Father and son are in the office. Eric is working on his computer, and my little boy is fast asleep. After giving each of them a kiss, I look for Simona, and, like two school girls, we settle into the living room to enjoy our favorite series.

Simona turns it on, and, ready with our Kleenex, we surrender to it.

My sister comes downstairs just as the last episode begins, and we pause it. If she watches this, she'll never stop crying.

"Raquel, if you want, take a swim in the pool. Maybe that will relax you, honey," I say.

But no, she knows what we're doing and drops down on the couch.

"I want to see *Emerald Madness* with you," she says.

Mother of God . . . I predict this will not go well. My pregnant sister, dismayed by the love of a Mexican, and *Emerald Madness*. Doesn't look good. Doesn't look good at all.

I try to convince her not to do it. I tell her the soap opera will remind her of her problems. But no. We wind up turning the show back on and leaving it in the hands of God.

The music makes her cry, and, when Mexico and the characters appear, it's Niagara Falls. Simona and I try to calm her down, but she asks us to just let her watch the soap. Mother of God!

We finally focus, and Simona and I enjoy attending Esmeralda Mendoza and Luis Alfredo Quiñones's wedding. At last!

They're so cute. They gleam. They deserve their wonderful happiness. The mariachis play, and those of us who've suffered along with them on the road to true love believe we deserve it too. Esmeralda and Luis Alfredo swear eternal love gazing into each other's eyes, and Simona and I cry. My sister wails. When their young son tells his dad, "I love you so much, Daddy," we join my sister, and all three of us lose it.

When the show finally ends and the three of them gallop away on a horse heading toward the horizon, the box of Kleenex is empty, and we, like three fools, are spent from our shameless tears.

That night, Raquel goes to sleep right after dinner. She's a tortured soul. I do the same. The whole ordeal is exhausting.

Eric and I go to our room, and, after giving the baby a bottle, he gifts us with a truce and falls asleep in his crib. We're getting to know him, and we know this will only last about three hours.

Weary, I throw myself in bed and close my eyes. I need cuddling. But suddenly I hear a song at a very low volume.

"Will you dance with me?" Eric asks in a barely audible whisper.

I smile, get up, and hug him.

We dance in silence. Neither of us speaks; we just dance, listen to the song, and hold each other.

We kiss. I want him, he wants me, and we want to continue with what we were doing the night before. But Eric's cell phone rings. I roll my eyes and protest furiously.

"Who could be calling now?"

He smiles. He understands my frustration. He kisses me and picks up. He talks to someone and quickly leaves the room. Without a clue as to what's going on, I put on a robe, and, when I go downstairs, I see Eric opening the front door and notice the lights of an approaching car.

"Who's that?"

But before I can answer, a taxi stops at our door, and I'm speechless when I see who emerges from it.

Mother of God, my sister's going to lose it when she sees Juan Alberto here.

"I'm sorry, honey, but I thought it best that the guy who created this situation should have to deal with your sister's hormones," Eric says.

Instead of bothering me, that makes me laugh.

An unshaven Juan Alberto comes in.

"Where is that woman?"

But before Eric or I can answer, my sister is upon us.

"If you come anywhere near me, I swear I'm going to split your skull open."

I turn around and see her in the middle of the hall, with a glass of water in her hands. I start to go to her, but my husband holds me back.

"Eric . . ."

"Don't move, sweetheart," he whispers, and I listen.

With his eyes fixed on Raquel and without fearing for his physical integrity, Juan Alberto goes right by us and straight up to my sister, though he doesn't touch her.

"You're going to kiss me and hug me right now."

365

She throws the glass of water in his face.

Oh God, excellent start!

But instead of getting angry, Juan Alberto takes another step forward.

"Thanks, sabrosa. The water helps clear my head."

Raquel raises her eyebrows. Oh . . . that's bad . . . very bad . . .

"You can go right back where you came from," she says.

Juan Alberto drops his bag.

"Why haven't you taken my calls? I've been going crazy calling you, my queen. I'm sorry for what I said the last time we talked. I got entangled, like a moron, imagining all sorts of things, but I love you, beautiful. I love you, and I need to be by your side and for you to love me."

Fuck . . . we're right smack in the middle of *Emerald Madness*.

My sister collapses. She has no resistance to these beautiful and sweet words. She's an inveterate romantic, and I know that what Juan Alberto is saying is shooting straight to her heart.

But I'm puzzled by her passivity.

"I know you're pregnant, and that baby is mine. My child. Our child. And I'll be forever grateful to my good friend Eric, who called to tell me. But why didn't you tell me yourself, my queen?"

Raquel glares at Eric.

I understand her. At a time like this, I would do the same.

Eric shrugs.

"I'm sorry, sister-in-law, but someone had to tell the father."

You can cut the tension with a knife. I don't speak. My sister doesn't speak.

"Tell me, beautiful," whispers Juan Alberto. "Tell me what I like to hear so much from your sweet mouth."

Raquel's chin trembles again. I fear the worst. She might smash that glass on his head . . . But, suddenly, against all odds, she wrinkles her forehead.

She whispers something back to him.

Juan Alberto hugs her; she hugs him and they kiss.

I blink. What just happened here?

Holding me in his arms, Eric tells me to be quiet and takes me straight to our room. Without letting go, he plays the song we were dancing to again and looks at me.

"Now, sweetheart. Now they'll finally let us."

I grin. At last everything, absolutely everything, is fine. I kiss him.

"Mr. Zimmerman," I say, "please undress."

EPILOGUE

In the same efficient manner my sister got an express divorce, she organized an express wedding.

In August, the whole family gathers at Sweetheart Villa to celebrate and party, not just for her wedding but also for little Eric's christening. We decide to just do both events at once. To bring everyone together is no easy task, but we didn't want anyone missing.

This time, we unite Mexico and Spain in a wedding and Germany and Spain in a baptism. My father's friends laugh and say our family is like the UN.

Dexter and his mother sing rancheras, and my father, with Bicharrón, offer their bulerías. When the clan starts dancing rumbas, it's chaos, and even the band conductor dances.

Wow, we sure know how to have a good time!

Raquel is madly happy. She deserves all of it. She's a married woman once more, in love with a man who deserves her and who's looking at the possibility of living in Spain. Specifically, in Madrid. Juan Alberto is organizing everything to transfer his work. For him, Raquel and the baby come first; there was never any doubt about that.

My father can barely handle so much joy. He's proud of his children and his sons-in-law. According to him, Eric and Juan Alberto are two true men who put on their pants feet first; they're responsible and judicious. There you have it!

You just have to take a look at his face to know he's tremendously happy. We need our mom, but we know she enjoys our happiness from heaven and is as happy as we are.

Frida and Andrés, together with little Glen, come from Switzerland. They're well and happy, and I laugh with Frida when she tells me they've already found people to play with in Switzerland.

Björn comes alone. But he's only alone for about five minutes. My sister and my friends drool over the German dandy. They've all fallen under his influence, and he takes them all on. Björn is incredible!

Sonia shows up with her new plaything, a man much younger than her. It's clear she wants to enjoy her life and love, and that nothing, not even her son's occasional disapproving looks, will stop her. As she says, live and let live!

It's taken a toll on him, but Eric finally understands.

You only live once!

Marta and her boyfriend, Arthur, enjoy the revelry. She dances until she's exhausted, and together we shout "Azúcar!" a few times.

While Susto and Calamar run all over Sweetheart Villa, Simona and Norbert make everything possible.

Dexter and Graciela continue their honeymoon phase. They haven't gotten married, but I'm sure it won't be long before they do.

After seeing Juan Alberto's express wedding to my sister, Dexter's mother can only dream about her son's nuptials. I know she'll get her wish, and we'll be there, as their friends, to accompany them.

Flyn and Luz continue with their mischief. What one of them doesn't think up, the other one does. They loaded the wedding cake with a firecracker and were saved from being punished because it exploded in the kitchen and not in the living room. I can't even imagine what would've happened if it had burst in front of Raquel and her new husband. I laugh just thinking about it.

My child, my precious baby, my little Eric, is passed from loving arms to loving arms during the wedding. Everyone wants to cradle the beautiful little boy, and he loves it. He doesn't cry, so I'm able to enjoy my sister's wedding with my love, the most wonderful man in the world who loves me madly.

Of course, we still argue. We're still like night and day, and when one of us says white, the other says black. But as Malú sings in our song, we give each other love, and we give ourselves life. Without him, my life would no longer make sense, and I know it's the same with him.

At the end of August, after spending several days in Jerez, Eric and I, together with Simona and Norbert, the little ones, and the dogs, return home. Some respite before starting the school year and going back to work is good for us.

Surprisingly and without my prompting, Eric asks me if I've considered working for Müller again. Honestly, I've thought about it, but now with my little one, I don't want to. I know I'll go back in a while, when he goes to preschool, but for now I want to stay home with him and enjoy it before he grows up, goes out with girls, looks at dirty magazines, and smokes joints, as my sister says.

Knowing my decision, Eric smiles and nods. It makes him happy.

One morning in September, we go out with our two boys to walk around Munich. It's a good day, and we want to take advantage of it. We're a family, and we've planned a surprise for Flyn.

Ever since little Eric came home, Flyn calls us Mom and Dad. His happiness is ours, and, on more than one occasion, we've had to hide so he doesn't see us get excited like two fools when we see them together.

When we park the car, the four of us walk around until we reach Kabelsteg bridge, where our lock is hanging. Eric and I walk hand in hand, while Flyn guides the stroller with his brother.

"Wow, so many locks!" he says, surprised.

370

Eric and I look at each other and grin. After locating ours, we stop.

"Look, Flyn," I say. "Look at the names on this one."

"Is that you?" he asks, amazed.

"Yes, it's us," I answer, bending down to his height. "This is one of Munich's love bridges, and Eric and I wanted to be part of it."

Flyn nods.

"What do you think?" Eric asks.

He shrugs.

"All right, well, if it's a love bridge, it seems good your names are here." He looks at the other locks. "Why are there smaller locks attached to the bigger locks?"

Crouching next to us, Eric explains. "Those smaller locks are the fruit of the love of the big locks. When couples have children, they include them in that love."

Flyn nods.

"So, we've come to put a love lock here for little Eric?"

I shake my head, and then my love, taking out two smaller engraved locks from his pocket, shows them to Flyn.

"We've come to hang two locks. One that says 'Flyn' and another that says 'Eric.'"

He blinks.

"That one has my name on it?"

I smile and hug him.

"You're our son in the same way Eric is, darling. If we don't hang two more locks, our family won't be complete. Don't you agree?"

He nods.

"Wow."

Eric and I smile, give him the locks, and explain how to put them on our lock. After we all kiss the keys, we throw them in the river.

My man looks at me and winks. We've always been a family, but now we're more. Fifteen minutes later, while Flyn runs in front of us and I guide the stroller, I ask, "Are you happy, honey?"

Eric—my love, my Iceman, my life—presses me closer to him and kisses me on the head.

"More than you could ever imagine. With you and the children, I have everything I need in my life."

I know; he lets me know every day.

"Oh, but not everything, no."

Eric looks at me.

I press the stroller brake and hug him around the neck.

"I have everything I want, sweetheart. What do you mean?"

"There's one thing you've always wanted, and I haven't given it to you yet."

Surprised, he wrinkles his brow.

"What?"

Trying to keep from laughing, I kiss him. Eric's delicious. I adore him.

"A little dark-haired girl," I whisper, just inches from his mouth.

He's blown away.

He's speechless, breathless.

He goes pale.

I crack up laughing.

"Are you going to drive me nuts with your hormones again?"

I playfully slap his ass.

"Don't worry, Iceman. You're safe for now."

I kiss him.

"But you know what," I say, "maybe someday . . ."

ABOUT THE AUTHOR

Photo © 2015 Carlos Santana

Megan Maxwell is the prize-winning author of *Now and Forever* and *Tell Me What You Want*. She credits her success to a stubbornness that kept her knocking on editorial doors for years until her first novel was published in 2010 and became the winner of the International Prize for the Romantic Novel in 2011. Since then she has published dozens of novels, including romance, erotica, historical fiction, and time-travel tales, and she has won many more accolades. She is a great dreamer who believes that to dream is to live. Born in Nuremberg, Germany, Megan has lived her life in and around Madrid, Spain.

ABOUT THE TRANSLATOR

Photo © 2017 Megan Bayles

Achy Obejas is the author of *The Tower of the Antilles*, a nominee for a PEN/Faulkner Award for Fiction; *Ruins*; and *Days of Awe*. She has also written for a number of publications, including *Vanity Fair*, the *Washington Post*, the *Advocate*, *Playboy*, and *Ms*. As a translator, Achy has worked with Wendy Guerra, Junot Díaz, Rita Indiana, and many others. In 2014 she was awarded a USA Ford Fellowship for her writing and translation. Born in Havana, she now lives in the San Francisco Bay Area. For more info, visit www.achyobejas.com.